Linda Hamlin

TOBY BARLOW is the author of *Sharp Teeth*. He lives in Detroit.

ALSO BY TOBY BARLOW

Sharp Teeth

Additional Praise for *Babayaga*

"Barlow displays a firm authorial hand while wrangling the book's large cast—an eternally beautiful Parisian witch who seduces her lovers without mercy, a detective who's turned into a flea—into a rip-roaring narrative." —*Vogue*

"The razzle-dazzle of the supernatural merely complements the beating heart of [*Babayaga*], a consideration of kinds of everyday witchcraft: advertising, affection, the lure of foreign lands. It makes for a story that's flat-out fun to read." —*New York Daily News*

"Elaborate, confidently written, and ultimately seductive." —*Detroit Free Press*

"At its best, Barlow's novel reads like a blend of the sensibilities of George Simenon in noir mode and Billy Wilder's cynical farce in *One, Two, Three.* . . . *Babayaga*'s blend of history, romance, and the weird has compelling charms." —*Los Angeles Review of Books*

"If his brilliant *Sharp Teeth* wasn't enough to make you read anything Toby Barlow writes, he's done it again, giving a well-worn story a tasty twist. *Babayaga* is a pulpy, magical adventure set in a Paris any reader would love to visit." —Stewart O'Nan, author of *A Prayer for the Dying* and *Emily, Alone*

"The pair of virtuosic, murdering witches at the heart of *Babayaga* are two of the most vivid and entertaining characters in recent fiction. Possessing the secrets of the ages and of the earth, the crone and the beauty upend the city of Paris with spells I can't believe aren't true. And beneath Toby Barlow's zany, persuasive conjuring runs a touching meditation on love. How did he do it?" —Sarah Blake, author of *The Postmistress*

"Eye of newt and toe of frog, wit and heart and mordant social commentary: this dark, delicious brew from Toby Barlow has it all." —Hillary Jordan, author of *Mudbound* and *When She Woke*

PICADOR · FARRAR, STRAUS AND GIROUX · NEW YORK

Babayaga

A Novel of Witches in Paris

Toby Barlow

BABAYAGA. Copyright © 2013 by Toby Barlow. All rights reserved. Printed in the United States of America. For information, address Picador, 175 Fifth Avenue, New York, N.Y. 10010.

www.picadorusa.com
www.twitter.com/picadorusa • www.facebook.com/picadorusa
picadorbookroom.tumblr.com

Picador® is a U.S. registered trademark and is used by Farrar, Straus and Giroux under license from Pan Books Limited.

For book club information, please visit www.facebook.com/picadorbookclub or e-mail marketing@picadorusa.com.

Illustrations by Matt Buck

Designed by Abby Kagan

The Library of Congress has cataloged the Farrar, Straus and Giroux hardcover edition as follows:

Barlow, Toby.
   Babayaga / Toby Barlow.—1st ed.
      p. cm.
   ISBN 978-0-374-10787-1 (hardcover)
   ISBN 978-0-374-70959-4 (e-book)
   1. France—Fiction.   I. Title.
PS3602.A775624 B33 2013
813'.6—dc23

2013008712

Picador Paperback ISBN 978-1-250-05029-8

Picador books may be purchased for educational, business, or promotional use. For information on bulk purchases, please contact Macmillan Corporate and Premium Sales Department at 1-800-221-7945, extension 5442, or write specialmarkets@macmillan.com.

First published in the United States by Farrar, Straus and Giroux

First Picador Edition: August 2014

10 9 8 7 6 5 4 3 2 1

Dedicated to Richard Peabody & Rob Stothart,
both poets & teachers & good, honest men

Man hunts and fights. Woman contrives and dreams; she is the mother of fancy, of the gods. She possesses glimpses of the *second sight*; and has wings to soar into the infinitude of longing and imagination. The better to count the seasons, she scans the skies. But earth has her heart as well.

—MICHELET

Women must tell men always that they are the strong ones. They are the big, the strong, the wonderful. In truth, women are the strong ones. It is just my opinion, I am not a professor.

—COCO CHANEL

Babayaga

PROLOGUE

There are facts and there are lies. There are true lovers with bad alibis. The world is a busy hive, filled with stories that have been retold over and again ever since our tongues learned to talk and our ears first opened. We hear all this, yet we are still lost, barely making out our path in the pale, inconstant light. As the ancient man said, we know nothing. But I can tell you this much is true, this happened. I know, because my elder sister wrote of it to me in a letter sent late last autumn, of how, behind the high walls of a fading castle, tucked in a valley not far from the northern border of France, a woman in her later years brought out an old guitar and, strumming it gently to find the tune, announced to the night, "I will sing you a song now about when the babayagas fled to Paris . . ."

Book One

When I was living in Paris, we had an expression, a very American one, which in a way explains it better than anything else. We used to say, "Let's take the lead." That meant going off the deep end, diving into the unconscious, just obeying your instincts, following your impulses, of the heart, or the guts, or whatever you want to call it.

—**HENRY MILLER,** *The Paris Review*

I

Time was bothering Zoya. She lay on the broad bed amid the crumpled silk sheets, listening to Leon scrub and gargle in the bath. There was almost a cartoon melody being composed in the various noises of his evening toilette. He always fastidiously washed and perfumed himself after they made love, immersing himself in soaps, talc, and a cloud of *eau de Lisbonne* before he returned home to face his wife. Even on nights such as this, when his Claudette was out of town, he performed the ritual out of habit. Usually Zoya did not mind, but tonight the music made her sad.

Coming out of the bathroom with the steam billowing out around him, he looked like some gray ball of boiling fat spit out from a cauldron. "What is wrong, *ma chérie?*" he asked.

She remembered the day he had first found her while strolling through the Jardin des Plantes. When had they met? Was it the spring in '45? Not long after the war had ended, when the Paris streets and nightclubs thronged thick with a mix of wide-eyed American and British soldiers fresh off the train from Calais and sniffing about for fun. She had her pick of any one of the swarm, but she found Leon instead, a stocky middle-aged Parisian of square chin and broad shoulders, far from the slouching fat man he had grown into. So much time had passed as she had watched his profile slip and slide steadily down from stout to rotund to fat, eyes growing cloudy, his bright blue irises dimming to a mottled gray, folding bloodshot beneath the heavy lids and puffy circles of wine-swollen flesh. When he was drunk on brandy, he loved to recount how he had once been a formidable athlete, back in his Catholic school days, but she had a hard time convincing herself of that, looking at him now, for he was simply a doughy old man, while she still looked as fresh as she had the day they first met.

"I have a small headache, I need fresh air," she said. "Why don't you get dressed and we can have a stroll before you go home?"

"At this hour? Ha! Have I not exhausted you yet?" As he toweled off his back, his vast white belly shook. It was almost too silly to watch.

"I slept all day," she said. "It is a pleasant night and it will do you good to move those bones of yours." She looked around the room— the tall dresser, the modest crystal chandelier, a framed dark oil of the dead red fox surrounded with ripe autumn apples that hung above her small desk. Though the artwork seemed merely decorative now, she could remember when still-life paintings of heaping bowls of blushed fruit kept verdant hopes budding during the bleak seasons of cold cabbage and cellar potatoes. Look here, the pictures said, and do not lose faith. Pear, peach, apple, and plum, all will blossom again.

Beside the painting, three silver clocks sat on the mantel. Leon had told her they were from the collection of Princess Mathilde. Zoya did not know if she believed him, her pompous and proud Leon was certainly prone to exaggeration. But she did enjoy the comfort each of these intricately designed timepieces provided. One clock counted the months along with the hours, another tracked the phases of the moon, the third was astrological, showing the zodiac arcing above the hours as the year progressed. Through the day and night the clocks' light, gentle chimes provided a charming accent to the quiet apartment, grounding her in her well-appointed surroundings and bestowing a small delight with their delicate tones. Over the years, Leon had periodically presented these precious gifts to her, along with perfumes, pendants, pearls, fox stoles, and soft leather gloves, repaying her undemanding patience, her indulgent good humor, and her generous physical attentions with luxuries that had, over time, soothed and almost succeeded in letting her forget what was coming. But it was never too far from her mind. She knew she would miss all these delicate and beautiful treasures; she would not be able to take much with her. Like the summer birds now instinctively leaving the branches of the Paris trees for their warm Mediterranean refuges, it was time for her to go. The river of time was loud in her ears now, foaming and surging, washing the whole room away.

That first day, so long past, she had been sitting with Elga, the squat old woman napping with her eyes half closed, sinking down into the bench like a fat, cooling scone on a baker's shelf, while Zoya relaxed with a novel. She tried to remember who it was, a Russian no doubt, Gogol or Turgenev. At that point they had not been in Paris long. She did recall very clearly how the shadow crossed her page, and how she looked up to find a grinning Leon standing there in the evening light. Zoya had offered a polite smile.

She shook the memory off and rose from the bed. "It is our last night together before your Claudette returns from the country. I want to walk with you. Don't worry, nobody will see us." Leon was always easy to read, simple to lead. "Come," she said, tossing him his shirt from the bed. "We can go down by the river. You can tell me about your week while we walk, and then I will tell you an old country tale as we return."

He smiled. Her Leon, like every man she had ever known, liked her stories, the old Russian sagas she would often spin to make the men grin or laugh or lull them to sleep. Many of her yarns were made up, while others were true, some were bawdy, others bloody, but she couched them all in the velvet warmth of folk fables. Each one held a kernel of a lesson, there to be found by the attentive and curious, but although Leon savored the adventures of lost children and dancing, bell-chiming bears, of damp, hungry soldiers finding false comfort in lone cottages, and of brides with serpents curled up in their hair, Leon never bothered to grasp any of the morals. Few of her men ever had. She had come to believe that fables and tales and even epics from history taught very little, they held not enough sting for their lessons to stick.

Leon squeezed his pants up around his wide waist, pulled his suspenders over his shoulders, and straightened his stiff collar as she gathered up her own chemise, stockings, and dress. It was a nice, unseasonably warm, autumn night; the season was coming on slow, but still she would have preferred to remain inside. If only he had not asked such a seemingly innocent question moments before, lying beside her and still breathing hard: "How do you stay so young?"

A small inner voice nagged at her, asking her to put it aside and wait. He was so dense, perhaps he did not know what he had noticed. They could lie together a few more nights, or maybe even two or three months, and she could listen to his fat snores gurgle, sputter, and snort—which she found endearing—if only for a few more dawns. What was the rush? After all, it had only been a muttered phrase, a pillowed kindness. She could make him forget if she wanted to, but what was the point? Over time, she knew, he would only notice more. Even a dull, blustering bull such as Leon was not that stupid. What once were clumsy compliments would echo and twist over the years into a wiser, sharpened suspicion. He would observe that his aches were not hers, his hazy, milky gaze would look resentfully down at her clear, pure features, her soft skin and ever-focused eyes, and then a low, seismic anger would slowly take hold in his thick mind. From that point, certain predictable difficulties would emerge. No, there was no need to rush, but better to attend to it now. As Elga often said, pluck out the troubling eye before it blinks again.

"Good day, mademoiselle" were the first words Leon had spoken to her on that long-ago day, bowing slightly and tipping his straw hat as a gentleman of the Old World might have done. The green abundance of the summer garden framed his body, so that in the twilight he appeared like a great topiary creature coming to life before her. Sizing the stranger up, the first thing she sensed was money—she had a well-honed talent for spotting that. Better yet, his flat, dull smile revealed a man with no great capacity for wonder, or even curiosity. He took things to be as he saw them, and he did not see very much. This was ideal. Added to that, there also was a grinning kindness and, it seemed from his eager gaze, a hearty appetite, too. She did like hungry men.

"My dear," Leon said tonight, "you are truly beautiful."

She hugged him, wrapping her arms around his wide waist and resting her head on his soft shoulder. If he were truly a sensitive man, he might have felt her deepening sadness. But he was not. Raised by servants and conditioned amid the rude, patriarchal abuse of religious schools, the only other intimacy he had ever known was the cold affection of a smartly arranged marriage, leaving him with all the emotional range of an old, seasoned workhorse.

As they headed to the door, she glanced at a framed picture on the mantel. It was the only photograph of the two of them that existed; they had had it taken on a night when they had been out for another evening walk and had stumbled upon a neighborhood carnival. Wandering past mimes and magicians, monkey grinders, flea circuses, and nimble jugglers, they had come upon a photographer's studio. Caught up in the spirit of revelry, Leon had dropped his usual guard and paid for a portrait. In the picture, taken with a gray velvet backdrop, she demurely held his hand, her black hair tucked under a hat, her eyes looking up at him with clear affection. He stood beside her, erect, grinning into the camera the way a safari hunter smiles while holding up the antlers of some magnificent, dead prey.

Leon was such a funny man, she thought, not brave at all (he had bribed his way out of the war), but kind enough. An adulterer, a liar, a larcenous man who clumsily cheated his clients and then paid to make the problems go away, he was all of that, but these were the burdens of most of the rich men she had known. She had stolen much from him, he had stolen much from others, and who knows where the first theft occurred? So few who touched a coin were pure or innocent. But as far as men went, his heart was decent. She knew she was being sentimental here in these final moments, painting him to be better than he was. She was like the farmer's daughter who lovingly watches the sweet, obese pigs lolling and snorting in the mud the morning of the winter slaughter. "Do not forget to turn off the light," she said.

Earlier, through the open apartment window, they had heard what sounded like distant firecrackers going off, but now the streets were quiet. They wandered up rue d'Ulm. The markets were closed, the bistros empty, a few automobiles rattled by. She held his hand, gently stroking the fat side of his palm with her thumb. She wondered if she had, in fact, ever loved him. They turned up rue Erasme. Leon complained, as he often did, about his frustrations with his ancient mother. Zoya had never met the woman, but Leon painted a picture of a stern, frigid creature who never appreciated her youngest boy, always favoring his older brother instead. "For me, she has only the most spiteful milk."

Zoya was barely listening. Her mind was busy trying to remember a foggy collection of words while her eyes glanced about, searching in the sidewalk's shadows for a sharp-tipped rail she recalled. It would be a handy place to stick his skull.

II

Will Van Wyck sat only half listening to Mr. Guizot; his mind kept wandering. He was trying to piece together what his life was going to be like now. He realized this was no time to be distracted, he needed to focus on whatever Guizot was going on about at that moment, because the little ball of a man bouncing around in front of him had just become Will's very last client.

Earlier that morning, Will had still been running two clients for the agency, while eighteen months before that Will had been personally responsible for every single client in the office. But over time the French directors of the company had slowly, deftly, ever so politely, reduced his involvement in their business. They always smiled as they took away his accounts, and it was always over a generous four-course lunch at Fouquet with a few good bottles of white burgundy. But try as they might, and they did try, they could not completely dislodge him. The home office back in the States wanted him to stay in the Paris office managing one very special client, and that is what he had done, with never a word of complaint and nary a missed deadline. He had quietly given in to his French colleagues' awkward and obvious Machiavellian politics, happily handing off responsibility whenever pressure was applied because, up until today, he knew his most important client kept him securely in place. The one unexpected surprise had been the loyalty of his other client, Guizot. This self-made mogul had started his beauty-care company only a few years before the war with a bathtub full of homemade hair tonic that he had tirelessly flogged until his empire stretched across western Europe. Even at that scale, his account was of no critical importance to the agency, not like their automobile, cigarette, or liquor accounts, and the senior managers grinned and nodded when he insisted that Will continue to run his account. "Americans know how to sell!" Guizot had proclaimed, and they happily agreed, but mostly because they could not stand Guizot.

"Watch! Boom! Yes! Bang! Our campaign explodes across the countryside! Perfectly timed, catching all our idiot opposition with their piss-stained underpants down around their ankles." Guizot could not contain his excitement, he was practically jumping around Will's office. He always acted this way as they prepared an advertising campaign. Will negotiated for him, deciding which newspapers and radio shows they would buy, while Guizot enthusiastically provided the product, the capital, and even the advertising copy, which he did not trust anyone in the agency to write. "What do your copywriters know about art or business that I do not know? If they are such great writers, where is their poetry, where are their literary prizes? And if they are so smart, why are they slaving away at their typewriters, working for me!" Will usually found Guizot's antics entertaining, but not today.

"We will completely blitz the opposition! Bam! Bam! Bam! It is a true campaign, not an advertising campaign but a military campaign, with military precision!" Guizot was almost shouting now, his fists flew wildly in the air like a punch-drunk boxer. "They won't be able to escape us, we have them in our sights! Because they are—how do you put it, Will? Oh yes, ha, our 'target audience.' See what I mean! See our target there, innocently opening the pages of *Le Monde*? Bam! There we are! Kaboom! The target opens *Bonne Soirée* or *Vogue*, ah ha! Rat-tat-tat! And when they turn on the radio, oh, Will, that is where our most secret weapon will be unleashed! Yes, ha ha, our sweet little girl's innocent voice will be sapping their strength, sucking them in with her song, *"Chase your pimples away. Chase your pimples away. Ah ha ha, Ah ha ha . . ."* He was dancing now, hopping and slapping the bottoms of his shoes for rhythm as he performed his self-composed jingle. Will stared blankly at him, barely listening, his mind still mulling over the very different meeting he had been forced to endure a little over an hour before.

The room had been much quieter during the earlier meeting, almost too calm, and his American client, Brandon, had spoken in much more sensible tones. Brandon had tried to seem nonchalant, making all the facts sound perfectly reasonable and logical. It was, Brandon explained, the kind of change that happens, priorities simply shift. "Listen, Van Wyck. I'm not happy about it either, but it's not the end of the world. They have accounts for you in Chicago, right? That's where you're originally from, isn't it?"

"I'm from Detroit."

"Perfect, see. Go get a job there. Those car accounts are strong." Brandon had leaned back in his chair; it was as if they were talking about a baseball game or a boxing match. His attitude did little to comfort Will. Will's previous Parisian clients had always been somewhat deferential. Not all of them worshiped him like Guizot did, but they all generally believed they could learn something from American marketing, and so they listened respectfully to what Will had to say. But being from the States himself, with an East Coast style and a crooked nose from playing football at Brown, Brandon had always dealt with Will as if he were little more than a foolish underclassman, there to be bullied or charmed, depending on the whim of the moment. "Detroit's got, what, AMC, Chrysler, GM, and Ford? It'll be a different game, sure, but you'll be fine. Marry a Michigan girl and buy a nice house outside of town. They have great suburbs there. You'll want to be in the suburbs. The niggers have taken over the city. But I guess you knew that."

Will was having trouble digesting the news. He reached for a cigarette. "Exactly how long before the billings stop?"

Brandon had shrugged. "After the election. Nothing will happen until Ike's out. No sense in pulling the plug till then. But no matter who wins, even if it's Nixon's fucking dog, this move is going to happen. The action simply isn't here anymore. The government's moving its spending to Asia. All our budgets are migrating there."

"They're moving you, too?"

"Me?" Brandon smiled a funny smile, surprised at Will's question. "They'd like me to go south with them, but I'd rather not. I'm cooking up a project that might keep me here at least a bit longer, but it's not going to involve any kind of advertising. So I'd say you've got a year, tops. But I'd start making plans now. Never hurts to be prepared."

Will had looked around the room. He was thirty-one years old with a corner office in Paris. He had worked hard to get here. If he went back home he would be stuck working for the old guard. He'd be trapped at a desk, listening to the old guard drone on about how things were done. The old guard would pile him up with dull research assignments before heading out to swoon their clients at the country club or screw their secretaries at the motor lodge. And in twenty years, if he was lucky, he would be the old guard. "Fuck."

His assistant, Madame Belec, poked her head in the door. "*Monsieur Guizot est arrivé.*"

"Thanks, we'll only be a minute more."

"*Il semble très impatient.*"

"He always is," said Will. She left and Will looked at Brandon. "I'm going to have to wrap this up. It appears I have a real client waiting."

"Aw, whaddaya mean." Brandon laughed. "I'm a real client. We pay you guys good money. If I could figure out how to keep you on the gravy train I would, believe me. But they're shutting down this side of the operation and the stuff I'm into now is way out of your league. You wouldn't want it anyway, it's grueling stuff, day and night." Brandon snapped his fingers. "Oh damn, that reminds me, here"—he reached into his vest pocket and pulled out two tickets—"I was gonna swing by this reception over at the Hotel Rothschild tonight, but I can't. The ticket's yours if you want it. It's up on rue Balzac, only a few blocks away. Full bar, and I bet the booze'll be the good stuff. Go get yourself drunk, take a girl with you or meet a girl there, or better yet, meet two girls there." Brandon laughed at his own joke as he rose to leave. "Seriously, you didn't think it would last forever, did you? Now give me that report so I can show my guys you still care."

Will had handed over the Rhône-Poulenc file. Meticulously compiled, the file was a summary of the chemical company's growth plans, its supply base, and its accounting, along with a separate analysis specifically focused on the company's current relationships with various branches of the French armed services. Brandon gave it a cursory glance. "Looks like you covered all the bases."

"We always do."

"You got anything else coming for me?" Brandon had said.

Will winced slightly; Brandon always wanted more these days. Not so long ago, he'd been content getting a monthly report on whatever

Will found of interest. The Americans used the reports to keep an eye on Europe. Will's other clients had had no idea that the secrets they shared with their advertising agency were being passed on to a foreign government, and they would certainly not have been happy to find out. The home office did a good job of keeping it a secret, even from the local executives. That's why they had kept Will there for the last few years. He was the only one who knew exactly what the reports were for, and who was receiving them. He knew he was, in essence, spying on these companies for Brandon. It did not bother him since it felt so far from sinister. There was nothing more than raw data in the files, reports on commodity pricing, production cycle estimates, supply levels, and shipping analyses. Lately, though, the requests from Brandon had grown more constant and generally focused on pharmaceutical, chemical, and medical supply firms. Will had given Brandon five write-ups on five different companies in the past six weeks, and he had two more reports in the works. Normally it wouldn't have bothered him, but it didn't seem right for Brandon to come in and basically fire Will and at the same time be demanding so much more. Still, the client was the client. "I'll have the one on Bayer ready next week," Will said.

"Great. Keep 'em coming"—Brandon smiled—"at least till we shut out the lights. You don't want to piss off the Central Intelligence Agency, right?"

Will nodded. "Right." Depressed at the thought of going back to America, he didn't even look up as Brandon walked out.

Mulling it over now, Will realized this was the final card in the deck; he no longer had enough business to keep him in Paris. It was only a matter of months before he booked one of the new transatlantic TWA flights back to the States. There was so much that he relished about Paris, from the bright lights of the brasseries to the wild parrots of the bird market to the garden view from Montparnasse. Of course, there were also the yellow-and-pink-pastel-skirted girls who looked as tasty as macaroons as they carried their books to their Sorbonne classes, and then there was this thick, little puffball of a man who was singing about pimples and dancing around Will's office. Watching Guizot bounce about, Will realized that he had thoroughly enjoyed, savored, and celebrated every single day he had spent in this city, and now it appeared it was over. "Fuck," he said.

Guizot stopped and held up his hands. "Come on, it's a good song!"

III

Standing in the finely furnished apartment, Detective Vidot felt guilty. Crimes were always bad, and all too often they were tragic, terrible, and truly awful things, and yet whenever they involved peculiar or unusual circumstances, Vidot inevitably felt a wondrously delicious feeling rise up inside his heart, a delightful sensation that bordered on giddiness, and one that almost always inspired him to break out in an enormous smile. It was a shameful habit that he had long struggled to suppress. He thought it stemmed from the fact that ever since he was a young boy, he had derived enormous pleasure from puzzles, crosswords, jigsaws, anagrams, word games, and riddles. The great mystery stories featuring Dupin, Holmes, and Lecoq had sparked the initial ambition that led to his career. But once he actually became a police detective the smile itself caused unfortunate results, especially when his duties included querying a victim's grieving relatives, neighbors, or traumatized colleagues. Too many times, that impish grin had slipped across his face, sending the sad souls he was questioning into even more wildly distraught states. Calls had been made, complaints lodged, and over the years, he had strained to erase it from his features, attempting to appear more consoling and sympathetic, yet the little smile always found a way to creep back, dancing at the corners of his mouth, mischievous, almost like a nervous tic.

It was a good thing no friends or family of the unfortunate victim were around now, because this case had him grinning from ear to ear from the moment he had first encountered it.

Atop the hill that rose in the 5th arrondissement, not far from rue Mouffetard, there had once, long ago, been a tall, spiked gate on rue Rataud that protected the chaste, devout nuns living within the monastery. Late in the nineteenth century, city life had grown too chaotic, so the sisters were moved away and the gate had been almost completely disassembled. But due to a series of arguments between the hired laborers, devotees of the protosocialist Saint-Simon, and the more conservative Catholic accountants, the final work was never completed. The gate's top was left intact, arcing above the lane, its sharp and heavy pointed hooks, primitive precursors of modern concertina wire, curling menacingly down toward the cobblestones below. It was here that they found the body of Leon Vallet hanging early on Monday morning, the iron spikes impaling his thick neck and skull. Blood was splashed down the wall and across the cobblestones like spilled paint.

"How did he even get up there?" had been the first, and remained the most, obvious question. There was no clear answer. One policeman suggested he had somehow fallen from the neighboring building, but Vidot could see that was impossible. The hooks faced downward: Leon Vallet must have been thrust up into them. The small team investigating the scene offered up various theories. Perhaps he was riding atop a tall truck that had driven beneath the gate. But a truck would not be found on these narrow streets, and besides, what would a successful man of finance be doing atop such a truck? Was he taking a hayride? No, no. Perhaps an explosion had thrust him upward? This was easily dismissed, as there were no signs of combustion, either on his body or on the ground below.

"Did anyone report hearing any unusual sounds?" Vidot asked.

"No," said a patrolman. "We have asked around the neighborhood. They said it was a quiet night."

Vidot nodded. He looked at the corpse that lay on the street. It had taken the team the better part of an hour to unhook and carefully lower the victim. It was incredible that his skull and neck had been able to support such heavy weight. Vidot would have thought gravity would have pulled the torso down from the hook, splattering the lower body's contents on the pavement while leaving the impaled head alone on top, but then, he realized, anatomy was a tenacious thing as bones clung to bones much the same way that life clings to life.

Over the following two days, the preliminary basics of the investigation had been covered. Vallet's wife, Claudette, was informed of the murder. She had been away, at their country château, and learned of her tragedy only upon returning home. She was grief stricken and though she remained a suspect, Vidot deemed it not likely. His one meeting with the woman had revealed a small, murine creature who was most likely easily frightened by strong summer breezes and afternoon shadows, not the sort capable of an act so macabre. Cursory professional inquiries had meanwhile pointed to a wealth of potentially vengeful enemies, as it was revealed that Leon Vallet had not run the most scrupulous business.

More promising still was the discovery, uncovered while inspecting his account books, of an apartment Leon Vallet had been paying for located only blocks from the crime scene. Vidot went to visit the flat, accompanied by three policemen. Entering the spacious rooms, it was immediately clear that whoever had been living there had been well provided for during their stay. There were oil paintings on the walls, expensive linens for the large bed, and a full set of fine Wedgwood porcelain in the sideboard. It did not interest Vidot that Leon Vallet had such a nicely feathered love nest. What did interest Vidot, as he sniffed in the empty dresser and poked at the bare closet, was that Leon's lover had flown away.

He stood in the middle of the bedroom, considering the various possibilities, as the other policemen continued their search, looking under the bed, behind couch cushions, pulling out the drawers of the small escritoire and knocking gently at the sides of the grand armoire, listening for secret panels. Smiling the way a boy being tickled grins before he finally breaks into laughter, Vidot walked over and examined a silver picture frame. He focused on the empty space inside the frame for a moment, as if observing details of the image that was not there. Then he moved down the mantel, turning his attention to two clocks perched near the center. He went up so close that his inquisitive nose practically touched their glass faces and then pointed at a wide space between them. "A gap," he said, turning to the young policeman who stood by the door. "You, what is your name?"

"Bemm, monsieur."

"Well, Bemm, I would like you to ask around at the local pawn shops and antique stores, anything in a five-kilometer radius, and see if you can find a clock, I am guessing it is a very rare clock, that has either been sold to the shop directly or left there on consignment. And if the proprietors have not received one recently, please ask them to keep their eyes open. Indicate, but do not promise, the possibility of a reward."

Vidot then went into the kitchenette. Looking down past the sink, he was excited to see that the policeman had not yet looked into the small metal garbage pail tucked in beside the counter. This was one of Vidot's favorite places to search. People tended to be thoughtless with their trash, and even the most cunning criminals had a habit of leaving a wealth of useful materials behind—notes, letters, in one case even a grocery list of various pharmaceutical poisons. Clues dumped in the bin were almost always forgotten by the guilty parties, as if all garbage vanished from reality the moment the lid closed shut. Vidot knew better. He had spent more than a few afternoons knee-deep in the dumps and landfills on the outskirts of the city, foraging for soggy and rotting evidence amid the rich layers of debris. He knew nothing really ever disappeared, it only changed form.

He dumped the bin's waste into the sink and began picking through it. There was no mail and no personal papers, only three eggshells; a few lemon rinds; scrapings of burnt rice; the unused ends of a baguette; cucumber, onion, carrot scraps; a hunk of moldy cheese; and some soiled sections of *Le Monde*. There were also fragmentary pieces of bone that at first he thought might be chicken, though they were oddly enmeshed in what seemed to be a tangle of peat moss. He carefully separated this mass from the rest of the trash and placed it on the counter.

The policeman going through the kitchen drawers glanced over his shoulder. "I haven't seen one of those in a while."

"What is it?" asked Vidot.

"We used to hunt for them on the forest floor out at my grandparents' country place. We called them owl balls."

Vidot grinned at him. "Owl balls?"

"Yes, they are the remnants of mice, voles, or baby rabbits, whatever the owl has caught and swallowed. The owl pounces on the creatures and gobbles them up whole. Later the owl coughs up the indigestible bits in small pellets. That's what you have there, I'd swear to it."

"Owl balls," said Vidot, looking down at the fragments while rolling the idea around in his head with a delicious sense of wonder.

IV

Although it had been almost two months since they had last seen or spoken to one another, neither had said much when the younger one showed up at the door. Elga had let her in and then put a kettle on the stove. Zoya dropped her bags and limped over to the couch. Before the water was even boiling, the younger one was fast asleep. Over the next few days the old one said little, cooking for them both and going out every so often to get stock for the soup and ice chips for Zoya's black eye. Elga only asked a few questions.

"He beat you?"

Zoya shook her head. "No. He would never. The words made him kick, his shoe caught me as he was going up."

"He went up?"

"The spell went wrong. There were spikes above me I didn't see. The words pulled him there. I was aiming for a gate on the corner. It happened fast and he kicked as he flew."

"Who can blame him for kicking? Nobody wants to go." Elga nodded. "Did you empty your place?"

"Mostly, there was too much to take it all. But do not worry, I was thorough enough. I tagged one trunk and shipped it to the Luxembourg Station, the taxi dropped another at the North. I'll send for them when I have a place to stay." Zoya felt the exhaustion of her breath crawling out of her body. Perhaps this was the end. That would be fine, her bones were so tired. Her stomach felt as if there were rotting weeds stewing at the bottom. Here she was again, counting on the patience and tolerance of this stooped and ancient creature who tended to be neither.

She realized that over the course of the years, the length of her stays with the old woman had shrunk to fit Elga's vanishing patience. Perhaps, after so much time, they had finally outgrown one another. But she also knew that she still needed and even wanted the old woman in her life. They were, as far as she knew, the only two left.

There had been many more of them once, and not only the women they had traveled with but still others, sighted and acknowledged in glances and knowing nods caught amid early-morning markets and in the busy, bustling streets, but the ones she had known by name had vanished long ago, and no new faces had stepped out from the crowd. So it seemed there were only the two of them, now too ill fitted to one another's company, and so after this small pause she would be off on her own again, probably before she had even wholly caught her breath.

Over the next few days, Zoya lay on the couch, listening as a tone-deaf accordionist practiced *bal musette* somewhere in the floors above. She did not know how Elga paid for her small basement flat, it certainly was not with money, the old woman was too tight to ever part with a coin when a trick would do. Perhaps she was dangling a sordid secret over her landlord's conscience. Or maybe she had convinced him that she did not even exist, though that would be an ambitious spell, even for Elga. This woman was hard to hide. The room brimmed over with stacks of dusty papers, piles of dried herbs, and long rows of packed bookshelves all lined with discolored jars stuffed with pickled organs, hoof and snout. A dank, permeating odor of mildew mixed with burnt ginger and soured cheese leaked from the walls, and there were constant rustling, scratching, and scraping sounds off in the shadowed corners.

Elga brought out another kettle and poured the tea. Zoya looked down at the old woman's spotted, knotted hands; the veins reminded her of the gnarled tree roots that clung tenaciously to the lichened boulders up in the northern forests.

"I have a present for you," Zoya told the old woman. Digging into her bag, she pulled out a large object wrapped up in a sheet. Placing it on the couch, she carefully peeled off the fabric and held it up for Elga to admire.

The old woman gave it a blank look. "What do I want with a clock?"

Zoya shrugged. "I thought you'd like it. Look . . ." She pointed to the small golden swan perched on the top. "It's beautiful, isn't it? Like the treasures from the palace."

Elga said nothing but took the clock out of Zoya's hands and shoved it atop a cockeyed stack on the shelf. The old woman had always been impossible to predict—Zoya had seen her cackle and hop with joy at the gift of a simple sugar cube—but these past few days her mood seemed even more erratic and dark.

The old woman sat down on the floor, shelling sunflower seeds, while Zoya lay back on the couch. A squeaking in the room kept her awake. Zoya opened her eyes and watched the scrawny black rat finally emerge from beneath the couch to chew at the corner of the rug. "Don't let Max bother you," grunted Elga. "I will send him out on his errands soon."

Zoya nodded and shut her eyes again. She felt as if she had been drugged, but she knew it was the spell that had drained her. Also, she always hated being without her own bed and her own room, wherever that might be. Being a guest always left her ill at ease, especially with Elga. Their journeys always brought them together for a handful of days, a full cycle of a moon, or even at times for years, but then they eventually diverged again, Zoya to the arms of another warm patron and Elga back to her busy stews.

When Zoya woke again from her nap the old woman was sitting across the room, her pudgy feet propped up on the cold woodstove, leafing through the pages of *Figaro*. "There's nothing in here about your Leon. I guess all they could say is, what? His wife is sad and the policemen are still snooping around."

Elga balled the newspaper up and threw it into the stove. Trudging over to the couch, she squatted beside Zoya. The old woman lowered her head and nodded, muttering to herself. Zoya waited. The room was silent, even the rat was finally still. When Elga looked up, it was as if she had come to a firm decision.

With one fierce stroke she slapped Zoya across the face so hard that the shriek was torn from the girl's lips. The old woman grabbed Zoya's hair, pulled her close, and stuck her red bug eyes up into the girl's terrified face. "There wasn't a train he could fall in front of?" she hissed. "Is poison too slow? You have always been too showy, too stupid, such an awful and tiresome creature. Mistakes can be avoided. They must be avoided. My god, you can disgust me." She slapped her again, harder this time.

Zoya's words fell out through her tears. "I'm sorry, I'm sorry. I panicked. He had noticed, Elga. I was frightened."

Elga let go of her hair and got up. "So what, he notices? Suck a man's cock and he forgets so much. It's easier than sticking his head onto a spike." She went back to her chair, leaving the girl curled up in a weeping ball. "Bah. Fine. Pull yourself together." She took a box of matches off the shelf and leaned over to light the stove, not even looking at Zoya anymore. "You make things too unsafe. Police sniff-sniffing around. We will have to leave town and begin again. Why do I want to waddle these bones of mine for you? I am fine here alone without you showing up and ruining it all."

"No, Elga, it's fine. I'll go. I won't bother you."

"Fine. Go soon. You make it hard for me to think, and the neighbors will notice you. I don't need their questions. So yes, go."

A little less than an hour later, Zoya was packed up to leave, relieved to be going. With no kindness in her gesture, the old woman shoved a grocer's bag filled with carrots, red potatoes, and a handful of leek sprouts into her hands and then tucked a pair of small white eggs into her pockets. Zoya thought Elga might offer a kind word too—not an apology, but perhaps some phrase laced with tenderness—but all the old woman said was, "Don't come here again. If I move, I'll let you know, but don't come back. If you need help, well, keep an eye out for Max. He'll be close. Now go." The girl looked down at the rat, which sat watching from the corner. She nodded to herself, her mouth set firm and determined. Elga was right, it was time. She had probably rested enough, and her injured eye's swelling had receded; there was now only a dark streak, more a smudge than a bruise, that made her look like a sooty chimney waif.

The old woman followed her out to the stoop and then stood watching as Zoya walked off down the cobblestone street. A nausea itched in Elga's guts. The girl boiled her blood. For so many years she had needed Zoya, leaned on her, used her to find safe harbor as they were pitched about the brutal landscape. It had been a tiresome journey for them both, from the far-off country quiet of long vanished woodlands through the black billowing exhaust and shrill screech of steel railway wheels as they made their way on, station to station, ducking and stepping between the dueling engines of empire wars and burgeoning progress. Civilization was ever encroaching, barreling down upon them, crowding them and clouding their path with the gunpowder haze and steam-engine smoke, pressing and pushing them down narrow lanes toward dead-end corners, forcing tricks from their hands and curses from their lips as they found a way to leap free over and again.

But things were peaceful now, now she did not see the girl for weeks at a time, even months, and never missed her. There was no need. The continent was as quiet as a sleeping lamb, and the two of them had settled down with it. The papers called it a "cold war" but that seemed an odd phrase to Elga, she knew cold wars, they were the ones where hatchets and knives wielded by frostbitten fingers chopped solid meat sides off frozen stallion corpses. Those true cold wars had nothing in common with what she found in the newspapers now, but it was certainly an easier time, and as the din died down, she found the pretty dark-haired girl with the slender hips and the fulsome bosom to be growing tiresome. Each time she saw Zoya it bothered her more, like some silly farmer's song you hate hearing but are forced to endure a thousand times until it claws at your ears. She could not place a reason for the irritation, but the feeling was so strong it felt almost cystic inside her. Time to cut it out, she thought, and good riddance.

The wind kicked up and she sniffed at it. Coal soot, sea salt, ham, yeast, and dog hair, nothing new, nothing to worry about. She stood there, distracted, random words tumbling round in her mind, until a neighbor noisily emerged with a crate of empty milk bottles. Broken from her daydream, Elga waddled back into her flat, shutting the door hard behind her.

V

The tuxedoed jazz trio was playing a bouncy tune he didn't know, there was no one in the black-tie crowd who he recognized, and the average age of the women there was somewhere north of fifty. But Will stayed on, seduced by the charms of an open bar. The event was ostensibly a book party for a Parisian politician's wife, but the chatty guests didn't look very bookish to Will. It seemed more like an up-and-coming chapter of Paris's down-market society crowd. The men's suits all seemed a size off, and the women's dresses were either drab and dull or taffeta loud. Beside him, an ancient pair of *grandes dames* wearing outfits that looked like they were cut from wallpaper samples prattled on about summer shopping in Monte Carlo. One of them caught Will listening and abruptly asked, "*Êtes-vous un critique?*"

"No," he answered politely, "I am only here for the cocktails."

The women both laughed, a little too loud. "Of course, we are too," said the one in blue. With their excessive makeup and painted eyebrows, they both looked like wax figurines caught melting in the sun.

"Are you British?" one asked.

"American," Will said.

"Ah!" The women both beamed at this news. "Are you a writer? An artist?" asked the red dress.

"Are you from New York?" the blue dress chimed in.

Will shook his head to both questions. "Actually, I'm from Detroit. I work for an advertising agency here."

At this news, both women made a funny face, as if they had each simultaneously bitten into a disagreeable dish. Will was unsure if it was the word "advertising" or "Detroit" that had ruined their high spirits, though he suspected both. He excused himself with a polite nod and began working his way across the crowd until he found a more peaceful corner by the table where the books were piled up. He lit a cigarette, listened for a bit to the jazz, and began leafing through a copy. According to the cover, *Rendezvous at Saint-Cloud* was a memoir of forbidden love in the French resistance. He was flipping through it, looking for pictures, when a voice speaking in a distinctively Brahmin American accent interrupted him from behind.

"A pretty piece of fiction, don't you think?"

Will turned to see a tall, thin man with sandy blond hair eyeing the book stacks with a slight grin.

"Excuse me?" Will asked.

"Their so-called underground resistance," said the man, gesturing toward the books. "Totally charming nonsense, absurd, nothing more than a collective hallucination, really."

Babayaga

Will was a bit taken aback and looked around nervously. "Well, I'm not sure I would go so far as to—"

"You know"—the man picked up the book and studied the cover—"I once met a former GI who had parachuted in here during the height of the Occupation. By the time I met him, this fellow was one hell of a drunk, the sort with the grand gin-blossomed beak that scares off small children, but in his prime he must have had real guts. He told me about how the OSS dropped him in with a crate packed with Browning rifles, revolvers, grenades, a couple of Thompsons, a veritable cornucopia really, all gifts for our friends in the underground. The problem was, once he landed he couldn't find a soul willing to take the stuff off his hands. Wandered around the city for weeks, and all he ran into were your usual run of perfidious black marketeers, reprobate collaborators, and more than a few fast Nazi bullets he had to dodge. In the end, he buried the guns on the southwestern side of town, down someplace in the catacombs, and then skedaddled back across the Channel. He and I had quite the chatty night at the Algonquin. He even gave me a map he'd sketched out of where his stash was hidden." The man placed the book back on the top of the stack. "Care to see if we can dig it up?"

"Excuse me? Dig up what?" Will felt a little confused.

The man smiled. "The guns, of course. They're out there somewhere."

Will was not clear if he was being kidded or not. "No, that's okay."

"Another time perhaps." The man took a sip of his drink and patted his lapel. "I do always carry his map here in my wallet on the off chance I ever find myself in need of a Thompson. Seems prudent, don't you think?"

Will looked around, nobody else seemed to be noticing this curious man with the strange ideas. The fellow stuck out his hand. "Hullo there, sorry. Oliver Pierce Ames."

"Will Van Wyck."

"'Van Wyck,' yes, like that new expressway back in New York. I hear it's marvelous. Say, what kind of cigarettes do you have on you?"

"Chesterfields. Want one?"

"Ah, yes please. God bless you. I can't stand to smoke any more of that nag hay they sell over here." Oliver managed to take the cigarette and light it without pausing in his speech. He was a talkative fellow. "You know, I saw you walk in and knew in a snap you were a Yank. You're too broad-shouldered to be French. And such American teeth. So what brings you to this corner tonight?"

"A friend gave me a ticket."

"A *friend*? What sort of friend sends you to a party like this?"

"Well, actually, it was a colleague; he got stuck with a ticket. Brandon must have thought it was going to be a different kind of party."

"Well, you never know with book parties. The better ones can be outrageously good." Oliver gave him a curious look. "Actually, when I first saw you I thought you might have been escorting those two *grandes dames* over there."

Will laughed. "No, no. I came alone."

Oliver sipped his drink again and looked around the room. "Brandon, you say? Wouldn't be Bob Brandon, would it?"

"Yes. I sort of know him through work. You know him?"

"Only slightly. It's a small town for Americans, you know. Seems like a good man. You work at the agency?"

"Yes, I do. I was transferred over from the States two years ago."

"Really?" Oliver said. "So what do you do there?"

"Not a lot these days," said Will. "I used to manage a lot of different things, but it's gotten kind of quiet."

"Yes, well." Oliver sipped his drink. "Can't say I know much about how the agency works. No reason to, I suppose. Golly, nothing's more boring than shoptalk, is it?" Oliver gave him a quick, curious look. "Though I am curious why on God's green earth Brandon ever thought *this* would be fun for you."

"Like I said, must have been some sort of mix-up."

"Either that or your friend has a bit of a cruel streak, throwing you out like fresh carrion for all these dusty dowagers to descend upon."

Will smiled. "How come you're here?"

"I know the publisher, we play belote now and again. I'd hoped to find some real writers here, but they are such an elusive bunch." Oliver looked at his watch. "Actually, I'm supposed to be meeting up with a couple of girls right around the corner in a bit. At Taillevent, ever been?"

Will shook his head no.

"There are two girls and only one of me. So perhaps you should join? The restaurant's a touch stuffy but the food's fabulous, and their crab remoulade is beyond words. Please, come. It's always nice to have a fourth."

Will felt a little uncertain if he should say yes. Oliver looked him in the eye and smiled.

Five hours later, Will lay stone drunk on a bench below the Pont Neuf, blearily gazing at the lights playing across the dancing surface of the night-blackened river. A few feet away, Oliver was humming a waltz tune as he slow-danced with the young brunette named Juliette. She was wearing a short white dress with matching pearls. The other girl, more beautiful than Juliette, and far too lovely for Will, had found a taxi home hours before. The yellow moon was verging on full and the stars up in the sky looked blurred and undefined, as if someone had splashed water across them before their ink could dry. Will tried to recall what day it was and prayed it was Saturday or Sunday. The sun would be up soon and he was in no condition for work.

The dinner had been enjoyable. Oliver had introduced Will as an old friend from America and the two French girls had quickly complimented him on his fluency. He explained how his mother's family had emigrated down from French Canada to Detroit ("Ah, Detroit!" exclaimed Oliver, "the Paris of the Midwest!") and so he had grown up with a rough-hewn colonial version of French bouncing around the house. It had grown more refined in his time in Paris, though it was far from perfect ("*Absolument!*" the girls laughed. "*C'est pas du tout parfait!*"). He was going to tell them more, but Oliver interrupted with one long anecdote that spilled into another, and as the evening progressed, that turned out to be just about all Will had a chance to say. Instead, he and the girls listened on while the seemingly ever-present sommelier popped bottle after bottle of '47 Clos Saint Jean's and Oliver bubbled over with gossip, rumors, anecdotes, and broad, flirtatious innuendos that made the girls blush and giggle into their napkins. Will did not mind, Oliver seemed to be both fascinating and humorously silly as, over the course of the evening, he described swamping his mother's vintage Jordan roadster in the Connecticut River, sang them a smattering of old Phillips Exeter fight songs, butchered some Keats verse in a slightly slurred attempt at oration, and then drunkenly reenacted the march he had made entering Rome with the American army.

"You were in the infantry?" asked Will, now a bit tipsy too.

"Yes, nothing very brave, mostly clerical work. Supply-line stuff. My father, of course, harbored much greater ambitions for me, firstborn son and all that, but it turns out the dreamy, poetic types make for rather poor officer material."

"Well, he must have been proud of you, you did your part."

"Oh, in the end he was proud enough. I sent him a photo of me with Patton. That positively thrilled the old man," Oliver said, refilling his own glass. "What about you? You look too young to have served then, did you do Korea?"

"No . . ." Will hesitated, feeling a little self-conscious. Coming out of a working-class family, he knew he had been fortunate not to have been drafted, and an academic scholarship had kept him from having to sign up to cover the costs of school. But he never felt lucky about it, especially when he was talking to a veteran like Oliver. It was one of the reasons he liked living abroad in France, he felt less surrounded by those pressures. The subject rarely came up; people in Paris tended to be quiet about what they did during the war.

"Well, maybe you didn't serve then, but you certainly serve now, don't you?" Oliver said, leaning over with a knowing smile. "We all serve."

The line puzzled Will and he was about to ask what Oliver meant, but instead his friend plucked up two spoons and made them dance the cancan, which again got their dates giggling and the moment passed, dissolving into various chocolate and meringue desserts served with fruit brandies and followed by more servings of Oliver's effervescent chatter, this time about a conspiracy he was obsessed with, a cover-up involving a silver flying saucer that had been found somewhere in the deserts of New Mexico. Everyone laughed at his imitation of a little green man from Mars.

The two girls began asking Oliver's opinion on various topics, and Will realized he should know a bit more about the range of subjects they touched upon, the fashionable filmmakers like Chabrol and Truffaut and the new authors he had never heard of—Robbe-Grillet, Butor, and Duras. He knew a little about current events, the situation in Algiers and the return of de Gaulle, but only what the headlines told him, not enough to have anything resembling an informed opinion. Listening on as the subjects went by, one by one, like train cars clattering along through the night, Will was aware again of how, despite the time spent here and all the things he had done, Paris remained vast and impermeably foreign to him. For the first time since that heady season when he was literally fresh off the boat, the city once again felt exotic.

When he had arrived, more than two years before, Will had earnestly planned to immerse himself in the arts, the museums, the theater, and great stacks literature, to become more cultured, even sophisticated. He imagined taking tours of the Louvre's galleries and attending lectures at the Sorbonne. But, wearied from the tedious days at work, he had wound up spending his leisure time focusing only on the food, the wine, and the women. He had spent more time chatting up the owl-eyed girls with the straight gray skirts and bare legs he met browsing the shelves at Shakespeare & Company and Galignani than he did reading the actual books. In fact, he rarely got to the books. But it was hard to feel guilty about it when even the basest pleasures of Paris were so abundant and entirely elevating. Tonight, though, he did feel a slight pang of guilt for all the time he had wasted. He nodded and smiled along, feeling the shame of his ignorance as he quietly scraped the last mocha out of his *pot de crème* while his dinner companions chattered on about protosocialist revolutions and structural linguistics.

To Will's relief, not only did all the intellectual conversation finally peter out, but, as the last cheese plate was picked clean and the table finally cleared, Oliver picked up the check too, with a reassuringly confident gesture indicating that he had it happily covered. Then, still laughing and chatting, the four of them crowded into a taxi and began a drunken, fruitless search for a mythical Latin Quarter jazz band. Oliver claimed to know the players in the band. "These cats are mad with talent! Their music is absolutely phosphorescent!" he kept shouting, though after many stops and drinks, it turned out the band wasn't playing at any place they could find, nor had any of the various waitresses or bartenders ever heard of them. Eventually, the prettier girl yawned and peeled off, leaving polite farewell kisses on Will's flushed cheeks. He wandered on with the other two as they eventually found their way to this secluded spot beneath the bridge on the Seine.

The last of the bottle of Drambuie that Oliver had bought off the last bartender had been finally drained dry and the Chesterfields were all ground dead into the stone. Will lay on the bench, listening to Oliver hum his little waltz to the girl as they danced along the gravel path. Gazing past them, across the water, Will watched a low barge slowly work its way up the river. To his sideways mind, the small glimmering gas lanterns on the boat's sides seemed to be heading off to a rendezvous with the flickering stars above, their luminous sisters in the floating constellations.

The sound of the water against the barge's bow reminded Will of being a young boy back home, standing on Jefferson Avenue, watching the massive gray cargo ships churn down the Detroit River on their way to the enormous and looming Rouge mills. Those vast, ugly ships, so large they seemed to barely fit bank to bank, were laden full of the raw, mined ore pulled from the Iron Range that would be forged and molded and stamped into the new industrial skin for the whole wide world. And what were these charming Parisian barges filled with? Sacks of grain for little baby lambs? Ground corn for pecking geese? Fresh-milled white wheat flour for warm morning croissants and baguettes? And why did he find the small boat so beautiful and romantic while those much larger ones were to his eyes only ugly and overbearing? Why do we love the little things so? Will grinned to himself. See, he thought, I can be philosophical. He drunkenly chuckled and his eyes flickered low as, one by one, a string of imaginary yellow ducks nimbly swam across the sea of his mind, each one kissing out puffs of vanishing smoke.

Babayaga

He awoke twisted up in his suit, as the dawn's first flush was tinting pink, yellow, and orange off the clouds and glinting gold and bronze off the Paris rooftops. He sat up on the bench, rubbing his eyes and glancing around. Only here, he realized, could one wake like a vagrant and feel so lucky and blessed. The city was dappled in light, looking Impressionistic and wholly refreshed from its own nocturnal slumber. Checking his jacket to make sure he still had his wallet, he found a note scrawled onto the back of the dinner receipt: "Pricey dinner. We'll sort it tonight. Meet me at 9 rue Git-le-Coeur at eight p.m. Be prompt. Ta, O.P.A." He studied the note. Was Oliver saying that Will owed him for dinner? That didn't seem right. What else did they need to sort out? Plus, there were a few other words scratched at the bottom that he couldn't make out. Finally, studying the handwriting carefully, he deciphered it: "p.s. bring a knife."

VI

Most French men, like his father and uncles, were completely happy to leave the kitchen work to their wives. But Charles Vidot enjoyed cooking with Adèle. Their kitchenette space was tiny and cramped, but after ten years of patient practice they now moved about one another in what felt to him like a smoothly choreographed routine. She diced while he mixed, she poured while he simmered. All while he recounted the details of his days to her, and with this series of small, brisk movements, Charles Vidot was able to unwind from his life at work and reattach himself to the cozy and satisfying comforts of home. The radio was whistling out Debussy. "You see," he said to her, "it seems Monsieur Vallet had a lover."

"A lover," she said.

He could not tell if she was merely repeating what he said or asking for more details. "Yes"—he put the pan on the burner and turned on the gas—"a lover who has utterly vanished, leaving nothing but the faintest trace of her scent on the pillow."

Adèle smiled. "You smelled the pillow?"

"Well"—he smiled—"I would not be much of a detective if I had not."

Adèle nodded. "And what did it smell like?"

Charles paused to think. "Citrus and jasmine . . . expensive."

"So, perhaps whoever killed him also frightened his lover away."

"Perhaps," he said skeptically. He put the two chicken breasts on the skillet, letting them simmer with the garlic and the butter.

"But you suspect her?"

"Probably, yes. She is certainly the most interesting element in this case." He told her about the girl's garbage bin and the strange remnants he had discovered there.

"A few mouse bones spit from an owl do not necessarily make her a suspect," said Adèle.

"That is quite true. And if she were present I am sure she could have provided a reasonable explanation. But she is not, so . . ."

There was so little room in the kitchenette that her waist slid against her husband's as he shook the pan. He smiled at this, savoring the small satisfactions that fed their life together. He watched as she squeezed lemon onto a bowl of shredded carrots and placed them to the side. She gave him a small smile. Was it a remote smile? A hesitant one? He could not tell. She had been difficult to read as of late. "Have your headaches been back?"

"Yes, earlier this week," she said, "but the new pills from the pharmacist seem to help."

"Better than the tea?"

"I don't know. Perhaps. The doctor tells me my tea recipe is merely an old wives' tale."

"Ah well, if it works, it works." Charles leaned over and kissed her on the cheek. "I am glad I could come home early." He had thought of staying at his office desk to peruse various notes on the case, there were interviews to comb through and the coroner's statement to study, but he hated being in the station of late. A new chief of police for Paris, Maurice Papon, had recently been installed. In Vidot's opinion, Papon was a thoroughly dishonorable man who, twenty years earlier, had stood out as one of the very worst of the Vichy collaborators. But history in France was a fickle thing, and as the nation healed from its great trauma, the powers that be had found a place for Papon. Once installed in his new office, this quisling had moved quickly, placing numerous other regrettable characters in various high positions throughout the department, including Vidot's new superior at the station, a stout, lethargic toad of a creature named Maroc. As a detective, Vidot had encountered many disagreeable sorts, both criminal and civilian, and he liked to think he had a patient spirit and could tolerate any soul so long as they did not obstruct his path; but Maroc strained his patience. The man's every expression insinuated either dishonesty or lethargy. Vidot found him nauseating and hated even being on the same city block with the man, and so this evening, after typing his case report in duplicate and leaving a copy in Maroc's in-box, he locked up his files and made his way home.

But he was not done with the case that day, for work was not something that Vidot ever entirely left at the office. He lived and breathed and often dreamt about his cases until they were done. "My husband is a man of passion," Adèle used to dryly joke with their friends. "Unfortunately, his passion is police work." So, there in the kitchen, his thoughts now turned to the puzzle of Leon's missing lover. Vidot did not judge the man too harshly for having a mistress. It occurred all too often in French society, it was as ordinary as the sliver of lemon rind that came with his morning espresso. But, in his opinion, it did signify a weak man and a dull mind. Any fool could seduce, but it took a true intellect to know and love his partner. Women, to Charles Vidot, were absolute and thrilling mysteries. They moved through the world as if a different gravity applied to them and answered to untranslatable calls of the body and soul. So many times, especially of late, Adèle had utterly befuddled him with her sudden moods and reactions to events. Tears would arrive and tempers would flare with no warning, vanishing again as if carried away by some unseen benevolent wind. He understood that these sorts of unpredictable mood changes often frustrated and shut lesser men down, sending them searching for other, seemingly more simple, beds; but to Vidot a woman's riddles were nothing to run from, each was another enigma to be solved, another curious knot to untie. He knew he could never completely comprehend the wonder, the strangeness, that was his wife—how could one soul ever know another?—but he did completely love every small challenge that she gave him, every shadowed and mysterious moment she delivered. They may not have been as physically intimate as they once were, in fact lately she seemed even more distant from his touch, but that was fine; after all, they were not lusty schoolchildren. As far as Vidot was concerned, their union was a complete one, encompassing all the harmonies and inherent contradictions any relationship could hope to hold.

They sat at the table, held hands, and said their habitual small prayer of thanks. Charles opened a thick volume of the encyclopedia to a chapter on owls and read as he ate. He found himself quickly distracted by a description of this strange bird's incredible powers of hearing (a high perched owl could detect the sounds of a tiny mouse moving beneath a foot of snow!) as Adèle slowly finished her food in silence. She never seemed to object when he worked at the supper table. In fact, it was how they spent many evenings. She was employed at the university library and would often bring him home books on subjects related to his cases. It made him happy to share his work with her, and he was always grateful for her thoughtful assistance and insights. To him, it was like they were one organism, different arms and legs carrying the two lobes of one great mind.

Adèle finally rose and began clearing the empty plates. "Perhaps the woman is also dead. They could have thrown her body in the river," she said as she headed into the kitchen.

"No," Charles said, looking up from his reading. "I am certain that Leon Vallet's lover is very much alive. Not only were her dresser drawers cleaned out but also the bottom of her closet was completely bare. And a dead woman rarely takes all her shoes with her, however much she might like to."

VII

Zoya chose the hotel down the hill from Place Pigalle because it was two stories higher than the other buildings on the block. Also, it was inexpensive and the block it stood on, though busy, had none of the loud nightclubs or neon that filled the rest of the district. In the small, yellow-tiled lobby, the man working at the front desk was not wearing a suit or even a jacket, only a sleeveless white T-shirt with a pair of suspenders. He itched at himself as she signed the register.

"That's not from bedbugs or fleas, I hope?" she said.

"No," said the man with a self-conscious grin. "It's only a little rash."

She knew a simple myrrh cure for his ailment but she was not in a mood to be generous. "I need a room on the top floor if you can, one with a bath."

"No problem," he said. "The top floor is mostly empty because the elevator is broken. I only have one room up there with its own bath, but it is our most expensive."

"*Quoi?* The most expensive? With no elevator?"

The man shrugged. "It's a big room. Lots of sunlight."

"Fine, I'll take it," she said. "But I will need some assistance with my luggage when it arrives from the station. I hope that will not be a problem."

The clerk smiled. "Not a problem for me. I'm off in ten minutes. The next fellow can take it up."

She counted out franc notes to him as he explained that each room had a kitchenette with an electric coil, but that the only working phone in the building was behind the front desk. "We do not let guests use it unless it is an emergency. Otherwise, there is a phone booth down the hill on the corner. They sell the *jetons* for it down at the tabac."

When she reached her room she found it was quite spacious. She ran the faucet. The pipes rattled and banged but the water came out clean. She opened the windows and, reaching into her bag, took out a small stub of a red candle. After lighting it, she removed a few small striped feathers from her pocket and placed them on the outside of the window. She dripped the candle wax onto their thin quills to fasten them to the sill, pressing them into place with a centime. The birds would find her, maybe not tonight, but soon.

From another pocket she took a piece of chalk and wrote a row of small words on the inside of the hotel room's door. Then she filled the tub and took off her clothes.

A hot bath almost always made her recall the fierce, frigid cold that had, through the years, so often clenched its teeth into her bones. She had to be careful with memories. When they flooded her unexpectedly, triggered perhaps by something as slight as the scent of blooming dianthus or the sharp taste of anise, they could overwhelm and debilitate her. But it felt safe to recall those deathly days of ice and cold when she was tucked in a warm bath. It was as if, enshrouded and cloaked in the thick cloud of rising steam, the ever-hunting frost could not find her.

There had been five of them when they began their flight west from St. Petersburg. They had watched every train pull out of the Warsaw Station, the cars headed west toward the Balkans, packed full of deserting soldiers, all pale-faced and drunk with desperation, impure vodka, and the mighty relief of escape. The city's spare horses were all gone—eaten or seized—and the handful of automobiles in the city had been taken too, commandeered by panicked priests and overflowing with the frightened remnants of their splintered congregations. Their faces stared out as they sped by, heading fast to the border in their stolen cars. Too tired to coax their passage, still exhausted from weeks of furiously wrought protective spells, the five women watched as all those in the city who could took flight, and then they followed, on foot, trailing the last vehicles' sputtering black exhaust, steadfastly heading down the frozen roads toward nothing.

The first lost had been Mazza, a day into the journey, shot dead as they stole a pair of mares from a barn. Zoya had looked back when she heard the gun's report and saw Mazza's eye explode out in wild, crimson red. They had not slowed their pace and the woman's body was left behind, lying crooked, facedown, with the snow staining scarlet around her as they galloped their new horses away.

Three days later, the hard-driven mares already dead, the women had been running across a frozen estuary when Lyda broke through, sinking with only half a gurgled shriek, the heavy hidden current hungrily gulping down her last gasp, her thick knit woolen clothes making the swallowing simple for the river. Again they did not pause—no one looked back and nothing was said. Any words spoken would only slow their momentum.

Basha was the last to go. Sneaking from their campsite into a nearby village to forage for food, she had muttered a small charm for protection and disappeared down the road. Elga had slept soundly that night, curled up in her guttural snore, but Zoya lay awake, staring up at the stark claws of winter branches looming above her, waiting for Basha's familiar footsteps to return to camp. When Elga finally rose the next morning and saw Basha had not made it back, she insisted they leave at once. Tucking her bulky Nagant into her belt, Elga patted the pistol. "We can sit here and wait, see who comes. But if it is not Basha, well, I only have so many bullets. You know, I always say the best plan is to run." And so they turned south, and they ran.

For the rest of their journey, Zoya could sense the three lost women following their trail, one bloodied and blind, one soaked, spitting fish scales, and one invisible, a ghost in a ghost. She could feel them at her heels, haunting and hovering over as she and Elga pressed on, bearing down side roads, hiding from passing armies, and digging out forgotten root crops and semispoiled cabbages from the hard soil. Finally, in the warrens and maze of old Krakow, she and the old woman slipped free from the noose of their past, finding a rich bounty in the classical warming comfort of wealthy men's laps and thick bankbooks. Pianos gaily played while she laughed and giggled, bouncing down into the deep plush divans and soft velvet lounge chairs, eating goose pâté, mushroom pierogi, and hot *naleśniki* topped with Finnish cloudberries while sipping bottomless crystal glasses of sparkling *Perlwein* and foamy steins of cold winter ale. The world was new once more. She remembered Elga laughing too, peering out from behind curtains and fogging service windows, staying back in the shadows of the kitchens and coatrooms while chuckling and clapping with relief as Zoya's snares caught their prey, watching her kiss, swoon, and giggle for the magistrates' fathers, the costermongers' sons, and every furrier's drunk uncle. Drowned out by the musical, mirthful tambourine jingle and bass drum din, Zoya's three ghosts finally receded, like water seeping away into the soil, though she sensed they were merely settling below the sediment, always close, constant in their waiting.

There was a knock at the door. Zoya rose from the bath and wrapped herself in her robe. The new desk clerk, a tall, sweating boy with acne, had hauled up one of her trunks. She tipped him and let him go.

Picking through the luggage, she found the white dress with the faded orange polka dots and the red high heels. It was not much, but it was all she needed. Krakow was long past, and now time had chased her into this corner, this bare room, this bone-stark poverty. But she had been here many times before. Looking herself over in the bathroom mirror, she saw over a hundred years of this race, this unending run. She knew its predictable rhythms, its steely electrical hum, she knew the necessary steps she would have to follow. She could almost hear the tempo starting up now, the tune that played for this dance she knew so well. It led to the unrelenting hunger of hearts, to lustful, searching eyes, and creeping, confident hands, to souls who believed that what they could touch they could own. She would give them all they wanted. There would be amorous whispers, false promises, ecstatic moans, and, if they wished it, even pleading, playful cries of pain. Every desire would be fulfilled, for night after night, and mornings too, until, in a snap or a sip, a slice or a shove, that final question, the greatest mystery, that which they had pondered for so long in their church pews and lecture halls, would finally be revealed for them. What a gift she would give. She smiled nervously at her reflection. Yes, she would provide them with everything. She always did. All her remembering was done. Now it was time to hunt.

VIII

Will checked his watch. It was only eight-twenty but the little nightclub was already a loud, crowded haze of Gitanes and Gauloises. A Cannonball Adderley LP bopped alto saxophone out through poor belabored speakers and people shouted in a rough cacophony above the music. Will was not surprised that his new friend was late. Oliver seemed to possess that sort of joie de vivre that did not lend itself to punctuality. Will was only surprised to find himself there. He did not particularly need to seek out new friends, as there were always nice ex-pat dinner parties to go to—the Lion's Club was hosting its weekly dinner that night, where he could have caught up with the many merry midwesterners who now lived here—and, even more preferably, he could have been on dates with pretty girls who were never too hard to find.

Though he had to admit, he had been growing a little wary of romance of late. When he had first arrived, he had quickly and happily embraced the ease of Parisian romance. Initially, he had only dated expat girls, but found that the British and Americans not only smoked too much (in fact, constantly) but also shared the habit of holding every cigarette in the same pronounced pose, as if they were about to say something of vital importance. Then, inevitably, they talked breathlessly and pretentiously and said nothing of interest to him at all. They were all young, overheated Rosalind Russells or Kate Hepburns, but without the scriptwriters on hand to supply them with decent material. Besides that, far too few of them remembered to relax enough to smile, and even when he got them into bed he found they were still affected, as if they were doing what they thought a woman was supposed to do, but nothing for which they had any instinct, or even desire.

Over time he built up enough confidence to start dating the local girls; they were more at ease with him, playing, teasing, and fun, and they enjoyed helping him improve his French. One girl called herself his "sleeping dictionary," and, in the depths of many nights, his fumbling attempts to convert his rustic French-Canadian into cosmopolitan Parisian had provided a good laugh. The Paris girls did make him feel a little self-conscious, like a redneck newly arrived in the big city, but they were almost all kind and generous girls, thoughtful and easy to get along with. More important, he enjoyed their boldness and their sexual style: they were much more physically open than the Americans or Brits; some insisted on being spanked like bad girls and others wanted to be wrestled down like wild animals, while still others simply swooned and sighed like modern dancers and then shared a cigarette with him after. But it was all entirely comfortable; they came into his life and then wandered off again with an ease he found surprising.

There were two of them, Marie and Nicole, whom he had dated for lengthy stretches, taking one skiing up in Morzine, the other sailing along the coast of Brittany, but in each case, the girls had drifted away, taking longer and longer to follow up on the messages he left until ultimately his calling cards went completely unanswered. He did not mind, for while he had been happy enough to buy them the cigarettes, silk stockings, and chewing gum they desired, he sensed they were aiming for the sort of men who also came with their own ski chalets, open cars, and cruising yachts.

Occasionally, he would see a girl he had once been with riding along down the avenue on the back of a Vespa or drinking wine with another boy at a bar, and they would all innocently wave and smile. It all seemed perfectly natural, but after a while it began to wear on him, leaving him feeling as though all he had been to any of them was an exotic treat, *"l'américain,"* or, as the menus in town put it, *"le dessert du moment."*

So, while he continued to date fairly regularly, going out dancing or catching a movie, he found spending a whole night with them to be what those pretentious British girls might have labeled an existentially empty event. He didn't quite know what to call it. All he knew was that when he woke up with some new girl sleeping beside him, either in his flat or hers, he often felt substantially less whole, as though he was losing a piece of himself through every encounter, slowly dissipating, dissolving, bits of him vanishing into the vacuum of the world, and, with every conquest, becoming in some manner more hollowed out. It was exactly the opposite feeling he had expected to feel with these sorts of heady, libidinal victories. He had been raised to believe they would provide him with some sense of validation; that's what he'd gathered from the way his uncles had talked about women ("babes," "honeys," "broads") when the men took him hunting up in northern Michigan. They'd boozily spit out ribald stories of stag parties and bawdy burlesque shows involving generous fat-bottomed and bosomy women who would put two tits in your face for a quarter but whose names no one could ever recall.

The emptiness was easy to shake off and move on from, but it had its effect. He had lately found himself less inclined to chase the pretty smiles of Paris and spent more time wandering the streets alone, eating in the bistros and reading the paper or sitting up late with a book, a Herman Wouk novel, Hemingway's Nick Adams tales, or a collection of Stephen Crane. He was not lonely, but he had grown isolated. He was ready for something different. Perhaps that was why he was here, he thought, glancing around the bar, waiting for his charismatic new friend who seemed like the sort who would come primed with volumes of trivial anecdotes, personal connections, and pertinent intelligence.

The couple sitting at the bar to the right of Will had been busily necking since he got there, and although it was still early, there was already a man at a table nearby apparently asleep though still upright in his chair. The sleeping man's head bobbed, either along with the music or simply out of reflex, it was impossible to tell. Will finished his Pernod and put out his cigarette and was rising to leave when he felt a tap on his shoulder.

"Hullo, hullo," said Oliver with a smile. "Sorry we're late. William, I'd like you to meet Boris and Ned." He nodded to the odd couple standing beside him. One of them—Will guessed it was Boris because the man looked like a parody of a Russian brute—loomed at a height Will guessed to be somewhere north of six foot six. This Boris was a lantern-jawed man with a chest as broad as a Klondike bear's and shoulders so wide they blocked Will's view of the rest of the bar. His features wore an unpleasant expression as if his face had been shoved into a dingy, wet dishrag. The woman standing beside him was as short as Boris was tall, maybe five feet at best. She wore her hair in a short brown bob, and her vulpine face held the same dismal, distasteful scowl as the Russian's. She was puffing a nickel cigar that made her look like an ornery cowboy from some old Walter Brennan oater. "Boris's real name isn't actually Boris," explained Oliver with a chuckle, "but it suits him to a T, don't you think? On the other hand, Ned here really is named Ned. Ha ha. She looks meaner than she is, Will, I promise, though I warn you she is an absolute terror at dominoes—play that woman at your own risk. So, then"—he leaned over conspiratorially toward Will—"did you bring that knife?"

Will was about to answer when Ned tugged at Oliver's sleeve and pointed to the neighboring table.

"Oh my, look! There's Jake!" Oliver shouted, grabbing Will by the arm and leading him over to where the sleeping man was still bobbing his head. "Jake, old man! Wake up!" he said, kicking the man's chair.

The man lurched awake and gave them a wild, disoriented look, then grinned and settled down again. "Oh, Oliver . . . yes . . . hello."

"Pull yourself together, friend, we have vital things to discuss. Come, I've reserved a private room for us in the back." Oliver strode to the far corner and dramatically pulled aside a black curtain, revealing a small, dimly lit table set for five.

Will followed as they filed in and each found a seat. "Let me introduce our new friend," Oliver said, pulling the curtain closed and sitting down to complete the circle. "This is William, he works with the agency. And, Will, these fine people all work with me in one capacity or another. We each have unique skills, passions, motivations, but what we definitely share is a collective dream of what this city could be, and what we can do here, so I'd like—"

"Wait, these guys work for you? I don't understand." Will did not mean to interrupt, but he was confused. He looked around at the cast of characters. "Didn't you say you were a writer?"

"Oh my. Did I? I am sorry, ha ha." Oliver laughed amiably. "You know, I thought the agency would have provided you with a bit of background. Honestly, we must be less important than I like to think we are. Fine, then, let me back up. I am a writer of sorts, yes, from time to time, but more pertinent to this particular conversation is the fact that I am the founder and editor of *The Gargoyle Press*, and these good people here are, in one capacity or another, some of my esteemed colleagues."

"*The Gargoyle Press*? Is that some sort of a magazine? I'm afraid I haven't heard of it."

Oliver forced a smile. "Ah, yes, Will, it is a literary magazine; we publish fiction, essays, good and bad poetry, interviews with whatever ambitious authors we can corner, and occasional artwork. But if they didn't tell you about all that, then I'm not surprised that you are ignorant of our journal's existence. At the moment, we enjoy only a modest circulation."

"'A modest circulation' is a modest exaggeration," muttered Ned.

"Ha ha, yes, thank you, Ned. Possibly so." Oliver grinned. "Which is exactly what we're here to discuss tonight."

"Okay, I see. I think I get it. You have some sort of a problem with your circulation?" Will said, slowly coming to life. So far, the entire gathering had been confusing him, but now he felt he was getting a grasp on the situation. Very often people approached him for advice on how to advertise their small businesses; in fact, only a few months ago the little Basque fellow who ran his neighborhood's corner bistro had asked for his help in attracting more patrons. Will had gotten the boys in the paste-up room to design some new window signage for the Basque, bolding the font up a bit and adding drop shadows so the name would pop out at passersby, and though it was unclear that it had actually helped increase business, the Basque was happy now and always ready to pour Will a Belgian ale on the house. He had then connected Will with a florist and a haberdasher, and Will had his people redo their logos. Will hadn't charged any of them a dime; his agency earned so much good money from their large accounts that even thinking about billing these tiny shops would be a foolish distraction. But these acts of generosity made him feel more like a part of the real Parisian community, less like a tourist who was merely passing through.

So now he sat up and happily offered his help again. "Listen, maybe the agency could give you some advice on your ad sales, or drum up some subscriber interest? I'm sure there's a whole bunch of action items we can put together. Have you ever thought about running some sort of a mail-in contest, or a sweepstakes . . ." By the time the last words had left his lips, the entire group was gazing at him with a set of stunned expressions that made him stop, suspecting that he had, in some inexplicable manner, gravely misspoken.

Boris coughed. Ned stared down at the table. "Gosh, well, a sweepstakes you say? I'm not sure that is exactly what we want," Oliver said slowly. "Actually, it's not even about wants, it's really about needs, and our needs are entirely . . . well now, I am confused, what I actually both want and need at this moment is a drink. How about I get some whiskey for us?" With that, he jumped up and dashed out of the room.

As the curtain settled behind him, a silence fell over the table. Will felt awkward. Nobody said anything for a few minutes until, finally, Ned turned to Jake. "While we have a minute," she said, "Boris tells me your doctor friend is looking for more help. I know the sorts he's been working with, he can do better. Boris and I are both willing to sign on, but the doctor will have to pay."

A sleepy-eyed Jake nodded. "I don't know if I'd recommend work-ing with the doctor, Ned. But if you want I'll pass the word on."

"Yes. Please do. With all these cuts, we could use the money."

Will had no idea what they were talking about, but felt happy not to be the center of attention. At that moment, though, Jake looked over at him, seemingly wanting to shift the subject away from whatever Ned had brought up. "So, friend, what department in the agency do you work for, anyway?"

Will smiled, feeling unaccountably nervous. "I run some accounts for the agency here in town. Well, I help manage one of our European clients here. I used to do more but, you know"—he shrugged—"politics."

"Clients?" said Jake. "Interesting. What sort of clients have you worked for?"

"Oh, I've worked for all sorts," said Will. "I've done research and media work for automotive, pharmaceutical, hotels, soaps. Anyone who wants or needs advertising."

Jake gave him a curious look. "Advertising? What do you mean, advertising?"

"Well, I've worked on all the kinds of accounts an advertising agency works on."

"So, you work at an advertising agency?"

"Yes, of course, where else would I work?"

Nobody answered Will's question. Jake sat looking stunned while Ned had a single snort of a laugh and Boris broke into a grin. This disturbed Will, especially when no one offered up an explanation as to what they found so entertaining. Except for Ned's chortling, the table once again was quiet. They all sat there in what Will now found to be an exceedingly uncomfortable silence until the curtain was dramatically pulled back and Oliver returned to the room carrying two bottles of whiskey precariously topped with glasses. Seeing their expressions, he stopped. "Well, well, well, what did I miss?"

"Oliver, I've got some news of your friend here," said Jake, pointing at Will. "He doesn't work at *the* agency, he works in an *advertising* agency."

"My gosh, really?" Oliver looked befuddled. "But I thought you said you worked with Bob Brandon at the agency?"

"No, I only, I only meant . . ." Suddenly understanding too much, and blushing with embarrassment, Will rose quickly from his chair. "I'm sorry, I probably need to go, you all have things to discuss and I . . . have an appointment. There seems to be a bit of a mix-up here anyway. I'm not sure I can help you. I actually only know Bob Brandon socially." Will's heart was racing, nobody was supposed to know the kind of work he did. This odd series of events had almost tricked him into betraying the very thing he was never supposed to disclose, a fact he had not told anyone the entire time he had been in the city. How stupid. He couldn't believe he had even let on that he knew Brandon in the first place. How had that happened? He remembered his conversation with Oliver at the party, how easily and innocently Brandon's name had slipped from his tongue, all because he was talking to another convivial American. Had either of them mentioned the Central Intelligence Agency that night? It was hard to remember. The sinking feeling got worse. Maybe it had all been a setup. What if Oliver was in with the Russians, and the two pretty girls at dinner had been agents too. If that was the case, then, Will realized, he was playing way out of his league. He should have stayed at his desk, working on reports. He was really better as a manager, no more than a glorified clerk, not someone who should be out wandering the streets of Paris, spilling his guts to any smart fellow who happened to cross his path. He should be home, working, he still had the Bayer report to finish, what was he doing out on the town?

"Relax, Will, it's fine, a simple misunderstanding." Oliver seemed to shrug it off. "How about a drink?"

"Thanks, but no." Will pulled on his coat as quickly as he could. "It was great meeting you all, really, thanks. Honestly, I've gotta run." Putting on his hat, he nodded a quick farewell to the slightly stunned table. Sitting together in the dimly lit room, watching as he stumbled over himself, the four staring figures collectively reminded him of a dark gathering from some somber Rembrandt. Will pushed the curtain aside and the sound of Cannonball Adderley's sax blasted loud in his face, sending his head spinning even faster as he bolted for the door.

A cold light rain was falling. The air was foggy and smelled of sooty chimneys. Looking up and down the street, he couldn't see any cabs coming so he walked fast toward the metro, hoping that the evening air would clear his mind. Shoving his hands into his overcoat pockets to stay warm, he jammed his palm against the long knife he had brought along to show Oliver. He realized he had forgotten all about it and thanked the Lord that it was folded shut.

The knife was sentimental: a fourteen-inch antique ox-bone folding knife his grandfather had given him for Christmas when Will was only six or seven, still too young for such a gift. He could remember his grandfather telling him it was from Toledo, Spain, which had sounded funny to Will since he was pretty sure Toledo was down the road from Detroit someplace. He remembered too his grandfather explaining that this particular knife was best for fishing, and that there was a whole range of other knives he could collect that were good for hunting, campfire cooking, and woodwork. "What about a knife for fighting?" Will remembered asking. "Oh," said his grandfather. "Every knife is good for fighting. Even a butter knife can kill a man, if you know where to shove it." Will remembered how all his uncles had laughed at that.

He had worshiped his grandfather, a sly-eyed wily French-Canadian who had worked the shipping lanes up in Sault Ste. Marie before moving south to open a boatyard on the shores of Lake St. Clair. He taught Will dozens of knots and was always pulling exotic gifts from his coat pockets: tortoise-patterned Petoskey stones, banded agates, and Sauk Indian arrowheads that he had found while sailing the Great Lakes. But the knife was the gift Will treasured most. He could remember playing alone with it in his backyard as a boy, opening and closing it repeatedly, mesmerized by its sharp, hungry mechanical snap. He would dance around in the shadow of the trees; in his child-ish fantasies he had moved with the grace of Errol Flynn or Douglas Fairbanks as he stabbed at the air in his imaginary swashbuckling battles, his knife the most potent point of realism in his whimsical adventures. As he grew, he had always kept that gift close, on the shelf at his bedside as a child and tucked into his desk drawer in college before bringing it along with him to Paris. Now here he was, out on a real misadventure, fumbling along and banging his hand with it. He remembered that Errol Flynn had died only the week before, he'd read it in the paper, and Fairbanks had died years ago. His grandfather was gone as well for almost two decades now. All the cavalier and capable adventurers were vanishing, and there were only awkward oafs like him left stumbling on the earth. Will wondered why Oliver had even wanted him to bring the knife in the first place. It didn't matter, he told himself, it was none of his business now. But he had a hard time putting the evening's events behind him.

As he stood beneath the white-tiled arch of the metro platform waiting for the train, his anxiety nagged at him. "It's okay, it's okay," he kept trying to calm himself: after all, nothing of importance had been revealed, the secrets were still safe. It was even sort of funny. How could you confuse the cloak-and-dagger world of the Central Intelligence Agency with a bunch of guys writing snappy jingles for laxatives and breakfast cereals? It was ridiculous. By the time the metro pulled in and he found a seat in the train car, he had finally begun to relax. It had been a simple misunderstanding, that was all. He could clear it all up. When he handed the Bayer file over on Monday he would tell Brandon all about it, if only to stay on the safe side. Maybe he could make an amusing story out of it, that's what his grandfather would have done, with a chuckle and some spit.

He changed to the Line 1 at Châtelet, boarding a train that was nearly empty. The only other passenger in his car was a solitary woman sitting on the bench halfway down. She smiled politely at him. As he found his seat, she said something to him he could not quite hear over the train's rattle. He had never seen strangers speak on the train except to complain or argue. It was one of the things he liked about Paris, people generally left you alone. But she was pretty so he moved closer.

"*Pardonnez-moi?*" he asked.

"*La nuit, c'est belle,*" she repeated. She spoke with an accent of some kind. Polish? Russian?

"Yes, it's a very nice night, if you like rain," he answered in French. He grinned and she smiled back. They did not speak as the stations passed. He looked at his feet and then looked up to read the signs posted in the car, but his eyes kept wandering back to her. She wore a red sweater, yellow scarf, and a simple beret that her long black hair spilled out, falling down around her shoulders. Her cheekbones were high, framing a pair of strong, clear blue irises that managed to find his gaze whenever it wandered back to her face. Then they would both turn away with a blush and a smile. A small dark bruise below her right eye made him feel instinctively protective. Had she been hit? Who would hit a woman?

Finally, as they approached the George V station, she said, "I'm sorry, have we met before?"

"No, maybe, I don't know, I think I would remember if we had." He fumbled his words, embarrassed and awkward. The train screeched to its stop and he rose to leave. He thought about asking for her number, but it felt too awkward, too sudden. Still, that gaze.

"Well then," she said, rising to go, "until we meet again."

He nodded politely. As they left the car, she turned toward the station's southeast exit. He thought about going back to stop her, to say something funny or charming, at the very least to catch her eye one more time, but it seemed silly and he was tired. Although it was still relatively early, it already felt like it had been a long night and he did not have time for any more foolishness. Up on the street the rain had stopped. He turned off the Champs-Elysées and walked up into his neighborhood, where the comforting scents of bread baking and simmering kitchens seemed to leak out from every apartment and café. It was late into the dinner hour and the aromas of roasting lemon chickens, garlic sausages, and peppered lamb all spilled onto the street, mingling there with the pungent petrichor that always followed an autumn rain. Will realized he had not eaten yet, so he stopped in at the Basque's place for a bowl of steamed mussels and a *pichet*. There was a newspaper lying on the table that he picked up and read. An article described how the world's leading nations had met at a conference and divided up Antarctica, cutting it up into slices like pie. He paid the check and went home.

There was no mail in his slot and the elevator was slow going up. When he finally opened the door to his dark apartment, Boris hit him hard in the face with the phone book, knocking him down onto the cold, tiled floor.

A light was turned on and he opened his eyes. "Hullo." Oliver stood above him, wearing an expression that reminded Will of the grin young boys give their captured butterflies right before they begin plucking off the wings. Then Will passed out again.

IX

Witches' Song One

Wait, wait, don't rush past too fast,
such the busy bolting red squirrel, you there
scurrying around the hard, bare field, to what?
That there? That nettled haven of a hedge?
Careful, teeth may lie in those shadows too.
Glance back here first, through the tumble of time
yes, here, see that bundle of dirty laundry
stuffed now with so much useless flesh,
all spilled about to soil the pure snow,
with deep red blood, leaking free
from my cracked, hollowing husk,
as sisters and life all gallop away
with freshly stolen horses.

Mourning, lonely and lone as the black moon,
I trailed the four, trudging till I found my Lyda
wandering lost like some untethered blinking mule,
a sole specter dragging wet
along those rough timbered banks of ice,
the shoreline stacked with bleached stone and winter branches
as gray as my drained, dried veins.

Lyda was sputtering, spitting out scales,
already talking dumb as a dead fish.
I told her to come along and she came.

The trails of the dead plod on,
we never stop for feast or song,
following beneath winter's skeleton trees,
our weight no greater than a hard frost's whisperings.
We finally sensed Basha too, looming
invisible, sulking, and brooding,

her only substance the shade of darkness
that comes to murderous concentration.
Silent as slate, hear me say solemnly,
her ghost frightens even me.

So, some company I've got,
a river's raw stew, a stomach's turgid gas,
the two each saying nothing I can fathom
but poking, pointing, divining a path.
Lacking the firmness of fates, we are no more than
broken pianos, warped keys, shattered hammers,
our sheet music dancing off with the wind, blowing
    loose and bleak,
but we have our certain melody, yes, we do, don't we?

See the girl meet the young man?
See the man meet the young man?
See the young man become what then?
Not yet? Maybe never?

All souls believe they make their own way
and spin out their path's filament through bold free will
and yet we are the spiders, aren't we, yes,
voracious and certain,
shuffling on, luring and stalking,
tracing out the perimeter
of those tautened spans.

Basha is the one guiding the way,
with the sure force of a cemetery's gravity,
she and we go here and there
and then she stops from time to time
to softly seethe with hissing vipers, to hoot with shrewd owls,
and to whisper with other sapient creatures.
She is our vengeful matchmaker

Babayaga

all thoughts set fast
on village death.

There is a set point, a marked destination,
And while we cook, chop, and boil,
I cannot say what its flavor will be.
But watching our busy Lyda, helping too,
I'm fairly sure it will taste like fish.

X

Exiting the metro early before work, Charles Vidot took his time strolling to the precinct house. Maroc, his recently appointed superior and now day-to-day nemesis, had posted the week's assignments the evening before and, spitefully it seemed, had assigned Vidot an extra shift. This meant for two nights a week Vidot would have to remain at the station until two in the morning. It was not an assignment an officer of Vidot's seniority and rank should have received, but it seemed he had, in some manner, accidentally initiated a battle of wills with his new boss and this was one of the consequences. Well aware of the dynamics of power, Vidot did not like the odds he was facing.

After pausing briefly to pick out his usual Reinette apple from atop the pile at the corner market and offering, as usual, to pay the toothless grocer for the fruit (the man would never take a sou), Vidot went on his way, continuing to mull over this slightly sticky political situation. He knew from experience that any sustained antagonism, even repressed, against a superior was ultimately going to be self-defeating, as bitter words could easily slip out and a carefully managed career could quickly be swept onto the ash pile. He knew he would have to find a way to extricate himself safely from this thorny dilemma. He was not worried, Vidot was a practical, pragmatic man with a keen strategic sense; quixotic idealism was far from his style, he knew full well that merely despising Maroc was not a plan nor was it an option. He had his retirement to consider, and a wife to provide for, so he knew he would stay focused, make a few prudent, tactical adjustments, and work his way to better ground. The bitterness within him began to subside, dissolving into that more familiar pleasure as the small smile crept across his lips and he found himself actually savoring this little riddle. Climbing the last steps to the station, Vidot was so preoccupied with his thoughts that he was almost run over by Officer Bemm rushing out through the doors. The young man looked excited.

"Monsieur! Good morning, I was trying to find you! I received a message this morning from one of the antiques shops, an old woman tried to sell an antique clock."

"A clock?" Vidot had to pause for a second before his eyebrows shot up. "Ah yes, a clock, I remember! Well done! Let us go immediately. Yes! Get a car. Right away."

Minutes later they found the antiques shop at the edge of the 6th. It was a narrow crowded street and they had to park more than a block away. The thought of making real progress in this mystery sent all of Vidot's issues with Maroc flying from his mind. Entering the store, he had to force himself to suppress his giddiness. Now was the time to act professionally.

Unlike the spacious and well-appointed antiques shops that sat toward the center of town, this store was a hodgepodge of clutter. As they worked their way down the narrow aisle of cabinets and bureaus, a small, fat man with a bushy mustache and bulging eyes popped out from the back of the shop.

"*Je peux vous aider?*"

"Yes, monsieur, you called the police station and left a message," said Bemm.

The man immediately switched into a state of extreme urgency. "*Mon dieu*, you're almost too late, she'll be here any moment. Quick, come into my storeroom, *vite, vite!*"

He led them into the rear room that was even more packed with antiques. They stepped gingerly around piled-up chandeliers, rows of paintings, and stacked-up jewelry boxes until they could find a space to talk. "She came in as I was closing up last night," said the man. "I told her I did not have the cash on hand and that she should return today. She has a mantel clock, late-eighteenth-century, very fine craftsmanship, rococo style. Worth more than a few thousand francs, I'm sure. How a Gypsy like her got her hands on it I cannot imagine. I called you right away, of course. I run a very honest operation."

The inspector nodded respectfully.

"So, what sort of crime is this?" the shopkeeper went on, rubbing his hands together. "Is she a thief? Some kind of gang leader? Is this contraband from the war? I only ask because I know the reward will likely be based on the nature—"

Vidot made a small tsk-tsk sound. He never liked to share information about cases he was investigating. He was relieved that the tale of the Parisian man impaled impossibly high on the irons above rue Rataud, had so far, miraculously, not appeared in the local papers. He did not need the attention. He would have thought an incredible death like that would have headlined as the crime of the year, but Mitterrand's scandal, Cuba's charismatic young Fidel Castro, and the ongoing unrest in Algiers continued to eat up the headlines. Vidot thought these were indeed amazing times, when a man could be hung high on the street with a spike through his neck and nobody paused to notice. He took the shopkeeper's hand and patted it gently. "Patience, sir. If the information proves to be useful, we will happily reward you. But first, please tell us, when is this Gypsy woman set to return?"

"At any moment! That is why I had to bring you to this room. Now wait here. When she comes in you can pounce on her!"

Vidot shook his head. "No thank you, we will watch from across the street. Simply pay her, and please act as naturally as possible."

He and Bemm went out the storeroom door, which opened onto the side street and, walking around the corner, entered a pharmacy located right across the street. There were no customers in the shop, and while Vidot explained the situation to the couple behind the counter, Bemm turned around the "Closed" sign in the front door. Then the two policemen positioned themselves discreetly behind the window and waited.

After a little while Bemm asked, "Would you like me to go get you coffee?"

"No, no," said Vidot, "this should not take long."

"Why don't we simply arrest her?"

Vidot smiled. "Do you think a weak old woman could hoist a fat man up onto those spikes? No, there is more to this story. Let's get to know her a little bit and see what we can learn."

Twenty minutes later they saw a squat ancient woman carrying a large heavy package work her way down the street and turn into the antiques shop. Five minutes later she came out again empty-handed. As they started for the door, Bemm said, "There's a radio in the car, I could call for assistance."

"Please," Vidot scoffed. "I believe we can handle her ourselves. You're in uniform, she'll easily spot you. So stay far behind and keep your eye on me, I can stay close."

Trailing behind her, Vidot carefully kept his distance, subtly gesturing back to Bemm, who was more than a block behind, to keep a proper length away. This proved to be wise since the old woman stopped and looked around every so often. Vidot could not tell if she was being careful or simply trying to get her bearings. He was not particularly concerned; after years of experience he knew how to follow a suspect unobserved, and with the streets bustling with midday shoppers, the officers had no trouble staying on her trail.

To Vidot, she seemed painfully old. Watching her swollen varicose legs work their way down the lane, Vidot sensed the ache of every step. As he slowly followed her through the maze of cobblestone streets—pausing occasionally to window-shop whenever she glanced around—Vidot found himself preoccupied with thoughts on the expansive arc of life, how slowly old age stretches out long after youth has flown by, and how, he thought as he watched her make her way, the nomadic people of earlier times must have built those first simple towns and villages for no other reason than to give their own ancient mothers and fathers a place to sit down and rest. Vidot dreaded the thought of aging, his own father had died relatively young, in his early fifties. But his mother was nearing ninety now and was cared for at home by a private nurse. Of course Vidot was glad she was still alive, not only because he loved her, but also because, after his father passed away, she had actually grown noticeably kinder, even gay. Every afternoon in her sun room, the nurse would play old phonograph records while his mother happily waltzed with invisible partners. Perhaps she danced with the memory of his father, Vidot imagined, or maybe lost suitors recalled from another age.

Following behind this tired creature now, Vidot had a feeling those legs of hers could never dance, let alone carry her another block, and, sure enough, she turned off into a small dead-end lane. Vidot peeked around the corner and saw her disappear down into a basement apartment.

Bemm caught up with him moments later. "Come," Vidot said, "let us see what our new friend has to say."

The old woman did not look surprised when she answered their knock at her door, and her eyes showed little concern or interest as they introduced themselves. Vidot felt as though they could have been electricians or plumbers she had been expecting. "Fine, yes, hello, come in," she said, shutting the door tightly behind them.

Vidot was immediately intrigued by the contents of the small, packed apartment. The light streaming in was tinted yellow and the air was heavy and mote-laden. Every nook was stuffed and filled. Stacks of books labeled in Cyrillic script were packed and shoved roughly into the uneven shelves, and more were piled crookedly in the corners, all topped and lined with tied bundles of dried herbs, jars of pickled roots, and bole-colored soils. Small growths of mushrooms cropped from mildewed cracks in the windowsill, and as Vidot peered into an open copper pot, he saw tiny orange minnow creatures swimming about in a brackish brown-and-mustard-colored liquid. The creatures seemed to glow.

"Bah, don't touch that pot. That's dinner," the old woman said, trundling off into her kitchen. "I was about to put a kettle on, would you like tea? Who did you say you are again?"

"I am Inspector Vidot and this is my colleague, Officer Bemm," he said, now trying to decipher the titles of the books on the shelves. "We have a few questions regarding the clock you offered the shopowner down the street."

"Mmmn," she said. "Did you say you want tea or no?"

"We do not need anything to drink, madame, but thank you for your kind offer."

Vidot and Bemm listened to the banging about of cabinets, dishes, and pots before the old woman emerged again from the kitchen. Now clutching a steaming mug, she brushed by them and sat herself down on a threadbare upholstered chair in the corner. "The clock? The clock? Mmmn. Oh, yes, that clock"—she shook her head with a scowl—"a girl gave it to me yesterday."

"May we ask who this girl is?"

"A girl, she is a girl, she is trouble, she is bad news. Her name is Zoya Fominitchna Polyakov. She was moving, leaving town, and she did not need the clock. I certainly did not want it either, look at this stupid place. Where would I put such a pretty thing?" She kicked the beat-up ottoman in front of her. "No room. Nothing pretty here. Ha. Plus, at my age, staring at a clock is worse than a dagger in the eye. It's like kissing the enemy. Ugh, I don't have to tell you about that. But as I say, this girl, Zoya, she owed me money, so I took this clock. You want to sit down? You two make me nervous."

Vidot and Bemm both sat awkwardly on the couch. Vidot tried to suppress his smile. "This is all very useful information. And can I get your name?"

The old woman leaned forward and pronounced her name very clearly, "My name is Elga Sossoka."

"You are Russian?"

"Yes, but I left there in, what, ah"—she counted in the air with her fingers—"1917."

"You've been here since then?" asked Vidot.

"I've been all over." She went back to sipping her tea, and then stopped. "Why are you grinning like such an idiot?"

"To be honest, madame, I have been working on this case for a little while now and we have had no real leads. So it is very refreshing to receive even this small bit of information."

"Ah! I see, I see. Ha ha." Her eyes lit up, suddenly she seemed bright and lucid, almost young. "So you're that sort, you like to hop about and think on puzzles, yes, of course, of course, hmmm, yes, then you should see it, a problem, a strange troubling problem you can help me with. You certainly look like a man who can figure things out, so this will be easy for you, I am sure." The old woman balanced her tea precariously on the ottoman and, stiffly pulling herself up, waddled over

Babayaga

to the bookshelf. Watching her reaching up to dig through the shelves, Vidot again sympathized with the woman's aches. He found himself wondering at the strange ratio between pain and age, how when we are young and without suffering we lead such careless lives, physically risking all without the slightest thought, and it is only when we're older, when we're given such misery in bone, joint, and tooth, when our sense of smell and taste are long gone, our eyes have clouded over, and our ears have waxed shut, it is then that we cling to life so fiercely, struggling to continue on when we are only little more than a compendium of agonies.

"Ah, there it is," she said. The ancient woman was up on her tiptoes now, grunting and reaching toward a dusty, thick tome perched high on the shelf. "I think I can reach it." Vidot was about to rise up to help when, in her clumsiness, the old woman knocked two jars down onto the floor. They both fell with a loud crack as the glass shattered and a dark, red dirt spilled out onto the rug. "Ah, forgive me, such an ass," she said, leaning over.

"Oh, no need to clean—" Vidot began to say, when suddenly she bolted upright, letting loose a loud raspy scream and throwing handfuls of the dirt into each of the policemen's faces. The mixture of dirt flooded his lungs, and immediately Vidot felt immobilized, incapable of even turning to look at Bemm. None of the words shouting out of the woman's mouth were recognizable, they did not even sound like language, merely a serpentine thread of barks, hisses, shrieks, and throaty rasps. Veins bulged out of her brow and neck as she lunged backward, grabbing another jar off the shelf and fiercely shattering it onto the floor. More dust billowed around them, blotting out everything but the thick streaks of ocher light streaming through the curtains. Vidot felt weighted shadows come crawling in around him; looking down, he was shocked to see his fingernails extending backward, running up his arm, splitting open his flesh. His body shook and his old skin smoked off him, like dry autumn leaves burning in a pile. Then his spine suddenly twisted and contracted as extreme cramps in his thighs and stomach caused him to lurch over and collapse onto the floor. He caught a glimpse of Bemm as he fell down, his partner reeling too, his face covered in a sheet of blood and his mouth open in a silent scream.

Looking up, the last thing he saw before it all went black was the old woman's pained expression and her hands madly weaving around in the air, as if she were playing some great and terrible harp. Then the pain ceased. He felt as though he slept for months, maybe years, and when he opened his eyes Vidot was stunned at how impossibly large the room had become.

XI

Zoya sat on the bench across from the apartment building and gazed up at the distant lit window. She was almost certain the man had not seen her slipping up behind him as he left the metro station. He had been easy to pursue, she simply trailed him at a short distance, sticking to the shadowed side of the street. After trailing him from the station to the restaurant, she watched him eat alone as she sat perched behind a column at the bar, disappearing behind the menu whenever he glanced her way. After that, it was only a few more steps of stalking to reach his apartment building. Moments after he disappeared into the lobby the lone light went on up on the seventh floor, so she assumed that was his home. She watched and waited and thought.

First impressions were critical to her, though she could not always articulate why she chose one prey over another. From his pressed suit and his clean-cut style, she had taken him to be a businessman of some sort. He seemed both a little less successful and also slightly brighter than poor Leon. Perhaps it was his American accent that drew her in; she liked the idea of an outsider who would not know the things he should be suspicious of, the subtle cues that might make a young woman from a foreign land too intriguing. Each of them had come a vast distance, from opposite horizons, which made every question and each curiosity that much easier to imbue with myths and fables and lies.

From time to time she wondered if she did not, in fact, get to choose her prey at all, if perhaps it was the long hand of fortune that marked the quarry. She did not like the possibility that she had no control. "Fate is as fickle as a drunk at a piano," Elga used to say. "Listen to it at your own risk."

Zoya saw shadows move up in the room, not one but two silhouettes. A lover? A wife? Wives made things easier, keeping men preoccupied and paranoid. Guilt came with the busy building of excuses and alibis, and often introspection too, and she preferred her men looking backward and inward, anywhere, really, so long as it was not too closely at her.

But there was also the chance that a wife might not bode well for Zoya, it generally depended on the man's predisposition. In their brief exchange on the metro, this one had left her with the impression of being almost too uncomplicated. Men such as this, once married, often worked hard to stay true. She didn't meet many such men. Still, one with a solid faith in his vows was never wholly unconquerable, she had plenty of tricks tucked in her charms, but it often took effort. She was more comfortable with men of duplicity. The sinister ones were so much easier for her to handle. After all, that was where she had first begun.

Her first adventure with a boy had been Grigori. She worked then at the estate belonging to Grigori's father, a prosperous but minor count who spent most of his time out hunting with his hounds. Her own father, Foma, managed the stables. Her mother had died giving birth to Zoya, and so she was raised alone with her father in a small cottage that sat behind the manor house. Grigori was the count's only child, and the household had let them play together; they enjoyed hiding games in the gardens and skipping stones in the fish pond. By the time she was old enough to begin making the beds, he had already been sent off to a military academy.

His school was too far away for him to return for every holiday, so she did not see him again until the late harvest break. Almost immediately she sensed a change. He was now stiff and formal with her, and she found herself ducking his gaze. When he did look at her, it was as if he did not know her, the boyish spark gone, as if the light in his eyes had been snuffed out. The change in his demeanor made her young heart ache in a disorienting way, but she went about her duties, washing and steaming and laying out the clean towels and linens. Instinctively, she avoided him, staying as much as she could in the back of the house, but she could still hear his voice, bluntly ordering the servants about, shouting for Foma to saddle his horse. Evenings were filled with the sound of Grigori's hard boots pacing across the floorboards of the large manor, walking room to room.

On the final afternoon before he was to return to school, she was changing the bedding in the guest wing when she heard his boots coming down the hall. She did not pause but kept focused on straightening the pillowcases and smoothing the duvet. The boots came closer, the echo of every step seemed almost deafening as he approached, until finally the sound stopped and she knew he was there in the room with her. She looked up. Grigori smiled at her. She smiled too, blushing with relief, for finally she had a sign of warmth from him. Then she paused, nervous again, sensing that his smile was not that of the boy she once knew. It came with a steel glint she did not recognize. "It is my birthday," he said.

She smelled the liquor on his breath as his cold hand grabbed at the back of her neck, pushing her down onto the bed. She did not struggle much, for if she hurt him she sensed there would only be more trouble.

Seven weeks later her angst-ridden and nervous father prepared to go talk with Grigori's father, the master of the house. Foma was a proud man, he wanted what was right, and as he stood in front of the small stove, rocking nervously back and forth on the balls of his feet, his hands shoved deep in his pockets, he carefully practiced what he would say. He did not expect Grigori to marry Zoya, clearly that was not possible. But Zoya had not asked for this, she was a good girl. They were a decent and God-fearing family, devoted and loyal. Foma knew incidents like these occurred in every big house, but he did not know what was supposed to happen. If his wife were alive she could provide advice, but alone, with a daughter, what could he do? Perhaps he could be moved into a new position in a relative's house, or caretake the patriarch's home in St. Petersburg? Or maybe there was a management position out among the field hands, with living quarters that were larger, to make room for the bigger family? Could they possibly arrange a marriage for Zoya to another worker? Foma was unclear what choices, if any, they had. But a solution would have to be found. He could only ask for his landlord's advice, father to father.

She watched Foma change into his best shirt, proper buckle shoes, and church coat. She did not expect he would be gone long, but hours passed. She sat in mute terror, rocking in the chair, her heart a cold stone. Finally a sharp knock came at the door. She opened it to find Pyotor, the farm's foreman and one of the few men her father considered a friend. His face held no kindness. "You need to be gone by sunrise, take what you can carry. Talk to anyone here, ask anyone for help, and you will be as dead as your father." All the emotion that was frozen within her suddenly transformed into a wild, burning streak of lightning and she was about to scream out when Pyotor slapped her hard across the face. "You have killed a good man, whore. Feel free to kill yourself, only do not do it here. I do not want to clean up any more of your family's blood." His spit hit hot on her face, and before she could unflinch he had already slammed the door.

At midnight she started off with a small satchel of quickly gathered possessions. Her path only lit by the star-pocked sky and a broken shard of the moon, she did not know her destination. The closest village was more than two hours away but it was not worth aiming for, she knew the town well enough to realize that no one would offer her any warmth. Even the road itself was not safe, only months before a pair of men had been attacked and killed by bandits. She needed protection, she needed shelter. Finding a trail into the woods, she disappeared into the absolute darkness of the trees, exhausted and confused, hoping to find some mossy, soft spot to lay her head.

Fifty years past that night, the same fractured moon was hanging low, slightly obscured in the overcast sky, when the team of horses pulling Count Yaroslavich's carriage suddenly stopped dead in their tracks. The driver waited as the stewards came out to watch the footman whip and kick at the immovable beasts. It was a quarter of an hour before the count himself finally stepped out from the coach. He did not want any more delay, he told the driver. He was due at his new grandson's christening in three days.

The air was crisp, a frost had come early. The driver was offering his apology for the stubborn horses when the count silenced him and pointed out across the rough burdock field. "Who is that out there?"

A group of figures was emerging from the darkness. Preparing to defend himself from a possible bandit attack, the count thought first of calling for his saber. But then he saw it was nothing more than a small group of peasant women, four of them in all. A young one was leading the way, and as she neared the road, she pulled the wool scarf from her head and offered him the warm, comforting smile of an old friend. Her gaze shook at the doors of his memory, but he could not place it.

"Grigori? Grigori Yaroslavich? Today is your birthday, yes?"

He looked again at the women and spoke with the condescension that came naturally to him. "Yes, it is. But how do you know me?"

"Oh, you are a very great man, many know of you, and today I wanted to visit you on your birthday."

"How—?"

"It does not matter. We are only here to tell you that though your journey has stopped, you will be the cause of much felicity and joy on this night. Your son may have died, but with every tragedy comes a bit of good, yes?"

He looked at her, puzzled by her words. He shook his head. "You're confused, my son is in Tver, his wife gave birth to a baby boy, my grandson, there is—"

"Yes, yes, you will be the cause of much felicity and joy tonight," she said again, and giving a quick bow, she turned and led her small group away. The count was confused, he felt like calling her back to ask her more questions or simply to slap her for her impertinence. The familiar tone with which she spoke to him, it was not right, especially not with the footmen watching. As the group of women slowly vanished across the field, becoming one with the cold darkness, he thought he could hear them singing in low tones out to the night.

Their song brought the wolves in. It was a large, hungry pack running fast, too many to fight off. The wolves curled round on every side, quickly closing the circle around the carriage. Someone tried to pass a gun up to the driver, from his perch he could have done some damage to the pack, but in his panic he lost his balance and slipped, falling down as the wolves dove in.

The count kicked at them, trying to keep them at bay. It was only once they had taken him down, when a wolf's breath was in his face and he could see the glint of the moonlight in its bright grinning teeth, that he finally remembered the girl. He could not quite believe it, it seemed impossible, but there was no time to wonder.

Sitting on the bench in Paris, Zoya shivered and shook off the recollection. To distract herself, she opened her purse and pulled out a small mirror. She was curious to see what those shadows in the American's apartment were up to. Muttering a tiny trick spell, she aimed the reflection carefully and coaxed the stubborn light to bounce and curve to her will. As she worked, the ancient echoes of Grigori's desperate screams faded into the folds of her memory, along with all the agonies of stallions, servants, and centuries.

XII

The happy sound of a clarinet was playing as Will came to. His hands were bound, his mouth gagged with some cotton cloth—what was it, a washcloth? A dirty sock? He hoped not. He looked around, trying to get his bearings. He was lying on the couch in his living room. Boris was standing against the doorframe, looking sleepy. The woman named Ned was busy at the desk, a tiny camera in her hands, taking pictures of what Will guessed was the Bayer file. An Artie Shaw record was playing on the turntable as Oliver stood by Will's open closet, trying on various hats. Hearing Will waking up, he looked over with a smile. "Ah, you're alive! Excellent, we were growing weary of waiting. I was just going to teach Boris here how to play pinochle, you know, to pass the time a bit." He came and plopped down next to Will on the couch. "Jake had to go home to rest. Poor boy suffers from narcolepsy and there's no medication for that. When I first met him back in school he would fall asleep on the football sidelines and the coaches all feared he'd had a concussion. Now he falls asleep in bars and comes off like the village drunk. Then last month he fell asleep in the front row of a preview for Roussin's new play, the result of which, my lord, the poor playwright almost killed himself. Can you imagine? Context changes so much. Care for a drink?"

Will looked at him in dumb disbelief.

"Oh, let's take the silly gag off. Sorry about that. It's only that I didn't want you going bonkers when you came to. What would the neighbors think? Boris, please." The Russian untied the table napkin from around Will's head and took what appeared to be a balled-up handkerchief out of his mouth.

"And my hands?" Will sputtered.

"Of course, of course." Oliver blushed. "Clearly, this sort of nonsense really isn't my forte. Boris?" The Russian untied Will's wrists and Oliver handed him a drink. Will sat there with a knot of rage in his gut while he tried to play along with their game.

"Want to tell me why your friend's photographing my file?" asked Will.

"Oh yes," said Oliver, looking over to the desk as though he had forgotten Ned was there. "Well, every Monday Ned here goes to the embassy and gives the agency—not your agency, mind you, but the one we work with—a packet. If they don't get the packet, they don't pay us. Used to be we were on a regular retainer, but lately, I have to say, the Central Intelligence Agency has not been acting all that intelligent."

Will sipped his drink and wondered what time it was. The record came to an end and the room was quiet except for the sound of Ned's small camera clicking away and the soft slipping of the ice melting in their drinks. Oliver wandered over to the shelves and started looking through the record collection. "You've got some great stuff here, Will. Oscar Peterson, Teddy Wilson, very impressive. I would have thought you'd be more an aficionado of those sexed-up Negro spirituals Elvis Presley sings so well."

Will still didn't answer; he was too busy stewing with anger at himself and the mistakes he had made. Watching Ned at his desk working with her little camera, he realized he should not have brought the Bayer file home, it was not secure there, the apartment had no safe or even a file cabinet with a lock on it. But then again, he reminded himself, there had been no reason to expect anyone would ever break in like this. Will thought about informing Oliver that the file was already heading to their mutual friend Brandon, but he sensed that offering any more information would not be prudent. Better to stay quiet. He wondered what Brandon would think if he knew Oliver and his friends had gotten hold of the file. It wouldn't be good. He could already imagine Brandon's condescending look. Will realized he might be sent back to the States even sooner than he had expected.

"What made you come here? How did you know I would have anything you'd even want?" he asked.

"Oh." Oliver shrugged. "At some point you mentioned that you were in research, so we thought we would pop by and see if you'd researched any subjects we might be interested in. Now, I don't know if they'll be interested, but it's worth a shot."

"How did you find my place?"

"Ah, a marvelous invention called the telephone book," Oliver said, lowering the needle on the turntable. Lionel Hampton's vibraphone started playing.

Will ignored his sarcasm. "Okay, well, so tell me this, how do you know I won't call the police the minute you leave?"

Oliver went over to where his overcoat hung casually on the chair. Digging into the pocket, he pulled out a brown paper bag. "Well, here's why. This bag contains your knife. We took it off you while you were resting and now it's covered with your fingerprints. So, yes, I suppose you could call the police, but the minute one of us is picked up, that very knife of yours gets stabbed right into the side of some poor Pigalle prostitute."

Will was shocked. "Wait, seriously? You'd kill a woman over this?"

Now it was Oliver's turn to look incredulous. "Oh heavens, no, that would be some rude work. First of all, we need the girl alive to tell the policeman how you attacked her. Secondly, we like the girl. You'd actually like Celia too, she's a zaftig one, quite roly-poly with a massive set of bosoms. They're like a pair of great pointy Luftschiff Zeppelins. She claims they were the secret to her splendid success back when she danced in the Folies Bergère."

"So, then you've done this before?"

"Boris has, Ned has, me, I'm only along for the ride." Oliver leaned forward. "Look, I am so sorry about all this. It was a terrible mix-up. I suppose I had too many in me the other night, we had quite a time, didn't we? And somehow I got the impression that you were with the agency. In fact I could swear you said you were. Anyway, I fear I've revealed some things I shouldn't have, a bit more than was proper. Not very professional on my part, but there you have it. So, what to do? Originally, I had a much more innocent plan for the knife, but now I'm afraid I need a bit of leverage here. You understand, right? I'd be pretty sore if I were standing in your shoes, I know, but I can't afford to have you running around like the proverbial loose cannon. Don't worry, please, be a good fellow about it if you can. You have to understand, I'm merely trying to manage a rather sticky situation."

Will was quiet for a moment, puzzled by Oliver's clumsy blend of justifications, rationalizations, and attempts at friendly sympathy. "I can't let you copy that file," Will finally said.

Oliver shrugged. "Fine. I don't want to be unreasonable. Give me some other shiny toy I can distract them with."

Will nodded. "I'll try. Tell me what they're interested in so I know what to look for."

Oliver shrugged. "Anything, really. Scraps on Algerians, hints on Russians, rumors of some potent or burgeoning movement, Fascist, Communist, doesn't matter. Bits and bobs and curiosities, that's all the agency wants. If it happens to be relevant to their work, they'll pay me a little more for it."

"Well, you're not going to find anything along those lines at the advertising agency."

"You'd be surprised. For instance, that Bayer file's nice because they've been specifically asking us for anything related to the pharmaceutical world."

Will wondered if that was somehow related to Brandon's request for the Bayer file. He had never provided Will with any explanation for the agency's various interests and Will had never bothered to ask. "Any idea why?"

"Ours is not to reason why, only do and die, yes?" He smiled. "I don't think they honestly expect substantial information from us; it's the evidence of our industry that counts. The key is to appear tireless and eager, to keep the action moving, keep the eye busy. We're like those Puerto Ricans with the three-card monte games up in Spanish Harlem. It's exhausting, really. Brandon's people used to be much more generous. But now the money's tight and they've got us sweating for every franc."

Babayaga

Will nodded. "The U.S. is spending more in Indochina now."

Oliver gave him a funny look. "Your friend Brandon tell you that?"

"Not too hard to figure it out from the papers," Will lied, not wanting to draw any more attention to his relationship to the agency. "With France pulling out, makes sense that we're going to have to go in there to keep things stable."

Oliver smiled. "You know, they call Saigon 'the Paris of the East.' I've never been there, but I'm fairly certain I prefer the original."

Across the room, Ned switched off the desk lamp and tucked the camera into her coat. "I'm done."

Will pointed at the camera. "You're not taking that, are you? I told you, it will be traced back to me."

"I need something, Will. I haven't got enough to make payroll at the journal right now and I desperately need that embassy cash." Oliver buttoned up his jacket and reached for his overcoat. "I'm happy to make a trade, though. We can give you twenty-four hours. Find us a good tidbit and I will give you Ned's film from tonight. Fair enough?"

"Not really, but I don't see that I have much choice."

"Yes, well, apologies again." Oliver grinned. "Of course you know it's all toward great and noble ends. And I am sorry for that bruise; at least it won't be a bad black eye. Take some aspirin and knock it back with some scotch, that should do the trick." He gave a half-salute farewell and followed the other two out the door.

Will listened to their footsteps disappear down the hall. Once he was sure they were gone, he got up and locked the deadbolt. He was surprised to find his initial anger already dissolving into some milder form of irritation. Why wasn't he more upset with the three of them? Shouldn't he be furious? Somehow Oliver's apologies, combined with his bemused and detached manner, made it hard to take the odd course of events seriously. The entire evening simply seemed preposterous. He walked over to the bar and refilled his drink, rubbing his sore jaw as he looked around the room. Lionel Hampton's mallets were bouncing across "Stardust" on the stereo and a few LP albums were spilled out across the table, empty cocktail glasses sat on coasters, a few hats lay on the floor, and the last of Boris's Gitane was still smoking in the ashtray. In the past two hours he had been assaulted, tied up, and blackmailed, and yet his apartment looked no different than if he had been hosting a few friends for drinks. Perhaps that was why he wasn't so angry, he thought. Maybe it had been nice to have company come over.

XIII

Elga pulled her head up from the sink and wiped the bits of vomit from her lips, sick with dizzy anger, her breath puffed full of hysterical rage. What a goddamned gutted sour fish, she thought, what stinking putrid marrow. That bitch. That horrible bitch. Zoya had led them here, she knew it, her bowels screamed and gargled this truth to her. Why? When they had first appeared at the door, panic's hammer had struck hard at Elga's tired heart. Policemen! In her home! What were they asking? Why? Their presence kicked her mind spinning, and now she could not remember much of what they had said, the echoes and static of their questions buzzed about her skull like honey-drunk bees. In her tangled thoughts, the policemen's words were clotted and mottled, wet bits of sonic matter that clogged her brain. She tugged at her ears, trying to unstuff the meaning. Her stomach cramped and she retched again, spitting gray and green into the basin. Think, think, get their faces back; when she tried to imagine them she only saw big sturgeon fish burping fat bubbles underwater. She slammed her hand on the counter, trying to remember. It was hard, the nosy policemen's questions were slipping away, like silver coins rolling off a sinking deck, every phrase drowning in the murk. She grabbed and grasped at the words before they went. Yes. Wait. There it was, it was the clock, the shit of a clock. Damn the little mite. The clock had been a snare. Zoya had given her the clock, like a piece of cheese baiting a trap. That bitch, that serpent, that double-crossing fork-tongued asp. Ah, yes, that reminded her.

Staggering up, she moved at a stumbling, sclerotic pace, fumbling over to the shelf where she pushed the books and vials about till she found the glass jar she was looking for. She dumped the teal powder on the counter by the sink, pulled a thin silver tube out from a pot of spatulas and mixing spoons, then leaned over and snorted up the dry dust of the snakeskin. Her head kicked back as electricity sprayed chaotically inside her head, bringing her heart racing fast to life.

Refueled and regaining focus, Elga supported herself against the doorframe and steadied her legs. The small rooms were choked with a dusty smoke that curled slowly in the weak light, filling the air with the sulphur stink of rotten eggs. After so long, she thought, to have so little, less than nothing. She glanced down at the empty police uniforms lying limp at her feet and the sight brought her small satisfaction. She grinned grimly to herself. Stupid trespassers, they were on their own now. Scum toads. She spat out more gray, and scratched the small, thin whiskers at the end of her chin.

With the snakeskin in her blood and the anger pulsing through her veins, she had enough to push her on. She crouched down and stared at the uniforms. So how did these two get here? Where did they begin? They must have followed her from the antiques shop, that was the only path that made sense. Logic was hard for her, more difficult every day, it seemed, but her mind could still follow a path and keep focused; it took effort but it worked, so long as she had some purpose, some goal. She imagined Zoya's head severed from her body, lying sideways on the pavement like a dropped melon. That did the trick, now Elga had her motivation. She made clicking sounds with her tongue and the sniffing rat came scurrying out from below the couch, joining her as she began searching through the pockets. Where was it? What was here? She found a black wallet. The rat emerged from deep in a pocket with keys in its mouth. "Good, Max. Wonderful." She emptied the cash out of the wallet and pulled herself up from the floor, sucking in her soured stomach to keep from heaving again as she reeled over to the bureau. Opening a drawer, she pulled out the old pistol. "Come."

Moments later, standing in her doorway with a stuffed satchel on her shoulder, she spoke a few sharp words that sealed her apartment safe from thieves and prying eyes. Then she locked up and headed off, still woozy and unsteady. A passing man in a plaid suit glanced over his spectacles at her, and she held back a hiss. Chart a course, she thought to herself, the way the sun sets its path across the sea, then follow it—or sink and drown. A few steps behind her, the rat scurried along the lip of the storefronts' gutters. She had only taken what she needed for now, yet her load was heavy and made her stagger with effort. She tried not to knock against the passersby. Her mouth was set open, her breathing raspy and hard, and her eyes had to squint to keep focus. Every spell takes its toll.

She turned left at the corner, past the bookstore and bakery and on up the hill. Three blocks up and she was close. She sniffed deeply— snot gargled in her nose—she wanted an odorous clue, but the air was empty of meaning . Step after step, passing Citroëns and Peugeots, she eyeballed each one quickly as she went. Keep looking, she scolded herself, it's here, those policemen would not have walked, they would not have taken the metro, she kept searching. She reached the antiques shop but staggered past without stopping. They would have come in a car. But where was it? Where? She circled around one block. Then another. There, finally, she spotted the police car, parked like a turtle sleeping in the sun, waiting to be cracked open for its meat. She tried the key and, sure enough, it worked. As she got in behind the wheel, the door still ajar, she sighed with an ancient relief. The rat hopped in behind her. She put the key in the ignition. Wait, she thought, wait. She put her fingers to her temple and felt a balled-up thought pulsing there, ready to be opened. There is no time—but there is always time. She looked down at Max; the rat stared up at her from the passenger seat. Yes, she thought, a loose thread to cut. She pulled herself up out of the car and started again toward the antiques shop. The rat waited behind.

One minute later, the dull sound of a shot rang out. Three minutes later, she climbed back into the car with the clock under her arm. She shoved it over onto the passenger seat and stuck the key in the ignition. Exhaling hard, she looked down at the dash. Elga had only driven an automobile a handful of times, but it wasn't hard to remember how they worked, the logic of both men and their machines were always painfully stupid. Bah, she thought, a wheel turns a wheel and they call it civilization. She gunned the engine, shoved it into gear, and lurched off down the street, cutting off a Renault, and receiving a sharp horn blast for her trouble. Nobody would stop her now, she knew she had the momentum. Elga muttered a few quick words to make her unnoticeable, to keep her safe, and the car became anonymous and indistinct as it zoomed down the street. Impulsively, she turned on the police radio: "Car number 17 . . ." Max squeaked, and she nodded. He was right, there was nothing to be won by listening in; she needed to concentrate. She turned off the radio and looked for the street signs that would lead her out of town. In a matter of moments, her squad car was gunning up the Champs-Élysées, heading northwest.

As she drove, the hate boiled and popped in her blood. Yes, I will kill her for this, Elga thought to herself. I will drown her in the frothing rapids and racing current of my anger's yellow bile. I should have held her under a long time ago. "The juicy tart set me up, mmn-hmm, that soiled hump-rag framed me but good," she said out loud. Max was silent. She threw a disgusted look at the rat. "Stay quiet. I know you. You fall for the big blue eyes, the fat tits. Yes, and look where that got you. Stay quiet, you little shit, or I'll bite you in two." She shook her head—that's right, she thought, I'll bite, I'll be the toothsome viper biting down deep into that girl's naked throat. I'll bite her palm, those tits, her thigh. I will bathe in her blood and eat her alive. You send the cops after me, donkey girl, and I will send so much more after you. Feel it in your bloodstream, you slime of slithering worm. For I am coming, I am on my way, quiver and wait for me, you pathetic bitch beast. I will get a friend to help me, yes, a nice, sharp little fox of a killer with an eye for the hunt. I will find her and then we'll both come for you, girl. I've got your big stupid clock. Oh yes, I've got it. I'm going to make you choke on it. Watch out, woman, because I am coming, and I am not coming alone.

XIV

Inspector Vidot could not stop hopping up and down. He was wild-eyed, he was exhilarated, he was tiny. It was a tremendous feeling, so much excitement, so much power, in an instant he was halfway across the room. Then, in no time at all, he had hopped back to where he'd begun. He paused to catch his breath. He stared at his strange, bristled legs in dumb wonder. Hearing noises, he looked up and watched the giant old woman as her mighty rat pawed through the cavernous pockets of his limp uniform, which lay like a vast blue mountain range across the floor. He watched her varicose-veined legs, so covered with moles they looked like the barnacled hull of a ship, stumble around the apartment as she packed and cursed and snorted up a blue-green powder before mumbling and belching her way out the front door. In his excitement, he felt the urge to follow her, but the chain of events had been too fantastic and disorienting; he had to stop and assess the situation. Besides, his partner was missing.

Vidot looked around the room for Bemm—where was the poor boy? How would he even recognize him? Vidot looked himself over: yes, no doubt, he was now in the form of some sort of insect. A hopping insect, to be exact. A louse? A flea? This was too shocking to be comprehended. Bemm must have been transformed as well. The simplest solution was that Bemm had been turned into the same kind of insect. And so, that was what Vidot looked for. He leapt up high onto the bookshelf and tried to get some perspective on the room. He scanned every corner, anxious for any sign of his colleague. Where did he last see Bemm? There, yes! Bemm had been sitting in *that* chair. Vidot aimed his jump well and landed on the stuffed arm. He tried to shout, but no words came out. This was fascinating!

Là-bas! He saw a small bug scurrying through the fabric of the cushion. Vidot hopped, aiming his descent so that he landed eye-to-eye with the creature. The pest froze and stared at him. Was it Bemm? Vidot attempted a small hop as a signal. The bug cocked his head. Vidot hopped again. He could feel his strange heart beating fast with anticipation. Could this be him? Yes! Yes! The bug gave a small hop back. It was Bemm! Poor little thing, he looked so frightened.

Fleas, Vidot decided, they were fleas, not because he could honestly tell the difference, but because the thought of being a louse would be too disgusting for words. However, being a flea, well, that flooded him with inspiration. He actually had a bit of experience with fleas, not entirely negative either, so a flea was definitely a more comforting thing to be. Yes, he thought, we decide what we are and then act appropriately; a man says, "I am a saint," or "I am a cheat," and there you have it, these conclusions determine our course through life. Well, thought Vidot, I am a flea, and it appears this other flea is

Bemm. He hopped once more, just to be sure. The other insect hopped in mimicry. Yes, he thought, now they could begin.

Vidot leapt a small distance and looked behind him. Bemm followed. Ah, what a good soldier, Vidot thought. He took a more decisive hop toward the door and the little creature was still right there behind him. One more jump and they began to crawl under the doorsill. He was relieved his transformation had come with an innate notion of how to manage his strange, new insect legs, for this was not unlike much of the training he had done in the army, crawling on hands and legs in the mud beneath razor wire. There might not be beer steins and barracks full of singing soldiers at the end of this particular exercise, but at least he knew what to do.

He remembered, a long time ago, as a small boy, being taken to a neighborhood carnival where, amid a warm chestnut afternoon of atonal organ grinders and pugilistic puppet shows, he had been delightfully transfixed by two English street performers, the amusing Sir Billy and his beautiful assistant, Dottie, as they presided over their little flea-circus stage. One by one, the fleas were introduced by sir Billy with great fanfare, as if they were stars in a Folies review. Then, as Vidot watched in awe, the small creatures miraculously came out dragging around toy cannons and chariots, writing out legible letters in wet ink, and hopping back and forth across taut strings to the rhythm of Dottie's warbling piccolo tunes. Watching as one fabulous act followed another, little Vidot had laughed and clapped along, gleefully cheering each new feat of the fleas. How magical and charming it had seemed, not merely the tricks themselves but also the fact that these two minstrels had transformed such pestilent nuisances into fabulously playful creatures of awe and amazement. Perhaps, thought Vidot, this is why I am not so bothered by my own transformation. But what of poor Bemm, how was he weathering? He looked back but could not discern much about the state of Bemm's mind. He saw merely a pair of insect eyes, beady and attentive, staring blankly back at him, waiting to be led.

Finally, the two made their way out from under the door. As the shadows grew long in the afternoon, they reached the edge of the doorstep. Having accomplished the escape from the old lady's warren, Vidot knew it was time for a plan, but he had no idea where to begin. He knew nothing of the woman or her possible destination, and he had no hope of summoning any help in his current state. Besides, there was some pertinent fact about his current condition, a piece of critical information about an insect's life nagging at the corner of his consciousness, that he knew he needed to remember. What was it? He thought hard, finally recalling again that long-ago day when he had returned to his family's modest flat with the thrills and delights of the strange flea carnival still alive in his mind. As he often did when he was in such a state, Vidot had gone straight to his father's crowded library and, after climbing up the ladder to take down book after book from the tall shelves, he began thoroughly reading every volume, poring through all the facts he could find about the fleas he had seen. What had he learned that day? Not much that he could recall now. Fleas have six legs, yes. Obviously so. Fleas are vampiric, absolutely, they are parasites that survive off animal blood, that he already knew. What else? What was it? Then there it was, the crucial fact suddenly returned, coming into clear and sharp focus after being obscured in his mind for so many decades: a flea lives, on average, for only ninety days. Making every single day for a flea roughly the equivalent of a human year, and two hours was a month and four minutes a day. Remembering this now, time immediately became a very different thing than it had ever been to Vidot, so absolutely present it was almost palpable. The need to find a solution was immense and overwhelming. At the one time in his life when he desperately needed to act, he felt paralyzed with panic.

He concentrated, reminding himself of the adage that had always sustained him in times of trouble: there are rarely any truly big problems, only collections of little problems that pile up. Also, one thing his investigations had taught him was that nothing ever disappeared; this was a rule of the natural sciences as well, substances evolved and transmuted but no energy was ever lost, it merely reformed itself, which meant the rest of him was out there in the ether, as gas or a shadow, existing in an unknown or unknowable shape, waiting to be reclaimed. So he could solve this. He had to solve it. It was, in all probability, the greatest mystery he would ever encounter. He tried to imagine his success, thinking of how, at the end of this journey, he would hold his Adèle's hand and kiss her pale forehead and tell her about his incredible victory over this strange and surprising adversity. Ah, sweet Adèle: the thought of his wife consoled him. He had ninety days to live, ninety days to find a way back into her arms, not as an insect but as a man. He would succeed, there was no choice. He would go to the station, rally the troops, marshal the resources of the entire nation, send legions of men out to scour the streets, search every basement and garret until they found that old wicked crone again and forced a cure from her. Now was the time to act! *Voilà!* He signaled to Bemm, pointing to a dog passing by, and then, blending intuition and calculation, they leapt out and jumped aboard.

In an instant he and Bemm were bouncing down the alley, riding a small bulldog out for his evening constitutional. Vidot carefully crawled to a spot in the middle of the belly where he felt he would be safe from any chance of the dog scratching. He checked to see that they were all heading in the right direction, yes, he could see the *boulangerie* they had passed, wait, no, they were now turning into a house, time to jump again. He leapt and Bemm followed. They landed in the crack between the street's rough paving stones. These stones that had once seemed to be a quaint vestige of his city's ancient past now had grown impossibly large, like massive dark mausoleums that loomed up above him. Quickly, they crawled to the side gutter and waited for their next ride.

Two dogs later (one an oversized mutt and the other a squat corgi) and they were at the edge of the river. He had been tempted during each ride, out of some vicious newborn impulse, to sink his teeth into the flesh of the dogs for sustenance, but he denied himself the satisfaction. I draw the line there, he said to himself. I am a man, not a beast. Having leapt off their last ride, Vidot and Bemm now waited by the Seine. He guessed they were only a quarter of the way to police headquarters, but he had no idea how long it would take them to get there. They were at the mercy of whatever creatures passed. It was dark now, not many dogs would be out for their evening walks at this hour.

There was the rustling of debris and then a small mouse appeared, scampering out and darting past them, busily following its own sniffing nose. "*Allons-y!*" signaled Vidot, and in a synchronized jump they both were on its back. Vidot felt quite satisfied, this was no worse than pushing his way onto the metro at rush hour. The mouse moved fast, making his way down the stone staircase to the water's edge and then along the masonry and then up again onto the Pont du Garigliano. Vidot checked to see that Bemm was still riding beside him. He knew he needed a plan for what they would do once they reached the station, but it was their best destination, as good a place to find help as any he could imagine. As the mouse continued on its path, crawling beneath the debris and pausing to sniff the garbage, Vidot felt an immense respect for all the tiny things in Paris that were forced to get by on whatever small crumbs fell their way.

He was mulling this over when, from above, he heard a deep thumping noise coming down. At first he thought it might be a passing bus or a burst of thunder, but as its volume rose, his brain ceased to wonder and his body intuitively reacted with an adrenaline burst that sent him jumping away from his host. Behind him, there was a massive tearing sound, like a fat wineskin being ripped open, as enormous talons tore into the mouse's flesh. A great piercing squeal of death filled Vidot's ears, like that of a locomotive train's brakes screeching as it slid to its fated collision.

Landing on the pavement, he quickly hopped around and looked back for Bemm. The sidewalk was empty and the great owl was already off, flapping its broad wings high up over his head. A few drops of the mouse's blood splashed loudly about him on the pavement as the massive bird carried its prey away. Owls again! First in Leon Vallet's apartment with those strange bony pellets, and now here. He had lived in Paris his whole life and never seen a single owl, and suddenly they seemed to descend upon the city. They were like a plague! Where did they come from? And where was Bemm? Had he jumped clear? Vidot gazed out at the broad flatness of the empty sidewalk and waited for his friend.

The night crawled on and there was no sign of life. The loss of his companion filled Vidot with a terrible loneliness. Finally, he decided to set out again on his journey, changing his destination to the one place where he knew he belonged. There was no need to head for the station, he realized: he would find no one to listen to him there. They would no doubt merely crush him like the bug that he was. So instead, he now headed to the comfort of home and his wife. He needed her consolation, as for the first time since this adventure began he found himself anxious and worried. Overwhelmed and vulnerable, he longed for the solace of his small living room, kitchen, and bed. He did not know how he could possibly communicate his situation to Adèle or what she would say. He imagined pulling off a series of tricks, improvised variations on the flea-circus acts those bohemian British street performers Sir Billy and Dottie had shown him so long ago, perhaps writing messages to Adèle on the steamed bathroom mirror or leaping from the inkwell to spell out his dilemma. Yes, that might work, he thought, realizing almost at the same time that this was an inspiring example of the power of love, as all he had to do was think of Adèle and the puzzles began solving themselves. She would be his muse, his soldier, his salvation. Together, they could solve "The Mysterious Case of the Flea Detective." The thrill of possibility again flooded his heart. He was ready to go. Vidot looked about in vain for a wandering rodent who could be his ride home. The cobblestone streets and gutters were quiet and empty, not a shape or shadow stirring. Ah, he thought, what a truly cursed city, the rats are never around when you need them.

XV

Witches' Song Two

Ah, look, so rash and wrong,
so sure and shortsighted,
watch Elga's little spells scurry,
see her black intention tearing into fortunes,
tearing like a startled, blind mare
breaking through a weaver's beaded loom.
Elga, Elga, oh, I've crawled alongside this crone
for how long now? Solstice to solstice, far back to where?
To there, when I eyed her quayside on that cold slimy wharf
arguing over a broken crate of rotting root weeds.

Orts and offal were her wrangled trade
    and at first sight I could see it all:
skunk cabbages, bleeding radishes, and a fistful of horsetail,
a telltale mirror to her tangled soul.
She traveled alone then, and, curious for company,
we gathered round, compared char-scribbled crib notes,
congealing into a dark hymnal congregation
all muttering, humming, and spitting for luck.
Ravenous for the musty, mystery spoils
we pulled from the clasp of those new found lands,
we tested and tried much, oft with bitter ends for the unlucky
(sailors shrunk to pea size, shrieking whores sprouting curled
    pig's tails).
Our effort was tremendous as our new age dawned,
never a belfry rung to our victory but hidden here in the
    cellars,
proud hard work, seeds dried, stews simmered,
round sounds married to sharp tones
and turned backward like a citrus peel until
our fresh curses were cooked and our efforts done.

The loot was split fair,
Elga loaded a half dozen bartered asses
and rode off, beating them down the lane,
laden with potent bounty.

It was only long later that she turned up again,
sprouting in our path like a drizzle-day mushroom might,
now pulling Zoya along, fresh bait for her fancy.
Elga was always a barb, you know her well enough now,
even a small taste of her bitterness lasts a cur's age.
And the young one too often caused us grief,
too pretty. Such wide blue eyes, such fulsome paps,
pulling like a strong northern tide.
Elga and Zoya were good enough companions
but at times so dark, too conniving for me—

Babayaga

their trick was idiot simple,
Elga dangled the girl,
first luring in arguably deserving devils,
then milking them of their shiny kopecks,
before cutting them free of life's loose grasp—

In these days our bickering was slight but needle sharp,
and so when we were chased to the fens, pauper poor,
or bulge-eyed with bare-bones famine,
I was more than happy to say farewell.

Thusly we would come, we would go,
and the years passed like bloody feathers
ripped by hungry hands
off a barnyard hen.

And now here we are,
death running fast toward fate,
fate running fast toward death
as a sour Elga waddles the cold cobblestones,
hissing out ancient maledictions.

XVI

Will found a tuxedoed Oliver in the back lobby of the Hotel Lutetia. He was sitting on a love seat with a lit cigarette and the remnants of a Bellini. There was a pianist playing in the corner, but otherwise the room was empty of patrons.

"Oh, hullo," said Oliver. He began to rise, and then, on second thought, settled back down.

Will sat down beside him. "Nice penguin suit."

Oliver forced a smile. "I've got a premier tonight." He looked at his watch. "My companion's in the powder room now, she shouldn't be long, then I'm afraid we've got to dash. So let's make this quick."

"No problem," said Will, pulling a fat envelope out of his briefcase, placing it on the cocktail table. Since it was a Sunday, getting the file had turned out to be a reasonably simple task. Will had spent less than an hour at the office going through the agency's filing cabinets. It turned out there was an abundance of material that looked weighty and substantive but was actually useless stuff.

Oliver took the envelope and slipped it under the black overcoat beside him. "What is it?"

"Hoffmann-La Roche's file. A sizable company. Swiss, growing. You said you could use something pharmaceutical, right?"

"Yes, exactly." Oliver looked at his watch and glanced around the room impatiently. "And they're a client of yours?"

"No, it's a competitive analysis."

"Good?"

"There are a few bits some might find of interest," Will exaggerated. He knew no one would find one iota of valuable information in that file. There were, however, a lot of words.

"Yes, well, this should be enough to feed the beast. The agency is stuffed to the gills with data addicts, pure and simple. Here, as promised." He pulled out a small silver film canister from his pocket. "These are the shots Ned took at your place last night. Cigarette?"

"Thanks," said Will, taking both the film and the cigarette. "I'd like that knife of mine back too."

Oliver slapped his hand to his forehead. "Oh gosh, that's right, your silly knife, I'm so sorry, I forgot all about it. It's at home, I'm afraid."

"That's not funny."

Oliver put out his palms. "I'm not joking, Will, honestly, it completely slipped my mind. I've been fairly distracted in the last twenty-four hours, and not only by our little misadventure. You see, I also met up with the most delightful old friend—" Suddenly, his face brightened. "Ah, here she is now!"

Will looked up. She looked familiar walking across the room, but he couldn't place her. Her dark hair was pulled back, her blue eyes sparkled, and she was smiling at him in a familiar way, as if they were old friends at a school reunion. He and Oliver both rose to meet her. "Will Van Wyck, this is the lovely Zoya Polyakov," he said.

She smiled. "It is nice to see you again."

Will paused, confused. "I'm sorry—"

"We spoke, on the metro last night, about the rain. Do you remember?"

"Last night?" Will remained confused even as the memory dawned. The accent should have reminded him, but her black hair pinned up changed her face, her cheekbones seemed stronger, her neck longer, and in her elegant low-cut black dress she only vaguely resembled the woman he had met the night before. He did recognize her eyes, though; they were hard to forget.

Oliver laughed. "My, that *is* amusing, what a small town, eh? People do have a tendency to pop up out of the blue. Right, well"—he slipped his arm around Zoya's thin waist—"I'm afraid we have to make our exit. I would invite you along, Will, but I'm not sure it's up your alley. It's a profligate and atheistic work, designed to shock, hence the Sunday screening. But I'm fairly sure it's going to be dreadful. We should be ready for a good strong drink afterward, if you'd like to meet up."

"No, that's okay, I—" Will's gaze was still stuck on Zoya. He was thrown by the coincidence, and, given all that had occurred that weekend, he didn't quite trust it. But more than that, the girl intrigued him.

"You stole my eye," she said, ignoring Oliver.

"Excuse me?"

"You have a bruise there, I put cover-up over mine." She touched her face where the mark had been. "Perhaps I should lend you my makeup?"

Oliver chuckled. "Yes, I heard you got yourself into a scrape aiding a damsel in distress."

She looked at Will with a small, complicit grin. "That's not really true, is it?"

"No. It's not," said Will. He didn't know what to add. He wanted to make her laugh, or at least smile. But all he could do was stand there, struck dumb. There was an essence to her gaze—the way her eyes connected with his—that took the simplest words in his mind and effortlessly broke them down into small, useless heaps of letters.

"Yes, well, dying to hear the real story but haven't got time, I'm afraid. And now you'll excuse us, Will, we're running late," said Oliver, guiding Zoya to the exit. "Thank you again. I'll call you later to—" The hotel's revolving door clipped off the end of his phrase as they spun away into the night.

Standing in the empty lobby, Will felt cheated. It was as if some captivating salesman had danced a collection of precious jewels in front of his eyes before whisking them away and locking them up in some unseen vault. Will played back the short conversation he had shared with the girl the previous night on the metro and then let his imagination jump to all the things he could have added to that brief exchange: the well-timed phrases he could have impressed her with, the little jokes to make her laugh and the observations to make her wonder, all of which could have culminated in Zoya Polyakov being on his arm tonight, looking up into his eyes.

There were charmed souls who always seemed to say the right things in the perfect manner, deftly slipping the precise amount of weighted meaning into every nuanced phrase and achieving their goal with a minimum of effort, squeezing every sugary drop of opportunity out of every ripe moment and always getting their way. That simply wasn't Will. But Oliver did always seem to know what to do, what to say. He was so silver tongued, he could blackmail you and steal your girl and it was still hard to hate him. Probably because, for Oliver, none of it was serious. Like the boys back home on the field at Tiger Stadium, he was simply playing a game while the rest of the world struggled on. He held the world in the palm of his hand, the same way pitchers like Hal Newhouser and Dizzy Trout held a baseball. Will wanted that control, he wanted to possess his share of the graceful victories that came easily to some and never to him. But it was no use, he could improve and try harder, but in the end he knew he was too earnest and straight, he didn't have the luck, the charisma, or the air of money that opened the secret doors and won the loveliest girls. He had been raised to follow the rules, and for the most part he had, knowing all the while that those rules were invented to keep everyone in their place. He had to live within those limits, he didn't know what else to do. Besides, sticking to those rules had gotten him this far. Here he was, living in Paris, after all. He had no right to complain. Still, though, he didn't have that girl, Oliver did. Will stood there for a few minutes, finishing his cigarette while staring down at his plain brown shoes. In the far corner of the room, the hotel's pianist was playing the final phrases of a Schubert sonata. Will didn't know the piece, all he knew was that its beauty hurt.

XVII

The rising sun sent bright rays of fresh light flooding across Zoya's room. She was still awake, though out of her party clothes. She sat perched on a stool, leaning over her kitchen sink busily picking apart one of the pellets the owls had left. She separated out the larger bones from the small, tangled ball and rolled the remaining contents to- gether in a paste with marzipan and chicory, spitting on the ball to hold it together. A pair of houseflies buzzed about as she dipped it into a teacup filled with elderberry wine, letting it soak before taking it out to dry on the sill. One of the houseflies landed on the ball and walked nervously along its surface. Go ahead, she thought, taste it, you will be surprised at what you find.

She went back to the bed and lay down, waiting.

Her plans for Oliver could not have gone better, he was so smug with his lofty attitude, so ready to go through all the motions of seduc- tion. It never occurred to him that he might be the prey. She enjoyed this sort of man wherever she found him; more than once she had seen empires undone by the ignorance that pooled around such grand, unflappable confidence. Where would the world be, she wondered, without all these blind and greedy men?

Two nights ago, she had sat on the bench with her small, enchanted mirror, bouncing and bending the thin light from Will's apartment. She watched as the tall man and his two accomplices had bullied Will. She had seen him tied up and gagged, she saw a knife flash. She could not hear anything, but it did not matter. Eventually things seemed to settle down. Will was untied. The tall man talked to him at length, clearly trying to make a point, while a short woman sat at the desk, taking pictures. Worried that she might be observed by some curious passerby, Zoya finally tucked her mirror away. She knew enough. Her path usually brought her into contact with the small, garden-variety deceptions people habitually dabbled in—hidden mistresses, larcenous accounts, or rude domestic violence. This was notably different. Will was like a rabbit she had been carefully stalking and tracking through the woods, only to have it stolen out from under her nose by another pack of predators right before she could pounce. This was interesting. She sat and waited.

When the tall man and his friends had finally emerged from the apartment building, Zoya fell in behind. When the three grabbed a taxi, she jumped in another. "*Suivez le taxi là*," she told the driver.

They drove out of the 8th, down the Champs-Élysées, and crossed the river. Driving up the Left Bank, she watched the short woman emerge at one corner and the large oaf of a man crawl out at another. Finally the cab stopped in front of a café and she watched the tall thin man pay the cabbie and head in. This would not be too difficult, she thought. For starters, he was alone. Also, he was handsome enough, lean, and sharp looking. She'd done her fair share of work with ugly ones in the past, men with faces so pimpled and flabby her stomach turned merely at the memory of them.

She found Oliver sitting at the bar, hunched like a thirsty crane over a Pernod. She sat down in the manner of an old friend, and with, six words, whispered backward, had him convinced that they actually had met before. Three drinks later, a few double entendres, and a hand on a knee had him convinced he would be seeing much more of her.

She had asked very little, but as he smoked and drank through the night, Oliver told her quite a lot. He was a writer and a publisher, he said. He had rowed crew in college, his parents had hoped for him to study law, following the family tradition (a grandfather on his mother's side had been a Supreme Court justice). Zoya had listened, smiled, and nodded along, though it all meant very little. He said he had fallen in love with Paris after the war and had lived here off and on, ever since then, now over in the 5th arrondissement.

"Decades of lessons and tutorials plus years spent here, and the locals still say my French is only fairly good," he said.

"You understand *my* French," she said. "That's good enough, *oui?*"

He smiled warmly at her. Testing the spell of familiarity, she had said that he seemed happier than he'd been the last time she saw him, but at this, Oliver shook his head in dismay. "Glad to hear I'm putting on an optimistic front, but no, the thunderheads are looming, I'm afraid, and nothing's panning out. My humble little magazine's about to go under, we've lost our biggest benefactor, you see, and if I don't come up with some grand stroke of genius, well, I'll have to pack it in and go home."

"Perhaps your writing will be successful."

"What writing?"

"You're an author, no? Did you not say—"

"Oh, yes, I did, didn't I?" This had made him erupt with a burst of drunken laughter, a startling sound that reminded her of a mule's braying, but then his face grew somber again. "Well, I was a *real* writer for a stretch, banging away at the typewriter every morning, big ideas billowing like thick cumulus clouds across the horizons of my mind, and all that bunk. Hemingway says the best writing is when you are in love, and it's true, but then something happened, a kind of personal tragedy, and I was forced to stop. You might say I was scarred. Anyway, since then, my mind's been a blank. Oh wait, I did have one idea, I thought I'd write down the crudest pornography I could think of, then hit the *Roget's* hard and doll it all up into a novel. Figured if I dead-on nailed it I could get the book banned in the U.S., a nice nasty scandal would erupt, and international sales would shoot through the roof. Miller and Nabokov both managed that trick quite well, of course. But then of course mother would want to see it and, well . . ." He stopped to sip his drink. "For quite a long time I felt guilty about abandoning my writing, but then I heard a story that helped. A taxicab driver told it to me—he was Russian too. You see, before the revolution there was a Muscovite writer, magnificently talented, who was known for his brutal realism, real hard stuff, like Gorky, only darker. His work exposed the callous ugliness of the tsars, the starving peasants, the pestilence and fever, the whole shebang. Then, of course, the revolution came and, like the rest of the true believers, he bought all of it, brotherhood, unity, fraternity, the works. Of course, then comrades began disappearing into Black Marias; the state was seizing journalists, neighbors, all of them, poof, vanishing like some sort of terrible magic trick, and this writer began to worry. So he worked up a canny little strategy to dodge the ax: from that point forward, he only wrote nonsense. Kitchen sinks barking recipes to mops, cattle mournfully mooing out tennis scores, salt shakers singing nursery rhymes—the man had no agenda, but he had to write, because all he knew how to do was weld verbs and nouns together into some kind of powerful harmony. In the end, of course, Stalin suspected this fellow was up to something, so bang, they shot that writer dead. End of story. Well now, this tale certainly shook me, but I also took some solace from it. When the revolution does arrive and the committee gathers to judge, they won't be able to hang me for any of my work, for I am the writer who never writes."

"I see," Zoya said. She was interested in the way he told his tale, beginning with an emotional truth, a point of clear vulnerability, and then quickly burying it under drunken tangents, glib humor, and randomly grabbed pages of history. Here, she realized, was a man afraid of his own heart. He would rather hide it beneath layers like some papier-mâché mask, pasted together for a carnival. He was simply a coward. This was not a condemnation; she genuinely appreciated it about him. The truly craven were, in her eyes, nothing to despise; she had spent much of her life hiding with them, cowering in the dank, dark corners of root cellars, hiding up high in the branches of trees, or cringing below the putrid edges of half-full latrines, listening as pillaging troops and blood-lusting rioters tore apart their homes and villages. She remembered looking into the cowards' quiet, knowing eyes as they huddled together, listening to the gunshots and the screams and then the receding din of the marching boots mixed with the clatter of looted spoils, all followed finally by the perfect silence of death. Cloaked there in that petrified darkness, crammed shoulder to shoulder with the breath of their fear on her neck, she learned that coward was often only another name for survivor.

"So, you never write?"

"No," he said. "Every so often I think about dashing off a stanza about the crystal winter frost or the blush of a girl's cheek, only to keep the blood going, but I rarely get round to it." Oliver finished the last of his drink and seemed ready to change the subject. "Say, look now, here's a thought. I've got two tickets for a cinema premier tomorrow night. Wasn't planning on attending, but maybe we should go?"

"Didn't you already invite me?"

"When?" He looked confused.

"Earlier." She liked shuffling the deck of time, keeping him off balance.

"Did I? Yes, maybe, who knows. Lord," he said, chuckling, holding up his drink, "I suspect someone slipped some alcohol into my cocktail. Ha ha. So, how about we meet up at the Hotel Lutetia, say at six?"

She had agreed and then excused herself, leaving Oliver with kisses on his cheeks and a warm smile promising more. As she was leaving she saw him shake his head, clearly a little bewildered and slightly thrilled by their encounter. She paused to look back through the window as he signaled the bartender for another drink; clearly she had excited nerves that now needed soothing, better with a bottle than another woman. Wives were fine, but other lovers tangled plans.

Arriving home that night, she had looked around for a sign of Max's visit, but it was clear he had not been in the apartment. She didn't think much of it, the rat often took days to make his way, sniffing over the rooftops and up the drainpipes until he tracked her down.

She found the two owl pellets lying inside the open window and placed them in an empty pickling jar. Then she prepared for her work. Inside a wide, shallow bowl she placed Oliver's handkerchief (which she had furtively slipped from his pocket), along with the calling card he had handed her as they departed. Before she placed the card into the bowl, she licked both sides and poured in a spoonful of honey, sprinkled tea leaves, ground star anise, white pepper, and cinnamon. Then she placed the bowl on the sill and, singing a quick spell, spit into it twice.

The next evening, she met Oliver at the hotel. She had not expected Will to show up, she had not seen or prepared for it, and when she came into the brightly lit lobby and saw him sitting there, she paused and thought, Well, hello, rabbit.

She felt the dust stir in her heart. Perhaps it was the simple pleasure of surprise, or the deliciously wicked feeling of having a plan surge ahead. But possibly, she thought, those wisps of girlish sentimentality that always floated around inside her had been blown to life, those gilded and hopeful fairy-tale notions that Elga always scolded her for harboring.

Stay focused, she thought, but it was all moving very fast. In the old days it would take eons of plotting star charts and memorizing stagecoach schedules to choreograph the right coincidences, but now, with combustion engines roaring and the sky scratched thick with telephone lines, gears meshed quickly and plans flew together. Walking toward him, she adjusted her dress, one of the few couture items Leon had ever bought for her (petite lace negligees had been more his style). She was tempted to toss a quick trick into the air but hesitated, reminding herself that spontaneous spells too often went awry (there were countless rows of countryside graves attesting to that); but also she was curious to see what she could accomplish naturally. Watching the slow recognition on Will's face as he saw her, followed by his realization that she was accompanying Oliver, made her wonder if this enchantment might work entirely organically; after all, coveting another man's possessions tended to come with its own dark spell.

Moments later, when Oliver put his arm around her waist and swept her out the door, she barely had time for a quick glance back at poor Will, still standing there, watching her go. The look on his face told her the deed was as good as done. The fish had swum into the net, the bear's paw had found its trap, and this little rabbit was now all hers.

XVIII

Elga steered the patrol car off the country road and bounced it up the farm's muddy driveway. She parked between a small flatbed truck and a shed. Getting out of the car, she paused to look around. Past the small farmhouse a yellow bicycle rested against the large barn. She walked up onto the farmhouse porch and, without knocking, went in. The rat scurried in behind her.

An old man wearing a priest's cassock sat at the table, eating a bowl of soup. He paused for a moment to look up at Elga, then returned his attention to the soup. The rat crawled from behind Elga's feet, jumped up onto a chair, hopped up onto the table, and started licking at the edges of the bowl.

"Tell him to stop that," said the priest, raising his spoon in protest.

"You tell him, he's your brother," said Elga.

"Max, stop it," said the priest, but the rat kept at the soup. The priest put down his spoon and watched as the rat steadily emptied the bowl, licking it clean.

"He was hungry."

"I can see that. Where's your Zoya?" said the priest, taking a green apple off the sideboard. "Curled up in her little love nest?"

"No. Zoya is dead."

This stopped the priest halfway through his first bite. Thinking about what she'd said, he slowly resumed chewing. "What kind of dead?" he said.

Elga rubbed her face with her hands. "Dead dead. Does it matter? She's dead to me."

The priest nodded. "Right. So she is alive."

Elga shrugged. "Only until I find her."

"What did she do now?"

"Bah, what didn't she do? First she kills her fat *lubovnik*, puts his head right through a spike, then she leads the policemen straight to my house. Two of them. Two policemen. Trouble. Much trouble. I tell you this too, I think she did it on purpose."

"Why?"

"Who knows? But she has betrayed me, and that comes with a cost." She dramatically crossed her throat with her finger.

"No need for the theatrics, Elga, I know what you mean." The priest shook his head. "But that does not sound like Zoya."

The old woman threw up her hands "She has always been a messy one. And I am tired of cleaning up after her. She makes me act like some ugly maid scrubbing the floor, working on my hands and knees with my fat ass up in the air, ripe for a kick. It is stupid. I am too old for this."

"You are the same age you have been for a century," he said.

"No, I am much older, you just do not see. It happens too slowly."

He chose to ignore this; he knew he did not understand the laws that governed Elga and her sisters. He had tried to once, but that was a long time ago. "Any idea where she is?"

"No. We left town fast, before Max could sniff her out." Elga dug her finger into her nostril and then flicked the snot on the ground. "Listen, I'm going to need you to send some of your village idiots with that truck to my place to pack my work up. It's safe there, should be no trouble, I put a curse on the door."

"No trouble? Really, Elga? I hear the word 'curse,' and I tend to think there might be trouble."

Elga was quiet. The priest scratched his head. "The farmer down the way has two boys who can help move your stuff. He has a better truck than mine. Whose car did you come in?"

"I don't know." She set the keys on the table. "You can have it if you want. I wouldn't drive it, though."

The priest looked at her suspiciously, then he went out the door. A minute later he came back inside. "It's a police car, Elga. You want to tell me where the policemen are who came with that car?"

"You got me." She shrugged.

The priest went over to the icebox and slid a bottle of vodka out of its small freezer compartment. He poured himself a shot and then splashed another shot into the empty soup bowl. The rat went at it. The priest sat back down. "Why don't you tell me what you want, Elga?"

"Maybe put the car in the shed. Then get those farm boys to clear out my place. I can store things here for the time being. And I need your help getting a new girl."

"A new girl? Why?"

"I told you, Zoya's dead."

The priest closed his eyes, letting the comment pass. "Where will we find this new girl?"

"That hospital in town. Get me a job there tomorrow."

"What if they're not hiring?"

Elga nodded. "One of their workers is sick, they're going to need help to cover for her. I can be that help."

"You're confusing me, Elga. The worker is sick? How do you know this? Are you talking about an event that has happened or will happen?"

Elga looked at him like he was an idiot. He knew time and tense did not concern her, they would be chopped and thrown in the stew with all the rest.

Max the rat was done with the vodka. He tottered around drunk for a few steps before slipping off the edge of the table. The priest deftly caught him in the palm of his hand before the rat hit the floor and placed him back on the table. "Seriously, Elga, you can't barge in here with so much nonsense. When will it stop?"

She dismissively shook off the priest's question. "There is no stop."

XIX

Vidot the flea arrived at his doorstep, near dead with exhaustion and hunger. He had briefly caught a ride on the back on a stray cat that had carried him less than a dozen blocks before it turned its tongue against him. He had barely escaped unharmed and had hopped the rest of the way, dodging deep oily puddles and fat automobile wheels. But now, finally, he was home. He crawled under the main entrance door to the building and through the large lobby before beginning the laborious job of jumping, one by one, up the three flights of stairs to his apartment. Finally reaching the top, he used the last of his remaining strength to crawl under his door and into his hallway. He was home. He knew no real remedy for his condition could be found here, he would work on that tomorrow. For now, he simply needed the solace of feeling safe from the nightmarish world of unexpected predators and oversized poodles that lay outside. For Vidot at this moment, no sight could be more reassuringly welcome than that of his beautiful wife. He longed to smell her hair, to fill his lungs with her perfume, find calm in her radiant presence.

The radio was on but the front room and the kitchen were both empty. In two hops he had leapt into the living room, where he paused to have a look around. He half expected to find Adèle sitting in her favorite red chair, reading one of the flowery romance novels he loved to tease her about. But the living room was empty too. It was then Vidot heard the sound of her voice.

It did not take much of a detective to realize what was going on. Hopping toward the bedroom, he was devilishly pleased. He had often wondered, on those occasions when he was stuck working at the station late into the night, if his wife ever longed for him and, fantasizing about his touch, brought herself to pleasure. He had always secretly wanted to see her in such a state. Yes, he thought mischievously, this was his golden opportunity. So, almost giddily, he hopped to the doorway to spy on his sweet Adèle.

She was there, but she was not alone. There was a man with her, wrapped up in her clawing arms, making love to her with a fierce and feverish devotion. Reeling from the sight, Vidot was not immobile for long, as the hurt and betrayal filled him with a wave of furious electric adrenaline. Without reflection or hesitation, a mighty leap sent him onto her naked lover's back, where Vidot began attacking the stranger with all the fury he could muster.

It was not very much. The man did not stop in his exertions and an enthralled and ecstatic Adèle kept her lover entirely focused. They were both utterly engrossed in their passionate wet kissing, biting, nibbling, licking, grabbing, and thrusting; with every rough touch this interloper elicited deep guttural moans from his wife. Vidot had never heard Adèle like this; it was as if she were a completely different creature, a feral animal bathed in sweat, wholly possessed by feverish lust and hunger. Boiling with rage, Vidot scrambled up deep into the thickness of the stranger's dark hair and, like a crazed Gaul in the heat of battle, vengefully sank his teeth deep into the man's skull. *Take that, you bastard!* Vidot wanted to scream.

Almost immediately he felt he was losing his senses. The flooding, intoxicating rush of the man's blood overwhelmed and disoriented him with its rich savory nourishment. Vidot's mind went soft and woozy and he found it hard to focus, his consciousness wholly immersed in the warm, pulsing waves of pure sustenance. Forgetting himself and his terrible circumstances, he sucked greedily, instinctively focused on absorbing all the blood he could. As his belly swelled his senses reeled and his head felt dizzy. His legs weakened and he scurried to reset his footing, trying to stay upright. As the man and Adèle simultaneously reached the peak of their ecstatic convulsions below him, the oblivious Vidot keeled over and passed out cold.

He awoke in absolute darkness. Was this death? Had he been pitched into the cold blackness of purgatory? He almost hoped so. He got back on his legs and tried to shake his tiny head clear. So many odd and terrible events had unfolded so quickly that he felt he was prepared for the worst. He began to make his way and though he was unable to see a thing he quickly realized that he was still in the dense, dark forest of hair atop the man's skull. He could make out a few muffled voices and then he heard a door slam. The surface he was riding on seemed to bob both forward and downward in a gradual sinking manner, indicating to Vidot that they were descending the stairs. It was then he realized he was being carried away from his home, away from his Adèle, away from every ideal he had ever possessed of love, harmony, and domestic happiness, trapped beneath the surface of another man's hat.

XX

Up in the Pigalle hotel, Zoya checked on her concoction. Finding it dry enough, she removed a long-stemmed clay pipe from the bureau and placed the small owl ball in the chamber. Tucking herself into the corner of a white cushioned chair, she struck a match and inhaled deeply. Then she lay there, waiting.

It did not take long. The ceiling above her soon dissolved from solid to liquid as the walls subtly ruffled like a theater curtain with actors busily moving behind it before the show. Spectrums of light flickered, casting visions that quickly pooled in around her. Soft glowing red and powder blue hallucinations rose from the floor, translucent figures finding their form, crossing past one another in a busy collage, some familiar, some unknown; street scenes and tiny sets of homes, offices, hallways materialized in different corners of the room, their motions choreographed by the rhythmic words of the whispering women wrapped and enshrouded in obscuring layers, ghosts from the ancient vanished covens who now crowded around Zoya. Each voice layered over another, narrating in cacophony the many-dimensional scenes playing all around.

Zoya kept control, maintaining her concentration; she was well practiced in this art. More than a century ago, when Elga first gently dropped the owl ball into the pipe for her, she had been taken on an anxiety-ridden journey into darkness that disclosed a wild and chaotic universe, purposeful in its intention but unfathomable in its cause, its myriad of forces so overwhelmingly powerful Zoya barely survived witnessing it all. But she lived, and learned, and now she could choose the thread she wished to explore amid the tumult, focusing on the ghosts' discordant tones until she isolated each tableau she wanted to follow. There in the corner, by the love seat, a miniature Oliver volleyed in an early-morning game of tennis, while over by the base of the sink she saw her rabbit Will making his way through the crowd to work, looking a little worried, but more steady in his step than he knew.

She looked around, trying to locate Elga. There was a street carnival and a small bedroom where two lovers lay entwined, a fog passed across their bodies, blown from the tops of rows of boiling beakers that sat in a busy laboratory; then trees grew up between the industrious scientists until they all disappeared into a dense forest. A parliament of owls flew out from the high branches, spreading their broad wings to clear the room of every vision, causing it all to vanish like vapor in the air. She looked around the empty apartment, frustrated; there was more to discover, she sensed it, some crucial element was lurking below.

She lit the pipe and inhaled again, this time more deeply and with subsequent greater effect. Flickering to life in the kitchen space, a rat's giant head stared out at her. On the rodent's forehead a man stood like a mountain climber on a peak, or a captain on the bridge of his ship. Not recognizing him, she watched as he leapt above her, becoming a giant now, far larger than the former dimensions of the room. He soared up into the night sky above, then looped and spun like a diver in the air, falling straight into the open mouth of an alto saxophone. Suddenly all the noises of the ghosts ceased and silence filled the room. From deep inside the brass horn a small noise emerged. Zoya could not tell what it was. She leaned in, listening closely, until finally she discerned the voice of a child, a little girl, who seemed to be crying, from fear or solitude. Then more voices joined in, another chorus like the ancient covens but this one somehow more familiar. They grew louder, chanting gibberish and calling out to Zoya. Her eyes went wide with recognition—yes, she did know these voices, she knew these old crones. The chorus steadily increased in volume until they seemed to be screaming. A trembling quiver took hold, sending her body backward onto the floor and shaking her breasts, arms, and thighs in an epileptic frenzy. The voices' pitch rose steadily inside her head, building in tempo until its harsh and screeching amplitude made her skin flush, her eyes roll back, and her jaw grind hard. Then, finally, in a flash, a great crack of light broke through, shattering the blackness like glass.

It was over. She blinked a bit and stayed there on her side without moving, thinking over what she had seen, what she had heard. She spoke to the empty room: "Mazza, Lyda, Basha, you old cows, back for what?" Then she was silent, as if they might answer. Her senses awake and alert now, she could feel the three, pulling at her the way tides draw in boats. What was their intention? What were they up to? She ran through the visions again in her head. There had been no sign of Elga, which was odd. Why would the old woman be hiding? Finally, she wiped the sweat off her brow and rose to light the kettle. She needed a cup of tea. Her mind drifted back to Will, not because of anything she had seen, but simply because that was where her mind wanted to dance. For amid all the gnarled knots of mystical weaving, he was the uncomplicated one, simply a strong and healthy rabbit, bolting about the field without any sure knowledge, only a bit of naïve wisdom and wholesome innocence guiding his way. It relaxed her to think about him. If only it could last.

Book Two

The whole fight is for the conservation of the individual soul. The enemy is the suppression of history; against us is the bewildering propaganda and brainwash, luxury and violence.

—EZRA POUND, *The Paris Review*

I

It was almost one in the morning as a still quite sleepy and bewildered Superintendent Maroc sat in his office, listening to his subordinate explain what had happened. Two officers, one an investigator and the other a patrolman, had vanished from the streets of Paris, along with their patrol car. Worse, there had been yet another strange murder, over on rue d'Astorg. Responding to calls, policemen had found the owner of an antiques shop with a bullet hole in the center of his forehead. Further investigation revealed that the man's tongue had been cut out of his mouth, and despite their searches through the shop's bureau drawers, ancient urns, hat boxes, humidors, and jewelry cases, the investigators had been unable to find it.

"So we are missing a pair of policemen, a police car, and a tongue," concluded the officer, summing up his report.

Superintendent Maroc said nothing. One of the missing policemen, the smug and judgmental Vidot, had always been a constant pain, and in any other circumstance Maroc would have been happy to see him gone. The other, Bemm, was unknown to the superintendent. Maroc had only recently been appointed to the station, did not intend on staying long in the position, and had very little interest in getting to know any of the men. The only reason he had taken any note of Vidot was because the man was so perfectly insufferable.

"Should we inform the families?" asked the officer.

Maroc shook his head. "No, not yet. Call tomorrow and tell them that Vidot and Bemm are off on an important undercover assignment. Maybe they'll turn up. I don't want any trouble or newspaper coverage on this."

Over a year ago, Maroc's benefactor, Papon, had been promoted to prefect of police and had promised to find a prominent position for Maroc in the customs section, where opportunities for furtive profit abounded. No suitable position had been available at the time, so Maroc had been temporarily assigned this job, while Papon arranged for personnel to be reshuffled. Maroc knew he had to be reasonably patient, all he had wanted was peace and quiet in the interim, and for the first few months he had gotten his wish: the normal parade of pickpockets, petty burglars, counterfeit rings, and abusive spouses (sometimes fatally so—wives were occasionally beaten and strangled, just as husbands occasionally ran into cooking knives) had done little to disturb the station's smooth operation.

But now, suddenly, a series of bizarre and inexplicable events had begun erupting all over Paris. On the same night that a machine gun had been fired out of a car at Senator Mitterrand, a few blocks away a man was found hanging dead on the spikes above rue Rataud. The first story had, fortunately, overshadowed the second, and while the Mitterrand case proceeded to quickly unravel into a farce (the politician seemingly set up his own assassination attempt in a foolish ploy to gain popular sympathy), the second case had only grown more complex. The loss of a patrol car along with two of the policemen who had been investigating the Leon Vallet murder was not a story that could be easily kept under wraps, and when it did come to light it would certainly not reflect well on the superintendent.

Through the open doorway, Maroc stared down the empty hall, thinking that while he had never enjoyed the sight of the self-righteous Vidot, with his sarcastic, all-knowing little grin, he sincerely hoped for nothing more than to see the man come sailing into his office now, smug smile and all. But looking at his watch and realizing he would not be getting home to bed until at least three, he suspected the chance of such a simple solution was small. His gut told him that solving this would be drawn out and complicated, and, he reflected with a heavy sigh, there was rarely any profit in complications.

"Tomorrow morning, go through the shopkeeper's inventory," Maroc said, returning his attention to the officer. "See if anything is missing. And tell Gilbert down in the morgue to keep both his and the corpse's mouth shut. At this point, any loose tongues will only confuse things."

II

"Surrealism!" shouted Guizot.

Will had returned from lunch to find his client bouncing up and down in his office waiting for him. Hanging his hat and coat up behind the door, Will sat down at his desk. *"Pardonnez-moi, Monsieur Guizot.* I'm sorry to have kept you waiting. I didn't know we had an appointment."

"We did not!" His client grinned and opened his arms as if ready for a hug. "I had a vision, Will! A magnificent bolt of illuminating lightning! I was smacked right in the brainpan just as you were smacked in that eye of yours! Ha ha. Really, though, what happened to your poor face? An angry husband?"

Will blushed, embarrassed. He had not come up with a good story for how he got his bruise. He was about to attempt one when, over Guizot's shoulder, he saw Brandon striding down the hallway. He had not expected the American until later, but he figured he might as well set things straight now. Thinking it over the night before, Will had decided that, despite all their drama, Oliver and his friends were merely silly and ridiculous creatures. There was nothing here that could not be managed. The knife, the Hoffmann-La Roche file, and all the other nonsense would get sorted as soon as Will had a chance to sit down with Brandon and lay it all out. All he had to do now was politely steer Guizot out of his office so that he could talk with his American friend.

"You know, Guizot, I hate to tell you this, but another client of mine has just arrived for a meeting. One that was actually scheduled."

Guizot looked out the window and saw Brandon. "Let him wait!" he said, eagerly rubbing his hands together. "I need to tell you about this. Two minutes is all I ask, simply listen. It is a story about my wife. My wife, you see, is far more sophisticated than me and she likes to spend all our money on cultured things. First-edition books, lithographs, etchings, rare photographic prints, any bullshit that seems important, she buys it up. So guess what she comes home with last week?"

Will shook his head. "I have no idea."

"She comes home from the gallery with a painting of a giant horse's ass sticking out of a wall. Unbelievable, right?"

"I never would have guessed it."

"Absolutely. I immediately hate this thing. I tell her this, I say, 'What is this absurdity? This is insane!' She says to me, 'It is not insane. It is Surrealism.' I tell her to get rid of it. She says no. I insist. She cries, a lot, but in the end she returns the painting and gets me my money back."

Will was only partly listening. He looked out past Guizot again and saw two men he did not recognize enter the office hall. They shook hands with Brandon and the three waited together.

"Stop being so distracted. I am your client, look at me, Will."

"I apologize, you have my full attention." He could not help smiling at Guizot's serious toue.

"Okay. Now, here is the incredible part," Guizot continued. "Two nights ago I dreamt about this painting. I thought nothing of it. But then, last night, I had a dream about it again! This damn horse's ass, I can't get it out of my head!"

"Maybe you feel guilty for making your wife return it."

"What are you, my psychiatrist? To hell with my wife. The point is, this Surrealism, it interrupts the way you think. It puts nonsense into your mind and disrupts your consciousness, twisting reality around. And this, Will, this is what my advertising must do! So, I want you to help me make an advertisement that is absolutely surreal, absurd, utterly insane, one that threatens to make my customers all go absolutely mad. That is what I want! Do you understand?"

Looking at the wild-eyed man jumping around before him, Will wondered if, despite the fact that Guizot himself was acting nuts, there could be the kernel of an idea here. But Will knew his client, and he knew he would be back in the office in two days' time with a completely different harebrained scheme. The important thing he had to do right now was wrap up this meeting and go talk with Brandon. "I understand, I get it, I will start researching this approach right away," Will said, escorting Guizot to the door. "Maybe check in with me a couple of days from now."

"Wait—" Guizot began to protest, but Will cut him off.

"I like your idea. Intriguing. But I have to wrap this up, as I told you, I have a client meeting." He gestured toward Brandon and the other two, whom his secretary was now guiding toward a conference room.

"Huh." Guizot sniffed the air toward Brandon. "What do you sell for those guys?"

"Pharmaceuticals," Will said, surprised to have come up with a lie so fast.

"Ah, I see," said Guizot. "Drug peddlers. I don't trust any of them."

"Well, they're certainly handy when you have a hangover. Listen, check in with me on Wednesday. I'll have some progress for you by then." He patted Guizot on the back and sent him off down the hallway. Then he went back to his desk, snatched up the Bayer file, and went to meet Brandon and his friends in the conference room.

Entering the room, Will looked at them seated around the table. He immediately took it as a bad sign that they had not removed their hats.

"Will, this is Mike Mitchell and Caleb White," Brandon said. "I asked them to join me here today, hope you don't mind."

"Sure. No problem. Can I get you guys anything? Coffee?" Will said, sitting down.

"It's fine, your girl is getting some for us," said Brandon.

Will set the file on the desk. "Well, I have the Bayer research right here for you but there are a few things I wanted to talk about first," Will said, wondering where exactly he was going to begin. When he met Oliver at the party? The scene in the back room at the bar? Or when Boris hit him with the phone book?

"Sorry, whatever you got is gonna have to wait," said Brandon, reaching into his briefcase and pulling out a thick envelope, which he tossed onto the table in front of Will. Picking it up, Will intuitively knew what it contained even before he opened it.

Sure enough, there was the Hoffmann-La Roche file, though not the report itself, only low-quality photographs of its contents. Many of

the pictures were blurred, others captured only part of a page—
whoever had snapped them had been in a rush. Will briefly considered
blurting out some attempt at an explanation, but a voice in his head
told him to wait, there was more bad news coming.

"So what is this about?" he asked.

"Well, we were hoping you could clarify that for us." Brandon's tone
was different, less like the arrogant collegial jock that Will had
known for so long and more like a stern border patrol agent, cold and
procedural. "Our people recognized it right away as one of your company's reports, the format is identical, the language is similar. Even
without any letterhead, that is easy enough to prove. Now the interesting thing is where we found it. An agent of ours managed to snap
these photographs this morning when the file was being shuffled
through the Soviet embassy."

"The Soviet—?" Will was confused.

"Yes," said Brandon. "Seems like the Reds have got their eyes and
ears working here in your shop as well."

Will let it sink in. He could not believe it. He had been both
beaten and betrayed. Why had he assumed that Oliver was working
on his side? The arch, upper-class accent had no doubt misled him; it
would never have occurred to him that someone as clearly aristocratic
and moneyed as Oliver would support the Communists. Not much
about that man made any sense, but still it seemed like there had to
be another explanation.

Will quickly ran through his options, for at the moment the idea of
coming clean with the truth seemed very unwise. He was apparently
guilty of handing over private documents to a Soviet agent. It probably
would not matter that he had been blackmailed into it. After all, a
great number of history's spies had undoubtedly begun as the unfortunate victims of set-ups and extortion, but the faultless roots of their
errors did not matter much to the firing squad. Will realized he
should have gone to Brandon immediately, he could plainly see that,
in the same way that he could also see, painfully, that it was absolutely
too late now. It didn't matter, either, that the files were, for the most
part, strategically useless documents; the enemy was the enemy, and
he had, somewhat inadvertently, but certainly not inadvertently

enough, provided the enemy with information. He needed time, and he needed to find Oliver. There had to be an explanation. "Of course, I want to help in any way I can. What are your next steps?"

"Well, right now I honestly don't have time to work on this. I've got some bigger things going on. But the agency is concerned about it, so I'd like to hand the case over to Mitchell and White here to sort out. If you could get them copies of your agency's personnel files, they'll sniff out where your possible leaks might be," said Brandon. "Of course, we can't arrest anyone ourselves, and bringing the French authorities into it probably wouldn't be smart. But once the suspects are identified, we can take the appropriate action."

"I see," said Will, nodding along. "Okay, no problem, I'll talk to personnel and have copies of the files for your guys the day after tomorrow. Wednesday afternoon at the latest. But I really don't think you're gonna find anyone of interest here. It is only an advertising agency, after all, it's not exactly thick with espionage."

Brandon grinned and got up. "Well, it's thick enough. The file came out of this office. That's all we know now. We'll figure out the rest. Thanks for your cooperation." He started to leave, and then stopped. "Oh, what was it you wanted to discuss?"

Will smiled and shook his head. "Doesn't matter, it can wait. Don't forget this." He slid the Bayer file across the desk.

"Right." Brandon said, picking it up. "Thanks again. We'll be in touch." He headed out, followed by his two silent colleagues, whose names Will had already forgotten.

Sitting there, Will's mind went back to Guizot, his wife, and the story of the painting. He felt like he was the horse's ass sticking out from the wall. But it did not feel terribly surreal, it felt all too real.

III

The ugly old woman had replaced Madame Vertan. She was quite different from the cold and efficient Madame Vertan, who had never said a word but only stared at the patients as she worked with a look of stoic judgment. This new woman never stopped talking, mostly to herself, as she changed bedpans, laid out linens and towels, and sloshed the mop bucket about. At first Noelle wondered if she was another one of the hospital's patients, because she seemed a bit loopy, raw and rude, even slightly frightening. But by the second day of having her around, Noelle realized the old woman was utterly harmless, even entertaining.

"Bah, all this piss smells like poison," the old woman said, dumping the bedpan's contents into a bucket. "It's the pills they stuff you with and the lousy food. It's a wonder you're not stone dead with the swill they make you choke down." Another time, as she was mopping the hall, she said, "What a bird knows, she flies south with. What a pig knows, dies in his sty. Ha ha." Later that afternoon, the old woman, down on her knees with the scrub brush, seemed almost lost in a reverie, going back and forth in muttering conversation with herself: "The prince's winter chalet? Remember? No, where? Prussia, you fool. Yes, yes, he fed us peacock with pickled radishes and sherry wine, there was stuffed goose and marrow, pigs' cheeks and oysters and abalone. Ha, that was a meal . . ."

Noelle could not believe that a woman scrubbing urine stains off the floor could have ever dined with a prince, and the food she was describing sounded disgusting. "Who eats a peacock?" she asked out loud, unable to contain her curiosity.

The old woman stopped her work to look up at the girl. "I'll barter a question for a question: Who ate the first egg that dropped out of a chicken's ass?" She paused for a moment, waiting for Noelle to answer. When the girl said nothing, the old woman blurted out the rest. "A hungry person, that's who." Then she went back to her scrubbing, still talking to Noelle. "But it's not always the fancy food that tastes delicious. My sisters and I camped for six seasons on a Yamna farmer's land. He would scoop eel out of the river for us and fry it with truffles he'd foraged and fresh sweet butter from his cows. Delicious. He was a dense and stupid oaf, but he was strong and big and he always smelled like horseshit. Oh yes"—the old woman paused again in her scrubbing—"nothing is as good as the smell of horseshit. You know, the streets are swept clean now, and all the horses are gone, so there is nothing in the air but the soot of your burning engines." She went back to her scrubbing. "That's why I like to sleep in a barn, to be close to real smells. Horseshit and horse farts. Those are the smells of life."

That made Noelle giggle. A little smile crossed the old woman's lips. Then she returned to her work and did not speak again.

IV

Witches' Song Three

Ah, ugh, agh, we pull at our skulls
and gnash our wasted teeth watching.
Why always the cracked cups, Elga, why never the whole ones?
The old woman's no better than a corrupt conscription officer
out rousting feeble drunks.
With bum dumb warriors such as these it is no wonder
we are only a few fingers' count from lost.
Our odds always long,
now here we are sinking low into polder bog,
desperately reaching and clutching at this single bare stalk
that looks far too weak to offer safety.

So many enemies, countless routs,
even our most sacred rites and pious celebrations of renewal
snatched up by that insatiable and foul pope beast.
See him sit proud and poised,
branded with the crusader's crucifix,
braying on about his mewling manger,
promising eternal life
and bottomless vessels of wine for all anointed.
Now there's a pandering peddler.
He forever extols the virtues of love and compassion
while his crusading Knights Templar
slice at the bare babes' throats.
He can bear no other tale, take no rival myth,
and in his absolute hunger to rule he tore down and cooked up
every sharp-tongued woman in his path,
even turning on his own, his blessed, his consecrated,
the poor, fevered nuns, no more than sick or delirious,

only mad with loneliness,
brokenhearted in their sunbaked convents,
suffering amid the spiraling vertigo
of eternal ennui.
There, standing stone-faced amid their magpie cries for grace,
the priest raised his hand for silence and said simply
and solemnly, burn
sisters burn.

Ghosts, they say, stay for three simple reasons:
they love life too wholly to leave,
they love some other too deeply to part,
or they need to linger on for a bit,
to coax a distant knife
toward its fated throat.

V

Vidot the flea was exhausted. He rested, hanging upside down beneath the couch of his rival's apartment. Over the past two days he had learned all that he could possibly want to know about the man. He had been certain that his investigations would unearth evidence of a great villain, but what he discovered was a decent enough individual with a perfectly ordinary life.

The man's name, which Vidot had painstakingly traced out on letterheads and various envelopes lying throughout the apartment, was Alberto Perruci. He was Italian, a philosophy professor working at the University of Paris. He had a wife named Mimi. She worked as an assistant photo editor at *Festival* magazine. She was a very attractive woman; in fact, Vidot had to admit that even she was more beautiful than his Adèle. Mimi clearly adored her husband and would wrap her arms around him when he came through the door, kissing his neck with warm affection before resting her head against his chest.

Why would such a man need another lover? How insatiable was his greed? Many Europeans—Italians, Spanish, and French—all kept lovers; Vidot did not understand it, but he accepted it as a fact. Still, this woman cooked, she cleaned, and she waited on her husband with a complete unwavering devotion that impressed Vidot. His Adèle was certainly, by all appearances, a good wife, but she never knelt to remove his shoes at the end of the day, she never poured him an aperitif and brought it to his side while he read his evening paper, she never sat in his lap and tickled his ears when they listened to the radio. His respect and instinctive affection for the beautiful Mimi made his heart ache in overwhelming empathy for all the betrayals in the world.

The first day, Vidot had gone to work with Alberto, riding high on his head, tucked safely beneath his hat. He had sat on the tip of the man's skull, looking out at the bored and listless students yawning as Alberto lectured them on Hegel and Marx. Later in the office as the professor graded papers, Vidot watched from above, mildly impressed at how thoroughly Alberto went through the students' work, marking it up in a diligent, thoughtful manner. Then, after a little more than an hour, the descending hat returned Vidot to a state of darkness, and when next he emerged he was in his own apartment again, watching this perfect devil once again embrace his Adèle.

He barely recognized his wife: in Alberto's presence this prim and proper woman instantly became a creature of lust; her eyes watered with hunger and her mouth opened wide as she avidly kissed him until she had to gasp for breath. Vidot felt sick and instinctively returned to his only comfort at hand, once again digging his jaws deep into Alberto for more vengeful—and succulent—sustenance.

About twenty minutes later, lying dazed and nearly unconscious amid the man's thick hairs, he was suddenly roused by the sound of his own name. Scurrying again up to the peak of Alberto's skull to listen, he saw his beautiful Adèle lying naked on the bed, recounting how a policeman had called to say that Vidot was off on an undercover investigation. She said that while this was certainly convenient for the two of them, it was also odd, as her husband surely would have mentioned it. Alberto kissed her cheek and told her they must make the most of this little vacation together. He rose to dress. Vidot was so distracted thinking about what his wife had said—why would the station say that he was off on some secret mission?—that he missed the critical moment and so once more found himself trapped beneath Alberto's hat.

When Alberto arrived home, Mimi had greeted her husband with the usual ardor, laughingly telling a tale of models running around the magazine's office in their frilly underwear. Alberto had laughed too, patting her bottom affectionately and pouring them both wine while she pulled a casserole out from the oven. Vidot was flummoxed by the casual ease with which his rival moved from scene to scene. This Italian was a marvel.

As they were retiring to the bedroom, Vidot finally leapt clear of the man. He did not want to witness any more of Alberto's amorous antics or be party to any more of his betrayals. Settling beneath the couch, he anxiously counted the days he had left. A flea's existence might be short but it could certainly be lively; since he had been transformed it felt as though he had already died a thousand times over. How fortunate he would have been, he thought, if only he had perished alongside poor Bemm. Being torn asunder by the talons of an owl seemed infinitely preferable to the slow, unendurable torture life brought to him now.

Vidot knew he would go mad if he did not find some new distraction. His mind went back to the puzzling thing Adèle had said. Why had the station misled her? It seemed highly suspicious. Not only that, but it was harmful too, for had she been told the truth, the news of Vidot's disappearance could have had a profound effect on his wife, she might have suddenly realized how devoted she was to her equally devoted husband. But, for reasons he could not understand, his superiors were covering things up. The shrieking sounds of Mimi's sexual ecstasy started bouncing off the walls of the dark apartment. Christ, thought Vidot, this Italian was unstoppable. Vidot forced himself to concentrate on his little mystery. Why had the station lied? He guessed Maroc was probably behind it, that hunk of swine was as fork-tongued as they come. Vidot realized he would have to make his way back to the station to uncover the answers. Sensing the long, laborious journey ahead, he sighed. It would be so much easier, he thought, to stay here in this warm, comfortable apartment, spending his evenings listening to the lovely Mimi enjoying her false and perfect heaven.

VI

Zoya sat at the restaurant bar with Oliver, listening to him chatter on as he drank his scotch and emptied a pack of Chesterfields. She laughed at his stories on cue. He was not boring, but he was only a means to an end and there was little reason for her to pay too much attention. As his tales rambled on, she was reminded that this was why she preferred married men, they already had someone to bore with their stories. As if to accent and punctuate his various points, Oliver's hand kept optimistically straying up her thigh. She let him have his fun.

At one point he paused mid-anecdote and looked her in the eye. "Zoya, my dear, you are intriguing."

"What do you mean?"

"I mean, you're a little strange."

She smiled. "Oh no, I'm not, it is only that I am from a foreign land, and you are confused by our cultural differences."

"I don't think so. I know plenty of Russians and you're different from that lot. Where did you grow up? Moscow? St. Petersburg?"

"A small town you've never heard of."

"Oh, I know that town very well, it's where so many pretty girls come from. But seriously, tell me about yourself, Zoya. I may come off as somewhat conceited and self-centered, and I suppose I am, but I can be observant too. At times tonight you've been absolutely luminescent, but in other moments, my God, girl, you get a look that is as heavy as an anvil."

"That only sounds like a Russian to me, Oliver."

"But—"

She patted his hand. "Maybe you should go home now, you're drunk and tired."

Oliver looked both amused and offended. "No, I'm most certainly wide awake. I feel like I'm Fred Astaire with Cyd Charisse in *Silk Stockings*."

As his hand slid farther up her leg, she laughed. "Oliver, you make your passes the way Americans kill Indians."

"What are you talking about?"

"Did you ever know any Indians?"

Oliver paused. "American Indians or Indian Indians?"

"The ones from your country, the ones you all killed." His hand slid down between her thighs.

"I'm sure I certainly didn't kill a single Indian. But I can't say I personally know any, either."

Zoya looked into her glass of wine. "But it's funny, don't you think? The way you Americans killed them. I read about it in a book once. How you would make treaties, yes? And then you would break the treaties so they would get upset and make war, and so you would kill them, and then there were new treaties? And you kept going and going, the same trick, over and again, until there weren't any more Indians."

"Well, they're not all dead," Oliver said, shaking his head. "But, of course, it was appalling."

"Yes, a tragedy, but rather clever too, no?" she said. "You almost made it appear to be an accident. Sloppy and offhand, like spilling red wine on a rug. It was the same way Stalin killed, a few here, a million there, a few sips of vodka in between. That is the way to do it. Now, Nazis, they were serious and efficient about it, so German and well organized, that it could not be ignored. If they were more like you perhaps they would have gotten away with killing all those Jews. But the Germans were simply too obvious and clear in their purpose."

Oliver looked at her with amazement. "Look, I don't think—"

She laughed. "Never mind." Now she placed her hand on his leg.

He smiled, shaking his head in bewilderment. "I merely want to say, as an American, that I believe our genocidal habits are well behind us."

"Well, you did drop that atom bomb."

He raised a tipsy finger. "Only to make a point."

She leaned over and kissed him on the cheek. "Enough talk, Oliver, we should leave while you are still reasonably sober. I don't like lovers who prefer their booze to my body. So, we go to your room now?"

"Yes," he chuckled, surprised at her frankness. He threw a handful of francs on the bar and wrapped his arm around her shoulder. "Cold war indeed."

VII

Seated on a bench on the hospital grounds, watching the gardener clip the hedges, the girl thought about what the old woman had been telling her. It was exciting, so many possibilities. The old woman had made her swear by the saints to keep it a secret, but even if she had wanted to share it, the other patients were too far gone to confide in. Even sweet Martine, who had her moments of clarity, was sure to break out into one of her nonsense songs before Noelle could get through the whole tale.

The old woman had become Noelle's only reliable company at the hospital. Nurses came and went with their shifts, their only concern being whether she had tried to hurt herself again. Her parents had not visited in a month, and the last time they were there her father had stood in his gray suit staring with a grim, pale expresssion at the scars on her wrists, while her mother rattled on about the tangled state of her hair. Now the two of them were off traveling to visit relatives in Brittany and would not be back for a few more weeks. At first her loneliness had been profound and she lay in her hospital cot with slack-jawed despair, but then the old woman had found her and now it seemed things were going to be very different.

It had happened a few nights earlier, just after her melancholy had crept back like a black beast coming to eat at her heart. Noelle was sitting up in her bed, looking out her hospital window and wondering if she would ever trust herself again, out there in the wilds of the world. Every thought that came into her mind tortured and oppressed her. Recalling her mother's eyes, or remembering the swarms of small children playing wild in the schoolyard, or even the memory of the sea of shiny black umbrellas that filled the rainy boulevards, all these random recollections made her chest ache.

"So, tell me, what do you see up there in that night sky?" said a voice behind her.

She looked and found the old woman standing by her bed. Noelle was not frightened, the staff often came through after-hours to check on the patients. "I don't see anything out there but darkness," she said.

"Ah," said the old woman, sitting down beside her and roughly patting her on the back. "That is good. Very good. I have known Gypsies that will tell you they can read your fortune in the stars. But they only do this to trick you into looking up. They say, 'Look close! There is the Leo, there is the Aries!' and while you are squinting up into the blackness, these Gypsies stay plenty busy picking your pockets below." They were both silent for a moment. "I hate Gypsies," the old woman said, and then she got up and waddled off, disappearing down the hallway.

The next day the old woman returned after the lights had been turned off, coming out of the gloomy blue shadows carrying a comb and brush. She reached into the pocket of her skirt and pulled out a *sucette*. "Here," she said.

The girl happily took the lollipop as Elga sat down on the corner of her bed and began working the knots out of the girl's black hair. As she worked, the old woman asked questions in her short, blunt way and, knot by knot, with a mouth full of the sweet *sucette*, Noelle told her the short, sad story of her life.

Ever since she could remember, she had wanted to be a ballerina. She had trained and practiced, starving herself to be as thin as those beautiful creatures she watched flitting about the spot-lit stage draped in silk ribbons and tulle. Her mother had been more than encouraging, pressuring her to always be top of her class, taking her to the city to see the Opera Ballet and then sitting in on all her lessons. Her father had paid sums far beyond what they could afford for the best schools and most highly regarded teachers. They lived outside Paris in a small country village, but there was a bus, and Noelle and her mother rode in for classes three times a week, often not returning home until long after her father was asleep. Finally, although her teachers intimated that she might not yet be ready, Noelle's mother insisted it was time to try out for a spot in the Academy.

The audition had been even more rigorous than she could have imagined. She felt tense and nervous and it all went wrong, her *battement frappé* was too weak, her *déboulés* awkward, and every arabesque painfully unsteady. As she finished her final routine she did not even need to see the distracted and bored expressions on the judges' faces. In fact, she knew she had failed before the music even finished.

Stopping there on the empty stage and listening as the piano's last small high note echoed out into the air, she felt the ancient theater creak, crack, and begin to collapse around her, breaking apart into a hundred thousand splinters that fell at her feet. The walls caved in and the ceiling came down as her entire world tumbled and crashed in around her—her little village, the rolling countryside, waves of sea and ocean, and every atomic element she had ever learned about in her science classes were bursting into smithereens, exploding around her on the stage. When the thunder finally subsided, the judges were still there, staring blankly as they waited for her to exit the stage, while her father and mother, seated near the back, sat grinning, entirely blind to her failure, their eyes aglow with the hollowness of hope.

Her first attempt to kill herself had been a botched and desperate affair: in a hysterical fit, she had gulped down a well of dark pen ink, and immediately vomited it up again like a squid, retching the blackness out all over her father's well-organized desk.

Next she had slashed her wrists, but they had found her in time, flailing and weeping in the blushed, warm water of her rose-tinted bath. That was what had brought her to the institution. And now here she was, scarred, ugly, and alone.

As she finished her tale, the old woman nodded. "Yes, this is bad. In my time, we would put you to work, slap you into shape, make you wake up from your miseries through the penance of toil. But this place makes you lie down on your cot, or wander the grounds like a stupid park pigeon, waiting for them to fill you with more treats from their pharmacies. They are not here to cure you, you know, they are only here to make the pharmacist's pockets fat."

Noelle nodded. She was only waiting for the doctors' signatures of approval, she said, so that her parents could take her home. There, she confided with a deep breath, she would surely try to kill herself again.

"Bah," said the old woman. "If you wanted death, you would have death. It's too easy. Bang your head into that stone wall there until you crush it. Right there." She pointed at the cold masonry. "Do it now." Noelle looked at her, wide-eyed and confused. The old woman shrugged. "See? You do not want death. I tell you what, we can give you instead a whole new better life, one more beautiful than any idiot ballerina's. What are dancers, really, but silly whores without the fucking? You give them money and they twirl around in frilly colored costumes before your eyes. They twirl until they drop. You don't want that. You want what we can give you."

"Who do you mean by 'we'?"

"We? Oh, from now on we is you and me." Elga patted her hand. "If you want it, we do this. I'll help you. But it is a great secret. And if you do it, you'll have to help me too. I will need your help with a very tough job."

"What job?"

The old woman rubbed Noelle's shoulder in a soft and reassuring way. "We have to kill a witch."

VIII

Tuesday morning, Will had risen early and tried calling Oliver; then he had tracked down the address of *The Gargoyle Press*, and now, having been pointed to an unsteady, uncomfortable chair, he sat waiting among the piles of books and galley proofs in the journal's "lobby." The office was merely a large apartment with a few desks and telephones. Papers sat stacked and bundled along its tables, empty chairs, and windowsills. There were five people there, none of them the ones Will had met with Oliver at the bar. One sat at her desk reading, one sat typing in a concentrated hunt-and-peck fashion, and two more were at the far end of the room, apparently having a meeting. The assistant who had greeted him, an attractive, narrow-waisted French girl in a red sweater, had briefly disappeared after letting him in and then returned to her seat, where she slowly, studiously paged through the thick copy of *Vogue* that sat beside the big black telephone on her desk. He assumed she had told someone to find Oliver, but no one appeared. After a few moments, the phone rang and the girl answered it. For the next quarter hour she stayed on the phone, ignoring Will while she gaily chatted with the caller. Will suspected she was talking with a close friend. He thought of interrupting her but found it almost relaxing watching a pretty girl laugh and gossip as if he were not even there. Finally, one of the other young women who had been busy reading came over. *"Je peux vous aider?"*

Will stood up. "*Oui, je cherche Oliver.*"

The woman smiled politely and switched to English, which came with a stern British accent. "You've come to entirely the wrong place to find him. He is almost never here, I'm afraid. You're a writer?"

"No."

She grinned. "So sorry, we always assume our visitors are writers; that is why we have Nicole leave them out here unattended. Sooner or later they wander away." She stopped to correct herself. "That sounds bad. It's not that we don't fancy writers, we adore them, honestly, only just not the ones who tend to stop by. What do you do?"

"I'm in advertising, but—"

Her eyes lit up. "Advertising! Oh, right, then"—she firmly took him by the arm and guided him toward the door—"we should get you to Oliver right away. At this hour he's probably at home still curled up with his coffee and a paper, it's only a short walk from here."

"I tried calling him at his home number earlier."

"He rarely answers it. Oliver says the phone makes him a slave of technology, though he does love dialing me up at two a.m. with his tipsy editorial tips. Most Luddites are so charmingly inconsistent."

Like many of the British girls Will had come across in Paris, she was chattier than she was friendly. Her name was Gwen Knight and she told him she had come over after graduating from Cambridge. She kept up a brisk pace and though she never stopped talking, she never smiled, even at her own small jokes. Will found that oddly reassuring. As good as his French was, a slight gauze still separated him from Parisian culture, and so, whenever the locals grinned at him or laughed, instead of reassuring him it actually made him a bit more insecure, since he was never sure if they were expressing sincere pleasure, indulgence, politeness, or, perhaps, mere amusement at the silly American.

Rounding the corner, she led him across the narrow street to an apartment building that had two small statues of lions sitting on either side of the door. She rang the buzzer and a fuzzy "Hullo?" came squawking out through the intercom.

"It's Gwen, I—"

The door buzzed before she could finish her sentence. Instead of taking the elevator, Gwen climbed the stairs. Following her up, Will thought there must be circles of heaven where all one did was ascend staircases behind slender women wearing tight wool skirts. On the third floor, they reached the apartment door. It was unlocked and Gwen walked right in.

Oliver's apartment was spacious, with a guest room by the side of the entrance and a long hallway of densely packed bookshelves leading down to the main rooms. Newspapers were stacked up in the corner, *Times Heralds* and *Le Mondes*. There were piles of opened baby blue airmail envelopes from America lying on the narrow hall table with their telltale red-white-and-blue-striped stamps. "In the back!" they heard Oliver call out from the kitchen. Gwen and Will followed the voice and, rounding the corner, they found a silk-robed Oliver smoking and leafing through a copy of *Paris Match*. Beside him, sitting with her morning coffee, was an only slightly dressed Zoya.

Oliver looked up with a bit of a confused grin. "Oh, hullo, Will, Gwen. What are you two doing together?"

"He came by the office," Gwen began. "Nicole was ignoring him but I took pity. When he said he was in advertising, well, considering the straits we're in I thought it could hardly wait—"

Oliver smiled. "Are you really here to help with our advertising, Will?"

Will looked at Zoya, her hair hung loose and tangled down her shoulders, and all she had on was one of Oliver's tailored Oxford shirts. She sat looking at him, a slight friendly grin on her lips as if she were waiting for him to speak. Then he realized they were all waiting for him to answer. He felt confused and speechless, surprised to find his feelings all twisted, like a clumsy boy tripping on his laces while chasing some elusive bouncing ball. He paused to restart his thoughts. "Yes. I mean, no. You were supposed to drop a package off at my office yesterday."

"That's right!" Oliver said, lightly slapping his forehead. "I was, wasn't I?"

"Right, so I'd like to pick that up, but I also need to talk to you, privately, about another issue. It's very important."

"Fine, fine, ladies, please excuse us for a moment." Oliver led him down the hall and into the main bedroom. Will could not help but notice the top sheet and blankets were all off the bed. He saw Zoya's shoes and blouse on the floor on one side, the skirt lay in a bundle on the other, signs of a night and maybe a morning's passion that caused some emotion, envy, or jealousy perhaps, to well up inside Will. He tried not to think about it. "What's up?" Oliver asked.

"Okay, well now, we have some trouble," said Will, focusing on the issues at hand. "In fact, we have some very serious trouble." He then told Oliver about the photographed Hoffmann-La Roche file and the Soviet embassy. As Will sketched out the details, Oliver sat down, stunned, on the corner of the bed and stared at the floor, quietly taking it all in. He looked as close to being serious as Will had ever seen him.

"How did Brandon know the file came from your office?" Oliver asked. "There was no letterhead on any of it."

"The agency knows what our files look like," Will said, feeling as though he was confessing. "They've seen a lot of them before."

"Yes, I see." Oliver gave Will a funny look. "You've been keeping secrets, Will."

"Here's the deal," Will said, ignoring the accusation. "I'm supposed to hand our personnel files over to the two guys Brandon has working on this—"

"What are their names?"

"I don't remember their names, Mitchell and something."

"Odd that Brandon wouldn't take care of it himself—you're his boy, right?"

"No, I'm not his boy. He says he's working on something more important, he says he doesn't have time for this."

"More important than espionage at the Soviet embassy? Very interesting. The man does stay busy."

"The point is, I'm not going to hand over personnel files to his guys so that they can go digging around in a bunch of innocent people's lives. Who knows what they'll uncover? Maybe they'll find our janitor's a member of the Communist Party, and then what?"

"Well, I doubt they'd be surprised at that. All the janitors in Paris are Communists," said Oliver.

"You know what I mean. It's serious, very serious."

"Yes . . . Christ, of course it is . . . it's the Soviets." Oliver didn't say any more as he drifted into thought, and then he nodded, as if reaching a decisive conclusion. "The wisest plan is to do as you say, confess the whole truth. Make a clean breast of it."

Will exhaled with relief. He had not expected such a straightforward and simple solution from Oliver. "Yes, okay, that sounds right."

"But of course," said Oliver, "the only way you'll come out of this completely unscathed is if you actually hand over the double-crosser. If you don't, they'll make you the fall guy. You see, a leak like this, it's too important, they'll need someone to go down for it. Lucky for us, we know who the culprit is."

"That big guy Boris?"

"Absolutely not Boris."

"He's a Russian, isn't he?"

"Boris hates the Russians because he hates Reds, and the Russians hate Boris because they hate queers."

"Boris is a homosexual?"

"My god, you're not very intuitive about these things, are you? They're both queers. Boris and Ned. That's what makes them such a good fit, they're like an inverted husband and wife. But Ned's the one we need to find, she was in charge of handling the drop-off, told me she was going down to the embassy personally. Foolishly, I forgot to ask exactly which embassy. I was never very good at details. Anyway, we'll have to track her down." He rose from the bed and began dressing. "Why don't we leave the girls here for a bit and pop over to the Monaco Bar, it's nearly lunchtime so she's probably already there, or if she's not, we'll find Boris and he'll tell us where she is. Either way we'll talk to her, that's probably our best shot at mopping this mess up."

"What, we're just going to ask her to turn herself in?"

"No, I sincerely doubt she'd do that, but I'd wager we can get some information out of her, she won't know that anyone at the Russian embassy has been talking to the Americans. Who knows who's playing whom here, this whole thing might be straight up or it could be as sideways and dirty as the damned Dreyfus affair. So let's get Ned's side of the story first. I wouldn't want to hand her over to Brandon's boys without giving her at least a chance to explain. Rather like your concern for those janitors, *tu comprends*?"

"Okay," Will said, though he didn't like it. He would have preferred if Oliver had simply picked up the phone and called the U.S. embassy to sort the whole thing out. But that did not look like it was going to happen.

Oliver smiled. "Excellent, let's go."

Back in the kitchen they found the two women sitting in awkward silence over coffee. Oliver clapped his hands together. "Pardon us, ladies, Will and I are going to pop over to the Monaco, see if we can't find a friend. Don't think there's much fun for you two, so . . ."

"Fine with me, I've got loads of work waiting at the office," said Gwen, getting up quickly.

"Yes, of course. I will see you later," said Zoya. As she said it, she gazed steadily at Will, giving him a broad, warm smile. He felt caught in the focus of her attention. Normally it would have been flattering, but with her sitting there in Oliver's kitchen, wearing Oliver's shirt, with Oliver standing only inches away, it was, at best, confusing. But she wouldn't look away. Gwen was busy putting on her coat, and Oliver was clearing the coffee cups to the sink, so nobody else seemed to notice.

It was then that she started moving her lips, as if speaking but with no sound; not even a whisper emerged. He knew the old trick of mouthing out a silent phrase, but this was different, she was making no effort to slow or overenunciate the shape of her words to help him comprehend whatever she was saying.

Finally she stopped and broke her gaze, quickly rising to kiss Oliver on the cheek as he put on his hat and started toward the door. Will didn't know what to say, so with a confused blush and somewhat flustered, he mumbled his goodbyes to both women and followed Oliver into the outer hallway and down the stairs.

Out on the street, waiting as Oliver tried to find a cab, Will experienced a curious feeling. The words Zoya had been saying moments earlier seemed to catch up with him, coming clearly to life in his mind, as if she were there beside him saying them out loud. Perhaps she had said them in the kitchen after all and he had for some reason been deaf in their presence then, but apparently nobody else had heard them either. It was strange but it did not matter, for he heard the words now, quite clearly. *"I will find you later, I can help. You feel foolish and nervous, even scared, but you are merely lost."*

IX

When the priest walked into his farmhouse he found the young girl sitting at the kitchen table, eating a bowl of hot stew. He went to the sink and poured himself a glass of water.

"So, you've escaped?"

The girl looked up at him. "Elga says you are not a real priest."

"Oh, I am real. Maybe not as much as most, but far more than some." He looked at the girl. Her hair was brushed out and she wore an aquamarine blouse that made her clear blue eyes shine. He could tell she would have grown up to be a beautiful woman someday. Perhaps she would still if she could stay alive. It was possible; Zoya and Elga had both survived against long odds and countless years. But even if she did, she would not be a woman until centuries had passed. Time had become different for her now.

"Elga says you are an old friend," the girl said.

"Well, I am old. That's true. I've known her since I was only a few years older than you." He finished the water and rinsed out the glass. "How is your stew?"

"It's delicious! She cooked it this morning while I was still asleep. She said I should leave it on the stove for you in case you were hungry."

"What kind is it?"

"She said it was a meat stew."

"Here is a little advice for you. Try to avoid eating things that are only called 'meat.' Especially when they're cooked by Elga." He looked in the pot on the stove. He could see carrots, small onions, and red potatoes simmering along with the meat, but he did not feel tempted. "Where is she now?"

"She is working at the hospital. She told me she will finish there today and then she will take me into the city."

"When do you plan to go?"

"As soon as she comes home."

"Ah. I see." The priest got up and went back outside. It was a cool day and he had wanted to get his tulip bulbs in before the frost came. He went to the barn and climbed into the loft where the bulbs were stored. He saw that Elga had filled up much of the space with her cluttered stash of jars, herbs, and old texts. She had not asked his permission, but he was accustomed to her using his property as she wished, coming and going at will. (More than once Andrei had awoken in the night to the rough stony sounds of digging in the yard. He knew it was most likely a night badger or raccoon, but there was always the possibility that Elga or Zoya was burying a corpse in the vegetable bed. Knowing there was nothing he could do about it, he would roll back to sleep, consoling himself with the thought that the cadaver's blood and tissue would be good for the soil.)

Andrei took the bulbs, found his shovel, and returned to the garden bed. Digging into the soft rich earth, he thought about Noelle, back in the kitchen, remembering how he had been at her age, so wrapped up in himself, waiting like a tulip bulb, through the cold and the darkness, for a blossoming season.

This was over a half century before, when the tsars still ruled Russia. Born to a struggling merchant and his pious wife who both passed away from fever, he and his brother had been sent off by relatives to seminary as young men, the last of the family money entrusted to their care. Neither Andrei nor his brother, Max, were impressive students, though Andrei certainly believed he had been more diligent than Max. He labored at the catechetical courses and zealously obeyed the rules and rituals of the order, while the more mischievous and prankish Max was regularly caught and beaten. Once they were ordained, they both lived in the monastery, where Max continued to try the elders' patience. When they were sent off on missions to other eparchies, the elders made them travel as a pair, hoping Andrei would be a moderating influence on his errant brother.

On their last mission together, their destination was a small, remote village in the northern Ural Mountains. They never arrived there. On the eighth day of their journey, Max absentmindedly let their small carriage drift off the edge of the road into a deep, dry rut, splintering the wheel and breaking the axle. In the blistering heat, the two brothers loaded their luggage onto the back of their bony gray mare and trudged five miles to the nearest town, Ivdel. Arriving at dusk, they found the blacksmith's shop closed and so they dragged their weary bodies to the inn for the night. The town was crowded and the innkeeper tried to gouge them at first, but ultimately, out of shame and reverence, he offered the two young priests a narrow room above the saloon with a small horsehair mattress to share.

Ivdel was a prosperous gold town, booming in those days, and the brothers had arrived on the night of a saint's festival. The bars and hotels were choked with loud miners, all scrubbed pink clean and roughly cologned with the scent of sweating vodka and pipe smoke, all of them hungry for rough stimulation after their deadening days of labor. Raucous music, shouting voices, and the rhythm of loud, dancing boots rattled and shook the thin paneled walls of the brothers' small room, keeping the young priests awake. A grinning, invigorated Max finally insisted they go down to investigate, and a nervous, tired Andrei hesitantly followed.

The bar was packed with the broad-shouldered miners and their rouged, laughing whores. Unused to scenes such as these, Andrei blushed at each flirty wink and batted eye, and the barman roared when he timidly asked for a pot of hot tea. Max meanwhile had wandered over to the far corner of the room, lured in and transfixed by the rattle of the ball on the roulette wheel. Later, Andrei realized it had been the perfect trap, neither of the two had ever faced any true temptations and yet here they were sunk deep in the bottom of the devil's great belly. Before the next clock chimed, Max had coaxed their last coins from Andrei and was busy, betting fast and winning slow; it did not seem like he would last long. Nobody appeared surprised to see a young man in a clerical cassock throwing money down on the table, and they only roared the louder as his winning streak began and then picked up its pace. "You're truly blessed, my father!" shouted the roughnecks, slapping him on the back as the nine other players dropped to five and then the five to one. When the last ball rattled and dropped into the red slot, Max's pants and jacket pockets were stuffed full with rubles and kopecks, and, in a sight that made his brother blush, he had his arm firmly wrapped around the waist of a full-breasted grinning brunette. Grabbing a tall bottle of beer, Max announced he was off to find them better accommodations, and amid cheers from the host of drunken miners, the young priest swept the girl out the side door. Looking back over his shoulder as he left,

Max held the bottle up, toasting an embarrassed and crestfallen Andrei with a wide, beaming smile. That was the last time the priest ever saw his brother, Max, in the flesh.

The next day, waking alone on his stiff horsehair mattress, Andrei had waited until midafternoon before finally going out in search of his brother. He was not worried at first, sure that he would find Max in some nearby brothel, sleeping off his sins. Wandering through the town, Andrei prepared a sternly worded sermon for the foolish Max. But by nightfall he had begun to worry. The desk clerk claimed not to have seen Max since he had first checked in, and the local constable only shook his head—it was the sort of town where people came and went all the time, the policeman said. Perhaps his brother had eloped? Who could blame him, after all. Why remain a priest when you can run off, rich and happy, with a pretty young girl?

Andrei remained a few more days in the town, walking up and down Ivdel's streets, knocking on every door, until the innkeeper finally lost patience with this penniless priest and forced him to leave. Loading up the gray mare, a bereaved Andrei led the horse out of town, beginning the long journey back to the monastery with a heart heavy with shame. He trudged down the dusty roads, making a rough camp in the soft beds of the arbor stands and washing himself in the cold spring water of mountain creeks. As he was setting up camp in the dusk of the fifth day, he heard the distant sound of low flute music drifting softly through the trees. Lonely for company, he poked his way through the saplings and brush until he reached the source of the music, a campsite with five women gathered around a small cooking fire. It was a curious sight. He wondered if they were the wives of prospectors or tradesmen, or perhaps part of a traveling circus. One was playing the dancing tune on the flute as two others danced by the fire. The remaining two were seated on the ground, clapping and singing along. Then, with a shock, he recognized one of them, the dark-haired woman with whom he had last seen Max. Impulsively, Andrei broke through the trees and stumbled out in front of them, now wild-eyed; with a shaking voice he cried, "Where is my brother? What did you do to him?"

The women froze, stunned, and stared at him for a long moment.

The woods were absolutely silent except for the bubbling rapids of a nearby stream. Then one of the women broke out with a snort and they all started laughing. Taking him by the hand, they drew him gently into their campsite. "Come sit. Come, rest by the fire." Still trembling and confused by their reception, he stumbled forward and sat down on a log. Tears filled his eyes and he began weeping at his misfortune as they poured him a mug of bitter coffee, stroked his hair, wiped the tears off his cheeks, and handed him roasted pine nuts and dried apricots to eat. "You will find your brother, don't fear, you will find him," they reassured him, their voices warm and soothing.

He held the hand of the woman who had been with his brother. "Tell me what happened. Please. Tell me."

She looked him in the eyes. "I will tell you, of course. I know where he is; your Max is safe, he is happy, but drink first, rest. It is a story, nothing more than a story."

The oldest one, a stout silver-haired creature with a face like a toad, leaned forward, into the steely light of the fire. Her question came with a wary tone: "How did you find our campsite, my friend? Were you following us from town?"

No, he insisted, suddenly a hair nervous, sensing the air of prickly suspicion that had slipped into the circle. He told of his lonesome journey and how he had heard their music through the trees. They looked at one another, as if weighing the truth of his tale. Then the old one nodded, seemingly content with his answer, and they all seemed to relax again. A bottle of wine came out and was passed between them; he timidly sipped at first but then the warmth of the alcohol flooded him with comfort and so he drank more fully. Soon the dark woods were swimming around him and the stars above him seemed wildly strewn, like clouds of yellow pollen blown across the night. As he giggled and then laughed with the women at their bawdy jokes, he could feel himself floating away from the burdens of his ordeal as, one by one, the binding and long-strained ropes of conscience and duty were severed. He felt relieved from all the responsibilities that had long held him down. Finally, the old one, grinning mischievously as she sized him up with her mottled eye, said to the pretty one, "Yes, I think he is ready now. Let us show him." He looked around, bemused, confused, but still laughing along. The younger woman reached into the pocketed folds of her dress and when her hand emerged again it was holding a black rat.

"Here he is," said the crone, pointing to the rodent. "Say hello to your little Max."

The mood of the group had shifted, this absurd joke seemed in poor taste, but Andrei awkwardly chuckled along until, as he gazed down at the rat, his laughter stopped. The creature stood up on its hind legs, looked directly into his eyes, and nodded. In that moment, Andrei recognized his brother. The rat not only had Max's posture, but his face held hints of his brother's features and expression too, and, leaning close to observe him, Andrei quickly saw how much of Max's poise was perfectly echoed in the bearing of the little beast staring up at him. Andrei gasped and fell backward in shock. The stars now streaked down like daggers descending upon him as the world above him spun widly. He heard the women laughing and a voice he knew as his own cried out, and then the heavens all reeled into blackness.

When he awoke, he was alone in the woods, lying by the smoldering gray and white ashes of the abandoned campsite's dead fire. He knew if he ran he could overtake the women on the road, perhaps rescue his brother, and turn them over to the magistrate. But instead he closed his eyes and slept again. His sleep was deep.

When he finally awoke again, it was nearly dusk. He rebuilt the fire and sat contemplating his path. He felt he could not return to the monastery, yet he had no other home. Walking on to the next town, he stopped only briefly, sending letters to his relatives and to the priests saying that Max had disappeared. He was certain those who knew his brother would simply nod knowingly, for Max was always the sort doomed to vanish through some misadventure or lapse in judgment. Then Andrei wandered west, finding harvest, market, and scrap work in the hamlets, villages, and larger cities, slowly working to absorb and accept the strange new truths he had learned about the world.

Along the way, the women crossed his path again, first finding him scrubbing laundry in a Kiev hospital. Andrei was not surprised when they showed up. After that, they made it their habit to come and go at their whim, whenever he could be useful to their ends. He did not know how they traced his trail, he suspected the wine bottle they had shared that night by the campfire was part of some enchantment, a binding communion, making it impossible for him to ever lose them, or maybe that rat simply had a very good nose. Whatever their methods, Andrei was amazed to see how they controlled what others called coincidence, not only finding people but drawing them in as well. They lured prey to their door when they were hungry, pushed rivals together when they needed blood, and drove lovers into fevered embrace when they desired entertainment. Once you crossed their path, any conceit of free will became a fanciful notion.

Still, he tried to break free. Always itinerant, he attempted vanishing into various careers and stations, consciously hoping that each transformation would help him escape from the past. At times a soldier, a baker, a vagrant, a drunk, he had finally drifted back to the priesthood. It had been a pragmatic decision, not any sort of idealistic reconciliation. He did not regain his piety; he felt alternately angry and agnostic toward God, suspicious of any theology that could not explain what he had seen with his own two eyes, but he felt comfortable returning to the familiar patterns of his simple roots. So, here he was, decades later, tending his small garden in the fading light. Brushing the red clay off his hands, he headed to the farmhouse. The young girl was gone and the house silent. He suspected that Elga had already packed up and taken her to the city.

In a few hours he would mount his rickety yellow bicycle and ride down the narrow road to an ivy-laden, crumbling château. Inside was a small chapel. There he would say evening prayers to a congregation composed of one very pious Orthodox couple. They were ancient and wealthy and, like him, they had been exiled from their homeland of Russia for nearly half a century. They would kneel at the analogion and confess their imagined sins as he patiently listened. Then, as always, he would read them their absolution, and they would meekly smile, and he would smile back, knowing that at the same time another ancient friend of his was driving a young child toward the city, intent on evils that no God imaginable could ever forgive.

Babayaga

X

After working their way across town, making many fruitless stops at empty bistros, cafés, and apartments where no one answered, Oliver had the driver drop them off on a bustling corner on Place Pigalle. Crossing the promenade, they entered a small café a few doors down from the Grand Guignol. The waitress lit up with a bright *"Ah, bonjour, Oliver!"* kissing him on both cheeks before leading them up to the second floor. A Line Renaud LP was playing low on the turntable in the corner. They made their way to the back of the room, where, amid a scattered assortment of oddly arranged tables, they found Boris playing cards with five other men. The thick smoke from hours of cigarettes and cigars bathed the room in various shades of milky gauze. Instead of interrupting the game, Oliver asked the girl for two espressos and led Will to a booth in a back corner.

"His chips are low, we'll wait here till he's done," said Oliver. "You gamble?"

"Not a lot."

"Probably a good thing." Oliver grinned. "You don't have much of a poker face, do you? What games do you indulge in?"

"I play a little euchre, some gin now and then."

"Any sports?"

"Tennis."

"Really? We should get a match on. It's getting too cold now for Coubertin but there is a fine indoor court over on rue de Saussure. Boris claims to have some skills, but I've never played him, that would be a sight to see, wouldn't it? Ha ha, that great Russian bear lunging up to the net?" Oliver looked over at the poker game as a player scraped in a big, noisy pot. "Gambling is funny, isn't it? I've never heard any persuasive theories on its roots, I suspect its some primordial residue from our early days, similar to how we still wear the belts that once held our hunting knives, while our women carry designer purses to store all those harvested berries. We think we're modern and civilized, but Lord knows we're not."

The album ended and the needle mechanically returned back to the beginning. As Renaud started singing "Mon Bonheur," Will wondered how long the card players had been listening to that one side of the album. He tapped on the table impatiently. "You know, I probably need to head back to the office."

Oliver shook his head. "Oh really? What, is the great wheel of capitalism going to grind to a halt without you?"

"No, but—"

"Relax, we'll get you back to the trenches soon enough," Oliver said. "Say, you wouldn't have any more of those Chesterfields on you? I left my cigarettes at home." Will gave him one and lit another himself. "Thanks," said Oliver. "I'll pick you up a carton at the commissary next time I'm at the embassy. So, tell me how you know that girl I was with the other night."

"I only met her in passing, on the metro," Will said, unhappy to have the subject brought up. He could remember the way Zoya had looked at him that first night. He had thought about it more than once in the past few days. There was a magnetic element to her gaze that had stayed tugging at him, a subtle but constant force that pulled at him, making him want to leave and walk the streets to find her right at that very moment so that he could see her or talk to her or grab her by the neck and kiss her breathless.

"What did you think of her?"

"I thought she was all right," Will lied.

Oliver nodded. "Oh, she is more than all right. She's an intriguing one, very beguiling. Easy on the eyes, obviously, and sharp-witted too, but also . . ." He shook his head, seemingly unable to find the right phrase. Will was impressed that even the thought of Zoya left Oliver speechless.

They watched Boris lose another pot and, as the winner stacked his chips, Will tried to push the girl out of his mind. There was no percentage in keeping her there. He should have stayed with her when they had walked off the metro that night. He could have asked her out for a drink and maybe found a way to go home with her, but he hadn't. And now he did not like thinking about another man's girl, it did not seem right, it was not the way he was raised. You respected those bonds, no matter what feelings you had or how strongly you felt them. These were the things that defined your character and, as his grandfather had often told him, your character was the only thing you ever wholly and truly possessed.

The waitress brought them their coffees while they kept an eye on the game. Will did not find gambling to be as romantic or intriguing as Oliver did, but, recalling his grandfather as he watched through the hazy layers of ghostly cigar smoke, he almost felt as if he were peering through some hole in time, as if he were a boy again peeking through the upstairs bannister as his uncles and his father played their poker, euchre, or gin rummy up at their small cabin by the northern shores of Lake Michigan. He realized it would be deer season back home and they might be up there right now. The temperatures would be creeping down below freezing at night and the thin pale skin of ice would be scratching at the edges of the shallow ponds and lakes, silencing the frogs and signaling the birds to start south. The dog-eared Bicycle playing cards would be slapped down and his father would be laughing as he raked in his own fat pots while his uncles smoked their short cigars, drank their beers and whiskeys, and fed logs into the old Franklin stove. The hunting rifles would already be cleaned, oiled, and stacked on the wall, ready for the next morning, while empty bottles of Stroh's, Early Times pints, and Old Grand-Dad fifths would lie sideways on the floor.

The thought struck him that this very scene was being played out all over the world, here above an empty café in Paris, and there in that small midwestern hunting camp, but also in the back alleys of Hong Kong, warehouses in Brooklyn, guard barracks in Siberia, and out on the remote Argentiniam pampas, where the dark gauchos gambled by the flickering light of their campfires. The kings, queens, and jacks on the card faces paid no mind to the reign of the clock or the map; they ruled a borderless world that existed outside of time. Their servants lived in every land and served at every hour, punished or rewarded for their efforts by the random caprice and whimsy that so many monarchs live by. Dawn and dusk came and went, women sat up waiting and worrying or gave up and moved out while their men played on, sitting transfixed over a handful of ever-shifting faces, waiting for an ace's late arrival or some serendipitous eight to slide in amid a broken row of sevens and nines. It was all a shorthand language for life's cascading fortunes, an attempt to ride the random waves of fate, pulling small circles together, geometric concentrations of luck where every soul sought to shift and maneuver for a bit of extra grace. Will wondered how he had managed to steer clear of gambling's pull while so many others had not. Watching as Boris's last chips were scooped away, Will thought it was probably because he had always had an innate sense of how much easier it was to lose than win.

"Ah yes, it appears the game is up for our friend," said Oliver.

Will looked across the room as the Russian pulled on his jacket, straightened his tie, and drained the last of his drink. Oliver gave him a bit of a wave and Boris nodded and started heading over.

What followed seemed to happen in a kind of slow motion as the simple steps Boris had to take to cross the room were asymetrically transformed into a mighty cataclysm.

At first there was a clattering racket of chairs as Boris seemed to misstep, stumbling into a table. He turned and, after holding himself in balance for a moment, lunged forward, quickly accelerating, shifting sideways and then tipping over. Reaching out wildly to steady himself, he collapsed, careening across another set of chairs like a massive cannon rolling loose on the yawing deck of an embattled warship. All the faces at the poker table turned with a kind of sleepy-eyed awe, watching as Boris disappeared down, tumbling onto the floor as tables fell crashing next to him. There was a shuddering, violent sound as his body landed, and then everything was still.

The other card players slowly rose from their seats, all of them apparently expecting Boris to get up and dust himself off, but he didn't. Oliver leapt across the room with a dexterity that surprised Will. He was already kneeling by Boris's prone body by the time everyone else arrived.

"Did he faint?" Will asked.

"No," said Oliver, feeling at the man's neck for his pulse. "He died." The men had now gathered around, and someone went off to call a doctor. Oliver was now rearranging the corpse, loosening Boris's collar and emptying his pockets. He took out a wallet, house keys, a pack of Gitanes, a comb, matches, some business cards, and a small piece of tinfoil. Nobody but Will seemed to notice Oliver palm the business cards and foil into his own jacket pocket as he placed the rest of the items in a line beside the body. Then Oliver rose and pointed down at Boris. "Nobody touch him or any of his things," he said. "The authorities will be here soon. Be sure to give them a full report." With that, he tipped his hat and headed down the stairs. Will followed, his head swimming with what he had seen.

Out on the street, Oliver quickly flagged down a taxi and they hopped inside. Events had unfolded so fast that Will only realized now how hard his own heart was beating. He took a deep breath and tried to relax.

"*Dix-huit rue de Tournon, s'il vous plaît,*" Oliver told the driver and then took the tinfoil out of his pocket and unwrapped it. Inside was a small piece of brown resinous material.

"What is it?" asked Will.

"Some narcotic, I suspect. Not sure what variety. You ever tried anything?"

Will shook his head.

"I liked hashish the few times I've tried it, found it fascinating," Oliver said. "Of course Huxley's written about the heavier stuff, peyote and mescaline, but even a bit of any mind-expanding drug can reveal a lot. Small wonder society tries to ban it. Too much illumination and people might find a way to connect the dots, they might start wondering why doughboys are dying to protect barons' bankbooks. Can't have that. So instead the state unscrews the tap on the greatest mind-deadening drug in the world, alcohol, while releasing the hysterical prosecutorial hounds on all that reefer madness."

"I don't know," said Will, amazed at how quickly Oliver could segue from witnessing a close friend's death to expounding a random conspiracy theory, "You might be overthinking it."

"Well, I don't know about that. Look at the facts, look at history, our own government got Willie Hearst's papers to spread wholesale, widespread panic about cannabis, laws were passed, people were hauled off to prison, the distribution effectively quashed. Meanwhile, people drink themselves dumb every night. Can't have the people thinking too much, right? So, maybe you're correct, and perhaps that's the point, we should all be doing considerably more overthinking."

"So was Boris a dopehead?"

"Who, Boris, what?" Oliver shook his head as if he had been suddenly pulled back to reality "A dopehead? No, Boris was not a dopehead. He was merely a man seeking solace in an incredibly hostile world. I suspect, though, he might have gotten his hands on a bad batch." He sniffed the resin again. "I have no real expertise here, but luckily I know a few who do. We'll take a little detour and visit some friends." He leaned forward. "*Pardonnez-moi, vous pouvez nous emmener au numéro dix, rue Jacob, s'il vous plaît.*"

"What about finding Ned?"

"Under the circumstances, she's going to have to wait." He gave Will a forced grin. "Invisible hands are moving pieces on the board right now and I'm rather curious as to why." As Oliver folded up the tinfoil and tucked it back in his vest pocket, Will noticed that Oliver's hands were shaking.

XI

Zoya entered her apartment and looked around. There was still no sign of Max. Now this was odd, she thought. Usually the rat would have sniffed her out within two or three days. She thought of checking in again with Elga. But the last few visits had been too unsettling, lately there seemed to be a constant undercurrent of impatience and anger that rose like winter sap out of the old woman's moods. Zoya wondered if Elga was finally going mad, perhaps from too many centuries of stewing those vestigial remnants of spent spells in the rotting murk of her mind.

Zoya caught herself in the mirror. She was in essence the same young woman she had been for so long now; little had changed. How long had it been since that day when she had almost died in those cold Russian woods, an exile, stripped of every bond and affection, her heart scraped raw and her ribs sore from weeping? She was so newly grown into the fulsome body of a woman as to be still only a child, two children really, the other nascent one not yet stirring within her, though already so hungry. She would recall that hunger, the only thing about her child she would ever know. (To this day, whenever she found herself in bustling Parisian brasseries, watching wealthy tourists abandon their uneaten baguette or cheese plates, it filled her with such a quick, intuitive anger that she would instinctively hiss maledictions at their heels.)

She could still recall stumbling upon that trace scent of food as she wandered, staggering, starving, and lost in the woods so many dawns ago. Venison, she had been sure it was venison, a thin fatty smell sneaking through the needled larch to find her. The faint aroma had caught her like a fish on a hook, pulling her step by step deeper into the forest until she finally came across the lone hut. Unlike in the fairy tales, the little house did not stand on chicken legs, but was raised instead on thick stilts of stunted birch. Stumbling out of the red twilit woods, Zoya kept her distance and quietly worked her way around the building, looking for any sign that she might be welcome. The hut was foreboding. Without any sign of a door or window, smoke crept out from the roof and sharp scratched lines of yellow light leaked out from the pitch-caulked cracks between the hut's timbers. She thought she could make out a woman's deep voice, either talking to herself or humming a tone-deaf tune. Zoya hid behind a thick patch of thistle, settling in, to wait for the owner to emerge. But all night and well into the next morning, no one came out. As she lay there, pains of famine now desperately screaming in her belly, Zoya dug and scratched at the earth, finally sucking on worms and beetles for moisture. Part of her wanted to bang on the cabin walls and beg for bread, water, and mercy, but another, stronger feeling urged her to stay where she was. So she kept waiting. But nobody came out. Instead, the aromatic scents from the cabin smoke grew deeper and richer; the air swam with the fragrances of clove, garlic, and ginger, all wrapped in the smells of simmering haunch fat and pinewood smoke. It was too much to bear. Drained now of all strength, Zoya collapsed flat against the earth, her tears turning the soil beneath her face to mud.

She slept there through the rest of the day. Then, late in the afternoon, as the sun began disappearing behind a wall of dark clouds, a flap on the lower edge of the cabin swung open with a hard bang. A baritone voice like a swamp bullfrog's called out. "You, in the dirt there. Come inside now. It's going to thunder." Then another trap door popped open beneath the house, beside one of the cabin's stilts.

Crawling close, Zoya found that there were footholds carved into the side of the birch leg. She climbed up into the dark room. While its contents seemed wondrous at the time, it was no different from the other lairs Elga would stitch together again in St. Petersburg, Warsaw, Riga, Ostrava, Kiev, and scores of other cities. There were rows of dead creatures, skinned and dried, earthen bowls of moldy bulbs and moss, stacks of fungi and gnarled roots stewing in open pots of luminous orange, pale gray, and olive green liquids. Volumes of loose-bound manuscripts, books, and papers were piled up, some pages torn out, hand-scratched and nailed to the rough walls. The small stone fireplace had a cracked chimney that the smoke leaked out of, making the atmosphere murky and hard to inhale. But the fire did kick out a strong heat, and Zoya was immediately drawn to its side while the old woman bolted tight the floor hatch behind her. Pulling up a stool, Elga sat down close to make a study of the girl.

"So, some villager told you about my home?"

Zoya shook her head no. Elga nodded. "You know who I am, then?"

Zoya shook her head again. Elga gave her a grin that was almost warm. "Well, you look hungry. I have good yarrow soup. Eat first, then we can talk."

Along with the warm broth and vegetables, Elga served the girl the simple truthsayer recipe Zoya had long since memorized. It worked the way liquor does, only more so, and after an hour the old woman had pulled out the girl's tale, her rape and abuse, her father's death, her germinal child, all of it streaming from Zoya's lips without a tear or a shiver. Every hardship of her life was reduced to batches of sounds that Zoya handed over to her hostess in exchange for more soup and a chance to stay by the warm fire.

When she was finished, Elga looked at her for a moment. "You would like help?"

Zoya solemnly nodded.

"Fine, fine," the old woman said, clearing the empty soup bowl away. "I will help you, of course I am happy to, but it will cost you, and we must decide now how you will pay."

"But I have nothing," Zoya meekly replied.

Elga shook her finger at the young girl and her eyes flared. "We all can pay, girl, and you owe me too. You think soup comes free? I broke my back carrying that wood to burn in that fire. By any honest count, you already owe me more than you know."

Zoya looked around, nervously realizing that she had trapped herself in a house with no windows and a locked door. "Please," she pleaded, "I have nothing."

"There, there, do not be so hard on yourself," the old woman said, shifting her hard expression to a crafty smile. She reached out and softly stroked Zoya's tearstained cheek. "Every soul with a breath has to pay someone for something. But do not fear, it will not be so bad. What, you think I want to hurt you? You believe those awful stories the village fathers tell their stupid children to keep them enslaved at home? 'Oh, do not go into the woods, there is a woman there who will eat you.' Bah. We are going to help each other, you and me. It's a small price, a little help. That is all I need. Only a little . . ."

Now, in the small Parisian apartment, methodically collecting the scattered owl pellets from the windowsill, Zoya reflected on what that exchange had, in truth, cost her. Elga had taken more than a little. The price staggered her mind and flooded her with dark emotion, so she tried, as she so often tried, to shove the thoughts away and shut a heavy door on the past. But she never could succeed for long, the memories always pushed their way through.

First, there had been the child buried in her belly. That decision was one she felt she had to make, but the memory lurked in her, a ghost that had never ceased to burn. Allergic to the past, whenever the recollection came it was so clear in her mind it caused her throat to constrict, making it hard to swallow. Only when she traced the memory thread along its twisted path, seeing again how stark her lack of choice had been, could she let go of the guilt and let herself breathe again. Elga had led her through the logic of that painful conclusion the very first night and then taken her through the bloody purging. The old woman nursed her to recovery in the days that followed, the ordeal creating a bond between the women, Zoya now feeling that there was one soul on earth looking out for her, while Elga observed the girl's grit and strength and silently counted the ways her newfound friend could be of use.

Whenever the sharp regrets stabbed at her, Zoya reminded herself that the child she lost had been conceived in violence, a bloody curse that had followed her from that moment Grigori seized her in the bedroom until the night she screamed as Elga tore it from her body. Every good thing since then had been tinged with the red stain of that violence. Time was not absolute, and even without witchery she could travel right back to that instant, loom above it, and watch the last vestige of her simple humanity pulled out of her, a dark mark punctuating the end of so much innocence. She came up out of that bath a new creature with a new path and purpose, and with Elga's guidance (which was always as twisted as a weed root in drought), Zoya began a course of action that had its own logic, rules, and blunt necessity.

As the season began to change, the two women had wrapped themselves up and begun journeying the cold roads together. They never returned to those woods. For decade upon decade they covered the breadth of the continent, rarely resting for long, a year here, a few months there. They went in all four directions, wherever loose fortunes and safe travel could be found. When armies advanced, they followed in the rear guard's wake, sharing spoils as their luck held solid. They had more than a few narrow scrapes but had always managed to escape clean, packing up and making their tactical retreats, before any real pressure was brought to bear. They were generally careful and quick, looking for sparks of suspicion in observers' eyes so that they could be gone long before the thought ever reached those watchers' minds.

Their exits almost always coincided with funerals, and Zoya could count her victims the way Homer counted ships. Legions of soldiers, brokers, barons, bailiffs, and fools had all fallen before her. Murmured instructions into the ears of sleepy-eyed Arabian horses led cavalry lovers to broken necks, and she had coaxed the arc of battlefield bullets and the aim of cannons' muzzles into many a cursed chest. Some farewells came with great repercussions—a fever sent up a sleeping vizier's knobby spine had once brought a whole kingdom down— though most were simpler transitions, a few even humane, merely a touch of the unwanted slipped into their tea or a fumbling foot on a loose stair, sending masonry hard against the victim's head.

No one had ever looked to her for explanation; if she was ever noticed, it was only as a discreet courtesan, a rumored inamorata, or a laughing, playful harlot, always so easily forgotten.

She did have a quiver of curses reserved to make the bad ones suffer, and the bullies and savage sadists ultimately met pains that came in larger dimensions than even their base and brutal imaginations could conjure. Some had cuticle nicks that festered until the arms withered off as minds went feeble, others went into lavatories and never returned, as bowels fell out with bowel movements and whole men disappeared, sucked down into their foul latrines. The ones she despised most she killed best, as in a nightmare, bare naked, rocking astride their sweating bodies, until that ultimate moment came when their bodies tensed, poised for satisfaction. That was when she put her finger to their Adam's apple and deftly pushed the windpipe shut. Their eyes went wide as she watched with grim pleasure, their one final victory eternally denied. Thusly, every exit was tailored to suit a nature: some came tinged with regret, others felt better.

There was one she had almost spared. He was a military engineer, an officer and hero from the lost war for Crimea. All she cared for was his kindness, the thoughtfulness he showed by bringing bowls of fruit to their bedside in the morning, the way his green eyes gazed at her with so much affection, and how his hand resting on her hip made her cheeks blush as red as a cut thumb. "Don't make me put this one down. I'll walk away, but let's let him live," she said to Elga. The old woman said nothing, simply undertook the job herself. Passing as a chambermaid, Elga slipped some echoing curses into the folds of his uniform. The spell seeped into his chest at a steady rate until the delirium overtook him. Zoya received the news as she returned one morning to their grand hotel. He had hanged himself, tying sheets to the bannister and tossing himself down the wide open stairwell. As he choked to death, a fumbling, terrified guest tried to cut him loose with a dull dinner knife. Elga later admitted to the spell, said it had to be done, and after that day Zoya had never tried to save another.

Wherever they traveled, Zoya always found a way into the bright chandeliered wings and the warm officers' quarters where the toasts came from crystal glasses and they cut their meat with silver, but Elga could always be found close-by, down in the scullery, or off in the servants' wing, or, after the long day's battles, out among the fields of the dead and dying, digging through the entrails of the infantry corpses, cutting out gall bladders, bile sacs, testes, and spleen for later utility. When doubts arose in Zoya's heart, and over the years they intermittently did, Elga seemed to have a knack for showing up by her side, consoling Zoya with blunt woodland wisdom, explaining how it was all righteous, even merciful. "It is only fair and only just," Elga would say. "Men have dragged us by our hair through the ages, and whether they give us crumbs or bright, shiny rocks, they truly give us nothing at all. If you have not opened your legs for them so that they could crawl out as babies or crawl in as men, then they will leave you to starve like a dog on the street. So now we are done playing the way they want us to play. Now we are moving to music they cannot hear, to a rhythm they cannot understand. They call it madness and we call it truth and find me the magistrate you can trust to judge between the two? Bah. So we dance on, we dance on." At this, Elga would start stamping her foot hard to an offbeat rhythm and flash Zoya a mischievous smile.

So they danced on. Still, lingering regrets and resentments of all those hard decisions stayed with Zoya, like gristle trapped in her teeth or wax in her ears, and now, when the feelings were rising again and she needed some reassurance, the old woman had sent her off to be alone. It frustrated Zoya. Fine, she thought, I don't need her, I certainly don't miss her; after all, I have stayed away these past few years for good reason.

She recalled how they would once scuttle from camp to camp, city to city, plucking bright gold from the bloodstained hands of doomed officers and shining silver from the soiled fingers of ill-fated miners who all soon after died, cut down by saber or buried beneath whole falling mountains. Back then, the world was its own boiling cauldron of constant violence, the wars and battles never ceased, one Balkan war rolled into another that spawned a world war and then one more. Industry and iron erupted from the earth, soldiers and cannon clogged the roads and crowded the stations, ore filled the hulls of ships, and crates of raw supplies stuffed the boxcars. Whole cities rose up from the earth, swallowing up the countryside and spoiling the landscape, in many places beyond recognition, and the birds' evening songs were now forever warped by the constant, shrill scream of the ubiquitous engines.

Now, though, things seemed to be settling down. The great threat of atomic annihilation had made all the European soldiers finally hang up their guns and go home, like chastened children worried that their overbearing brute of a father might slap them around. Perhaps, thought Zoya, this is why Elga is so angry, because she misses the busyness and scheming that came with the great din of battle, for now there's nothing to distract and drown out her own rattling mind; perhaps it is the silence that is driving her mad. But no matter the reason, thought Zoya, I do need to stay away from her, for good, if I can. She has used me and haunted me and taken too much. I do not need her around. The anger flared in Zoya's mind. Why, if that rat showed up now, she thought, I might bite him right in half.

She smoked the owl pellets and sat with her mixture of visions. Afterward, she felt better. Applying her makeup before the small vanity mirror, she prepared for the evening's errands. She was a little concerned about moving around the city so openly during the time when the streets were most crowded; she preferred to go out later at night, or even in those mid-afternoon hours when people had finished with lunch and were trapped at work or napping at home. She knew she had already been out too much this past week, exposing herself almost recklessly, but Zoya also knew she had to keep moving and stay on her toes, for now she had her prey marked. She needed to bring Will in soon, before he grew confused, or some other woman got in the way. She had a small window to build a strong and simple bond with her busy rabbit, which she planned to do by mixing the two ingredients men enjoy most, lust and conquest.

Her concerns for caution turned out to be valid. As she walked down St. Germain, a little old man sitting at Café de Flore, who was trying to dim the racket of his busy week with a few strong glasses of Fernet-Branca, happened to see her pass by. She did not notice him, although, with his eyes bulging and his mouth agape, he would have made for an amusing sight. "My God," he said after she had passed, "I swear I have seen a ghost." The sleepy mule sitting beside him looked down at the old man's empty drink and said, "My friend, keep putting that poison down your throat and you will be the ghost."

XII

"Is this really a police car? Can your rat understand what I'm saying? Where did this bone come from? Where are we going to sleep tonight?" The young girl had Elga's small satchel open in her lap and was going through it randomly. Her hands were everywhere, waving items around, fiddling with the dials on the dash, asking so many questions that Elga was tempted to pull the car over, strangle her, and leave her body on the side of the road. "What's this little book for? Is this pink vial makeup? What does this knob do? Is this some sort of perfume?"

"No, that is a concoction for my gas."

"Does it work?"

"I do not think so," Elga said, releasing a tremendous fart. "Do you?" That quieted Noelle for a little while. They were heading back into the city. Elga wanted to act fast, before Zoya got suspicious and fled town. It would not be enough merely for Zoya to leave; Elga knew she had to see her die. She knew she was not being rash; it was time for Zoya to go. Why, look at the harm she had already done, putting the man's head on a spike? Leading the police to her with that stupid clock? Zoya had always been spoiled, always aimed too high, too fond of the chocolates, the rubies, the furs, and the smoked salmon with the caper cream sauce, especially that. But her latest actions were surprising even for her, and even if they weren't malicious, they were certainly dumb. That woman was bounding around like some wild doe with an arrow stuck in her ass. Taking her down would be an act of mercy, for clearly Zoya was losing her mind. Or, Elga thought, maybe I am losing mine. She shook that idea out of her head with the quickness of a burned finger lifted off a hot pan and looked over at the young girl riding beside her. Noelle now had the rat in her lap and was stroking Max's head as he lay curled up, sleeping. Yes, thought Elga, it is time for Zoya to go, this new girl will be so much better. "Go ahead, little one, ask me another question."

"How old are you?"

"Ah, that is a good one. I do not know."

"Before cars?"

"Before trains, before guns. Before people stole the curves from the high clouds and the angles from the flying flocks to build all their little alphabets."

Noelle pondered this silently for a moment before returning to her questions. "And where are you from?"

Elga chuckled. "You're going for the tough ones, huh? You are clever. I am from the far away, way beyond that edge of the sky where the sun rises."

"But where were you born?"

"The place I come from has changed its name many times; I don't even know what it is called now. When I lived there, it was named for the colors of the bay's water, then it was given the name of a fire goddess and then a soldier, then a saint and then again another soldier. You want to kill a place, name it. A name only draws the people there who will kill it again. They slice it up or tear it down; they rape the women, burn everyone on pyres, and then, thinking they own it, they name it again. Stupid. Enough to know 'there is a hill and good water, a cross in the road and a strong oak tree.' But do not say it out loud. A home should always stay secret or someone will come to steal it."

Noelle was quiet again. Elga suspected the girl was frustrated with the answers she was getting. Tough, the old woman thought, the real answers are never what we want them to be. She would teach the girl all she needed to know, how to read and write properly, how to curtsy and blush, how to slow time so that a wrinkle takes a century to grow, and how to cast the curses so that men would give you their fortunes, and their lives. As they reached the outskirts of Saint-Denis, Elga hoped that the spell she had put on her police car was holding, she did not need any attention. She only had to get to a bank, find a hotel, and set Max off on Zoya's trail. Perhaps they could do some shopping at Les Halles too. There were some market stalls where Elga knew she would find the necessary ingredients.

She looked down at the girl. Noelle was a little young, much younger than Zoya had been when she had made the change, but that was fine. A lot of snares could be set with this kind of bait. The girl would learn or die. It was too late to go back; if the girl did not want to take the lessons, or if it turned out she had no aptitude for it, Elga would put her down. But her intuition told her this one had skills. They could hole up and work on simple lessons while the rat tracked down Zoya. Elga would start by showing her small tricks, how to pack whispers in hats, whistle for snakes, catch an idle eye, raise a fevered boil. Elga felt this little one would be easier to control, no adventuring off on her own, no appetite for trouble. How many scrapes and scandals had she pulled Zoya out of? Too many to count. That girl was too softhearted and too clumsy in her affections, always falling for lousy men like stupid Max.

She remembered the morning that Zoya had shown up back at the campsite with the rat. It was still before dawn and her dress was torn, her skin was scratched, her hair undone. She had crawled into the bed of their caravan wagon and collapsed, sick, doubling over with dry heaves and in a cold, clammy sweat until finally she had rested and was calm enough to pull a terrified Max out from her pocket.

As always, Zoya had a good story. Earlier the past evening, bored with all the haggling and hissing between the women, she had left their campsite and headed into the nearby town. She had longed for dancing and music and the reassurance of friendly eyes, no more than that, she said. She had met a boy there, a young priest broken fresh from seminary, drunk off berry wine and flush from his first lucky run at the tables, who now wanted to taste his first woman. Zoya was willing to oblige, she was intrigued at the idea of playing naughty with a priest, especially a young one, and she also had an eye for the rubles loose in his pockets.

The trouble started moments after they finally found a room and shut the door. The drunken boy had pulled her close and began kissing her roughly. She had laughed and tried to slow him down a bit, but instead he had pushed her hard against the wall and started tearing at her clothes, ripping the fabric. The force of his body kept knocking her head against the wall, and she tried to pull away but he would not let go. He had a funny look dancing in his eyes, one that she recognized all too well. Deciding that she had made a mistake, she had kicked him hard in the balls and lunged for the door, but he had reached out and grabbed her, pushing her against the wall and banging her head again. "You are a real handful, aren't you? Some kind of devil's woman?" he had said. She was dazed. He threw her down on the floor. She began crawling again toward the door, but he grabbed her by the hair and pulled her to the foot of the bed. He tried slipping off his belt, but drunk as he was he could barely manage it. Sitting up, he fumbled around, clumsily attempting to unbutton his trousers, muttering, "My wise elders showed me where to stick it in troublemakers. Now I'll show you." Zoya went for the door again, but this time he grabbed her by the neck and pulled her back. "I will make it hard to run," he had said, pressing her to the floor and lying down on top of her. He reached under and squeezed at her breasts roughly with one hand while pulling down his pants with the other. "Yes, now you are going to have a hard time running," he said. She squirmed and struggled and screamed out for help but he slapped her harder and then she stayed silent. She knew nobody would come. Her head cleared enough so that she could recall what to do. She had been taken against her will before, but that was a different time. She had been weak then.

Turning and taking his head in her hands, as if she was finally succumbing, she put bloodstained kisses up his cheek and whispered the spell into his ear. He paused in his fumbling action and scratched at his nose as if he had a twitch. Then it began. She rolled free to the side of the room, and watched with relief and exhaustion as his flesh started its snapping and shrinking down.

The same people who had ignored Zoya's desperate shout for help now paid no attention to Max's, though his were far more terrible. He shrieked and clawed, whined and rasped through the whole messy, wet transformation; a high tearing wail screeched like a chorus of screeching kettle whistles as his vocal cords shriveled down and his throat constricted. Bones snapped as they were condensed and the room filled with the smell of the burning marrow and melting flesh as the heat of the boiling blood filled the room. His eyes changed last as he lay there, small weakened, and still pink from the raw, throbbing change. Then the black fur came out and a last shrill-pitched squeal emerged from him, but it was Saturday night in a mining town and everyone was deaf to the cries of a girl being raped and a rat being born.

Once changed, he had not run away but had lain still on the bare wood floor, looking up at her through terrified eyes. The sickness and dizziness from the spell overcame her and she vomited in the chamber pot. Then she curled up in a ball on the bed and fell asleep. When she awoke, the rat was still there, sitting up as if waiting for her. Perhaps he thought this was a temporary condition, that she would help him now that the lesson had been learned, or perhaps he was simply terrified of the new, unknown wilderness of hungry house cats, birds of prey, and dogs trained to slay vermin that lay beyond the door. She had thought of killing him then and there, she told the women, but that seemed too merciful an end. Still angry, she wanted him to live out his days as the pathetic little rodent he was. So she tucked him into her dress and staggered back to their campsite.

The rat ended up being useful. Through the unpredictable twist of spells, he had wound up capable of sniffing out any trail across every landscape and in all seasons, no matter how hard the frost or how flooded the roads. They had lost and found Max numerous times over the years, for at the first sign of real trouble he would always run off scared, disappearing for weeks, even months. But then he would pop up again, sniffing his way back to their side. His brother, too, the once innocent Andrei, who had found them at the campsite, proved to be bonded to Max by some tenuous but true sense of loyalty that made him, from time to time, a handy tool. Two bewitched brothers, she thought, each living a very different life from the one they had each intended, all because of a woman whose path they stumbled across, a woman they made the mistake of underestimating. Therein lies so much of history.

Elga pulled the car to a stop in front of the bank and looked down at the rat, who was now awake, sitting glumly in the girl's lap. "It's not so bad, Max. Think where you would have wound up if you'd never met us? A block of ice in some Siberian grave, tucked in with all those other bad Bolsheviks." The rat did not answer.

Inside, Elga found the bank empty of customers. She walked up to the lone teller sitting at his window, a bright and ambitious young man named François Collet. Elga quickly went to work. It was merely a matter of transferring between accounts to cover some bills, she told Monsieur Collet—and cash, she needed some cash too. She had an account, but stupidly she could not remember the number. But she had already been there earlier that morning, did he not remember her? She was quite positive he had written the account number down for her. He smiled politely and said that he did not recall her but then again perhaps he did. He felt confused. The morning had been a busy one. He proceeded to look through the ledger. She hummed high and low notes, and clucked with her tongue. Anyone listening would have thought she sounded ridiculous. But François did not seem to hear her. He did, however, almost absentmindedly, hand over every franc note he had in his drawer, a considerable sum. He even waved as she waddled off, shouting after her, *"Au revoir, madame!"* And that was the very last day of François Collet's once-promising career in banking.

XIII

Vidot found the morning and midday travel through the city infinitely easier than his original nighttime journey had been. He was almost proud of how quickly and completely he had acclimated to life as a flea. He hopped from soul to soul, pet to pet, tucking in for a bit of sustenance whenever he found himself on an undersized dog (the morning's trial and error had taught him that small ones were the sweetest, though breed mattered too; beagles were the best, while basset hounds tasted bitter.) His biggest surprise was that he found every animal he rode on appeared to be completely free of all other vermin. He deduced that this was not actually the case, as there were telltale signs (red bites, raw rashes) that other creatures had been riding and feeding on the dogs. Mysteriously, though, there were no other fleas, ticks, or lice to be seen. He guessed that they were in fact there all around him, but laying low and hiding deep in the fur, as his arrival had no doubt come as a bit of a shock to these simpleminded creatures of habit. For, as unfamiliar with his condition as he was, he therefore undoubtedly moved, acted, and behaved himself like a very unusual and suspicious flea. I must be like a gorilla dropped onto a city street, causing pedestrians to scatter and flee, he thought to himself. This idea amused him greatly as, very quickly and with an almost military efficiency in his hops and small scurries, he steadily approached the station.

Time was of the essence, if only because he did not know how much time he had. All he knew was that the clock of a bug's life ticked exceedingly fast and if he did not keep up his pace then the clock would run out. But he remained optimistic, reminding himself that he had raced against time on other important cases: running to Gare de Lyon to catch the fleeing embezzler Martel; dashing to the hospital to save the poisoned bride Castrillon; rushing so many places across the various landscapes of Paris that he wondered if he had not always lived his life like some wild, hopping flea.

There was one problem: he still did not know what he would do once he arrived at the station, but even that did not bother him. He knew the station's rhythms and hours, when the officers came and went, its every corner and corridor, and he knew that, at the very least, he could find safe harbor there. If he got hungry, he thought, he could simply go suck some blood off the skull of that cow-witted Maroc. That fool had it coming. It still nagged at Vidot that the station had not told the truth about his disappearance to Adèle. Maroc was most likely stalling, hoping Vidot and Bemm would miraculously reappear so that he would not have to face the scandal of losing two policemen. Such things did not look good on one's record. So Maroc was probably trying to buy some time. It was understandable, but it was not right, and as hurt as he was by his wife's adultery, Vidot did not like to see her deceived by an ass like Maroc. He wondered if she would be worried and if Alberto would comfort and console her. Vidot did not like where such thoughts went. And so, like many men who have troubled lives at home, Vidot energetically hopped off toward his office.

Luckily, it was a pleasant day and his journey was proceeding nicely. Things were not so bad, and the farther he got away from Alberto and Mimi Perruci's apartment, the more content and confident he felt. He understood that some other souls might be panicked or even overwhelmed with grief at the thought of being trapped in a small insect's body, but, he thought, these were generally the same people who felt cursed when there were only plain croissants at the market, or complained when the lunch waiter was slow. Whereas he believed life, any life, was a curious adventure, and if you merely kept your wits about you and stayed alert and in motion, you could find your way to a satisfactory conclusion. Instead of feeling cursed, he amused himself by thinking of how his hops resembled the arcing phrase marks on music sheets and, in fact, how he was not so unlike that American actor Bobby Van who had hopped so memorably through an entire small town in the film *Le Joyeux Prisonnier*.

Of course, this was no musical comedy. He remembered his fallen friend Bemm. While he had not known the young man well enough to be able to guess what Bemm felt about their peculiar metamorphosis, he did know how Bemm had responded to the crisis, standing right beside him, wholeheartedly jumping and following him through the streets, seizing hold of every house pet and rodent's belly with panache and gusto, both of them swinging like magnificent twin Tarzans through this immensely unpredictable and oversized wilderness. Too bad what had happened, it was tragic really, but Vidot had long ago learned one must not grieve too hard for the loss of comrades in action. The battle of life rages constantly on, and while Bemm was gone, Vidot had been fortunate enough to survive. Ah yes, he thought, and now I am once again in control of my own destiny. All I really have to worry about now is time, and time simply happens whether we worry about it or not.

At that moment his journey took a very sudden and dramatic turn. Momentarily lost in his philosophical reflections, Vidot was caught unaware when the plump and delicious little mutt upon which he rode was suddenly plucked up and shoved against the dog walker's chest, trapping him by pressing him snugly against the fabric of the owner's wool coat. Vidot squirmed, but the pressure was tight and he could not get loose. He heard a door slam and felt them ascending a staircase. He counted five flights until he heard the keys rattle as they entered an apartment. Vidot was not particularly worried, he was sure that this was only a temporary detour, and when the dog needed to go out again, as small dogs often do, he would once again be free.

It was a setback, to be sure, but he did not believe it would impact his race against the clock. What happened next, though, was as vexing and disturbing as it was utterly astounding.

Released from the owner's tight grasp, Vidot had every intent of immediately leaping free, hoping to find a high perch from which to survey the situation. Instead he found that, bizarrely enough, the dog was being held down beneath a white hood made of what appeared to be old parachute fabric. Stranger still, leaning over the mutt was a fat-faced man with a pair of spectacles made of magnifying lenses, who possessed the largest, greenest eyes Vidot had ever seen. The man's pupils looked enormous and distorted behind the lenses; Vidot felt as though two immense tropical planets were descending down upon him. The man's fat fingers busily worked through the fur, in a deft and practiced manner. The sight was so bizarre that Vidot found himself frozen with fear, cowering behind a follicle of dog hair like a frightened soldier crouched behind a cannon-blasted tree. But the all-seeing big-eyed man quickly found him, pouncing upon him with the tweezers and almost crushing him as he lifted Vidot off the prone beagle, dropped him into a test tube, and firmly corked the top. The man handed the test tube to his accomplice, a woman many years past young who, as she stared into the vial to make sure he was alive, appeared vaguely familiar to Vidot. As he tried to place her in his memory, she placed him on a rack on a high shelf surrounded by a long row of other fleas trapped in their own tiny vials.

Vidot looked down and watched as the man and the dog remained wrapped up together in the fabric, clearly a method designed to make sure no flea escaped. The man, hunched over his work, removed the fleas one after another and handed each bottled captive to his assistant, who then lined them up next to Vidot. Soon there were more than twenty test tubes on the rack, each one possessing a single flea. But to what end? What were they up to? Were they some odd variety of home scientists? Microbiologists? Curious collectors? Culinary experimentalists? The detective had no solution. Finally, the jowly man emerged from his labors, freeing the little dog to his food bowl and neatly folding up the parachute tent.

It was when the man took off his magnifying spectacles that Vidot realized with a jolt exactly who his captors were. What a strange and startling coincidence. It was Billy and Dottie, the theatrical English pair who had so transfixed and thrilled him with their carnival flea circus when he was only a boy. Now, thirty years on, here they were again, still busy at the old game. Vidot immediately began hopping about in his test tube, immensely thrilled by the wonder of it all.

After he calmed down, he proceeded to carefully observe the two through the rest of the afternoon, growing increasingly impressed with the tender harmony of their existence. Having finished their labors with the fleas, Dottie went and opened a bottle of wine. Meanwhile, Sir Billy donned a smock, set up an easel, and waited for Dottie to come sit before him. As Billy painted his wife's portrait, Vidot looked around the tiny, cramped apartment and discovered that the room was filled with what were perhaps hundreds of paintings of Dottie, canvases documenting her in every mood and era. There were other subjects tucked in among the portraits, rooftop views, country landscapes, and small still lifes, but the vast majority were of the progressively aging lady who sat before him now. The styles had changed, from realist to collage to Cubist to the melancholy style that was Billy's manner now, one that Vidot was not versed enough in to identify by name, but which he would perhaps call exceptional realism. It was as though as they began to approach the end of their life together Billy was trying to capture every small pore, every subtle detail of the woman he so clearly cherished. Or perhaps it could be that after a lifetime of staring at tiny fleas through his giant glasses, Billy lived wholly in an exaggeratedly magnified world.

Clearly, Vidot realized, the flea circus had only been a sideline for the couple, a way to cover costs until their paintings found a market. With the support of a canny dealer, a popular gallery, or a passionate private collector, they would have long ago left this downtrodden existence behind them. Perhaps they had dreamt of moving into a much larger flat or a mansion like Rodin's, or of sailing off as Gauguin did to some distant exotic land where they could devote themselves completely to their art. But judging from the canvases stacked ten deep in every corner of every shelf, Billy's paintings never sold. And so the circus lived on.

After about an hour, with much of the canvas still in a rough state, Dottie went to sit beside her husband. Billy kissed her forehead. She gave his hand a warm squeeze and looked over his progress, pointing out the parts she liked, and planting more affectionate kisses onto his cheek. Her husband blushed with pride. Their perfect affection almost broke Vidot's heart as he remembered all the agonies of his own cursed marriage, painfully recalling the succumbing sounds of ecstasy his Adèle had made as Alberto held her down and crushed her in his strong arms. Vidot tried to blot out those terrible thoughts and focused instead on the simple harmony here, the smiling, loving, eternal couple, together so long, imbued with such gentle, artful, and considerate spirit, who now rose, hand in hand, from their quiet idyllic contentment to turn their attentions to the orderly arrangement of vials containing fleas that sat on their shelf.

And here the real horror began.

XIV

Will followed Oliver into the jazz club. It was early in the evening but the chairs were still turned over up on the tables while the service staff sat in the far corners, smoking and idly chatting, apparently in no hurry to get the place ready for the night. The room smelled of cleansers and stale smoke. Oliver led Will to a red-leather back booth where they found three black men in matching blue suits sitting with their drinks, playing knock rummy. Oliver slid into the booth next to them, and Will looked around for a chair.

"Hullo, boys. Cigarette? Sorry, all I've got are Gitanes." Oliver held out the pack and they all politely refused. Oliver took one and lit it. "Flats. Kelly. Red. This is Will. He's an adman, but he's a good egg too."

The man called Flats raised an eyebrow. "Adman? Meaning you make advertisements of some sort?"

"Yes, sort of. I help make them."

"So, you draw the pictures?"

"No, I oversee all the other stuff, the research, the client relations, strategic thinking, you name it."

"That's interesting," said Flats, mulling this over, "because I can't honestly say I've ever noticed anything resembling 'thinking' in any advertisement I've come across."

Will couldn't tell if he was being joshed or not, but before he could reply, Oliver had changed the subject. "Listen, we're here with a bit of hard news. It seems Boris—you know Boris, yes? Ned's friend? The oversized Russian with a face like a bad dog's?" The men nodded. "Yes, well, he dropped dead in the middle of a card game today. Quite sudden. Suspect it was foul play of some sort, we're looking into it now. Anyway, the gist of it is, we're wondering have you all heard of any other funny stuff going on around town these days?"

The three men locked eyes with one another, as if some shared thought had simultaneously popped into their minds. The man called Kelly looked as though he was going to say something when Red put a hand on his wrist and stopped him. Leaning forward, Red looked at Oliver and Will. "Now, before we share any of our own observations on this particular subject, one thing I'm curious about is why you and this ad guy here are asking? Not exactly your usual beat, is it?"

Red had the slow, careful manner of a person who is always distrustful, and Oliver was cagey with his reply. "It's a mix really, a little personal, a little business. First and foremost, Red, Boris was a friend, a good friend. Also, coincidentally, I think whatever is going on might be decent material for a story, and a writer such as myself needs those. Chicken in the pot, and all that. If I did get a story, I could possibly squeeze a few francs out of my pals over at the *Herald Tribune*. Of course, if you helped I'd be happy to provide you with a cut."

"Sounds reasonable, though you never looked much like a man who needed to hustle for his chicken," said Flats.

"Oh, you'd be surprised," said Oliver with a grin. "A well-tailored suit is awfully good at hiding an empty stomach."

Flats nodded, as if this were an acceptable enough answer, and Kelly leaned forward. "The next question is, why you coming to us? Why do you think we can help?"

Oliver moved around in his seat a little nervously as he answered. "Fair enough. The truth of the matter is Boris might have been passed some bad medicine, if you know what I mean."

Flats nodded again and Kelly looked around the table. "Okay, bad medicine. I get it. Fact is, there has been stuff happening. Ugly stuff going down. More than a few folks keeling over of late, yours here being the third in only these last three days, which is a pretty high mortality rate, even for users. The other two were residents over at the Arc Hotel, long-timers. Be good to know what your friend was taking."

"Yes, well, we found this . . ." Oliver reached into his pocket and took out the tinfoil. Unwrapping it, he placed the small resinous ball at the center of the table. The five men looked down at it like rare gem merchants studying a precious stone.

"Looks like opium resin to me," said Kelly. "And I ain't about to do anything other than look. They say one of those fellows at the Arc flipped into some crazy convulsions till his body stopped cold, and word is the other went running out the window like he was being chased by voodoo spirits." He tapped the edge of the tinfoil.

"Yep, pretty clear there's bad medicine going round," said Red.

"Be a good time to stay clean, if you could," said Flats.

"If you could," agreed Kelly, nodding.

"That's all very interesting, yes. Funny, though, I hadn't seen any news about these other deaths," said Oliver, folding up the tinfoil again and putting it away in his pocket.

"Well, there generally isn't a lot of talk when a user kicks," said Red.

"That's true too," said Kelly. "Though word tends to get around to those who need to know. Good time for caution and all that. One other interesting piece of news these days is that lots of people who shouldn't have any coin at all have been flashing some pretty serious money. I only mention it because I hear they found a whole bundle of franc notes in that window jumper's wallet. And he was an absolute nobody."

"Right," said Oliver, looking at his watch, "very enlightening. Quite helpful, thank you for your time, gentlemen. If I do get myself hired as a stringer for this story, I will make sure to pass along your cut." He stopped as if a thought occurred to him. "Also, one other thing: we're looking for Ned. She been around?"

The men shook their heads.

Oliver leaned over and crushed out his cigarette in the bright-orange ashtray. "Well, there's some money in that for you too, if you can find her."

"We'll ask around," said Red.

"Wonderful. Give me a call if you have any luck," said Oliver, handing Red his calling card. He looked at his watch and hopped up out of the booth. "Oh, you'll have to excuse me now, I've got to find a phone. I'm supposed to call an ex–merchant marine who's got a duffel full of poetry he wants me to look over. Word is it's hot stuff. Take your time, Will. I'll meet you outside in ten minutes." He tipped his hat and headed toward the service doors.

Will felt a little uncomfortable being left alone with the three strangers. He didn't know why. They seemed like perfectly nice men. "How long you been in Paris?" Red asked.

Will shrugged. "A couple of years."

"Quite a while, then. You like it?"

"Sure. The music is great, the art, you know, there's a lot to like . . ." His answer trailed off as he realized it was nothing more than their blackness that was making him uncomfortable. He could have easily talked about how much he enjoyed this town, he could have spelled out the specifics of all the things he loved, from the thyme- and sage-scented smells of the coq au vin that spilled out of so many kitchens to the buzzing sounds of the Vespa scooters whizzing by to the chiming of the bold church bells through the days and nights, all of this had been top of mind of late as his looming departure from the city made him sensitive to how much he adored being here, like a man with a death sentence painfully aware of the final moments of life. But he felt tongue-tied in front of these dark men who sat patiently staring at him, waiting for a response. It wasn't that he felt superior in any bigoted manner, but rather because in all the time he had spent growing up in Detroit, he never mixed much with its Negro population, sizable though it was. Even when he was out on the town, exploring the different scenes, hanging out at bars and clubs that had a mixed clientele, he still rarely found an occasion to mingle with them. In fact, he realized he had never sat at a table and talked with three Negro men before in his life.

Flats seemed to sense his nervousness and gave him a reassuring grin. "You know what I like most about this city?"

"What?" Will asked.

"The tubs," Flats said.

"The tubs?" said Kelly.

"Yeah, the bathtubs," said Flats. "See, when I was growing up down South, we didn't have any kind of proper tub or shower or bathroom, we were, you know, what's the word for it?"

"Poor," said Red.

"That's right. That's the word." Flats smiled. "We were poor. Dirt poor. So I won't even tell you how we washed up back then. But in the army, they put us in those big shower rooms with all the other men. It was all right, but it was the military, so how good could it be? But now, here, in my little flat, I have got this white Parisian-style tub, and I tell you, it fits me like a glove. I dig getting in there, crouching down and scrubbing in all my nooks and whatnot. I tell you, it keeps me familiar and intimate with every bit of myself. You take a shower, your head is up, far away from everything, lost in the clouds, but down in the tub, man, you *know* who you are."

Red and Kelly both chuckled, Flats grinned, and Will smiled too. Thinking Oliver was probably finished with his call by now, he started to get up to leave, but Red stopped him. "Don't let us make you nervous, son. There's no rush. Your friend's not done yet. Tell us a little bit more about yourself. Stateside-wise, where exactly are you from? New York?"

"No. Detroit, Michigan."

"Oh yeah? No kidding." Kelly slapped his hands together.

Flats started singing: "*Michigan water tastes like cherry wine . . .*"

Kelly ignored him. "Listen, I'm from Detroit too. Black Bottom, you know it?"

Will nodded. "I grew up over on the west side of town, but, yeah, I know it."

"Well, if you know it, forget it." Kelly's smile disappeared as his face slid into a bitter expression. "Black Bottom ain't no more. They bulldozed the whole neighborhood. Paradise Valley district, gone. Club Sudan, gone. Sportree's, gone. They erased the entire history. I mean, Floyd Patterson grew up there, right? You've seen him fight, right? They should be building a statue to that man, not tearing down his damn home. When I hit this town I couldn't believe it. I mean, Paris has got whole city blocks and neighborhoods that have all been up for centuries. The place where I live is three hundred years old, beautiful place, older than Napoleon. Hell, I bet even Flats's little bathtub is older than Napoleon. But back home, they raze it down to dirt or pave a tollway through it. That's why I ain't never steppin' foot in Detroit again, 'cuz there's no Detroit there left to step onto."

Will was unsure how to respond. "I know, it's too bad."

Kelly nodded hard. "Yes, it is, son. It's too bad. It's like that magic trick where the magician tears away the tablecloth and leaves all the glasses standing. It's exactly like that, only the opposite."

Will felt silenced, he got up and nodded an awkward goodbye to the men and headed out to the street. Stepping through the double doors, he found an evening rain had started. Will lit a cigarette while Kelly's words about Detroit rang in his ears. It wasn't news. He would get long letters from his brother and mother describing how the whole city was falling to pieces, pulled apart by forces they could not quite explain. Each had their own prejudiced suspicions: his brother blamed the Negroes, while his mother blamed the auto companies, still stinging from the UAW's wins and hell-bent on beating the workers back down. Will did not know who to believe. He'd been to all the joints Kelly had mentioned, and over a dozen others, enjoyed his first legal drink at Sutree's, saw Johnny Hartman sing "Lush Life" at the Sudan. Will knew those clubs had been boarded up. The former patrons—ex-GIs with their new government loans, and union line workers enjoying their latest concessions—had all rushed out to the velvet quiet of the ever-expanding suburbs, while the downtown players, their old haunts, shuttered and abandoned, found their new gigs here as exiles in the City of Light. It seemed Paris somehow managed to absorb all the beautiful things the rest of the world discarded; it was a sparkling and bejeweled box of lost treasures, a wondrous cabinet that hummed with soft horn harmonies played against a grand piano's minor chords.

"Well, those boys raised some interesting questions," said Oliver, coming up behind him.

"In what way?"

"You heard it yourself, multiple deaths, eerily similar circumstances.

Boris may have had a bad heart, who knows, but there's no doubt he was helped along in his exit. I don't like it. I'm sensing a rare pedigree of wickedness, some peculiar evil looming here in our midst."

Will tried to ignore Oliver's dramatic overtones. "Should we check out this Arc Hotel?"

"Oh, perhaps we should, though I'm not too excited at the prospect. I happen to know the Arc quite well, it's a terrifically shabby place. We went there last summer to interview an American poet in from Morocco. The man was so high on kef he couldn't finish a single thought. We literally spent hours patiently sitting at his feet, waiting for something resembling coherence to emerge. From what I saw, the entire place is packed to the rafters with that sort, nodding-off junkies, hashish-chewing automatons, and a pathetic calico that's relieved herself on every rug in sight, making the whole place absolutely reek of cat piss. Very dingy stuff. But, given what the boys said, there's probably no avoiding it."

"Wanna go now?"

"Ha ha, no." Oliver smiled and patted him on the back. "I've got to run, meeting up with Aga Kahn and a Hollywood friend of his for a game of bridge this evening. Do you play?"

"No, I'm more of a euchre guy."

"Yes, you mentioned that. Shame, really, we're in desperate need of a fourth. Look, I'll ring you at the office tomorrow and set up a time for us to visit the Arc. Sound good?"

Oliver didn't wait for a response but instead bounded off the curb into a waiting cab. Watching the car whisk Oliver away, it occurred to Will that he had wasted an entire day on this wandering journey, and instead of finding answers about the missing file, the missing knife, or even the missing small lesbian, all he had discovered of any note was a very large and very dead Russian. It did not feel like progress.

Will had no umbrella, and as he looked down the street for a cab, he realized that Oliver had taken what appeared to be the last unoccupied taxi in Paris. So instead, Will endured a long, humid, and stuffy journey in the metro, pressed in shoulder-tight among stoic businessmen, sleepy clerks, and pale, long-faced tradesmen all heading home. An impressive, and pungent, range of body odors filled the metro car and the stout woman Will found himself shoved up against wore an overbearing perfume that somehow only accentuated the various smells instead of masking them. It was a reminder that there were a few aspects of the city he did not entirely adore. He distracted himself by recalling the night he met Zoya on the metro. He remembered her little smudge of a black eye, how surprising it had been when she had spoken to him, and how he'd thought about asking her out for a drink but hadn't, because he'd been too tired. He suspected that would be the single scene he took home with him as his mental postcard of Paris, the memory of talking with a pretty girl alone at night on an empty train.

When he climbed back up to the street he found the weather had gotten worse. He trudged the rest of the way to his apartment building, with the percussive drizzle of the cold rain hitting hard against his hat as the cold, chilling water soaked into his clothes.

Inside his lobby, he found a small card tucked into the corner of his letterbox. The message was simple and concise: *Je voudrais vous voir. Rencontrez-moi au Novy à 20:00. —Zoya.* As he looked down at it, the raindrops dripping down off his brim blurred the ink. He stood wondering in disbelief. How did she find his address? And why? What did she want with him? A warm vigor pulsed in his blood and he smiled to himself, at that moment especially delighted not to be playing bridge with Oliver, Aga Kahn, and his Hollywood friend.

XV

The owner of the Novy loved to work the crowd. He would come out from the kitchen belting out old folk songs from Little Russia, energetically coaxing the diners to sing along with his happy choruses about love and spring. Zoya liked it here; it felt sentimental. She drank a glass of water and waited. He would come, she was certain of that. The plan was working like clockwork, for after so many years she knew all the mechanics of this sort of clock. There were plenty of times when she did not use what Elga called "the decoy duck," when she simply went home with a Leon, or stayed with the soldier who grabbed at her ass, or let the bookseller have her in the shadowed back stalls; she judged each man as he came. But this Will was one who needed a rival like Oliver to make the gears mesh. She had already jarred him out of his ordinary rhythm of going drink to drink and girl to girl, and now she would be more to him than simply another catch.

She knew too she would have to be careful that he did not fall too hard. Overly devoted men could be trouble, often the worst. She always sought to be kept, but never owned. It was a fine line, and at times tricky to navigate. But if their hearts became too enflamed or driven to obsession, well, a carriage accident or cholera could take care of that.

She came out of her thoughts when she saw Will come into the restaurant. She found herself happily waving to him, surprised at how pleased she was to see his face. She knew a kernel of absurdity lay at the center of this cycle—fascination, flirtation, enticement, passion, satisfaction, and then, well, the wheel always turned. But there was no reason to be restrained in her joy: knowing winter is returning only makes the spring that much more wonderful. But she knew too that it was not quite so simple, her pattern was more like that of the soldiers of the great armies lusting for the green, fertile lands of conquest, who then took those fields they had pined for and scorched them down to char, poisoning them until they were nothing more than barren acres of death. Yes, that was the cycle she had always followed, as she would ever and again, yet still here she was now, grinning, flush-cheeked like a little schoolgirl.

"Am I late?" he asked, bright-eyed, kissing her cheeks twice.

"No, do not be silly, you are on time. Please, have a drink." He wanted scotch but she said, "No, no," and made him order vodka. "I like this place, they let you have the whole bottle. We'll start with two shots each, one right after the other, the way it is supposed to be done," she said, "and then we can talk." Zoya cut the owner off before he could break out in song and sent him scurrying off to bring them a bottle. She wanted Will to talk tonight, though she liked the fact that he didn't always fill the air with unnecessary words. He reminded her a little of other taciturn men she had known, including her father. They were instinctively reticent and always careful with their phrases, for they believed the words they said mattered. Now, with the telegraph and telephone and newspaper presses going all the time, words spewed out relentlessly, in the form of facts, gossip, and endless opinions. She remembered the hope and idealism with which people greeted each of these chattering new innovations, as if more words had ever solved anything. Sure enough, the words poured out and the wars grew worse, the corpses stacking up until they were as high as the silent mountains.

"I thought you'd be with Oliver," said Will.

Zoya shook her head. "Oh, he does not need me tonight, he has his friends. In any case, Oliver likes Oliver, he really does not ever need other people."

Will smiled at this. The bottle came to the table and Zoya poured. They downed the shots fast. Will seemed to get comfortable. She sat at the table, her legs set wide apart, her shoulders hunched over, as if she were an old friend about to tell him a secret.

"So tell me," she asked, "what are you doing here in Paris?"

"I work in advertising."

"Oh yes." She nodded. "You mean those posters, and the pictures in magazines?"

"Yes, those." Will smiled.

"Of course I see the posters everywhere, all those smiling girls with nice round bottoms holding out champagne or cold cream. But I don't pay much attention to them. Do they work?"

Will shrugged. "Research shows they can work very well."

She was intrigued. "Really? How so?"

Will seemed happy to find someone who was even slightly curious about his livelihood. "Well, there are lots of ways they can be effective. For instance, I've got a client who likes hitting his customers right between the eyes, as if he's smacking them in the face with a two-by-four."

She looked confused. "What is a 'two-by-four'?"

"Sorry, a beam, a wooden plank. The point is, he likes to be very direct, to the point of being irritating. He'll write a terrible jingle and play it on the radio nonstop until the listeners completely give up and surrender, run out to the stores, and buy all his products. For him it's an assault: he works to break down their resistance. Research shows that can get results in the short term, but I don't think it's very smart. Now, his latest idea is to use Surrealism to cut through the clutter and—his idea, not mine—to make his customers go insane. I'm not sure that's so smart either."

"What do you think works?"

Even though Will had answered this in presentations to clients a hundred times before, it made him blush to answer the question now. "Seduction."

"You seduce them?" Zoya thought about it for a second and then her eyes brightened. "Yes, I see, so this client of yours believes it is a kind of war, but you think you can win with love. Maybe you're both right. People can be conquered, certainly, but your idea is more like those pretty women I hear they have put to work in the airplanes now."

"The stewardesses?"

"Yes," Zoya said. "You see, it's not enough of a miracle to be flying high up in the air, even all the way across the entire ocean, that magic isn't enough, so they put someone pretty and seductive on the plane, now there's a possibility of sex or romance, a temptation to lure you in. It's right out of a folktale, a beautiful girl with a fool in a flying ship."

"Well, I don't—it's a little more simple than that," Will stammered, her mention of sex making his heart skip a beat. "You really only have to show them a bit of a life they admire or desire, a story they want to be a part of, paint them a picture and then invite them into it."

"Ah, I understand." She smiled, almost to herself. "So it's not love, it's merely a spell. So, then what? Tell me, what happens after these victims of yours buy your product and the spell is broken? When they awaken to find their life is as empty and sad as it was before, only now a little poorer too?"

Will seemed suddenly self-conscious. "Maybe they feel that way, maybe not, depends on the product. But I wouldn't call them victims. I think—"

"I'm sorry, I am being rude." She put her hand down onto his leg to reassure him and began to shift the conversation. "I am only trying to understand, your world is so very different from mine."

"No, it's fine. I don't get to talk about this stuff much outside of the office." Will collected himself. "But it's all boring, really. Tell me about you, where are you from?"

"Russia, a small country town."

"And what brought you here?"

Now it was Zoya's turn to shrug. "Oh, I came here for my studies. For school."

"What do you study?"

"Life, different kinds of life. I was interested in botany and for a long time I investigated various plants." She refilled their shot glasses. "Insects and bugs too."

"Bugs?" said Will, his eyes brightening with bemusement. "I have to admit I've never been very interested in bugs."

"Oh, I know a lot about bugs, the ones in the sky, below the earth, in your hair and beneath your skin, even the ones churning now in your stomach. There are so many bugs, but I don't want to talk about them tonight," Zoya said. "Let's try this, we'll make it fun, you ask me a question about you." She leaned in closer, she could smell him now. "Go ahead, ask."

"Okay," said Will, thinking for a moment. "Why did you say I was lost?"

"Oh, when did I say that?" she said with a wry smile.

"At Oliver's apartment, when he and I were leaving."

"Yes, I remember. I didn't think you heard me. I said it because in the times I've met you, you did seem lost, like the autumn leaves that float so uncertainly in the sky. Even when I first saw you on the metro, I noticed it. There was some confusion in your eyes, a need for answers. I don't think it's a feeling you're used to."

Will sat back in his chair and looked at her, wondering how she saw so much. Finally he said, "You're right. I'm not used to it."

She smiled. "Well, too much certainty is never wise. You must always be ready for the chaos, bend with it like a tree in the wind. That is how you survive." She poured him another shot. "You know, in Russia if you open a bottle it's bad luck not to drink it all."

"The whole thing?" He took the shot and slammed the glass down, feeling light-headed.

"Come." She refilled the glass. "Drink more."

"Wait, wait, there's also the other thing you said."

"When was this?" she took the shot. Her eyes grew wide as the liquor went down, and then she smiled.

"Back at Oliver's, you told me you had the answers. That's what you said. What did you mean?"

She slid another shot toward him. "Drink again. Then we talk."

So he drank. She had drawn him in with such simple tricks: the promise of easy conquest and the vague offer of solutions, these were the tides that always pulled men in, even simpler than the promise of flesh or money. Now all she needed to know was what troubles he was knotted in, for once she untied him from those, he would be as sealed to her as the silver rings that encircled her fingers.

He talked and as she listened, she was filled with delicious wonder. Whenever he slowed in his narrative she would pour him another shot while, at the same time, gently tapping out truth spells under the table. Over the next hour and a half, he revealed a lot. There were so many twists to his tale, even she was impressed: a knife, a dead Russian, a missing file, and too many other details for her to keep track of, light-headed as she was from drawing out spells and drinking down clear liquor. She had seen so much over the years that mankind's mischief almost never amazed her. She had watched brilliant financial virtuosos ensnared in the intricate nets of their own weaving, and charismatic politicians impaled by the bloody revolutions their own rhetoric had sparked; there had been double spies shot at dawn and duplicitous dauphins poisoned at dinner, but she rarely came across anything as oddly convoluted as what this poor Will was enmeshed in. It amused her how, in an almost endearing fashion, he had fallen into it with a guileless innocence, reminding her again of a rabbit, dashing across a hunter's field, bewildered by all the buckshot flying about. As he kept talking in their little drunken corner, the details continued to confuse her, but she knew she could sort them out once she had a clear head. There were other matters to attend to first. She pushed the bottle out of their way and leaned her dizzy forehead up against a wobbly Will's. "I think we need a taxi now."

Babayaga

She was upon him the minute they were in the back of the cab, barely pausing to let him tell the driver *"numéro vingt-quatre rue d'Artois."* Then her lips were on his. Immediately he surprised her, for she liked the way he kissed, like a man who wanted to swallow life. He pulled her tight in his arms, his hands grabbing up the length of her nylons. His desire was clear, but also his pressing need for some concrete thing to ground him amid all his current confusion. His left hand held her thigh, his right hand pulled her waist close against his. She smelled the soap in his hair as she bit at his ear while pushing hard against his body. He grabbed her face and pulled her lips against his mouth, the force of his action surprising her again, releasing an instinct in her that yearned for a kiss that could devour him too. It felt bestial, like the statues of the lions in the Tuileries gardens, attacking one another with a mutual muscular ferocity. She paused to catch her breath and pressed her palm against his chest. He was breathing hard too, his eyes wide, seemingly stunned and thrilled at this sudden encounter. You poor Americans, she thought, you will never learn to drink like Russians.

A little over an hour later she lay naked in Will's bed. She felt a soreness on her shoulder where Will had gripped her hard and she was bruised on her hip from where their bodies had collided. Yes, she thought, this is one reason I always come back to these beds, because intimacy changes the scale of the universe, folding down the vast and overwhelming horizon until there is only the small world that is my body, upon which toothsome storms, sweating floods, and soulful earthquakes break their mighty forces, and I lie ravaged and raw and blissfully alive. She surveyed her landscape, running her tongue across her lip, still slightly numb from pressing so tightly against his, tracing with her finger the small blue bruise on her arm. I meet these men and we draw these maps together, over and again, roughly exploring and intimately claiming our bodies as some kind of shared territory and then naming these with terms of deep affection. But maybe, she thought warily, it really is here, now. Or maybe it's that something worse. She turned on her side and lightly traced her finger down the bridge of a sleeping Will's nose, thinking, I am going to have to be careful, for this is no happy folk song.

XVI

Witches' Song Four

Yes, lust and love, yes, licking and sticking,
yes, sweat and saliva, yes, yes, all that pent energy exploding
into crystal white light. Me, I stuck with Lyda
for all of that sugary goodness.
Sweet fun and fat-cheeked, a hungry lover,
a lusty girl, skipping over borders and boundaries
and hauling around that fat dancing bottom
that teased so many for a slap and pinch.
No wonder the old river opened up
and sucked her down, wet and hungry, I'm sure.
Oh, we rode out many a waxing moon
in our crooked attic lairs, perched high over
the narrow streets of Moskva, Petrograd, and Minsk,
sweet sybaritic dreams, devilish fantasies incarnate
we wove, yes, seducing soldier, sailor, and monocled trader
as we wrapped them up warm in our generous flesh.
Luthiers brought us violins, butchers brought us tenderloins,
we cooked, shocked, and burned, and whoever we lured in
found themselves falling into our sweaty, writhing
triumvirate cocoons as we unveiled, and indulged,
always and truly good, attentive bacchante girls.
In the moments of high tempo
while she kept tongues tied up
and firm limbs enthralled
I would sneak and whittle chunks of fat
from their ruble-thick wallets.
Not the most honest way
to make them pay their fare
but we returned in kind, honestly, so,
with benevolent blessings
whispered into their sleeping, bare backs,
kissing their shoulder blades over and again

Babayaga

in fair and noble exchange.
Truly we were better charms
than any other diptych saints
they stumbled upon.

Nearly every crone bleats like a goose,
"Oh, I didn't choose to be this way,
my papa went heavy with a spiked belt,
my husband fucked my virgin daughters."
Ah, cry at the hurricanes, spit at the storm.
You could pile these melancholies higher
than all the tsar's dead armies.
We never had patience or time for complaints,
such wasted words, tiresome as a winter's rutabaga.
Flee the darkness of the past, run or drive or fly away.
Too many fools bear the burdensome bad of what was,
it spills out of their saddle bags and stuffed steamer trunks,
as they travel along slow bearing a heavy load,
while life itself flies fast by.
Running through nights with us you learned right,
to ride light and keep your history shut tight,
or leave it on the roadside far behind
for the village clocks count in chimes
all the time that is wasted,
nursing grief to no profit.

Elga never burdened us with her tale,
and we respected her restraint,
for the scars of fortune's razor were not hard to see.
And I never asked Zoya, either, nor did she talk,
though we had guessed the shape of her history
long before the beasts finished
ripping out that old man's throat.
That's about it, as for the rest, bah,
our pack grows weary of the bitches' barking,
on and on sobbing sagas so sad any bard

would bash his head in rather than recite.
Cynical, yes, but we chose this life
not because we were beaten or broken,
not angry or aching—
no man ever put me down, no—
we picked this path only
to drink at life's fresh spring,
ever and anon.
We thirsted for the ripeness
of a thousand soft fruits,
oh, let me put my hands on a peach ripe this day,
but, alas, see here, my palms are nothing but air now,
and there would be tears in my eyes too
if there were eyes for weeping.

XVII

Rita Hayworth, Monique Chevalier, and Belinda Lee all stared up at Noelle from the covers of the movie magazines that were strewn across her big hotel bed as the little girl sat, propped up by pillows, biting into another éclair. It was her third of the morning and the sugar had her bouncing. She had also gone through five butter cookies and two fruit parfaits. She was so excited by Paris. This was truly the life of a fairy princess. She had never stayed in a place so elegant; the suite had two separate bedrooms and a large center room with a crystal chandelier and a full, deep fireplace. She had asked Elga if they could always live like this but the old woman said no. "Enjoy it now, but this is not the way we will live. Money attracts too many curious noses. We get what we need but we stay low, out of sight. Like hedgehogs and moles. But there will be nice treats like this from time to time"—she patted the girl's head—"so gobble them up when they come." Then she let Noelle order any dessert she wanted off the big room-service menu.

When the clattering cart had arrived, the hotel boy placed the tray at the end of the bed and Elga signed the bill. Then the old woman took her doctor's bag and disappeared into the bathroom, with Max at her heels. The room-service boy had given the rat a curious look, but Noelle had said, *"Ceci n'est pas un rat."* The boy looked a little confused but left without asking a question. Alone in the room now, Noelle was wiping the last traces of chocolate and powdered sugar from her lips when she heard Elga call out.

"Noelle, are you finished?"

"Yes!"

"How was it?"

"Delicious!" the girl gleefully shouted, kicking her little legs with joy.

"Ha, good. Come here, girl, I need your help."

Noelle jumped up from the bed and skipped across the room. Pulling open the bathroom door, she found Elga sitting on the edge of the claw-footed bathtub. Towels covered the floor and a few of the old woman's odd jars of colored powders lined the counters. The steaming water looked funny to Noelle, it was same shade of deep dark green as the little slimy salamanders that lurked in her mother's country garden.

"Come child, I need you to take a bath now."

"Can I take it later?" Noelle edged away, scrunching up her nose. The room smelled like rotten eggs.

"No, now," said Elga, patting the side of the bath. "Hop in the tub and I will comb those knots out of your hair."

From the time she had spent in the country hospital, Noelle was used to disrobing and bathing in front of strangers. And so, resigned, she pulled her nightgown over her head and stepped naked toward the steaming bath. Elga had promised her shopping later in the day, so while the dark waters did not seem inviting, Noelle did not want to cause any trouble. Slipping her toe into the water, she quickly pulled it out.

"Oh, it's much too hot!"

"No, it is not." Elga spanked at her bare bottom. "Get in there."

There was a firmness to the old woman's words and a sting to her slap that made Noelle slightly nervous, so, despite the almost scalding temperature, she slowly squatted, wincing, down into the swampy bath. Her skin was scorched pink from the heat, but she got all the way in without complaint and rested her head gently against the rim of the tub.

"Good. Okay," Elga said soothingly. "Now if you close your eyes and count to three, you will get a big surprise."

Noelle, uncertain but excited that perhaps this meant more treats, shut her eyes tightly and began, "One, two—"

Suddenly, she felt the firm hands of the old woman pushing down on her skull, shoving her head forcefully under the water. Noelle squirmed hard to break free, thrashing to get out from underneath Elga's grasp, but the woman moved quickly, pressing one palm against the side of Noelle's face while her fist pushed the girl's bare torso down to the base of the tub. Noelle kicked and opened her mouth to scream. Gagging, she sucked in a lungful of the green water. It burned against the inside of her throat. She twisted and pushed with all her strength, thrashing like a caught fish, but she was no match for Elga. Terrified, the girl tried screaming again. Looking up out through the murky water, she saw the stern shadow of the old woman's face staring down at her. Noelle reached out to pull at Elga's arms. She was so confused, the water entered her lungs again; the dark green was growing black. It felt as though acid was being dragged through her veins. Then she saw nothing.

In her dream there was a russet red chicken. The two of them stood in a large circular clearing in a birch forest. Noelle was wearing her nightgown. The pine needles tickled her bare feet. The chicken stepped around her toes, pecking randomly at the soft ground. Then it looked up at her and spoke: "You are a dancer?"

"No. I was a dancer," corrected Noelle.

"Yes, I heard about that. The ballet, the audition, tut-tut," said the chicken before returning to its pecking.

Noelle looked around the forest; it seemed to be quite early in the morning, though perhaps it was twilight, she was unsure.

"Excuse me," said Noelle.

"Yes?" said the chicken.

A strong breeze came blowing through the trees, making their branches creak. Noelle started shivering. She looked down at the bird, who was waiting patiently for her to speak. "Do you perhaps have something to tell me?" Noelle asked. "Is that why we are here? I would like to know, for I am getting quite cold."

"Yes. I have something very important to say," said the chicken, pausing between pecks to look up at the girl.

"What?"

The chicken cocked its head as if trying to recall. "Well, I believe I am supposed to tell you to—" At that moment there was a blurring flash of red as a fox suddenly darted out from the trees. The chicken squawked and jumped, thrusting its feathers out wide in a panicked attempt to escape but the fox pounced upon the bird and, with a quick hard bite, snapped its neck. Then the fox dashed off into the woods again, carrying the bird's limp body in its mouth. The wind stopped. Noelle looked around at the vast solitude surrounding her and called out a tentative "Hello?" The lonely sound of her small, worried voice echoed in the woods.

Frightened, she woke up. She was in the hotel bed again; Elga was sitting at her bedside. Noelle immediately jolted up, desperate for escape, but the old woman grasped her tightly in a warm embrace. "There, there, do not worry, it is over, you are fine. You are good now. Look at you, you are fine." Elga stroked her hair as a terrified Noelle beat the old woman's sides with her tiny fists. Finally, Noelle stopped struggling and burst into tears, wrapping her arms around Elga and letting her whole body shake with grief and relief. "Why did you do that?" pleaded the girl through her tears. "Why?"

"It had to be done. Relax. You are safe now, you are safe forever," said the old woman.

The girl cried hard until it seemed as though she had drained her body of all its tears. Then, finally, she relaxed and lay back down again. Elga leaned over with a dingy handkerchief and roughly wiped Noelle's cheeks dry. Sitting beside her for the next hour, she massaged Noelle's back as the girl rested. Looking out the window, Noelle noticed the sun had set. There would be no shopping, she had slept through the whole day. "We missed going to the stores."

"Do not worry, there will be plenty of time for stores. You rest," said Elga, playfully tugging at the girl's earlobe. "But first tell me, what did you dream about?"

"A chicken."

Elga stopped rubbing her back. "Mmn. You are sure it was a chicken? Not a duck or a rooster or—"

"I know it was a chicken."

"Fine. So what did this chicken say?"

"Nothing."

"Nothing?"

"No. But it wanted to. It tried to tell me a very important thing, but then it was eaten by a fox."

"A fox? Hmmm." Elga gave Noelle a final pat on the back and stood up. "Okay. Well, a fox is not so good." The old woman shuffled out of the bedroom and shut the door, turning out the light behind her and leaving the girl in the dark.

XVIII

It was a simple trick that saved Vidot. For two consecutive days he watched as Dottie took the slender vials of fleas down, one by one, and handed them to Billy, who then disappeared with each into his hooded workbench. Billy wore his unusual pair of thick magnifying spectacles as he labored, making him resemble some sort of massive and diabolical insect god each time he emerged to take hold of a new subject. Billy would then vanish again beneath the white cloth, working for less than a minute, before reappearing with a carefully harnessed flea. A good number would be attached to carriages while the rest were hooked up to small silver balls. After observing to check that the flea was relatively undamaged by the operation, Billy would carefully hand the flea to Dottie, who would box the creature and place it in a traveling case.

The process was simple in theory but its actual exercise was, like any effort involving the collision of creatures with conflicting desires, fraught with violence. A good portion of the fleas taken beneath the hood were often simply brushed out, landing on the floor, mortally injured or dead, many torn to pieces. Occasionally, Vidot watched the silhouette of Billy's hooded fist come down with a force that shook the whole table, after which the debris of what must have been an unruly and uncooperative flea would be swept out onto the floor. Vidot surmised that Billy had an uncanny ability to predict a flea's motions, gathered over a lifetime of wrangling these simple creatures. Of course there was no remorse or even pause amid the constant carnage; these were merely bugs, common vermin, nothing more. The couple and their dog blithely ignored each death, stepping all over the fragments of flea debris as they worked, until they eventually crushed the corpses into dark smudges resembling no more than ink stains on the floorboards.

The entire exercise took about an hour. After they were done, Billy applied wax to his mustache and fastidiously put on his threadbare suit and tied his red-and-black-striped bow tie while Dottie rolled up her net stockings and zipped up the black petticoat with the pink trim. Watching her, Vidot could still remember the budding sexual thrill that had struck him as an adolescent watching the much younger version of Dottie assist a then much handsomer Billy in front of that small carnival crowd. To the enthralled and childish Vidot, she had been as captivating as a blossoming flower, teasing the bees crowded round with the succulent honey lurking there beneath the edges of her pink skirt. She must have been barely twenty then, if that, at the time of her life when every expression she adopted could not help but be coquettish and tempting. Now, though, she was of an age where it was almost too bittersweet to watch her dab on her eyeliner, brush on her rouge, and paint on the black vanity mole above her lip. The two gathered their carnival cases up in their arms and left, turning out the one bare lightbulb as they went, leaving all their captured bugs in the pale shadows nervously tapping against the walls of their slender glass prisons. Vidot did not hop about. Instead, he laid his head against the vial's cold surface and waited, feeling the hard pressure of time closing in.

A little after the church clock chimed ten, the two would come home. Each night it was clear that they had been worked to the edges of their endurance. Dottie would immediately lie down on the bed, tired and silent, and proceed to undress while remaining horizontal.

Across the room, a slouched Billy emptied his pockets of small bills and coins onto the kitchen table. Then he unpacked his black boxes. As they were dumped on the table, Vidot could see that in each case all the fleas lay still, without the slightest twitch or sign of life. They all had perished, worked to death in the course of a single day's performance. With a quick, efficient bang, Billy would knock each box's contents into the dustbin. Then he would strip off his suit and perform his evening toilet before finally coming to bed, where his wife, still in her makeup but now naked, already lay fast asleep. Billy would pull the blanket up over her body and whistle for their little dog, who would leap up onto the foot of the bedspread. Then Billy would curl up beside his wife, kiss her cheek gently, and switch off the light.

The Paris skyline sparkled through the window, its twinkling illumination bathing the room in a dark cerulean blue. The city's glow seemed to be taunting him, thought Vidot, like the visions of silver crystal kingdoms that arise in the deliriums of fever-crazed soldiers. Vidot stayed awake, hypersensitive to everything around him, the rhythm of the nervous hopping fleas reminding him of deep African drums beating before a savage blood sacrifice, a percussive prelude to the certain doom that awaited him when the circus master rose again to don his terrible magnifying glasses. For tomorrow was the day; there were only three bottles sitting to Vidot's right, and Billy used more than a dozen to prepare for every show. Vidot knew that he would have to come up with some sort of a plan if he wanted to survive.

Regrettably, Vidot's flea-sized brain was at that point utterly devoid of any ideas. He knew that once Billy set his tweezers on him beneath that white cloth, his life was over. He thought of all the things he would miss: listening to football matches with the chef at Chez Barbe, playing dominoes with Claude Attal, walking through the market in the April spring when the cherry and the pear blossoms colorfully bloomed overhead. He thought of the comfort of a glass of Brouilly and the grace of Satie's *Gymnopédies* and, finally, the warmth of Adèle's kiss, a memory laced with bitterness now, but one that still defined his greatest ideal of happiness.

The tap-tap-tapping of the fleas on the glass kept distracting him from his thoughts. He wanted this to be a moment of contemplation, his last night on earth, and yet these persistent pests kept breaking his concentration as they leapt about in their little vials. As he gazed down the row, his neighbors' ceaseless jumping reminded him of Camus's Sisyphus, forever pushing his boulder up the hill and eternally happy in the futility of his effort. Then he noticed that a few of the fleas next to him, instead of frantically attempting to leap to freedom, merely were crawling about at the bottom of the glass. He watched to see if they would hop at all, but they did not. These fleas simply paced around, circling endlessly, as the condemned often do. Vidot thought at first they were merely depressed or discouraged, but then, looking closely, he observed that, in fact, the rear legs of the creature were shaped slightly differently. Vidot found this very interesting.

The next day began as the days had before: Dottie put the water on, Billy and the dog went out and returned soon with a single loaf of bread. They ate silently. Then Billy chose a pair of small oil paintings from a stack in the corner. Perhaps he was going to a dealer, Vidot thought. Whatever the errand, it was an unsuccessful one, as Billy returned an hour later with the same canvases tucked under his arm. As he placed them back in the stack, Dottie said nothing—it had clearly been too long since any paintings had sold for any comment to matter now—instead she kissed him on the cheek and heated up some carrot soup. A little later Dottie boiled a large pot of water and filled the bath, a narrow steel tub that sat in the corner of the loft. Billy combed her hair while she soaked. When she was done, Billy took their dog out again for a long walk, and when he returned, the mutt's fleas were meticulously harvested, bottled, and placed up on the shelf. In the afternoon Dottie sat and modeled again while Billy painted. Debussy's *La Mer* played on the radio.

When Billy rose from the easel and put away the paints, Vidot knew it was time. He sucked in his breath and waited, watching as, one by one, Dottie reached for the bottles on the shelf. The first bottled flea caused Billy no problems. Within seconds the flea emerged attached to a harness and was swiftly put away. The fate of the second one, however, was exactly what Vidot most feared. After disappearing beneath the white hood, his neighbor's mauled carcass was quickly swept out, falling to the floor before it had even finished its final convulsions. Vidot had no time for sympathy, for at that moment Dottie reached for his vial.

The moment Billy shook him down onto the hard white paper Vidot began his charade. You're going to have to force yourself to march, he told himself, march, march, march, though it is against your instinct, though every microgram in your exoskeleton is begging you to leap, to soar, to break free and escape the doom that awaits, this is the time you must march. He tried to remember what it was like to march in unison with his fellow cadets in his youth brigade. But that brought other memories that were even darker than his current condition, so he blanked them from his mind and kept marching beneath Billy's careful gaze.

Observing his neighbors the night before, Vidot had come to the conclusion that while most fleas jumped, there were some fleas that could not jump at all, and these, he assumed, were the ones that Billy put into the chariot harnesses. Vidot knew his only hope at outwitting a man who had been outthinking fleas for more than thirty years was to convince the man that he was the wrong kind of flea. As he marched across the table, he prayed it would be enough. Vidot saw the gleam of the tweezers coming down. Then he jumped.

The fist came smashing down hard on the table behind him as he leapt. He had spotted a fold in the tenting where he knew he could hide for a moment. When Billy lifted the fabric to find him, Vidot leapt again, right over his captor's head, through the small opening and out into the rich, warm kaleidoscopic light of freedom. He did not pause to look back, he did not know if he had enraged the circus ringleader or if his escape was being shrugged off as a minor irritation. He thought he heard Billy curse, and the little mutt barked, but Vidot did not pause to worry as he leapt, jumped, and practically flew up to the most beautiful thing he had ever seen, the great wide open window.

Only after he passed across the threshold and began tumbling and spinning down toward the cobblestone street below did it occur to Vidot that leaping out from a fifth-floor apartment's window might not be the most prudent path to liberty.

XIX

Witches' Song Five

Oh no, oh no, tut-tut, look and scream,
your pretty pest has gone,
flailing and flying over the abyss
heading to be flattened,
most certainly flat, on the solid surface below.
So, tell me, do, who will you pray to now, pious ones?
What divine hand swoops in for the rescue?
Ah, let me guess, some manly shade, yes?
Some broad-shouldered musky balled spirit?
A pretty boy Jesus? An undaunted Allah?
Or some wizened circumcised Jew with neat sea-parting tricks?
Boys, boys, so many boys you have placed
in control of your dreams, destiny, fortune, and fate, why?
Tell me this too: where was your own father
when you stumbled and fell?
Who scooped you up and set you right on your path,
swatting your bum for luck as you ran off, weeping "waaa-waaa"
through your lush ivy gardens?
See there, it was a woman's hand that set you right. Yes.
Your mother or matron or nana who watched and nurtured.
So why this faith in the swollen and awesome
all-present phallic-bearing force?
Why do you pray for what you've never known?

It's not that we're envious or spiteful, no,
frankly we don't much care,
Lyda spits out her distaste for Poseidon
in fish scales on the floorboards.
But I am curious, why so many gods come
bullish, hirsute, and bearded?
What bullies and brutes elbowed them there?
Yes, women are tucked in amid your marginalia,

Mary, Sarah, Hagar, Hera, Hestia, I can name each,
sulking there in the testaments' shadows, outshone
like Diana by Apollo's ever-bright aura,
or shunted to the side like Jacob's two patient wives,
waiting there past the river's ford as he wrestled his angel
the way boys will do, the same way this stupid flea
now wrestles against gravity.
Oh, watch him descend.

Book Three

I've come to consider bravery as just about the
most pernicious of virtues. Bravery is a horrible
thing. The human race has it left over from the
animal world and we can't get rid of it.
—JAMES JONES, *The Paris Review*

I

Superintendent Maroc had an important errand to run. But he was a procrastinator by nature; in his experience if you put off most things you found in the end you didn't truly need to do them. But this errand was most likely not going to go away. Yet still, he stalled. He sat behind his desk, watching the big yellow clock tick its way around and listening to the little old detective rattle on: "This was, I don't know, thirty years ago now, between the wars. I was then working for my father, who was prosperous then."

"Your family had money?" Maroc said, not really listening.

"Before the war we did, yes, a bit. Mostly in property speculation, apartments out in the sixteenth. In any case, I was sent up to Frankfurt to meet with a group of Jewish bankers. Typical of business travel back then, they insisted on entertaining us every night. We'd start in their fine, fancy homes, I'd meet their wives and children, the butlers and maids would serve the thick coffee, I'd pet the little dog, hello, hello, et cetera, but afterward the bankers always wanted to take us out for a bit of additional entertainment. Their wives would never come along. You see, this was their time with their mistresses. We would meet up with them in the city's various cabarets. It wasn't so bad, there were lots of dancing girls, we'd drink champagne and sing along with "Das Lila Lied" and pretty women would come along and shake their round asses on my lap and, well, it was fun."

"Good for you."

"Yes, well, one banker, Jacobson, he had this girl. Amazing. A drop-dead beauty. Big dark eyes. She was a Russian but unlike any Russian I'd ever known. I'd always found them lean and angled, but this one had full breasts, the kind you want to drop your face into, and a sweet round apple of an ass as well, maybe not the type for everyone but I liked it. Just looking at this girl stole the breath out of my lungs. Every night out with the bankers, I found a way to dance with her, and more than once—probably too many times."

"I cannot imagine you dancing, Lecan."

"Ha, ha, me neither now, that would be a pathetic sight. But you remember how it was then, jitterbugs and Charlestons and lots of legs kicking high. Jacobson's girl was so mesmerizing, positively hypnotizing. I knew it was rude, trying to monopolize her like that; it did not look good, especially night after night. But I still can remember one waltz we danced, my hand on the soft flesh of her hip, the other hand aligned with her shoulder blade, her little smile, the delicious glint in her eye . . . well, looking back, I can see that the banker was jealous. I'm pretty sure that's why I came home without the loan. Papa was very upset. We could have used that money, it turned out we needed it pretty desperately . . ." The little man's story tapered off.

"So why are you telling me this?" Maroc yawned.

"Oh, because I saw her," said the little man, becoming animated again. "Last night. I swear it was her. I was sitting outside at Chez Loup and she walked by. Not a ghost, and not a girl that looked like her, but Jacobson's girl, looking exactly as she looked thirty years ago. I swear to the saints, the woman has not aged a day."

"Lecan, you are an idiot." Maroc chuckled as he rose to put his jacket on. "Either you had one too many last night or your mind is rotten for good. Now, do you want to come with me or do I have to do this alone? It's time to go." Lecan gave him a resigned shrug as they gathered up their overcoats, hats, and umbrellas and went out into the wet night.

The first stop was a half hour from the station. It took a few moments before an older woman answered the buzzer to let them up to her flat. She met them at the door.

"Yes?"

"Madame Bemm, I am Superintendent Maroc. This is Detective Lecan. I'm afraid we have some terrible news." Maroc quickly explained the situation, how her son and his partner, in the course of a critical investigation, had disappeared without a trace. He said they did not have any suspects now, it could be Algerians, possibly the National Liberation Front, it was hard to say. Maroc tried to wrap up as fast as he could, generously ladling out words like "noble," "brave," "valiant," and "heroic" to describe a man he had barely ever noticed.

As he talked, the old woman silently looked up at him, her eyes widening with confusion, and then refocusing, as if the various sounds Maroc was making were only slowly assembling into words she could comprehend. When he finished, her face went pale. She placed her hand on her chest and inhaled deeply, pausing mid-breath to suck in more air. Watching this small woman gulp up what seemed to be all the oxygen in the room, Maroc had a bad feeling about what was coming next. He tried, as best he could, to steel himself from the inevitable, looking nervously to Lecan for support, but when it came it was far worse than he had imagined, a loud, piercing wail of grief so shrill that went on for so long it seemed as if the old woman was intent on utterly destroying his eardrums. In the middle of her glass-cracking shriek, she lunged out and grabbed hold of him, pulling him close until her cry finally broke into choking sobs that she buried in his coat. Gingerly putting his arms around her, Maroc gave her an awkward, hesitant pat. "Now, now, have faith," he said, despite being sure that the situation actually was hopeless. She could continue to weep and pound her small fists against his chest all she wanted, it would not change the fact that Bemm—and Vidot—were most likely dead.

After a while, the old woman finally calmed down. She sat on a chair, staring glumly at the floor as Maroc explained the next steps, how they would wait a bit longer to be sure, and then, if no better news arrived, there would be a small ceremony at the station. The mayor would come, of course, and her son would be posthumously awarded many honors and medals. She would also receive standard insurance compensation, and her son's pension would help her weather this great loss. When Maroc finally began to make his excuses to leave, and he and Lecan started for the door, she watched them go with a desperate, silent sadness. Her eyes looked like spoons brimming over, ready to spill again. Maroc could not get out of there fast enough.

Vidot's apartment was not too far away, but by the time they got there the light drizzle had grown into a deluge and they had to jump over swelling gutters to reach the building's front door. Luckily, they did not have to wait out in the rain as they were buzzed in right away. They climbed the stairs to the flat and when they knocked at the apartment door, a woman quickly answered. Her bright smile faded instantly at the sight of them. "Yes, can I help you?"

"Are you Madame Vidot?" asked Maroc.

"I am."

"I am Superintendent Maroc. This is Detective Lecan. I am afraid—"

The loud buzz of the downstairs doorbell interrupted him. She did not answer it.

"I am afraid we have some unfortunate news," Maroc continued.

"Oh?" she said, her face turning white. "Is this about my husband?"

Again, the doorbell buzzed, and again she did not answer it.

"I'm sorry." Maroc smiled politely. "Are you expecting company?"

"It is nothing, no one," she stammered. "Please, go on."

Maroc was about to continue with his speech when Lecan stepped forward. "Madame, perhaps you should invite us in. The news we have is serious and inappropriate for hallway conversation. And please, let up whoever is waiting. The weather is terrible and we would not want to be the cause of their inconvenience."

"Yes, I'm sorry, please come in." She opened the door for them. As they entered the modest apartment, Lecan gave Maroc a knowing look. "But I am sure," she said, "whoever is outside will go—" The buzzer rang a third time, its duration implying a certain impatience.

"Please," said Lecan, "invite him up."

Blushing, Madam Vidot pushed the front door button. The three of them waited in the silent apartment, listening to the rain against the window and the footsteps climbing the stairs. When the knock came at the door, Adèle went to open it. Before she could say a word, the man burst in and immediately started removing his soaked hat and coat. "My God, it's terrible out! Were you napping? Oh, my little dove, I can't wait to get out of these wet clothes and—"

It was only then that he looked up and saw the two policemen.

"Good evening," said Maroc with a grin. "I am Superintendent Maroc, and this is my colleague, Detective Lecan. And may I ask who might you be?"

Less than an hour later the two policemen headed back to the station, huddled beneath their two umbrellas and engrossed in a rigorous debate. Maroc was convinced that Madame Vidot and this Alberto Perruci, who was undoubtedly her paramour, were now the primary suspects in the case. Clearly they had murdered her husband and probably Bemm too, perhaps as an unintended consequence. Lecan insisted this was not necessarily so. Maroc pointed to the statistics, how in most murder cases involving married couples, it almost always turned out that the spouse had done it. Lecan agreed that history supported Maroc, but also pointed out that this was France, where, if adultery led inevitably to murder, then piles of new corpses would be lining the streets every morning. Lecan told Maroc that he suspected a more sinister end, perhaps related to the case Vidot had been investigating. By the time they reached the station, Maroc had agreed with Lecan that while infidelity did not necessarily lead to homicide (if it did, he agreed, most Frenchmen would be dead), he still needed answers, and this pair was the closest thing he had to a lead. The death of Leon Vallet was proving to be a dead end, with no clear leads to follow. But these two were acting suspicious right under their noses. Therefore he would put the wife and her lover under surveillance, as it was the only constructive thing he could think of to do.

"Of course, maybe in the end we will find that Vidot simply ran away with a lover of his own," suggested Lecan.

"Yes, maybe he ran away with Bemm," Maroc said, and they shared a good laugh at that.

II

Tumbling down toward the street from Billy and Dottie's apartment, Vidot realized that his whole life would not, as the cliché put it, flash before his eyes. In fact, he had abundant time for regrets, second thoughts, and even philosophical ruminations, for, thanks to the air pressure and the updraft, what would have been a plunge of mere seconds for a heavier mortal man took substantially longer for a falling flea: it was as if he had tumbled off a tall cliff perched above a kilometers-deep canyon and it would now take considerable time for him to cover the vast distance before he reached the bottom. So, as he fell, he could contemplate all the many lapses in judgment that had brought him to this grim and unfortunate end.

Then, unexpectedly, a brisk breeze picked up from below. This gentle but firm wind, buffeting off the side of the building, completely ceased his descent and began forcing him up and aloft. In fact, as it quickly billowed him out over the rooftop, he found himself at an altitude of such atmospheric activity that it quickly became evident that he would not be returning to earth anytime soon. In surprising bursts and swirling currents, curious eddies, and elliptical wafts, he proceeded to spin and sail up across the high terraces, tiles, and chimneys of Paris, his soul now laughing in a nervous ecstasy of relief as he sailed over the spires of churches and soared past garret windows and bright tin peaks. In absolute amazement, he glided over the spider-webbed alleyways of the Marais and then out past the Hôtel de Ville. Cars and pedestrians clogged the streets beneath him. He was high up now, gazing across to where Montmartre itself gazed out over the city. He was swept along in the wind, admiring the twin steeples of Notre-Dame as he passed, along with the dogged, devilish gargoyles of St. Jacques.

Relaxing in his good fortune, he began to figure out how to surf the wind's current. By twisting, turning, and balling himself up while extending his long legs out into the air, he found a way to achieve some slight control. Aiming himself down the length of the Avenue Montaigne, he rode a buffeting gust and was shot clear across the river. Then, gleefully aiming himself again, he floated between the iron latticework of the Eiffel Tower. He soared out, up along Haussmann's grand boulevards all the way to Montparnasse. There the spinning wind's pressure changed and took him swooping down so that he found himself dancing along only meters above the black and gray hats of a small crowd of people. The breeze sped up again, and as he sailed over the street he caught a glimpse of a pretty blond girl selling newspapers, followed by a man pushing a movie camera in a baby carriage. What a marvelous city, he thought, captivating and mesmerizing even in its most pedestrian moments, those scenes composed of singular beauty that were almost camouflaged and lost amid its myriad wonders.

Babayaga

The gusting wind now shifted direction as it shot him up once more, blowing him back hundreds of meters above the Champ de Mars to where a lonely red balloon floated by. The sight reminded him of those first heroes of flight, his countrymen, who, long before the airplane, rose from crowded and cheering Parisian courtyards in their gilded and satin hot-air palaces. Filled with delight, and flying now back over the river, he passed the Tuileries. He tossed and turned in the cool breeze. He was beginning to think he could happily spend days up above Paris, riding high and repeatedly crisscrossing the Seine, a tiny observing angel keeping a keen, watchful eye on his fair city and its sweet and sinful inhabitants, when suddenly, as he was passing over the courtyard of the grand Hôtel de Crillon, the capricious winds absolutely died and Vidot found himself falling once again, straight down until he landed smack in the middle of an overflowing garbage can.

Stunned, quite happy to be alive, and, as far as he could tell, miraculously uninjured, Vidot roused himself up from the piled debris and hopped out onto the base of a nearby drainpipe. He had barely time to catch his breath before he saw a large, lumbering shadow passing by, and, without any hesitation, he leapt onto it, wholly intent on resuming the journey to the station he had been pursuing before he was waylaid by Billy and Dottie.

Quickly determining that he was riding the rear end of a common rat, Vidot scurried below to the safety of the belly. There, the warmth of the rodent's flesh struck another intuitive nerve. Vidot realized that, amid all the drama, he had not eaten in a couple of days. Without pause, he sank his teeth in and sucked deeply, filling his abdomen with warm blood, which caused him to slip into the familiar rich ecstasy of semiconsciousness that often accompanied his more gluttonous meals. In his daze, he failed to notice that his rat was not, in fact, carrying him down the streets but instead had ducked through a sewer grate and crawled up though a small hidden hole that led directly into the side of the building. Slipping behind plaster walls and climbing up the frame of the service-elevator shaft, the rat made its way steadily along the narrow warrens, finally emerging from behind a radiator inside a sumptuous hotel suite.

Coming out of his dazed stupor, Vidot was entirely shocked to hear a familiar voice in the room, one he had never expected he would ever hear again. "Ah, there you are," said Elga. "Been out playing in the gutters, eh? You are such the little man, Max, you go out for your evening stroll and you come home smelling funny."

III

Guizot was weeping, his head down on the conference room desk, banging his fist against its polished surface. Will tried to offer him his handkerchief, but Guizot ignored the gesture. It was fine with Will, he was happy to wait. At that moment, Brandon was on his way over to Will's office from the embassy, and so Will was happy to kill time listening to Guizot's hysterical theatrics, knowing that this meeting was going to be better than the next one.

"I am the destroyer, Will, the destroyer!" Guizot wept.

"I honestly think you're being a little dramatic," Will said.

When Will had left his apartment, hours before, Zoya had still been sleeping. After showering, shaving, and putting on his gray suit, he had left a short note on the bedside asking her to call him when she woke. He drew a heart on the note and then kissed her cheek before grabbing his hat and heading out the door. The minute he reached the street, he had regretted leaving her side.

It wasn't only the physical intimacy he had enjoyed, though they had fit together like perfect puzzle pieces and the passion had charged and thrilled him in a way it had not for a long while. But the conversation they shared at the restaurant had made him feel better too. He was a little foggy on exactly how much of his story he had shared with her (he had lost count how many vodka shots they'd put down), but, walking down the street, he felt relaxed and unburdened for the first time in weeks. He remembered the good-humored way she listened to him, a sly smile crossing her lips as he talked (what *had* he said, exactly?). Continuing along the avenue, a part of him longed to turn around and race back to his bed. He wanted to crawl between the warm sheets again, to feel her skin, to slide between her legs, to flutter her eyes awake.

He wondered how many men found such intensity in a woman's arms. Most of them thought they did, no doubt, that was the spark that drove lust onward. But did they really, or was it usually some thinner, cheaper version? And when it was good like this, how long did the feeling last? Is this how married men felt? Did those husbands still ache and pine to roll in their wives' embrace as they went through their tedious days, and when they were out with their wives, did they inch closer so that their fingers were never far from touching? He had felt he was being a little ridiculous, like a daydreaming character out of some silly romantic movie, but these were refreshing emotions for him, so he savored their rawness, sucking at them as one does a candy, wondering if he should give in to his desire and rush back to her side. If he turned around now, in five minutes' time he could be naked, holding her in his arms, kissing that perfect soft spot below her collarbone and still only be an hour or so late for work. But as tempted as he was, practical realities held him in check. He had already wasted the previous day gallivanting about town on Oliver's wild adventure. He needed to get back on top of things.

Thinking of Oliver reminded him that Zoya had not clarified much there. Was she seeing both of them now? Or had she smoothly switched over like a busy traveler changing trains? What would Oliver think, or say? And should Will even care? After all, the man had been nothing but a whirlwind of distractions and destruction since they first crossed paths, and now he had managed to tangle himself up in both Will's professional and personal life. No, Will decided, he wouldn't worry about Oliver.

Once Will had arrived at the office, he immediately buried himself in the distraction of work. Since he was not responsible for much these days, it didn't take long to catch up with his reports. The media buying for Guizot had been completed in his absence, and the first-quarter estimates had all been done; still, he gave all the work a thorough review and then attended a pair of brief meetings with his colleagues in which they were all given updates on their clients' general health. Then it was lunchtime.

As was often his ritual, he sat alone at his desk, eating the ham-and-brie his assistant had brought in for him. Most of the office went out at lunch; many would not return till it was almost three. Will had long ago come to terms with the fact that the French did not embrace his same slavish devotion to office hours that Americans did. Looking out at the empty desks, Will was of two minds: on the one hand, he was happy that Americans like him worked so hard, clearly it allowed his country to remain at the vanguard of industrial leadership, the captains of capitalism, stewards of the modern, civilized world. On the other hand, he envied the French their serenity. After all, they too had, at one time, ruled much of the world like their American cousins did now, but it seemed they had abdicated that role with only a little regret, finding more than enough consolation in the various pleasures that could be found in a nice, long lunch.

But no matter where they were, he thought, not one of them was experiencing anything like the strange misadventures and exquisite pleasures he had known in the past twenty-four hours. Then again, he thought, who was he to guess? Maybe two or three were out there in the throes of wild cataclysms that would make his recent escapades seem positively provincial. Chewing his sandwich, he enjoyed thinking that some of his staff were, at that very moment, caught up in riotous, bawdy, action-packed exploits involving various disguises, swashbuckling swordplay, suitcases stuffed with franc notes, the whooshing sound of throwing knives, loose prowling circus lions, or fleeing half-naked lovers racing across sunny, aristocratic courtyards. Perhaps that's what they were all doing right now, out on their lunch breaks, desperately trying to extract themselves from their absurd situations in time to make it back to their desks before anyone noticed.

Eventually, though, they did return and the afternoon went on, and though he waited for the phone to ring, Zoya never called. Finally, as the clock neared five, he filed the papers away in his desk and prepared to head out, wondering if she would still be there, waiting for him. She might have found an apron somewhere, poured wine, thrown together a cassoulet, and put it in the oven. No, he smiled, he could not imagine that. No cassoulet. But he felt his pulse pick up at the thought she might still be undressed, waiting for him there beneath the white duvet, her skin still warm and soft. He closed his eyes to savor the image. When he opened them again the first thing he saw was Brandon's two men heading down the hall, aiming straight for his office. Will realized he would not be going home any time soon.

"Hello, Mr. Van Wyck?"

"Hi, boys, what can I do for you two?" Will said.

"Brandon sent us over. You promised us those personnel files."

"Of course, I remember." Will lit a cigarette. "Say, what were your names again?"

"I'm Mike Mitchell and this is Caleb White."

"Right, well, Mike, look, I really haven't had time to—"

They both gave him a cold smile. "You did promise us the files," White said.

Something about their manner bothered Will. Both of them were a few years younger than him and they each seemed to share the same smug expectation that he would unquestionably acquiesce to their authority. Brandon, at least, had always been collegial and chummy, like they were fraternity brothers just goofing off. But these two took it seriously and played it straight in a way that made things both clear and ugly. They honestly irritated Will, and so, before he had thought through the possible repercussions, he said, "Well, here's the thing. I've been thinking it over and I'm not entirely comfortable handing those files over. After all, I don't really know what you're going to do with them."

He watched them take this news. They gave him a pair of official grins.

"We're only going to look them over, see what we can learn, and then give them back to you," said Mitchell.

"I understand that's what you want to do. But it doesn't seem right to me. So I'm not going to turn over those files."

He was surprised at his resolution. He wasn't sure what had caused him to be so headstrong, but he could see that, without the friendly presence of Brandon overshadowing them, Mike Mitchell and Caleb White both looked like small and mean men. These were not the sort of fellows you wanted digging into anyone's past.

"You mind if we use your phone?" said Mitchell. "We need to call Brandon."

"Suit yourself," said Will.

"He'll probably want to come here and talk to you."

"That's fine."

"He's not going to be happy. He's got another project right now that needs his full attention. We're supposed to take care of this for him."

"Well, do what you gotta do. But I'm not giving you those files."

Will realized that there was not much they could do. There was no one they could appeal to; no one else in the entire building knew about the agency's relationship with the CIA. Will was their only guy, and if he refused to play along, the only thing they could possibly do was fire him, which they had actually already done a few days before when Brandon had come by for his visit.

Mitchell dialed the phone while White worked on giving Will a hard, mean stare. Will could tell the guy wanted to look like a killer, but he didn't. He looked like an overfed Boy Scout, fresh-faced and cocky in his sense of righteous justice. Will did not care, he was not afraid of these two, he was experiencing his own sense of certainty, one that was coming together to make perfect sense of the present moment.

Will was reminded of the Hollywood writers he'd seen in the papers who had been called before various committees to rat out their fellow members in the Communist Party. A few of them had refused, even when they were threatened with jail. Will didn't know if they were really Communists or not, but he knew it took some character not to talk. Whatever their ideology, their resistance had shown a rare kind of integrity. Will thought about all the other people who had, over the ages, gone the other way, turning in people they actually knew were innocent: the ones who dodged suspicion by passing it on. The Nazis and Stalin were the most recent examples, interrogating and torturing innocent citizens until, finally, desperate to mollify their tormentors, the accused denounced their equally innocent neighbors. In the end, how many scapegoats were herded up? And when did this nightmare of evil arithmetic stop? Crystalizing within Will was the realization that what he was being asked to participate in now was in a way no different, it was the awful conveyor belt of history, a butcher's carnival where ultimately no one innocent escaped, they lost their jobs and homes, or their throats were cut and they were dumped in bloody piles. The only ones who ever seemed to get away were the guilty.

At that moment, as if punctuating his resolution, there was the loud cheerful ping of the elevator arriving and around the corner came Guizot, with outstretched arms and tears rolling down his cheeks. "Will! Will!" he cried out, oblivious to the stares of Mitchell, White, and the other employees in the office. "We are the destroyers of the world!" Guizot cried out. Will almost had to smile.

"You'll have to excuse me for a moment," he said, getting up and leaving the two men there.

A half hour later, Will was still sitting with his inconsolable client. Between sobbing and loudly blowing his nose, Guizot told him his saga, about how, after the terrible argument over the Surrealist painting, his wife had packed her bags ("So many shoes, Will, when did she buy them all!") and stormed out of their flat, leaving him shocked, appalled, galled, and completely brokenhearted. After a few days of suffering from inconsolable grief, he had rushed out to her art dealer and purchased every Surrealist painting he could lay his hands on, de Chiricos and Ernsts, Klees, and Mirós, along with countless others that the dealer, sensing a vulnerable moment, pawned off on him. Then he drove to the hotel suite where his wife was staying and begged her to come home.

"I was on my knees," Guizot said. "I pleaded. 'You are the most important person to me!' I groveled. 'You are the best part of my soul!' I kissed her ankles over and over like a desperate supplicant at the feet of a great princess, crying, 'You are the first woman, the only woman, I have ever loved in this way!' And you know what she did, Will? She looked down at me—oh, those eyes, so cold they could turn a mountain into ice, and she sneered at me, Will, she sneered. *'Oh, Guizot, listen to yourself, "most," "best," "first," how pathetic, you sound like one of your cheap little advertisements.'* I am telling you, I crawled out of there a destroyed man."

Since then, Guizot said, he had been holed up alone in his apartment, with the nightmarish shapes of Surrealism's asymmetrical jungles and melting timepieces looming over him as his wife's bitter words burned inside his head, quickly driving him mad. "Then in an instant, it hit me! I saw it! She was right! She was absolutely correct! Listen to the language we pepper people with, Will, listen to how our advertisements are ripping all the meaning from the world, tearing it out! How can a sacred word like 'adore' mean anything between a man and a woman when we say 'You will *adore* this creamy butter! You will *adore* this smelly fragrance! You will *adore* this fruity, delicious cherry cream soda!' What is adoration when our advertisements are done with it, Will? What are we destroying with our absurd and exaggerated creations? We are monsters, and we are sucking out the marrow from the world!"

With that, Guizot collapsed into a flood of tears on the desk and, in between sobs, fired the agency. Will could hardly believe it. Guizot vowed that from that day forward he was only going to sell his product personally to retailers, one to one, with no television, radio, newspaper, or outdoor advertisements. "All I need is a handshake, the handshake of a man, eye to eye, that is how I will sell! That is all!" He pulled himself together, wiped his eyes, and, giving Will a warm embrace, excused himself. "My friend, you should get out of this racket too," he said. "While you still have a soul."

"Yes, well, I appreciate your sentiments, and I very sincerely hope you work things out with your wife," Will said, sounding stiff and awkward even to himself.

"Ah, Will, you are a vampire. No, we are both vampires!" Guizot gave him a bittersweet smile. "But I have put the stake through my own heart." Then Guizot walked off down the hallway, his head hung low.

Will watched him leave, unsure of exactly what had occurred, other than having been fired from his last and final account. Perhaps Guizot would come to his senses. If not, it did not matter. Will's career in Paris was over. There was not much left to do.

He headed back to his office. He knew Brandon was there by now, waiting. He did not know if Brandon would be tough with him or friendly. He did not care. He was not handing over the files.

So, as he walked into the room, he was not surprised to see Brandon sitting with the two others, staring up at him as he entered. He was, however, surprised to find Oliver sitting with them.

"Oh, hullo," Oliver said, looking up from behind Will's desk, where he had clearly made himself comfortable. "What a nice surprise, I stopped by to pick you up for our appointment and ran into these fine fellows. Have you all met?"

Will gave a nervous smile. "Um, yes, Oliver, they're sitting in my office."

"Well, then of course you have!" Oliver laughed. "Turns out Caleb here hails from Cleveland. You two must have a lot to talk about. Ohio's got the oil and the tires and you've got the automobiles in Detroit, so there's a nice symbiosis there, right? But then there's that funny football rivalry and the war you two fought against one another back in the 1830s. The Toledo War, wasn't it? Yes, well, happy to chat all day but look, boys"—he slapped his hands together and stood up— "I must borrow Will for a bit. Your business can wait, can't it?"

"Listen, I don't have time to joke—" Brandon began to speak, but Oliver stopped him with a raised hand.

"I'm as serious as a saint, I won't take no for an answer. In return I promise you a substantial round of drinks. I do need him, you understand."

Brandon just glared as Oliver took Will's hat off the rack, popped it on Will's head, and swiftly guided him out the door. Will went along, a little confused by Brandon's silence. From what he had been able to gather, everyone did Brandon's bidding, not the other way around.

Two minutes later they were in a taxi, where Will was still trying to work out how they had gotten away. Maybe Oliver's sudden appearance had taken Brandon by surprise, or perhaps Brandon had felt he did not have the authority to stop them, or maybe the man was a little wary of Oliver, which maybe made sense; Oliver might come across as a bit of a foolish dandy, but he did seem to know a lot of influential people.

"Well, that went well." Oliver straightened his cuff buttons. "Glad I found you, because, you see, the jazz boys rang me up. They finally tracked down the whereabouts of Ned, and they tell me she's not doing so hot. I promised I'd phone when we were on our way. You have any *jetons* on you?"

"No," said Will.

"Well, your place is only up ahead, right? I'll have the driver wait while we dash up and make the call."

Remembering that Zoya was probably still in his apartment, Will tried to avoid the awkward encounter. "Oh, I bet we could find a *tabac* and get some phone tokens there."

Oliver chuckled. "Don't be daft, we're only a block away from your building." He leaned forward and told the driver, *"Prenez une gauche et laissez-moi à côté du trottoir."*

IV

A dazed Noelle sat cross-legged on the hotel bed, watching Elga dig through the oversized canvas carpetbag. The old woman had been bustling about the room for over an hour, muttering phrases to herself and barely acknowledging the girl. From the bottom of the bag the old woman hauled out a large bundle wrapped in an old sheet. Inside was an exquisite-looking clock, which she set on the table; then she went back to searching the carpetbag. After a minute of rummaging, she pulled out a pistol.

"Look around carefully and weigh all things, weigh them right, like a butcher weighs meat," the old woman said, giving Noelle a raised eyebrow as she waved the pistol in the air. "Especially dumb toys like this. People think guns are important—ah, so much fear and lust over this chunk of steel, right? But like so much else, they are very wrong, guns are not important; they are stupid. But . . ." She held up her finger to make a point, then suddenly went back into her carpetbag, searching and digging until she came up with a box. "Bullets yes, bullets are important."

"What do you have a gun for? What do you shoot?" asked Noelle.

"Oh, I've shot lots of things. Mostly food, animals, some trouble-makers," said Elga. "The other day, I had to shoot a stupid pig to shut up his big pig mouth. I was careful, though, I only used one bullet, see?" She pulled at the loading gate on the gun, unslid the rod, and the chamber popped out. Noelle could see it was full of bullets except for one empty casing. Elga popped the empty casing out, took a bullet from the box, and refilled the chamber. "First, I walked into the man's store and put the gun right up to his head and pulled the trigger. No chance of missing there. Then, to be sure the idiot stayed quiet, I cut out his tongue."

"Ew, what did you do with it?"

"Mmmn, well, um, tongues are tender," said Elga. "They taste good in a nice meat stew." She chuckled, set the gun down on the bedside table, and went digging into the bag again.

Noelle knew she should be frightened or shocked, but instead she was numb to all these new surprises. She simply took them in. She had been sleeping for much of the last day, still exhausted from her baptism in the hotel bath. Each time she had awoken, the old woman had been sitting by her side, stroking her hair and rambling on with strange lessons. "Listen now, where other people see trees, you should see fire, and if they look up to the mountaintops, you watch their feet." And then: "Men are like lakes, broad, big, and easy to navigate; women are rivers, small, narrow, with deep, twisting currents." And then: "Reading is important, but all kinds. When we learned how to read words, we forgot how to read dirt." Sometime in the middle of the night, Noelle had awoken briefly to hear her still talking: "Remember, the earth is angry, it bristles with weapons. So don't be slow, seize them, rip them up from the soil, and shove them right into your enemy's throat." Noelle had fallen back to sleep and dreamt of being a ballerina standing at the barre again, practicing her demi- and grand-pliés until her blistered feet were soaked in blood. When she awoke it was still dark and the old woman was looking out the window muttering at the night sky. "They think by reaching the moon they will discover some big truth. Idiots. They go so far for what? For handfuls of dust. If you want the moon's secrets, ask a fish."

Noelle noticed that the rat came and went, disappearing for hours at a time through a small crack in the baseboard. Every time Max returned, Elga fed him some breadcrumbs. The final lesson she had said that day was: "You will find each time you use your power, it hurts. Like a giant fighter with big fists punching you. The pain is good, though, it feels like"—the old woman paused to search for the right word—". . . I do not know."

It was the next evening that Noelle learned her first spell. It was after room service had arrived and Elga had washed down a dozen escargots with a bottle of Riesling. After a long burp, she walked across the room and put the empty wineglass on the mantel. "There, see that?"

The girl nodded.

"Make it vanish."

Noelle looked at her, bewildered. "How?"

The old woman took a vial of pink-colored sand out of the pocket of her dress. "You clap some of this, and when you do, you tell it to go away."

"The glass can hear me?"

"How am I supposed to know what a glass hears?" Elga scoffed. "I'm not a glass, stupid. Just try."

The girl held open her hand and Elga poured the sand into her palm. Then Noelle stared at the wineglass for a moment, trying to concentrate on it. It seemed odd and impossible, but the old woman was insistent. Giving the glass as evil a glare as she could muster, Noelle clapped the dust together in her hands and shouted, *"Disappear!"*

It vanished. The mantel was bare. Noelle did not have time to be amazed before the nausea came up fast and she retched onto the rug. Elga sat down beside her and patted her leg. "Good, good. Don't worry about that," she said, nodding toward the vomit on the floor. "The maid will get it." Then Elga took the Riesling bottle again and went back over to the mantel. As she poured the wine, the glass reappeared.

Noelle looked confused. "So it was only a trick?"

"Did it feel like a trick to you?" said Elga, returning to the couch.

"No," said Noelle, rubbing her sore stomach.

"Then it wasn't a trick." Elga went over to the closet. "Tricks are for Gypsies. You know what one of the charlatan Gypsies' favorites is? They sneak a worm under their tongue, then they find someone sick and tell them, 'I can suck the illness out.' When they suck at the sick person's flesh—shoulder or arm, it doesn't matter—they pull that worm out of their mouth, show it to the sick person, and tell them that was the illness. The charlatan gets paid and the sick person dies."

She pulled out the rest of their bags. Her luggage looked ancient:

the carpetbag's canvas was faded and restitched; her other bag's leather was stained with mud and cracked wax streaks. Both were covered in a hundred scars and scuffs as though they had been kicked across the entire continent. Beside them, Noelle's unsullied new suitcase gleamed as white as an egg.

"I am so sleepy. I don't understand anything you're saying," said Noelle, crawling up onto the bed and curling herself around a pillow.

"I'm telling you, don't trust the Gypsies, don't trust anyone. That's what I'm saying. Bah. It doesn't matter, sleep if you want," said the old woman. "But Max will be here soon and then we have to go."

"Go where?" asked Noelle, sitting up. "Are we leaving?"

"No," said Elga. "But we'll pack the camp up in case we need to leave in a hurry."

"Where are we going?"

Elga gave the girl an impatient glance, clearly tired of her questions. "Well, first we have to find you a damn chicken," Elga said, emptying the bureau of clothes.

"Are we eating chicken?"

Elga stopped and gave her a frustrated look. "What are you, some comedian? No, we won't be eating the chicken."

Noelle pointed to the gun on the bedside table. "Are we going to kill it?"

"Oh no; well, yes, eh, we are going to do a little killing." Elga looked at the pistol for a moment, thinking it over. "But I don't think I need that stupid gun."

V

She lay in Will's bed for a long time, contemplating staying there all day, not ready to rise and go through the motions again. Her muscles and bones were tired and sore from their passionate exertions, and she was not sure if she was strong enough for all the spells. Also, she was tempted to see if she could do it without tricks, perhaps this time the simple bond of affection could work? The thought was hardly new, she had often been tempted, and even tried it from time to time before the doubts struck and she found herself once again lacing her lovers' chicory coffee with nutmeg hallucinations and spitting spells into the pages of their Bibles.

But there was some element of what she and Will had both shared, and the way they were together, that made her wonder if this was not different. She had liked the way his hands had held her, pushing and pulling her body. There was reassurance in such strong, demanding need. She had liked the rhythm they had found, steady and forceful without feeling in any way automatic. She liked too the way his eyes moved over her body as they made love, not staring or overly attentive—which some men were out of their pure wonder at the luck of being with her. Nor did he make love with his eyes shut tight—which she had always found insulting—but instead it felt as if they were two animals running wild through some thick, shadowy wilderness, repeatedly catching each other's glances as they raced on, always reassured to find they were still so close together.

Amid all this, she sensed the seeds of a pure bond with him that she knew her many tricks would only taint and dilute. But the heavy rhythms of history called to her as she lay on the bed, tugging at her the same way she imagined the past pulled at opium addicts and alcoholics. No matter what the scientists say, heartbeats and appetites show that we are made as much of habit as either blood or flesh, she thought to herself as she rose from the bed and began to retrace the practiced patterns of old.

She began by pacing out the perimeter of the apartment, thoughtfully plotting all her careful geomancy. Then she sang knots of simple spells into the apartment's corners. She hummed and chewed on strands of his hair pulled from a hairbrush and then opened a tea bag and sprinkled the dry leaves on a pair of old family photos she found in the desk. After letting them soak up the image, she collected the leaves and steeped them in hot water with mustard seeds and drank it down. Afterward she opened the kitchen window and stood over the sink, burning three fifty-franc notes. She heavily doused the ashes with black pepper and sang the old backward songs as she washed it all down the sink. Squatting, she urinated in the doorway to the bedroom, then sprinkled white flour across it. It left an ochre paste that she scrubbed into the floorboards while she sang some more. She wrote out a pair of small, crooked blessings—the first she wrapped between the tines of a dinner fork and hid it in the recesses of Will's sock drawer, and the other she slipped into the inner band of a gray fedora that hung by the door. She pricked her finger with a pin and squeezed a drop of blood out, which she meticulously dabbed above the bathroom mirror. Sitting at his desk, she sketched a primitive drawing of Will surrounded by abstract oval shapes and, folding it up, tucked it into the back of a picture frame. She placed a complete suit of his clothes out on the bed and, lying naked on top of them, brought herself to another sexual climax. Then she hung the clothes up again, chanting softly as she set them neatly back into his closet. After that, she napped, exhausted from her exercises, rising a little over an hour later to shower and dress.

She was combing her hair when she heard the key in the lock. She didn't know if Will would be happy or upset to find her still in his home, but she knew much of their new relationship would be defined by whatever expression he wore when he found her there. It was the moment of first return, a critical test in any union. She tried to fix a simple look on her face, nothing too intense, no needs or expectations embossed on her gaze, only the sort of simple, friendly expression you'd like to see as you walk through your door, a smile that only says, "I am yours."

What she saw was Oliver.

"Oh, hullo," the tall man said, briefly pausing for a double take. Will came in behind him, taking the key out of the door.

"Hello, Oliver. Hello, Will," she said with a small but friendly smile.

Clearly embarrassed, Will looked beet red. She could tell Oliver had invited himself over and that Will was awkward and uncomfortable. But then Will made a gesture that surprised her. Striding over in a couple of steps, he gave her a warm hug and kissed her forehead. It was only a moment, but like every embrace, it told a story, and this was a most surprising one. It said he was glad to have her there, he had missed her, and he was sincere and even devoted. She had not expected him to be that strong, or even that clear. Perhaps he was not such a lost rabbit after all.

Then he stepped back and blushed again, grinning. She watched

Oliver observe it all, a slightly bemused smile crossing his own lips as his head cocked slightly to the side. He understood. It was decided. Theirs was not the bourgeois romantic triangle that the modern cinephiles might expect. It was a much simpler thing: she had been with Oliver and now she was with Will. The small wordless gestures, Will's touch, holding one another, had made it all apparent to the three of them in the room within seconds.

"Well, then," said Oliver, raising an eyebrow as he glanced around the apartment, "where is your telephone hiding? Oh yes, I remember. Excuse me for a moment." He strode over to the desk phone and dialed a number. "*Salut, je suis bien à l'Arc? Je suis à la recherche d'un homme noir qui porte un costume bleu et est assis dans votre hall. Oui, pouvez vous me le passer* . . . Hullo, Red, it's Oliver. I picked up Will. We're headed over now . . . I understand. Thanks. How is she? Any better? . . . Oh dear. Well, maybe see if you can coax anything coherent out of her. Very curious what she has to say . . . Yes, I'm sure you're doing all you can. All right, then, we'll be at the hotel in ten or fifteen minutes. Thank you." Then he hung up. "We should get there soon, but first I need a moment," he said, leaving Will and Zoya alone.

Will shook his head, embarrassed. "I'm so sorry, he wanted to make a phone call and I thought you might be gone."

She kissed his cheek. "It's fine, he doesn't care. Oliver is one of those modern men, you know, he's used to passing women around like candies at a party."

He pulled her close. "I'm not like that."

"Really?" She smiled and kissed him again.

The toilet flushed and Oliver came striding back into the room. "Will," he said, "before we go, I suggest you use your washroom here, they've got one where we're headed but it will make your flesh crawl."

"No thanks, I'm fine," Will said. Zoya suspected Oliver was trying to create a moment alone with her, which she was happy to avoid. Jealousy could be declawed and defanged with simple tricks, though she suspected Oliver only wanted some token acknowledgment that despite her moving on, their exchange had not been completely superficial. She found even the most cavalier sorts still hated to let things pass completely unspoken. Everyone wanted to put a meaning to things.

"Okay, then let's be off. The cab should still be out front. I'll go make sure. Zoya, what a nice surprise to see you. Amazing and wonderful." Oliver kissed her on the cheek and left, clearly in a hurry.

Zoya took Will by the lapels of his jacket and kissed him hard. "Why don't you come to my apartment tonight, whenever you finish with him."

"I don't know how long we'll be, last time I went off with Oliver, I was gone all day."

"Later is probably better, right?" She smiled. "Come by anytime; if it's after dinner I'll give you dessert."

"Okay, after dinner, then." He grinned and kissed her.

She scribbled down the address and slid it across the table. She felt bad playing this trick on him, she could sense it was unnecessary. But again ancient habits drove her to a well-practiced routine, for whenever circumstances allowed it, she liked to have new lovers stay in her bed for one night. When they saw the sad conditions she lived in, generally shabby, run-down lodgings in unsavory quarters, the men's protective impulses took over and they pulled her in closer to their lives. She remembered how poor Leon had spent less than an hour in the squalid hovel she had behind the park stables before announcing that he would lease her that apartment in the 5th.

She felt a little guilty watching Will fold up her address and tuck it into his wallet. She was still tempted to stop him, to hold back the spells and let things unfold naturally, if only to see where they would go, but she knew it was too late for that and so she bit her tongue, staying silent as he took his gray hat off the hook, kissed her cheek, and went out the door.

Once she was alone, Zoya caught her breath. The work was done. There was no room for romantic sentiment, she reminded herself, it was only about survival. But the feeling that she had committed some unseen error nagged at her, for the emotions she held for her rabbit were becoming quite real and substantial; small lightning sparks jolted about in her blood at the simple thought of him. This wasn't good. She sniffed the air, and all she smelled was trouble.

VI

Riding along in the taxi, Oliver was already focused on other things. "Do you know anything about dementia?"

"Not much." Will shrugged, relieved that they wouldn't be talking about Zoya.

"As you'll recall, I asked Ned's friends, the jazz boys, to keep an eye out for her. Well, they found her, or rather the hotel owner did and called them up. Apparently Ned was discovered lying in the common bathtub at the end of the hallway talking incoherent gibberish. The woman said she is sounding completely bonkers. Ned, I mean, not the hotel owner. Actually, the whole thing is a bit loony. First Boris and now this, well, one doesn't need to be paranoid . . ."

As the cab took them over the river and they headed up toward the Latin Quarter, Will tried to recall all that had happened over the past week. If these really were the last days he would spend in France, it was quite a way to go. Paris had always provided more than he could hope for: from afternoons spent walking in the Parc Monceau to evenings with hot beef bourguignon to nights with curvaceous brunettes taking off their cotton slips in his apartment, the city had given generously. Now, though, he was experiencing bewildering new dimensions of life here, far beyond anything he had ever imagined.

He had read somewhere about how reporters during the wars grew addicted to the intense, chaotic drama inherent to battle and once peacetime arrived these journalists slowly lost their minds amid the quiet and solitude, eventually throwing themselves out of windows in the capital cities where they'd been covering various slothful legislatures with their various voluminous farm bills. Will wondered if, once he returned to America, life in those quiet suburbs of Detroit might drive him mad too. After all, once you've raced through the streets of Paris rushing from a sweet, sexy Russian valentine to a delirious lesbian double agent, backyard barbecues might lose their charm.

A block off the river, they pulled up in front of the hotel, a run-down-looking four-story building. There was no sign. "This is the Arc Hotel?"

"Afraid so," said Oliver, handing the cabbie some francs.

Inside the small lobby, they found Red waiting. The musician filled them in as he led them up the stairs. "She has been going non-stop like a broken record. I thought one of the jokers staying here might have slipped her something, but the lady says Ned only came in yesterday and didn't talk with any of her neighbors." Red pushed open the door to the small hotel room. "Take a look."

Inside, the small woman lay on the bed, curled up tightly in the fetal position, her eyes wide open. Flats was sitting beside her, holding her hand. The only sound in the room was her rattling on in a raspy voice, the words barely discernible. Flats got up and Oliver gingerly sat down on the edge of the bed and, leaning over, put his ear to her mouth.

For the next fifteen minutes, none of the men said a word as Oliver sat listening. Other than Ned's noises, the room was as quiet as a Quaker meeting. Finally, Oliver sat up, shaking his head. "I don't know why, but I had imagined she would be more lucid."

"She was talking better earlier, clearer anyway, though it still didn't make any sense," said Flats. "It's probably worse 'cause she's tired now. It's like she's stuck under some spooky spell."

"No need to be superstitious," said Oliver, getting up. "There's always a logical explanation." He began poking around the room, opening the bureau drawers and digging into her pockets. In her small black purse he found some business cards. Will noticed him discreetly tuck one into his vest. "Has a doctor been called?"

"We were waiting for you."

"Why was that?" asked Oliver.

"Well, if the doctor came and took her away we felt there was a solid possibility you wouldn't pay us what you promised."

Oliver grinned, took out his wallet, and started counting out bills. "My, my, Red. I'm sorry you ever doubted my word. I thought we were friends."

"Yes," Red said, taking the cash. "You are my friend, Oliver, that is true fact. A hundred percent. But that is only one thing you are. And I was raised never to trust white people, and never to trust rich people, which is another two things you happen to be."

"Oh, you overestimate me." Oliver smiled. "But I suppose you do make some sort of anthropological sense." He looked at the woman lying on the bed. "In any case, there's probably no harm done. She seems beyond any doctor's abilities. Maybe a shot of adrenaline would wake her up. Any idea where we could find some?"

The black men shook their heads. Oliver got out his fountain pen and wrote an address down. "Okay, well, let's try this. Since all our accounts are now squared, ask the manager to let you use the phone and call this number for an ambulance. Ask for Jerry, he can take her to the American Hospital over in Neuilly."

Oliver gave Ned's curled-up body a pat, then put on his hat and headed out the door. Trailing down the stairs after Oliver, Will suddenly felt like a young, earnest Dr. Watson scrambling behind a distracted Sherlock Holmes. Will had loved those detective stories as a boy, but he realized there was one significant difference: Holmes's cases always involved a single mystery that he plucked apart with logic, grace, and wit, whereas Oliver never solved anything, each riddle only perpetuating deeper ones, which he clumsily fumbled at until they all came down on both their heads like piles of hatboxes tumbling off some great armoire. It was annoying.

As he reached the street, he saw Oliver striding fast down the block, past the busy sidewalk cafés and bars. Will ran to catch up.

"What's the hurry?" asked Will.

"I have an appointment."

"An appointment?"

"Well, a date actually."

"Really?" Will was confused, there was still so much to sort out. "But—"

Oliver spun around sharply. "But *what*? You thought perhaps I'd be too lovesick pining for your precious Zoya? Really? Don't get me wrong, she is a fine catch, easy on the eyes and exotically skilled in ways you've no doubt discovered by now. But, no, I wasn't planning to mope about like some kind of sad Leporello to your lascivious Don Giovanni. Believe me, I have infinitely better ways to occupy my time."

"No, that's not what I meant at all," said Will, slightly taken aback.

"I was only thinking maybe we should sit down somewhere and talk about Ned. And Boris. And that file the Russian embassy has. And my knife. There's a whole host of problems we have to sort out, Oliver. Especially since Brandon and his boys are not going to go away."

"Oh yes," Oliver said, quickly softening his tone. "I apologize. Don't worry, we'll attend to all that tomorrow, first thing. I can't do it now, I've got to attend to my other responsibility, that poor, long-suffering little journal of mine."

"I thought you just said you were going on a date?"

"Not a very romantic one. The woman has both the thickest ankles and the most equine features you've ever seen, but she does know a few writers I need to meet. I'd put it off if I could, but I can't. Come by my place first thing tomorrow. I have a few notions on our case that I think will interest you."

Will shook his head. "I can't come by tomorrow, I've been out of the office too much."

"Well, then, we'll find some opportunity to catch up over the next few days, and in the meantime I'll do some poking around on my own. For now you'll have to excuse me. I would offer to share a cab, but I'm sure we're going in very different directions."

With that, Oliver gave him a small smile, jumped into a taxi and was off, leaving Will once again bobbing in his wake. This pattern was growing absurd. Will looked at his watch. He had told Zoya he would come after dinner, and it didn't seem right to show up early. So, feeling a bit stranded, he wandered down to rue Monge and found a bistro where he ate a pile of moules marinières and drank a half carafe.

Afterward he hailed a taxi and gave the driver Zoya's address. As the cab took him toward Pigalle, Will thought about Oliver's last little outburst. It had only been a quick flash, but Oliver had seemed honestly hurt, angry, and almost human there for a moment. Will smiled to himself, it had been a refreshing sight.

When the cab finally pulled up in front of Zoya's building, Will was a little taken aback. The hotel made Ned's seedy Arc Hotel seem luxurious by comparison. He walked in and saw the clerk fast asleep at the front desk. Will looked down to double-check the address written there and found the room number, 5A. The elevator was out of order so he took the stairs. A little winded by the time he reached the top, he paused and looked down the hall. The door to 5A was slightly ajar. Inside he could see flickering sparks of light. Feeling a little cautious, he walked down the hallway, gently pushed open the door, and ran into a tremendous amount of electricity.

VII

Witches' Song Six

Ah, you wonder what we've been busy with,
how we're poised now?
Oh where, amid all the whirling, weaving,
and dark conniving of these impatient players,
we have cast our cursing lots?
I know, it is hard to find us, to be sure,
for while they flail and fly, we simply lie
like grubs beneath the soil,
brooding on our certain purpose.

VIII

Vidot was quite pleased with his perch. Elga had tucked Max the rat into the space between her sweater and blouse, resting him in her shirt pocket. Vidot had crawled up from the rat's belly and now stood high atop Max's skull. He felt like a Persian satrap riding atop a great elephant. The top of Max's head sticking out from Elga's hefty bosom gave Vidot an almost unobstructed view of the street ahead as they walked.

Vidot had been especially happy to leave the rat's belly. Though it had felt warm and safe, he wanted to see what Elga was up to. Also, his belly ride had grown uncomfortable when another flea had crawled up beside him. This flea had not actually acknowledged Vidot's presence, but it was the first that had dared to emerge from hiding, and it irked Vidot that he had become vermin enough to no longer frighten all the other vermin with his strange ways. He did not want to fit in with these creatures. Perhaps this flea also bothered him because his presence reminded him of his long-lost companion Bemm. He knew, however, that this was not the flea's fault, and Vidot bore him no ill will. In fact, though he did not like being near him, observing this flea's simple, focused manner did impress him. The creature reminded him of a monk in repose, only taking what he needed from the world. While human beings battled one another for iron, oil, and gold, this simple flea asked for no more than a soft bit of flesh to ride on and a bit of warm blood to drink. As far as the flea was concerned, the bare rat's belly was a land of plenty. Were it not for the many pleasures he missed of cheese and wine and afternoons at the orchestra, Vidot realized he might be happy to remain there as well. But the thought of the joys he would have to give up were too great. He had to fight on. The taste of a good sausage alone was worth the struggle, not to mention the pleasures of a nice fat novel and the kiss of his sweet wife. He winced at the last thought, and scolded himself for allowing his memory to trick him into forgetting her betrayal. Vidot vowed he would get her back, he would win her heart again, he knew it was possible, it was merely another devilish puzzle to be solved. First, though, he had to stay with this Elga and watch her every move. Sooner or later an answer would show itself.

The old woman's voice broke him out of his thoughts. She was talking to the young girl, who was now holding a live russet-colored chicken.

"Why did we get the chicken?" asked the girl.

"Because you dreamt of the chicken."

"I also dreamt about a fox," said the girl. "It would be fun to have a pet fox."

"No it wouldn't," said Elga. They had arrived at the car, which Vidot immediately recognized as his own police car. He could not imagine why the people passing by didn't notice an old crone getting into a squad car with a little girl. Then again, he thought, there was a time not so long ago when he could not imagine being turned into a flea.

"Does everyone dream of chickens?" asked the little girl.

"No. Sometimes they dream of snakes, or deer, owls, otters, beavers, marmots, maybe moles. Reindeer, rats, lots of rats, mules, horses. Never dogs, never wolves, and I've never heard of foxes showing up before."

"What do you think it means?"

"I don't know. I hope nothing." They were in the car now, driving through the streets. Elga had the windows rolled down and Vidot noticed that Max was keeping himself busy. The rat would look and sniff constantly, systematically reaching up with his little paw every now and again to tap Elga's chest. If he tapped her on her left breast they turned left, if it was on her right breast, she turned right.

The little girl kept going with her questions. "Are there any bad things to dream about?"

"It's bad if you dream of dragons."

"Why's that?"

"Because all the dragons are dead. So they're no help to you. Whales are tricky too, they are never there when you need them. If you dream about whales or seals, you are going to have a very wet, cold time of it."

The car stopped and the rat scurried up over Elga's shoulder and jumped out the open window. Vidot held on tight, and as they landed he tried quickly to decipher where they were. Peeking out from behind the rat's ear, he saw neons brightly blinking and flashing above restaurants, cigarette shops, and nightclubs. Maybe in Pigalle? The rat scurried up a doorstep and sped across the faded parquet floor of the bright lobby before stopping in the shadow of a moldy-smelling chaise longue. Apparently they were waiting for the others. Eventually, Elga and the girl came up, the old woman carrying a beat-up canvas bag, the girl clutching her chicken. Vidot watched the old woman pause at the front door and trace out an imaginary line around the doorframe, muttering a few words before they entered. Vidot looked over at the clerk sitting at his station reading a hunting magazine. The man seemed oblivious to their presence. She must have cast another spell, he realized, so that they could pass unnoticed. She had made them all, in essence, invisible. Vidot wondered if this might provide him with some tactical potential, but then he realized that, for all intents and purposes, his size already made him unnoticeable, even to the rat he was riding on.

Distracted with these thoughts, Vidot lost count of the floors as they climbed up the stairs and did not notice which floor they were on when they finally started down a hallway, the sniffing rat leading the way until he stopped at a door. The old woman leaned forward and ran her fingers along the edge of the frame as she carefully inspected the door from top to bottom, sniffing now like a shopper suspicious of cheese. Finally, she pulled a white envelope from her pocket. She poured out a handful of a brown substance and, crouching down, blew it beneath the doorsill. Vidot could smell it, cinnamon. He couldn't imagine how that spice could possibly help Elga and his brain was feeling sorely taxed from trying to make sense of so many irrational events. He decided it was time to stop swimming against the currents of all these nonsensical details and simply ride along in this wild and fantastical flood.

The old woman was now stooped on her knees in the hallway, picking the lock with a hairpin. The noise of a door opening down the hall made Vidot look up and he observed a small, balding man emerging from the neighboring room. Vidot felt his tiny heart skip a beat, certain that they would be discovered. He was not sure why he was nervous—he was, after all, the most insignificant player in this caper—yet when the neighbor walked past without a second look, Vidot exhaled with relief. He had to respect the audacity of this old woman, so confident in her camouflage that she had not even looked up from her work as the stranger passed by. The lock clicked and the door creaked open. "You go in first," the woman said to the girl.

"Me? Why?" asked Noelle, clutching her chicken close to her chest.

"Because you are innocent. Now go. This is the last time this trick will work for you," she said and pushed the girl forward. Elga and the rat followed.

Vidot watched as Elga quickly took charge of the situation. First, she took the kitchen chair and stood it in the center of the floor, facing the door. "You sit there, so you are the first thing she sees. When she comes in, you start saying these two words, 'knife light,' over and over, like a chant."

The girl sat hesitantly down on the chair. "Why 'knife light'?"

"Why, why why? Why does your finger fit so perfectly in your nose? To get the buggers out. Do not ask so many stupid questions.

Do what I say, repeat it over and over, no matter what happens, no matter what occurs. There may be smoke, fire, blood, I don't know. But do not be scared, do not let yourself be distracted, repeat it over and over again. Got it?"

"I think so," said the girl.

"Good." Next the woman took a piece of chalk out and went to the door. With her elbow she erased some chalk marks written there and in their place she scrawled a new hieroglyphic. "If you do this well, we will go buy you a new winter coat. Maybe one with a fur collar. You would like that, yes?"

The girl's eyes grew big. "Yes, I would."

"Right. So be good. Remember, 'knife light, knife light, knife light.' Repeat it like that." Elga went to unpack her case. From its depths she brought out the clock. How had she gotten her hands on that? He recalled that day so clearly, finding Bemm on his way to the station, meeting with the shopkeeper in his storeroom, watching from the pharmacy as she dropped the clock off and then following the woman home. Yes, he thought, Elga must have gone back to the shop. He did not like to think about how she got the owner to hand the clock over. It was a sobering realization, reminding him that he could not let his habitual bemusement distract him from the fact that this woman was perhaps the greatest single evil the city had seen since the mass murderer Petiot preyed on his victims. Vidot squinted his small insect eyes at her and waited for what was to come next.

For the next hour he watched as Elga took a small screwdriver and systematically dismantled the ancient clock, meticulously removing its escapement from the frame, then carefully disassembling the springs and hands and all the other mechanical features until finally a hundred or so pieces were spread around her on the rough wooden floor, as if she were the center of some marvelously ordered brass universe.

After that, nothing happened. Elga set herself down in the middle of this vast circle of parts and remained seated there, completely quiet. The girl called Noelle seemed apprehensive, watching the door nervously, waiting for it to open so that she could begin repeating her mysterious phrase. Even the chicken was silent. They all sat there, the old woman, the young girl, the chicken, the rat, and the flea, surrounded by the discrete metal pieces of a deconstructed clock. Propped up on top of the rat's head, with an unobstructed view of the still and silent hotel room, Vidot could not help feeling as though time itself had stopped.

IX

Zoya walked up from the metro to her hotel. It was too warm. Over the years she had become accustomed to most things being within her control, but the weather was always mysterious. She had heard of women who could make it hail or draw thunder, but despite many attempts, those spells had always eluded her, the same way that some children cannot master the violin or a foreign language.

She entered the lobby and went to check in with the desk clerk. It was a different man from the one she had met when she had first moved in. This one was a thin man with yellowed skin who always seemed a little worried.

"I'd like to know if I have had any visitors or mail," she said.

"No, mademoiselle, none, but there is a note here saying that you are late with your rent."

She nodded. Then she started whispering. Confused, he leaned in close to try to understand what she was saying and then she reached out and softly touched his clean-shaven cheek. Immediately he fell fast asleep. She laid his head down on the counter and whispered some more, feeding his dreams and confusing them with reality. With that, she had paid the rent.

As she walked up the stairs she got her key out. Later she would remember the scent of cinnamon, but at the time it had barely registered. She was distracted, worried that the owls might not have left any pellets, and wondering if Max had found her yet.

Upon entering the apartment, she noticed the girl first, seated there, holding a red chicken in her arms. It was a confusing sight and she dropped her guard for a moment. It wasn't until the girl started chanting that Zoya realized it was too late. "Knife light, knife light, knife light . . ." Zoya turned to flee, but the door slammed in her face. Then she heard a familiar voice speaking to her in Russian.

"You cannot leave," said Elga.

"Knife light, knife light, knife light . . ."

Zoya looked back and saw the old woman sitting on the floor, surrounded by small pieces of metal. It was a curious sight, even for someone as odd as Elga. "Why are you here?"

"Because Max said you would be here," said the old woman.

"Knife light, knife light, knife light . . ."

"But, Elga, why did you want to come find me?"

"Because," said the old woman, "you betrayed me. You sent the police to my house."

Zoya shook her head. "I did not."

"Knife light, knife light, knife light . . ."

The old woman shrugged. "So you say. You lie a lot. But it does not matter. I have reached my decision. I brought you in, I can take you out, and it is time for you to go."

"To go." Zoya nodded. "You mean to die?"

The old woman did not answer.

Zoya started trying to think, but no ideas were coming to her. She knew without even trying that the little girl's chant was a trick that kept her from employing her own. "I see, yes, every journey has an end and this has certainly been a long journey. So"—she put her hands on her hips, trying to look resigned—"how would you like me to die?"

Elga grinned her old wicked grin. "I am going to feed you this clock."

"Knife light, knife light, knife light . . ."

Zoya knew her options were very limited. Elga would have thought of as many angles as she could come up with herself. Zoya felt like a bug crawling across the dusty floor and her two uninvited guests were the curious chickens about to peck her to death. There was a movement in the far corner and she looked across and saw the rat sitting there, watching. Ah, yes, she thought, my old friend Max. Maybe he can help. She looked at the old woman. "If you would let me smoke some pellets, I could go out in a dream. That would be kind, Elga."

The old woman shook her head. "No, that won't work, I don't know where you go in a dream."

"Knife light, knife light, knife light . . ."

Babayaga

Zoya wanted to smash that chanting child's face. "I see. Then, perhaps I can have one last glass of water?"

The old woman studied her for a moment, weighing this indulgence. Zoya knew that Elga was not, by nature, merciful. But they had crisscrossed the borders of countless countries in the span of more than two centuries. They had ridden in private locomotive cars to aid in the looting of conquered cities, and they had trailed dying asses in retreating caravans, trudging past corpses through snowbound passes. There had been exotic palaces, expansive suites, and countless garbage pits where they were forced to dig for mildewed scraps of sustenance. They had been through enough together that she was sure she should be granted this small, last request.

But she wasn't certain, for who could comprehend what went on in Elga's mind? Zoya had no idea what madness was driving the old woman to this bloody deed now. Zoya suspected that it was the accumulation of all the many ages, now balled up like sewage debris jammed in a dam's drain. But it really did not matter. What mattered was getting to the kitchen. What mattered was Elga's answer.

"Knife light, knife light, knife light . . ."

"Fine," the old woman grunted, warily watching Zoya for a trick, but still confident, like a knowing spider eyeing the struggling fly stuck in her web, "you can have some water."

"Thank you, Elga." She got up and walked over to the kitchenette. The rat was her only option. Elga and the girl were steeled with charms, ready to withstand her attacks. But if she could find a way to break their concentration and distract them from the spell . . . "You know, on the metro tonight I was thinking about those saltpeter collectors back in Kiev, the two who came to dig out the cellar." Her eyes desperately scanned the counter and the shelves. There it was, an answer to her prayers: the cleaver was lying on the drying rack, right next to the glasses. It could not have been better placed. "Do you remember them? They were a funny pair: one was a dwarf, the other was so tall he had to duck to get in the doorway . . ."

In one complete and dexterous motion, she spun, releasing her left hand full of nothing toward the girl on the chair and, following that feint in perfect succession, she grabbed the cleaver, spun, and released a whirl of steel across the room, splitting Max's skull right between the eyes, spattering the rat's blood and brains against the wall.

"*Knife—*"

At the sight of the rodent's sudden explosion, the young girl screamed. Zoya hissed and held out her hand, sending a concussion of air toward the child that knocked her into the doorframe. Elga was hissing now too, with the loud sound of a fat steam pipe bursting, and Zoya ducked to escape the condensed balls of electricity coming at her. Two windowpanes shattered, spraying glass everywhere. She saw Elga pinching her fingers together. Zoya grabbed the cutting board off the counter, holding it up to block the shocks. The lightning blasted the board to smoking splinters. Knowing what was coming next, Zoya quickly looked for another shield. If she rolled she could duck behind the girl, now curled up in a screaming ball of panic with her hands over her ears. But Zoya had no doubt that Elga would take them both out, the little girl was a small price to pay. There was no defense in sight. The old woman's face was drained of all color, her eyes bloodshot and bulging, her hair shot out frazzled and wild from her skull, the final spell forming on her lips, when, for a fraction of a second, she paused, looking over as the front door creaked and a curious Will poked his head in.

"Hello? What the—?"

His entrance had distracted Elga long enough for Zoya to leap across the floor, landing hard on the old woman's body. Without the slightest pause she immediately began striking the old woman's face with her fists. After less than a minute of this, Will pulled her off.

"We have to go!" said Zoya, stumbling to her feet.

Will looked around, taking in the bloodied rat with a meat cleaver solidly wedged in its skull, the small child balled up and crying in the corner, the unconscious, battered old woman sprawled out, nearly dead, before them, and the chicken pecking at smoky wood scraps that covered the floor. "There is a reasonable explanation for all this, right?" he said.

"No," a nearly unconscious and reeling Zoya said, grabbing his hand with the last of her strength and pulling him out of the apartment.

X

As soon as they were in a taxi Zoya grabbed him and held him close. She was whispering some indecipherable words into his ear and, kissing his cheek, then whispered some more. Eventually, she stopped and lay down on his lap. She rubbed his cock through his pants and gave him a sleepy smile and then shut her eyes. He let her rest. It had been a crazy night. Already her whispered spells were making the memory of the fight and the old woman and the little girl fade from his mind, the spectacular becoming clouded out by the ordinary. What did they do tonight? Had they seen a movie?

The taxi sped along rue de Rome. Will looked down at his lover's face. Even with the deep, sunken circles under her eyes she was unimaginably beautiful to him. He took her hand in his; it was ice cold. He remembered how his mother would complain about her cold hands throughout Detroit's long, mean winters and how she would soak them in a sink filled with hot water at the end of each day. For some reason, that memory reminded him of the time when he was first living in Chicago, right out of college. He had a client who worked in the fashion industry selling chiffon ladies' gloves to department stores, and one day, over a long lunch, they arrived at a discussion about how women were always complaining about the coldness of their extremities. Will remembered arguing that evolution must have centered the blood in the middle of a woman's body, there where the warm womb and waiting eggs lay, nature's primary interest being in protecting whatever came next as opposed to ensuring the comfort and happiness of what existed now. The client, a flat-nosed former pugilist from the South Side who only worked in fashion because his mother had founded the company, insisted that nature had designed women's hands with poor circulation to keep them weak and unable to fight off the men who wanted to seize them, assault them, and, as the client bluntly put it, "pump them full of their dark demon seed." They were both cynical theories, the second one especially brutal. Looking out the taxi window, Will wondered how many human truths were that horrible.

As the shuttered Parisian storefronts sped by, his thoughts returned to the day, such a carnival of unexpected scenes, the course of events skidding beyond the realm of his reasoning, and in the end it was pretty hard to recall all the details (what movie had they seen?). The one thing he did remember was that he had begun that morning waking up next to Zoya for the very first time. He clearly remembered kissing her sleeping cheek as he had departed for work. He thought about the feeling that had hummed about in his bones as he had walked to the office that morning, as if the arrangement of spinning molecules that defined his body had momentarily unbonded and, in some harmonious anatomic Busby Berkeley choreography, magnetically rearranged themselves into some new, minutely heavier, more substantial element, literally harmonizing him with the universe. Perhaps that was what love really was. Maybe that was why it felt so real, because, like the ultraviolet light or the mysterious, invisible radiation waves vibrating in the air, love actually existed. But only in small and undetectable quantities, impossible to synthetically mimic, composed of only the most thin, fragile actuality that would absolutely vanish if you tried to contain, catch, or even observe it, like those awkward and inscrutable physics conundrums he had never been able to comprehend in his *Popular Science* magazines. If that's what love is, decided Will, then he now possessed it. He rubbed Zoya's hands, hoping to give them some warmth.

His thoughts suddenly stopped meandering as the car turned the corner and he saw, down his block, a dark figure step into the light for a moment before disappearing back into the shadows. *"Continuez dans cette rue,"* he told the cabbie. *"N'arrêtez pas."* The driver nodded in the rearview mirror. As they passed by the spot where he had seen the man, Will peered into the darkness. There, thought Will, was Brandon's boy, Mike Mitchell, hanging on the edge of a courtyard doorway, sheltered from the light, dutifully awaiting Will's arrival. Will looked out the rear window of the cab up into his apartment, where he spotted a light on. Mitchell's partner, White, was probably waiting there, maybe with Brandon. They must have gotten impatient with Will's stalling, done a bit of arithmetic together, and were now searching his place. Either that or they were waiting to ask some very pointed questions.

Will thought quickly, racking his brains about what he could do. He had no leverage, no answers, and he didn't have any connections to call who could get Brandon and his goons off his back. He realized there was only one person he knew who could manage his way past Brandon. Reluctantly, he gave the cabdriver Oliver's address.

Ten minutes later Will was holding up a sagging Zoya and ringing the doorbell.

"Hullo?" said a sleepy voice.

"Sorry to disturb you, Oliver. It's me, Will. I'm afraid I need a little help. I have a—"

The buzzer cut him off midsentence and he took Zoya inside. Fortunately the elevator was working, so he dragged her in, pulled the metal gate across tight, and pushed the button for the third floor. When they arrived, Oliver was standing at the open door, wearing a blue bathrobe. When he saw Zoya, his face dropped. "My lord, what happened to her?"

"Long story," said Will. "I was going to take her to my place but Brandon's people have it staked out. One of them was watching the door, and I think the other was upstairs, probably tossing the place."

"Tossing it? What do you mean exactly?"

"You know, looking around, searching it. Or waiting for me to come back so they could grill me. Either way, I didn't want to stick around. Here, help me get her inside." Together the two of them carried her into the apartment and into the guest room.

"Of course you're welcome to spend the night; it's actually timely that you're here," said Oliver, pulling a stack of clean towels and linens out of a closet and throwing them on the bed.

"Why's that?" said Will.

"I'm going to need your assistance with an errand tomorrow. I'd like to say it won't take long, but honestly I don't know."

"That's fine"—Will shrugged—"I can't go to work anyway. Brandon is going to have his goons waiting there too."

Oliver nodded. "Precisely. Besides, I believe you're going to find our errand to be an interesting one. Now, I'd offer you a nightcap but I'm afraid I have to attend to my other guest."

"Your other—?"

Oliver smiled. "Sweet dreams," he said, heading for the door. Then he stopped and paused. "You know, it's funny that they only went to your place. After all, they did see you with me. Perhaps they'll come sniffing round here in the morning."

Will was amused that Oliver seemed to be feeling left out of things. "They're probably afraid of you, you can be quite intimidating. Plus, you're connected."

Oliver nodded. "Probably."

"But thanks for helping. I really had no place else to turn."

Oliver patted him on the back. "Of course, my friend. We're a bit like Harlequin and Pierrot, aren't we?"

"I guess," said Will, with no clue who Oliver was referencing and too sleepy to care.

A few moments later Zoya lay soundly sleeping beside Will in the undersized guest bed as he listened to the sounds from the next room. There were faint whisperings accented occasionally by a woman's cooing laughter. Will recognized the voice: it was Oliver's British assistant, Gwen. No wonder she had seemed to dislike Zoya that first morning they met; Oliver was sleeping with her too. When the voices finally died down and the creaking of the bedsprings started, Will switched off his light. That Oliver, he thought, what a cad.

XI

Back in the battle, perched on Max's forehead, the flea's moment of decision had come fast. Distracted by the brunette's feint, he had glanced over to see what had been thrown at the little girl when the flash of the silver blade caught his eye. The rat, too, had clearly fallen for the same sleight of hand and was looking completely the wrong way as the cleaver came straight at them. Vidot felt Max tense as he recognized his fatal error. Vidot leapt to freedom, knowing there was no hope for the rat. His own desperate jump had him spinning in the air, giving him one last glimpse of Max. Vidot was in awe that a creature that had once appeared so small, scurrying beneath his feet in the gutters and alleys of the city, could now seem to him such a massive leviathan beast. Oh, how great the small things can be, observed Vidot, arcing high up in the air as the rat's skull was smashed in behind him with a thunderous splintering crack.

Vidot landed on the cold floor, blood splattering all around like hard rain. Without pause, he jumped again, aiming now for Elga. He landed right on the peak of her scalp. With the sounds of screaming and exploding glass now filling the room, he found himself caught up in the momentum of the battle and wholeheartedly joined in, siding with the brunette against their common nemesis. Using his only weapon, Vidot vigorously sunk his teeth into the old witch's skull.

Immediately he regretted it.

The fiery blood flooded in, not sanguine warm like he was used to but instead an acidic mix that blurred and burned, kerosene raw, blinding Vidot and sending him into shaking convulsions. He felt a red rage explode in his abdomen as a wall of serpent's eyes suddenly opened, the snake's shimmering green scales becoming the interlocking shields on a horizon littered with dead soldiers strewn helter-skelter across the amethyst twilit field. The serpent opened its mouth and a farmhouse burned inside, wild with full yellow flames raging thickly out the windows. The smoke rose up to form billowing ferns as will-o'-the-wisps crackled and exploded. Seven tiny skulls seeped up from the surface of the storming muddy swamp and snails dripped out of their eye sockets while slugs slid from their ears. A huge bottomless blackened mouth opened, showing rows of razor teeth, and a seething mass of speckled beetles came flooding out in a scream.

Then Vidot was running, lost, through the rows that were now tall reeds. Desperation gripped his heart, the boiling purple sun was sinking against the shadowed cattails, and he kept running. He sensed he was not escaping or fleeing, he was not chasing or hunting, he was searching, fruitlessly. As he ran, unseen forces pressed on him, compacting him down, harder and harder, into a substance dense as coal. The pressure came from all sides, it pressed on his heart, his chest, his brain. It felt like the collapse of all virtue, all goodness, all humanity.

At the point where he was almost lost forever into this feverish and dark hallucination, a great, violent, seismic shock knocked his fangs loose from the old woman's cranium and sent him spilling out to the floor, shaking him to his senses. He lay there stunned, gazing up, as he watched the brunette leap onto Elga and furiously and unmercifully beat the old woman's face with her fists. Eyeing the action carefully, and desperate to escape the melee, Vidot leapt again, this time onto the younger woman's head.

Landing amid her dark hair's roots, he immediately had to hold on tightly as she continued smashing Elga. Finally, the woman was pulled off by a man Vidot did not recognize. He tried to understand where this new fellow could have come from, but he didn't have time to figure it out, as they were now running out of the building and getting into a cab.

His head still woozy, Vidot was tempted to tap into the young woman's skull to wash out the traces of Elga's burning blood. Then he remembered scenes from the battle. How exactly did this woman overcome that old woman's magic? Perhaps the brunette was not so pure herself. So Vidot delicately hopped over to the man's skull. Vidot had come to apply only the slightest criteria in choosing his victims: dogs, cats, or vermin like his wife's lover—it did not matter to him as long as they were warm-blooded—but after his experience with the old woman, he decided he would try to stick to well-bred gentlemen from now on. This fellow certainly seemed decent, pulling the girl out of the battle and all that, so it was worth a try. He tapped in and tested. Yes, it was pure and sweet, not unlike a new Beaujolais. Chalk another victory up to the well-educated guess.

As the taxi drove through the streets, Vidot realized that by leaving Elga behind he was perhaps losing his one final chance to solve the mystery of his transformation. The old woman was, he was certain, the only person on earth who could turn him back again into the man he truly was. Without the solution she could have possibly provided, he would probably not last long—he would either be clawed by a beast's scratching paw, blown by a strong gust into the frigid Seine's waters, or perhaps even scooped up like Bemm by a fearsome predator. Even if he survived all that, the great mortal clock, the timepiece that had begun ticking the moment he had first awoken as a flea, would soon simply wind down to a halt, leaving him to expire in the dust, unnoticed as he was swept away by a bored grocer's broom. He had just barely survived yet another terrible cataclysm, this one the most frightening by far, but he had also hopped away from his only known possibility for salvation, and time was running out.

XII

Elga lurched up and spat, scratching a bite on her head. She looked at Noelle, sitting on the floor by her side. Her eye felt like it was starting to swell. "Get me some ice."

The little girl went to the kitchenette and looked around. "There's no ice."

Elga nodded and got to her feet, surveying the scene. She paused to take in Max's dead body. "I need a moment." She limped to the bathroom and, putting her head in the toilet, vomited and heaved for the next twenty minutes.

Coming out of the bathroom, she looked at the girl. "Okay, it's time to go."

The girl pointed to the clock pieces on the floor. "Should we collect our things?"

"No," said Elga, "leave them. It doesn't matter. But bring your chicken."

They headed down the staircase together, Elga wincing with every step. She was furious with herself. Noelle looked at her with eyes sunk with exhaustion and guilt. "I know I made a mistake. I'm sorry," said Noelle.

Elga shrugged. "No, it's fine. You're only as good as your teacher. We had her trapped, you know that? We did. I should have ignored her request for water. So stupid. It's my fault. And I should have left Max in the car. Dumb. But you"—she clumsily patted the girl's head—"you didn't do so badly for your first time."

Reaching the bottom stair, she made Noelle wait as she peered around the corner. The desk clerk had his head down on the register. She loudly cleared her throat but still he did not move. Elga and Noelle walked across the lobby and out the front door.

"I'm so tired," said the girl, sinking to the stoop.

"Yes. I told you, spells drain you, even little ones. Now wait here, I'll pull the car up." The girl only nodded, closing her eyes and wrapping her arms tightly around the chicken. In her dazed confusion, it took Elga a moment to remember where she had parked. Then she dug out the key and limped down the street toward the car. The cafés and nightclubs were closing, sending their tipsy, laughing customers out weaving along the sidewalks. A couple stopped to kiss beneath an alley lamp. All these accidental lovers, she thought, will wake up ill from poison in the morning, their hearts filled with black regret. She knew she probably looked drunk to them too as she stumbled toward the car. Though she used it occasionally as a base for potions, she had always found alcohol to be a poor enchantment. It made the banal beautiful and warmed cold hearts, but it was unwieldy and possessed no finesse. She had watched alcohol work like a cudgel through the ages, smashing lives and homes, even kingdoms and empires. It was too base and rough for her taste, but there was no denying the power of its spell; they even let you sip it in the church.

Reaching the car, she heard a voice behind her. "Madame, a moment, please." She ignored it, a beggar no doubt. But then a hand fell on her shoulder. "We need to ask you some questions." She turned and found herself facing a pair of policemen. They must have been watching from the shadows.

"Mmm-hmm," she said. "What is it?"

"This vehicle—"

Ugh, she looked at the car and realized that the spell must have worn off: now instead of being nondescript and ignored by all, the missing police car had revealed itself and been discovered. That was the problem with great taxing exertions like the fight with Zoya, they expended so much energy that the power was often pulled out from any surrounding enchantments. One had to remember where one's work had been and then go double-check after any struggle, or even a serious shock, scare, or fall, to make sure the important things were still held spellbound. Thankfully Zoya had only had time to give her a black eye, Elga thought, or who knows what other tricks would have been undone.

This had been a simple spell to begin with; she had never intended to hold on to the car so long, but it had proved to be too useful to part with. She quickly tried to think of which tricks she could use to escape these policemen, but her mind was fatigued and cloudy and even if she could think of one, it would be too dangerous with the late-night pedestrians passing by. She realized she would have to go along with the officers and find her opportunity later. A chance always opened up. "This? It's not my car," she said. "I found the key on the street."

The policeman nodded. "You will please come with me, madame. We can ask our questions at the station."

In her dazed exhaustion, forgetting for the moment the girl she had left sleeping on the hotel stoop, Elga limped off with the policemen to their waiting car.

A few hours later, after she had told the same lies repeatedly to a parade of different officers, she sat waiting in the dimly lit corner of the station's jail cell. There were three other women in the cell with her, all prostitutes. Elga shivered in the cold. She had never been arrested before, though she and Zoya had occasionally been detained and questioned. Usually it didn't take much to be released; Zoya could always distract them with a flash of leg while Elga hissed out the appropriate spell.

This time was different. This time she was tired, alone and vulnerable. She hugged her knees and thought about Noelle, whom she now regretted abandoning back at the hotel. How would she find her? Elga had never worried about Zoya in all their years together, that one had a fierceness in her that could be frightening. But little Noelle was unproven. She had allowed Zoya to get the upper hand in their battle, and she would need to be taught many more things or she certainly wouldn't make it. But was she smart? Did she have the right blood in her? Perhaps it was not worth the time, perhaps she should be cut loose or put down? Elga wondered what the right move was. Yes, it's simple, Elga said to herself, if she finds her way back to the suite, then she lives. If not, forget her.

Elga shook her head with dismay at how protective she was letting herself feel toward Noelle. She knew soft feelings were weakness, and that girl made her feel soft. Zoya had already been a woman when they met, fully formed, already betrayed and abused. But Noelle was still in possession of an innocence that, like green shoots in spring, stood out against the bleak, starved landscape. Elga thought for a moment of her own daughters, the three of them, but then stopped as she caught one of her cell mates preparing to squat.

"Piss in the pot, not on the floor," Elga hissed.

"Shut up, old woman," slurred her mascara-streaked cell mate, unsteady on her feet, either drunk or drugged.

"Piss in the pot, not on the floor," Elga repeated, staring at the woman. Her cell mate looked away and then stumbled over to the chamber pot in the corner. Elga slipped back to the past.

So many memories had flowed by, she was amazed at how much was dim now and what stayed sharp. The only child of older parents, she had grown up close to a loud sea. She remembered playing on the red sand shore and the roar of the waves when the winter storms came. Her father ran an inn of sorts, more like a barracks for traders who stopped to barter at their little crossroads. Her earliest memories were of late-night lanterned meetings where travelers with sly, wary eyes toyed with colored stones and sniffed pungent samples as they sat drinking and spinning tales around the rough wooden table. Her father weighed and measured while her quiet mother refilled the visitors' cups with wine and put out dishes of dates and lamb.

Elga helped with the chores, but where her parents were reserved, taciturn, and careful, she was boisterous and loud. She enjoyed staying up through the night, teasing the traders and taunting them with barnyard jokes until even her father broke into laughter.

The years were not counted, so she did not know how old she was when her father sold her. All she knew, looking back, was that it was in a thin season when desperation hung heavy, like spiderwebs off the broad-beamed rafters. One windy night some traders came through and as she watched the haggled exchanges, she failed to note one shallow-cheeked trader who had set his eyes on her.

The next morning, climbing out of her sleep, she heard her mother's voice barking her name. She blinked awake only to find the man standing with her mother beside her cot. Without warning, he plucked her up and carried her through the house and out to the horses. His stallion was laden heavy with saddlebags and the mare had a small pack her mother had stuffed with a handful of her possessions. She tried to recall now what would have been in that bag. Some rags of clothes? Perhaps some toy? No. She dimly recalled a small carving of a bird. Was it there? She was unsure.

She rode on the stallion with the trader, listening for the roar of the sea for as long as she could until the horses led them up into the mountain trails. Finally the surf's sound disappeared into the folds of the wind and her childhood vanished back behind an arbor's bend. Then she felt alone. The horses climbed on. When they finally stopped, he walked them off the trail and made camp. There was no fire. The waning, bloodred light was slipping behind the distant dry peaks as her new husband set out their bedding. Frozen with fear, she lay down. He was not gentle, and the moments that followed were worse than any nightmare she could imagine. Her mother had never warned, or even intimated, that this is what marriage could bring, and her father had always been reassuring and gentle with her. As Elga screamed out in those dark hills, the most unbearable pain she felt was that of her parents' betrayal.

Two days later they reached her new home. Her husband, Oman, came from a shepherd clan, with three brothers who tended their goats together. Life was not easy; she was the only woman working for the four of them and the chores were onerous, endless, and came with no gratitude. She labored hard at backbreaking tasks, receiving no tenderness from her husband, a man who was absolute, resolute, and methodical in his actions.

Soon she bore a son, and this pleased Oman greatly. The arrival of a child into their home brought the tender side of Oman to the surface. After his work was done, he would sit out in the field with their son for long periods, watching the light leave the day.

Life was still brutal and hard, though it was only after she was pregnant a second time that the absolute horror of her existence arrived in full. She gave birth on a feast day. It was a painful, tearing birth, and when it was over she held the baby girl for only a few moments, watching her squeak and cry at the new light of life, before Oman took the child from her arms and told Elga to rest. When she awoke, her husband and the baby were gone. Her brother-in-law told her that the child had died in the night and her husband had gone to bury it.

Over the next five years, three more sons were born, each of them healthy, and two more daughters came who did not live a day. Each girl she briefly held and comforted, and each one was taken from her hands. In the morning, the men always told her the same story. But by then she had been living with the tribe for nearly a decade, she knew their trades and how they bartered and dealt with the strangers passing by. She knew how to read her family's eyes, and this was a tribe of bad liars.

Oman's youngest brother, Elon, was a sweet, foolish man. He was the one ready with song and drum when the wine was poured. She would work chores with him and gossip about the family. One day, as they were combing wool for the looms, she gaily chatted and led him down to her trap. "You are so good at this! I think I've changed my mind, I agree now with what my husband says."

"What does my brother say?"

"Oh, you know, how he grumbles and says, 'Bah, women are a waste of food.' I say, 'No, Oman, though I do not mean to dispute you, I say we women are very useful.' Now, look at you, Elon, you are showing that he is right, you are so much better at even this chore than I am."

"Well, I am certain you women are better at some tasks."

"In the towns, perhaps. But not here. We need men for all our tasks. I can help with cooking and the wash, but you only need one woman for that. Too many women would be more useless mouths to feed, right? And even if our neighbors could pay enough for a wife, we get too few visitors looking to strike that kind of a bargain. Why, look how far my husband had to journey to find a woman."

"Yes, he went a long way and he still got a fat, ugly bride," Elon said and both laughed.

"Yes," she said, "I am only good for making him sons."

"You have given him strong sons."

"I know. It is good too that those daughters of mine did not live. My husband did the right thing there."

"Yes, he did," said Elon. He was about to say some other words, but stopped himself. That was when she knew the truth.

"It is all right, my friend," said Elga, shaking her head as if it were nothing. "He is a wise man, he is very wise. But tell me, where did he bury them? He never told me."

Elon was silent for a moment and then he answered her question. "In the river swamp. He buried them down in the reeds of the swamp."

She nodded and said no more. Then she waited, almost three

moons, simmering and stirring her plans in her boiling and turbulent mind. She would wander the muddy wetland trails in the dawn's bleak mist, amid the shrill, disturbed cries of waking starlings, searching, wild-eyed, for a sign of where her daughters might be buried. She would at times collapse and kneel on the ground, blinded with anger, a grief hot inside her that felt like molten metal. At dusk, after feigning her way through the day, she would return again to the swamp, clawing at the earth for graves she could not find. Night would come and the screaming wind would blow as the tall reeds swayed thick, looming above her like hissing serpents. During these trying days, she kept her face serene at home, and when she went on trips into the village, she was chatty and friendly. The horse trader found her full of idle questions about the roads and trails that ran out of town. When she asked for ways to kill off the squirrels nesting in her lofts that were eating at her grain, a bullman's wife gave her a recipe for poison.

Finally, the spring moon turned and Oman rode off, his mare topped with goatskins for the new season's trade. Only hours after he was gone, she went round and invited his brothers to her house for dinner. "I have a seasoned boar that needs roasting." She put out bulgur stew, sausages, radish, and blackberry wine. As she was setting out the meal, Elga told them that she had woken that morning from a nightmare in which her husband faced terrible trials on his journey. She raised a glass: "We must frighten this bad dream away with a toast to his safe return. All of us. Even my boys must drink this toast for their father's safe return," she insisted.

"You're going to make the little ones drunkards," teased Elon.

"Ha ha, no, I have mixed some water with the wine, so indulge a superstitious woman; let us drink and shout the devils away."

They all drank the wine and soon the men were unconscious, their heads heavy on the table. She pulled each one down from his chair and lined them up next to one another on the floor.

She killed her sons first, hammering a long fence nail through each of their hearts. Then, taking an ax, she methodically beheaded each one of her brothers-in-law. Going out to the pens, she drove the livestock into the barn, bolting it shut, and while the goat kids and spring lambs panicked and brayed, she put all the buildings to flame.

When she took Elon's strongest horse and rode off, the mad screaming of the dying livestock burned in her ears.

She was sure Oman would try to track her, but she never saw him
again. She felt no sense of guilt, no sorrow. Her husband had brought
that pain to the world, she had merely set the scales to balance. Still,
she was wise enough to keep running, blazing over the mountain
passes and across the high plateaus. She wrapped herself in shawls to
cover her eyes from strangers' questions and risked the bandits at
night to cover as much ground as possible. On some loose and rocky
flats she lost her horse to a sprain and then continued on foot, lying
down on her belly to sip from the streams she passed, rarely pausing
for long.

As the eighth sun rose, now starving, thirsty, and dizzy, she found
herself following a strengthening scent of woodsmoke down a broken
ridge of alder and pine that led her into a bustling encampment. A
group of women were busy caring for a field full of injured soldiers.
The women paid her no mind until the leader of the group whistled
loudly and signaled for her to approach. Without introduction, and in
a blunt tone, the woman told how the forces had already advanced
over the next rise, harrying a retreating army. Supply horses were supposed to bring up the rear, the woman said, but for now they were
alone there and overworked, with three of their own ill from fever.
They needed help. "What about you?" the woman asked. "Did the
soldiers attack you?"

The woman pointed at the blood that was still splattered on Elga's
dress. "Oh," said Elga, looking at the stains. "No, I was only slaughter-
ing animals." Already a good liar, Elga knew to wrap her deceptions
in vestiges of the truth. The woman nodded, and Elga felt as if a con-
ditional trust had been achieved.

The woman pointed her to the campfire and she began helping,
washing rags and filling pots while watching the other women work.
They cleaned out the dirt, gravel, and pus from the open wounds, applied herbs and poultices to fight infection. Some of the women sang.
The men writhed and screamed. Over the next few days, most died,
but some were saved. Elga took directions well and could feel the
women observing her out of the corners of their eyes, judging her

strength as she worked. When the riders came to tell them of the battle past the next rise, the women packed up and went off to find the injured. Elga traveled with them. This is where her long life began. These nurses had skills and secrets.

XIII

Witches' Song Seven

Here they are, gawking ones, a pocketful of curses,
not empty spells cast by angry incompetents,
red-faced over banquet tables, nay,
but sordid troubles embroidered well
unfurled in spells untoward
able to ignite the great metamorphoses, yes, you've seen well,
but subtler spoilers come in handy too,
right spit words that make you miss crucial connections in distant
     stations,
leaving you as lone, soft, and vulnerable prey
for salivating wolves who dine on lamb and ewe.
Or you drool yourself, dripping constant stains,
     or spilling through passing palsy drops of shame
from pewter spoons and crystal bowls,
splotching dress shirts and fine silks,
     all now spoiled for public judgment.
Then fun too: rich, pungent flatulence summoned
     at intimate times,
with counterpoints of noxious belch and burp,
and rich myriad tapestries of ill blushings,
lavender rashes, and textured boils,
a plague of unreachable itches
desperate for their needed scratches,
all indulgently accented with lasting urinary burnings.

Not enough? More, then, more.
     Grave addictions, the harshest needs,

the barest raw hungers, all voracious
open-mouthed, and panting to fill a gaping hole
with alcohol, baccarat, horse cocks, or the poppy scar's sap, yes.
Then of course taunting self-doubts,
gnats of insecurities, shaming anxieties
that flash white and hollow like lightning bolts tearing
through sturdy hilltop elms.
A vague but constant sense of forgetfulness,
always nipping with haunt
or a shadowed guilt for an imagined crime
that chews and frays at your tired mind.
Oh, a fierce envy for new polished shoes or great worthless land
    tracts,
a fevered lust for rubies, sapphires, pearl, and other beachcombed
    stones,
a gravitational attraction and steady pull
toward expensive strangers.

A gift for spilling teacups and dropping china,
a tendency to catch cloth on lit candles
or absently forgetting hearth and stoves
till cherished cottage and castle have all turned to cinder.
A strong wind for ill rumors,
the instinct to fold both winning hands and good enterprise.
Thick ears, stubborn pride, intolerance for strange skin and
    foreign tribes.
A profound, waist-swelling and spine-splitting constipation,
thick running noses spilling green, infused with muck,
or, worse, eyes weeping ceaselessly till red, bloody, and blind.

Our choice, we can pick, between sullen disappointments of
    impotence or the sorry prodding signals
    of poorly timed erections,
and even better yet, a splendid epilepsy
    of unending ejaculation.

Babayaga

A constant aching and swooning in extreme sexual longing
for the inappropriate people and inanimate things.

Then there's the murderous, a matricidal hunger, a patricidal
    bend, or, to be simple again,
we can loosen an indiscreet tongue
providing an unwanted gift for grave offense
and a penchant for fouling any convivial humor.
Yes, more than once we've been known to bestow the naked
pining for limelight,
the stark drive for a crown,
and the false nobility of immortal ambitions.

Finally, and darkest of all, the most elegant curse,
a numbing inability to sense or comprehend true virtue:
constancy, patience, generosity, and dear kindness,
when they are held in the palm of your very own hand,
seated by your hearth, lying in your bed,
when all that could fulfill your own heart's hope
until your last and final day
is standing by your side, bright-eyed and true,
while you, so oblivious, set your hungry eye
a-wandering . . .

XIV

Noelle awoke cold and shivering on the stoop. The chicken was asleep
in her arms, its head tucked under one russet wing. The old woman
had said she would be right back but now the streets were almost bare
of traffic and the sidewalk was empty, so she guessed some time had
passed, and yet Elga was nowhere in sight. Noelle rose and, hauling
the chicken up under her arm, began making her way down the street
with tentative, sleepy steps. A glowing green clock on the wall of a
shuttered café told her it was three a.m. Perhaps Elga had driven off
and forgotten her. That seemed possible, the old woman was moody

and hard to predict. Noelle knew she had disappointed her in the fight with the bad woman, but Elga had seemed kind about it afterward, even forgiving. So it did not make sense that she would have abandoned her. There must be some other explanation.

Noelle walked down toward what she thought was the center of the city. She knew if she followed the lights of the Eiffel Tower she would eventually reach the Seine and there, somewhere near the Louvre, she would find the hotel. All she wanted was to crawl into warm sheets and sleep. Oh, such a soft bed, how nice it would be. She looked down at the still bird in her arms. Was it dead? She paused to lean over and listen to it. It was breathing, making a barely perceptible soft, trembling sound as it slept. That cooing made her feel better.

She had never walked alone in the city, and after she had continued for a few blocks she was surprised to find a particular comfort in the late-night emptiness. At her home back in the village, her parents had always spoken of Paris as a dangerous and forbidding place, seething with vague horrors. They never explicitly enumerated these terrors, though whenever there was talk of the city, her mother's eyes would grow wide as if she were describing a goblin's lair. Yet near her own home, Noelle would often find herself frightened in the woods, where there were spiders hanging from trees and writhing centipedes waiting under rocks. There in the forest, the wind creaked the bony branches, thorns scratched her face, and thick mud puddles sucked at her shoes, threatening to swallow her down. The city, by contrast, seemed quite predictable, paved and chiseled, with wide, smooth concrete sidewalks leading past the finely lettered windows of confectioners and tailors, bookshops and tobacconists. Even though they were closed, they were still comforting. All you had to worry about in cities were people, not the creatures of the wicked wilds; and for some reason, right now people did not worry Noelle very much. The chicken in her arms kept her warm, and she felt so content on her little adventure that she was tempted to start singing old nursery songs.

It was only as she came near the Galeries Lafayette that she began to feel slightly nervous, because that was when she began to hear the clipped footsteps trailing behind her. The pace was the same as her own, and when she slowed to let the person pass, no one passed. She did not want to turn around, and she did not want to run, but she picked up her pace again and tried to walk faster. The footsteps behind her kept up. Perhaps, she thought, it was a policeman, or merely a grocer on his way to the early market. Still, she would not look back.

She tried to distract herself by thinking about the Galeries. She had been there once a few seasons past when her mother had brought her into the city for Christmas shopping, and Noelle had hoped Elga would take her there as well. It was the most beautiful place, every little girl's dream, like being inside a sparkling diamond or a sugar-tiered birthday cake. Her mother had bought her powdered beignets and currant scones—

—Noelle's thoughts froze as the footsteps behind her came closer still, so close that they were right behind her. Her heartbeat was racing fast as a hummingbird's. She did not have any money or she would have run out into the street and flagged down one of the lonely black taxis that were occasionally passing by.

"Good evening, mademoiselle."

The sound of his voice made the hair on her neck stand on end. She now felt as small and weak as a ladybug cowering beneath the shadow of a great descending boot. She dared not look up at the stranger. She kept walking, her eyes focused straight ahead. "Hello," she said, hoping not to offend.

"Do you have a spare sou?"

"I do not," she said, though she would have given the beggar any change she had to make him go away.

"Oh," said the stranger. "Very well then . . ."

This short conversation had distracted her long enough that she had not seen the darkened gap of a courtyard that lay tucked between the approaching buildings. But the stranger had noticed. In one sudden motion, he pulled her up off her feet, his hand over her mouth, and shoved her past the building's gate, into the blackened darkness. The first thing she did was drop the chicken and try to kick at the man's legs and bite his hand. The bird squawked loudly as it hit the pavement. Noelle's assailant was breathing hard as he pushed her up against the wall. It was then she saw his terrible, thin face, his stubbled skin, weathered and oily, with acne scars running down the sides of both cheeks. His expression up close was mean and hungry. He leaned in toward his little prey, his breath stinking of bile, tobacco, and sour wine.

"I only want what's in your pockets," he seethed. "Give me—" He was cut off by a wild screeching and a thunderous batting of wings, as if an entire kettle of hawks had dropped out of the skies. The man screamed out in a spasm of agony and released Noelle. She fell down and scampered away fast, looking back with fascination as the two silhouettes struggled in the shadows.

The chicken was attacking the man with a frenzied fury. Blood was already thickly streaming down from his clawed eye sockets as he tried to shield himself. The bird twisted and fluttered, its beak attacks alternating between the man's now tattered eyes and his Adam's apple, pecking hard with quick success so that the man's howls of pain were soon subsumed by the wet, gurgling sound of drowning. Finally, the bird's screeches and its victim's cries caused neighboring lights to come on. Noelle ran off down the street, nursing a strange thrill in her heart.

A little over an hour later, with the verve of excitement still tickling her veins, and her ribs sore from the attack, an exhausted Noelle turned the corner of the avenue and saw her hotel, down at the end of the block. With its broad façade and fluttering flags, the building looked reassuringly paternal, as if it had been patiently waiting up through the long night to comfort her upon her return. She exhaled, pleased and relieved that she had found her way home. She knew the night manager would let her into her room; he was the one who had brought her warm milk on the first night they were there.

She was surprised at how calm she felt, remarkably untouched by the puzzling series of events she had endured—the fight at the apartment, the death of the rat, Elga's disappearance, and, finally, the awful assault on the street. She knew she should be a bundle of frayed nerves, ready to be put back in the asylum bed where Elga had first found her. But, truth to tell, she felt perfectly fine. She turned and looked back down the boulevard to where the chicken was coming along behind her. The red bird paused occasionally to peck at the pavement's cracks.

Babayaga

XV

Will was awoken near dawn by Zoya's soft kisses. The woman who had seemed dead to the world was now feverishly alive, her lips running across the top of his collarbone, biting at his ear. In no time her attentions had him completely alert. He clutched her tightly, pulling her against him. She held him fast, her hands joined at the base of his neck, her forehead pressed against his chest. He grabbed at her breasts and nipples as she bit his shoulder and pulled his hair, gasping as he found his way inside her. They rocked the bedframe and knocked the headboard hard against the wall. Her legs were above his body as she pressed up against him, burying her cries into his neck. They rode each other, ignoring the racket they made, finally finishing with a high breaking moan and strong shudder. Then she fell off to his side.

"Where are we?" she sleepily asked, her eyes already closing again.

"Oliver's."

"Oliver's?" Her question was barely a breath. "Why?"

"There was someone watching my apartment. It wasn't safe."

Her brow furrowed as if these words worried her, but then she slipped back to sleep, resting against his chest, her eyes shut fast. He watched her sleep for a bit and then crawled out from under her to go to the bathroom.

He found Oliver in a bathrobe and striped pajamas, sitting up in the kitchen with a cup of coffee and an early edition of *Le Monde*. "Well, hullo," said Oliver. "Couldn't help hearing you two exerting yourselves in there. At first I thought it was Madame Boillet's poor cats yowling from the flat downstairs."

"Sorry to wake you. I thought I heard someone else here?" Will couldn't help prodding.

"Oh, Gwen could sleep through the running of the bulls. And, anyway, you didn't wake me. I was actually coming to roust you when I heard your little commotion."

"Right," Will remembered, "you mentioned some errand last night."

"Yes, take a look at this." Oliver took two business cards out of his robe pocket and laid them out side by side. They were identical, reading:

"One of those cards was in Boris's pocket when he collapsed. The other I found in Ned's room. As far as I can discern, it is the only common thread they share. Now, I've never heard of Poitier's and I've asked around a bit and gotten nothing. Even Red and the rest of the jazz boys didn't recognize the name, and those boys are usually fairly knowledgeable in this area."

"What area is that?"

"Pharmaceuticals."

"What makes you think that's what this is all about?"

"Boris had that odd opiate in his pocket, remember? Got it from somewhere, and this drugstore certainly seems like the right place to start. Worth a look, anyway. So I thought we might go sniff about the place, no need for any subterfuge, though mustache disguises would be fun."

Will ignored Oliver's theatrics. "It's probably only a regular old pharmacy."

Oliver shook his head. "No, it's definitely a suspicious outfit. The shop isn't listed in any directory I could find, and when I dialed that number the phone was picked up but whoever was on the other end of the line did not say a single word. I'm telling you, that silence gave me chills."

Will shrugged. "Maybe their telephone's busted."

"Doubtful."

"It's probably perfectly innocent, Oliver. Maybe it is where Boris and Ned both bought their toothpaste. Think about it, criminals don't generally hand out business cards."

"Yes, but turn that argument around—when you buy toothpaste, do you generally pick up a business card?" Oliver downed the last of his coffee while Will prepared to accept the inevitable. "Shall we head out then?" asked Oliver.

"Give me a minute to get dressed," said Will, shaking his head with disbelief at his willingness to go along.

"Yes, of course, me too," said Oliver. "I'll leave a note for the girls and tell them that, in penance for abandoning them, we'll take them out tonight for a nice dinner, someplace fun like Le Procope."

A few minutes later, the two headed out. As they reached the street, Will put his hand up for a passing cab but Oliver pulled it back. "We can't very well do a stakeout perched in the back of a cab, the fare would be astronomical. I borrowed that from a friend." He pointed across the street to a parked Bel Air. "Don't worry, I'm happy to drive."

It was early and traffic was light so they crossed town quickly and, after turning down a few backstreets, found the desired block. Cruising slowly by the building, they saw no signage, either on the windows or hanging above the door. The shutters were drawn and there was no sign of life. Oliver pulled the car up to the far corner of the block and parked.

"Now what?" asked Will.

"Now we wait and see."

Will looked around the abandoned street. "Why'd we have to come so early?"

"Well, if one wants to see who opens up the shop, best to be there before the shop opens."

Will couldn't dispute the logic, but he was tired and it was chilly. For the next hour he wrapped himself in his wool coat and tried to get some rest while Oliver watched the pharmacy in the side mirror. Eventually Will dozed off.

He wasn't sure how long he slept, but when he came to, the neighborhood was busy amid its routine morning bustle. The small markets had opened their doors, cafés had placed their chalkboard signs out on the sidewalk, and cars, pedestrians, and bicycles all rushed and rattled by. A group of children in their Catholic school uniforms headed off to school. The smell of country bacon cooking somewhere made Will hungry. He looked over at Oliver, who was still intently focused on the pharmacy. Will dug out a pack of Gitanes, hoping to kill his appetite. "So, what is the story with you and Gwen?" he asked.

"Please, let's keep the office gossip to a minimum."

"Sorry, just trying to make small talk."

"You'll find I take my work very seriously when I'm on the job, doubly so when I'm being paid overtime."

"Wait, you're getting paid for this?" said Will. "What am I getting?"

Oliver took a cigarette and lit it. "You're getting answers."

They sat in silence. After all the running around of the past few days, Will was enjoying this slow, peaceful morning. Instead of murder and intrigue, they were merely sitting in a car, watching a door. The quiet was comforting. Will leaned back in the seat and replayed highlights of old Tigers games in his head.

He finished his cigarette and fell back into a light sleep, only coming to when Oliver nudged him. "I've got to find a *pissoir*. Keep your eye on the shop." Oliver hopped out of the car and disappeared down the street. When he was gone, Will slid over to the driver's side to watch the pharmacy. He recalled his grandfather telling him that the only success that mattered was having a job where no one had to cover for you when you went to take a leak.

He glanced at his watch, it was almost eleven. Looking up again at the rearview mirror, he noticed a figure approaching the pharmacy. The man seemed familiar to Will, though he could not remember from where. The man gave a quick glance around before ducking in the pharmacy's front door. Will tried to place him, but he had no luck. He wasn't very good with faces, a fact, he realized, that did not make him particularly well suited for intelligence work. He was relieved when Oliver finally came back to the car. Sliding over to the passenger seat, Will told Oliver about the man.

"You say he looked familiar?"

"Very."

"But you don't know from where." Oliver drummed his fingers on the steering wheel. "You think he is from the agency?"

Will was confused. "When you say 'agency,' do you mean my advertising agency or the Central Intelligence Agency?"

"Either will do. Now think, who is he?"

"I don't know."

"Okay, it's fine. When he exits, you'll have a chance to try again."

So they sat there, watching and waiting. No one emerged from the pharmacy. "Well, I'm fairly certain of one thing," Oliver finally said. "That man is not here for his toothpaste." Will nodded, a little disappointed. He had actually hoped this errand would be a dead end; sitting doing nothing in the car had been a nice idyll. Now, though, he could feel the wheels coming to life, all the complexity churning into motion again. It made him feel slightly sick and queasy, reminding him of the feeling he had as a young boy in his West Detroit Little League uniform, standing alone in the peaceful serenity of right field amid the heavenly quiet, which would inevitably be horribly punctuated by the crack of some slugger's bat hitting a ball out toward him. He remembered watching the ball fly up high in its arcing, parabolic pop-up before coming maliciously back down, bringing so much chaos and mischief hurtling right into the heart of his awkward, uncoordinated life. Ever since he met Oliver, he felt like that, clumsily stumbling around, trying to chase down one fly ball after another.

His nausea was only made worse by the car's stale air, a thin haze of cigarette smoke having permeated everything. Also, it didn't help that Oliver was starting to smell. Will closed his eyes and tried to think of other things, imagining Zoya's scent, her skin and neck and hair, and the taste down between her legs, which, for some reason, at that moment brought to mind a savory Moroccan tagine. He smiled at the thought, which also made his cock stir, and then suddenly he felt self-conscious, hoping his friend would not notice. An erection in a moment of close camaraderie like this could be tricky to explain. Will opened his eyes and sat up, suddenly impatient to get out of the car and stretch his legs, but also not wanting to move. He was concentrating on trying to relax when Oliver shot up straight with excitement.

"My gosh, you're right, we do know him," said Oliver. They both looked out the rear window as the man emerged from the pharmacy. "It's Jake."

"Jake?" Will said.

"You know him, Will. You met him the other night." Then Will remembered, Jake had been the fourth member of the meeting at the nightclub, the sleepy one. "Question is, what in the good Lord's name is he doing here?" Oliver said, watching Jake disappear down the street.

"Why don't we go and ask him?" Will offered.

"No, considering Boris's and Ned's recent experiences, I don't think the direct approach would be the wisest course," said Oliver. "However, I am curious if his superiors know what he's up to."

"His superiors?"

"He works for your friend Brandon."

Will scratched his head, a little befuddled. "Really? Him too?"

"It's a small town for ex-pats and the agency is thinly staffed these days, so Brandon's working as the case officer for both the cultural and industrial sides of intelligence here, which includes Jake and you, and me too, technically. So, let's see if we can't get someone to help put two and two together for us. There's a phone booth on the corner, I'll be right back." He popped out of the car and disappeared down the street. Will sat trying to think through what he had just been told, but Oliver was back before he could come to any conclusions.

"That was fast," said Will.

Oliver started up the car. "Yes, I was lucky to catch Brandon at his desk, though he was a bit tight-lipped. Didn't want to talk on the telephone, he said. Suspect he's nervous about agency wiretaps, or maybe it's that mole they always fear is listening in, who knows? We made a date to meet up at our old handoff spot tonight, out in the Bois. He also said I should bring you along."

"He knows I'm with you?"

"Well, I didn't offer it up, but he asked and I didn't see any point in lying, especially since the last time we saw him I was dragging you out of your office. In any case, sounds like it's for the best, he said he's got some good news for you."

"Really?" Will was curious. "Wonder what that could be."

Oliver lit another cigarette. "Dunno."

Will looked at his watch, happy with the feeling that things were beginning to sort themselves out. "Looks like we have a couple of hours, maybe we can meet up with the girls for a drink first?"

"I'm sure the girls are fine; if we're lucky they spent the whole day shopping for lingerie at Victorine. We can catch up with them later. I say we get some oysters and wine over at Le Chat Noir, it's on the way."

XVI

Zoya woke after the sun had set. She pulled herself up in the bed and tried to piece together the last twenty-four hours. What had happened? Why had Elga attacked her? What was the meaning of the disassembled clock? How had she possibly escaped such a perfectly designed attack? She remembered the small girl who had been there, trying to trap her with a spell. The girl's presence was easily explained: needing to make the killing stick, Elga had found a malleable little urchin and pulled her into the scheme. Zoya realized that this was why she had survived the attack. Elga worked fast, but she was an unreliable and brutal woman who would as easily cut a hungry soldier's throat as hand him a cold potato—and she was the same with the girls she trained, pulling their hair one day, gently combing it out the next. Zoya knew such inconsistency made for poor training. If it was rushed, the girls would pay the price. Along the way, she had seen Elga try to train a few others, but the old woman's uneven methods made for shoddy work. There might be some out there still on the road, thought Zoya, but she doubted it. She had seen most of these unlucky students fall before her eyes, either from forgetting precious words or from sticking out too far for suspicious eyes to find.

Zoya knew she had been on a razor's edge of losing the skirmish, and if Will had not shown up she doubted she would have lived through it. She still could not believe the sight of his sweet face with its quizzical expression popping in the door at that fortuitous moment. That was too odd a twist of fate; she suspected those ghostly witches were pulling strings again. But to what end? What were they weaving? It did no good to guess. All Zoya did know was that being saved by a man was not an entirely comfortable feeling. Normally it was her task to pull them back from the abyss, confusing the auditors, poisoning the prosecutors, covering her lovers with shades of invisibility as they rode into battle. Men had occasionally tried to aid her as well but they were almost always the worst, appearing later with grim, avaricious smiles that said, "Debts are meant to be paid." She could not recall ever having been rescued like this by a man before, ever. It annoyed her, for it implied a debt and she did not like owing anyone.

She had to admit, though, Will was different: he had fallen into the situation unaware, like the rabbit he was, once again hopping blindly into the middle of the hunting party. It was not even clear if he had any sense of where he had been, and thanks to her whispering spell, now he would never recall it. So, yes, she thought, I can owe him, for he was not one who would hold her to any obligation. She knew he was happy simply to have been there for her in a time of need. She smiled to herself, recalling how relieved she had felt as they made their getaway, wrapped up in his arms, safe in the taxi, driving off from the chaos of the fight, the world around her seeming to close down into warmth and darkness. She realized that the sense of comforting protection he had given her, held there in his reassuring embrace, was an almost exclusively feminine feeling, one that most men only experienced as babes in their mothers' arms.

On the bedside table she found a note Will had left: *Out on a long errand, be here by dinner, rest, kiss, Will.* Putting on her clothes, she went out to the kitchen. She was startled to find Gwen sitting by the stove, wearing one of Oliver's oversized shirts and reading a slender novel. "Oh, good day, lazybones. Oliver left a note saying you'd be here. He wants to take us all out for dinner in a bit." She looked up with a pleasant smile. "There's a pot of Earl Grey there if you want a cup."

Zoya gave her a polite smile in return. "Thank you." She poured herself some tea. She looked out the window and saw that it was dark. "What time is it?"

"Nearly eight, you two must have had quite the boozy night."

"Mmmn." Zoya nodded to herself. So much sleep and she still felt weak. She knew it would be a day or two before she was fully recovered. "So, you are with Oliver now?"

The British girl smiled. "I never like to say I'm *with* a man. It sounds too much like I'm sick *with* the sniffles or down *with* the plague."

"Yes," Zoya said. "I suppose I should have asked, 'Are you having sex with Oliver?'"

Gwen gave a forced laugh. "Yes, but only occasionally, here and there. He asked me over last night to review some galleys, and then, well, you know, he's such a chatty flibbertigibbet. It took nearly two bottles of wine until I could finally shut him up."

Zoya looked at Gwen. She had known many women who actually were what Gwen pretended to be, and she respected those genuinely independent and capable women, the ones with great confidence, intelligence, and self-reliance. Zoya could never call these women "friends"—for almost all were so sharp and intuitive that Zoya had to steer clear to avoid being too closely observed—but she liked the ones she had known in passing, all too aware of the fact that making one's way as a smart, fair creature in a patriarchal culture took some deft choreography. The men would not let you fight them on their terms, for if you were as strong as them then they painted you as ugly or called you cold, while if you tried to succeed by promoting your merits they labeled you as vain. Some of these remarkable women did find men who could live with them as equals, and sometimes they found partners who even accepted them as superior, but even then, too often, those men fell victim to that darkest of instincts, pride. Then Zoya watched as these "gentle" men wore their women down with those soft and cruel weapons—jealousy, mockery, absence, neglect—often with lethal results. Men might be apelike and plodding, Zoya thought, but they were not entirely stupid beasts, they knew how to climb back on top.

"Of course, a real relationship with a man like Oliver would be impossible," Gwen went on. "He jokes about making an honest woman out of me, but I know he won't. You know, he had his heart horribly broken some time back and I think it's limited his ability to feel any deep emotion, really. It's fine, though, it's not like I'm in any rush to create some pathetic simulacrum of a happy marriage like my poor mother suffered."

Zoya nodded politely and sipped her tea. Many marriages she had observed seemed to her awkward, strained arrangements, often painful to be near. But she was not entirely cynical and had seen, too, a rich variety of marital bonds that worked well. One extreme was where the man rose to his slippers late, almost at noon, and stayed busy nearly to dawn, while his bride awoke earlier than the birds and retired to sleep only a little after sunset, their lives thusly arranged so as to barely touch, and when they did it was warm and affectionate, like running across an old friend while traveling through the station. At the other extreme were the partnerships where every engagement with the outside world was a blending of one another's thoughts and words as they harmoniously, almost clairvoyantly, completed one another's sentences, wishes, desires, writing in one another's diaries and signing each other's letters. There was a spectrum of working, functioning examples lying between these two extremes as vast in its richness as the many species of butterflies in the wilderness.

Zoya had to agree that Gwen and Oliver had no chance of that. For starters, Gwen was slightly false-faced, the tone of her pronouncements came off as a pretender's, finely schooled and well-read but a long day's journey from wise. Zoya had not heard of any broken heart in Oliver's past, but in her brief experience with him, his actions focused more on conquest than chemistry. She recalled how, in the throes of the sexual moment, his face held almost a boyish pride, as if the final act of consummation was equivalent to planting a flag on a snowy mountain peak.

Looking at the shirt Gwen had on, she realized it was the same one of Oliver's that she herself had worn the morning after she slept over, the very day, in fact, when she had first met Gwen. She was wondering if the girl had put it on as some sort of statement when the phone's ringing startled both of them. Gwen jumped up to answer it. "Hello? . . . Oh, hi . . . Yes, she's up, we're chatting now . . . Where? . . . Of course, darling, of course." Gwen hung up the phone and sat down again. "That was Oliver. He wants us to meet him over in the park. Not exactly clear what he's up to, but I told him we'd be there. A rendezvous in the woods," she giggled. "How exciting."

Zoya tensed slightly. Gwen's casual and happy tone held a nuance that worried her, and her voice on the phone had seemed wrong. One of the things Zoya had grown very good at over the years was spotting deception, and Gwen was a liar. She could not tell what precisely this lie involved, but she knew it was not an innocent one. There was danger in the room now, it was moving in Gwen's distracted eyes and dancing in her nervous fingertips as she snapped her cigarette case shut. Had that really been Oliver on the phone? Zoya doubted it. Was it a trap? Probably. Why? And who would care that Zoya was there? Who even knew who she was?

Zoya tried to stall. "Perhaps I should wait for Will here."

"Oh, don't be a silly stick-in-the-mud like that," Gwen said and teasingly punched her on the arm. "Oliver said Will's with him, and besides, we both need some air. It smells awful in this place. Come on, we'll have fun."

So Zoya nodded and Gwen went to get dressed. Zoya was not too nervous. She was confident that, even with her fatigue, she could handle what lay ahead. After so many years of playing along these mortal games, it was never too difficult to simply evade and escape. But she did not like heading into obvious and unknown deceptions. The only reason she went along was that, as was the case all too often, it was the only direction to go.

XVII

Witches' Song Eight

So you see,
like water spinning round
down the drain,
we suck up these troubled and toiling souls,
pooling them thickly together,
for now is the time
to set prey against prey,
and watch as these our proud planets,
rotating both near and far,
pass over our sun's brilliant surface.

The small moons we have spun
will cross too, providing an illuminating eclipse
down into the pit
of dear darkness.

XVIII

Vidot was getting hungry. He sat on the peak of Will's head, listening to Oliver talk on endlessly as they strolled into the unlit city park. "You've never been here? Really? The Bois is incredible, there's no place like it in the world. See that sign for the zoo over there? During the Siege of Paris the besieged citizens took the animals out of their cages, cooked them up, and served them at Paris's finest restaurant, on their best china. I had never thought of a zoo as an exotic larder before, but I suppose it is, potentially at least."

Riding along, the flea's mind wandered; he had his own memories of the Bois, for this was where he had first wooed Adèle. They had met a few months after the Occupation, he was a patrolman whose bruised sense of pride and patriotism was only beginning to recover. She was younger than him, a student of the classics at the university. They had met at the library. Adèle lived with her widowed mother in a one-bedroom flat where they drank ginger tea and ate very little. Vidot lived with two other patrolmen in a small apartment a few neighborhoods away, which made courtship difficult. So the pair of them would steal away for walks here in this park, the infamous Bois de Boulogne. He recalled kissing her against trees and slipping his hand beneath her blouse, how the feel of the warmth of her soft skin against his touch deliciously confused him, separating his body from his mind and taking him to a realm where the only things that existed had to be felt or tasted, like heat and flesh and desire. As the tender recollection returned, he desperately wanted to keep hold of it, the way one savors a delicious flavor before it vanishes from the mouth, but as hard as he tried, his grasp of the memory was slipping away, because this man Oliver would not shut up.

"Oh, and gosh you wouldn't believe it, in the nineteenth century they had an exhibit of human beings in the park. Live ones, Zulus and

Pygmies. The whole city came out to gawk. I suppose that is what people now do with their *National Geographic* magazines, ogle the natives' bare black buttocks and fulsome breasts, but it strikes me as particularly surreal to have it happen live and in person. Do you think any of the sophisticates strolling in that human zoo looked into the noble savages' eyes and found a universal brother? Seriously, one has to wonder, in that particular scenario, which side of the iron cage the savages were on."

As they made their way along the familiar path, the flea looked over to a passing row of benches. He could not recall where specifically, but he knew they had been sitting near here when he had decided to propose to Adèle. It was a Saturday, he recalled, and while they had often laughed and joked about the funny people who strolled by with their parasols, their little pets, and their ill-behaved children, that one particular day Adèle had seemed more thoughtful than usual, almost distant. He had wondered if she was sad, or perhaps distracted, but then he noticed that she was simply paying very close attention to all the things around them, the textures, the light, the nuance of each distinct element, the blossoms and the buds. Probing with some seemingly lighthearted philosophical question, he learned that Adèle did not see life as so many did, a mere entertainment to be enjoyed or blindly consumed, and she did not see it as Vidot did, a great series of interlocking puzzles waiting to be solved. Instead, she described her vision of life as an enormous great act held within an infinite and immutable instant, one where she was present both as a witness and a participant. He was stunned, recognizing this idea of existence was the most logical and true interpretation he had ever encountered, and he knew that he had to marry Adèle and become one with those eyes and that mind, or else he would never experience what it meant to be present in the world.

"And right over there, back in 1900, they held the tug-of-war competition during the Olympic Games. Believe it or not, tug-of-war was quite the competitive sport back in the day. Incredible, isn't it? I believe Sweden won. I recall reading that someplace, as a child I was quite the encyclopedic sports trivia wunderkind."

Listening to Oliver rattle on, Vidot was reminded that he himself could also talk too much, especially about his work. He wondered if this had driven Adèle away. He recalled how he was always diving into details about his grisly cases. Even once they were solved, he kept the stories alive. How many times had he told the tale of the wedding groom found with the hatchet in his head (the priest did it). He wondered if he had been curious enough about Adèle's life, toiling there amid the long shelves and crowded stacks of the library. He always assumed that his work, with its stories of thieves, cheats, scoundrels, and scourges was something she would want to know more about. But perhaps that was a false assumption; yes, probably so. Thinking about it now, he wanted to slap himself.

"Once upon a time, these woods teemed with criminals. Pierre Belon was murdered by highwaymen right down that path. Do you know Belon? Remarkable man, an explorer, naturalist, artist, actually he sketched out one of my most favorite drawings, a scientific comparison of a man's skeleton and a bird's. Amazingly parallel, bone for bone. Pierre Belon, my, my, what a fantastic person. Now, if memory serves, this is where we tuck into the brush to get to Brandon's little meet-up spot. He's rather fond of this cloak-and-dagger stuff."

Vidot knew he had to stop obsessing about Adèle and concentrate on the matters at hand, but being back in the park had brought all the memories of their courtship blossoming to life, and now his small mind could not stop recalling how energetic Adèle had been when they were first together. He remembered her loving him so completely, so generously, looking up at him afterward, the sweat covering both their bodies, their breathing still hard. "Was that nice for you?" she asked, adding coyly, "Is there anything else you want?" He had not been a particularly adventurous lover, he did the things he believed one was supposed to do, diligently attentive, sweet and romantic, not clinical or cold but certainly not as imaginative, ravenous, or physically demanding as what he had witnessed between her and Alberto. Of course, over the years the constancy of their passion had abated, growing more intermittent and a bit more predictable, but in all that time he had never stopped desiring her; the beauty of her naked body, even as they aged, always thrilled him.

Thinking about their life, though, he realized that there was an imbalance between her desire and what he had provided. Clearly, he had left her wanting more over time. When she had asked, "Is there anything else you want?" she was speaking of her own needs, longing for a kind of affection he had never provided. She had wanted so much more than even what they shared when they had first hungrily groped, lusted, and kissed beneath these dark, obscuring trees. Instead he had given her steadily less. How had he ever let that happen? Perhaps he had let his intellect play too large a role in their life, and, instead of embracing, devouring, and taking her, out of some pure animal need, he had been too rational, analyzing her moods and desires, merely appreciating her when he should have been loving her. He realized that while he had been approaching her body like it was some dry tome, there to be studied and read, someone had come along and snatched the book off the shelf.

The anxiety of all this guilt-inducing second-guessing left him light-headed and hungry. Once again, he reminded himself that he would have to find something to focus on other than Adèle. But first he had to eat. Scrambling deep into the brush of Will's hair, he dug in his fangs. The woozy satisfaction came fast and hit hard, blurring his senses, the warm blood washing all thoughts of his wife away. He wondered if this is what the hashish and heroin addicts experienced, cured from the daily pains of existence as senses dulled down and the mind clouded over. He was almost unconscious when, like a napping child hearing guests arrive, he vaguely registered a number of new, unrecognizable voices. Curious, he stumbled sleepily down the crest of Will's skull and fuzzily tried to focus on what was happening in the woods.

A small group of people stood around a clearing in the trees. He counted seven in all, including Will and Oliver. The only other one Vidot recognized was Zoya (he had learned the brunette's name earlier that day when a lustful Will had been earnestly repeating it during their early-morning exertions). Across from her, another young woman was pointing a gun at Zoya. Another man had a gun pointed at the woman. He, in turn, had a gun pointed at him. What the hell is happening? thought Vidot. I turn my back for one minute and the whole world gets a gun? Then he noticed that while everyone was speaking English, only one of them, the young woman, had an English accent. The rest were Americans, Ah yes, thought Vidot, Americans do like their guns. People started talking fast and he had a hard time following what they were saying.

"Let the girl go."

"What's come over you, White?"

"I love her."

"Don't be an idiot, White, you've never even met her."

"All I'm saying is, you have to let her go."

"Why don't we take care of them all and be done with the whole damn thing?"

"No, that's sloppy."

As the small crowd bickered over who should shoot whom, Vidot noticed that Oliver was nervously keeping his eye on one of the men in the group. Then Vidot noticed why, because that man was pointing his gun in their direction, and, more specifically, he was aiming directly at the very head Vidot was perched upon. Now a bit nervous himself, Vidot began surveying the scalps in the group, seeking the most prudent place to hop next.

His thoughts were interrupted when, off to the side, there was movement within the thicket of brush. "Hello? Hello? Are you there?" A high-pitched voice speaking English with a thick Swiss accent came out of the trees. "Excuse me, my, my, I am so sorry I am late. I seem to have lost the trail. Excuse me very much!" Then, after pushing branches out of his path the way a master of ceremonies might part a red curtain, one of the strangest-looking men Vidot had ever seen emerged. He was quite petite, only about a meter and a half tall, wearing a pair of round glasses and a baby blue seersucker suit with a neatly folded pocket square tucked into the breast pocket. Perfectly bald, his pale skin was covered in various roseate and pale pink blotches, much like the belly of an ailing dog. It only took one look for Vidot to realize he did not want to taste that man's blood.

"Why are you late?" grumbled the American whose gun was still trained on Will.

"Ah, good evening, Brandon, I am afarid I had a very difficult time following your directions. What seems to be the trouble here? I thought you had things under control."

"Nothing we can't handle, one of our men here has gone a little soft and romantic," Brandon said, gesturing toward the man called White.

"I see." The little fellow walked over to White. "What seems to be the matter here, my friend?"

"I'm sorry Mr. Bendix, I can't let them kill that girl."

"But you know she's critical to the plan. We all talked about it before. We kill her, then Brandon arrests the other two fellows here. It's simply one of those *ménages à trois* that's turned into a horrible *crime passionnel*." The little man walked a slow circle around the group, stopping in front of Oliver. "Later, before he can call a lawyer, this fancy one with all the connections hangs himself in his cell, the unfortunate victim of star-crossed passion, while the other"—he looked at Will—"this innocent man from nowhere, he tries to tell his story to the police, to the judge, to anyone who will listen, but of course nobody believes him and so he vanishes into a cell for the rest of his days. Everyone wins, you see? Well,"—he looked over toward Will and Oliver—"almost. So you see, White, it has all been thoroughly thought through, so why the delay?"

"I love her."

"That's stupid. He doesn't even know her," said Brandon.

"He says he loves her but he does not know her? This sounds very mysterious to me, or perhaps it is normal. I do not know. I abandoned my appetite for women so long ago, it is easy to forget how bewitching they can be. But this does sound unusual. Hmmn." He walked over to Zoya, stopping less than an inch from her cheek. "She *is* lovely. May I ask your name, mademoiselle?"

"I am Zoya Fominitchna Polyakov."

The little man looked shocked. He stepped back, his mouth hanging open wide. "Zoya . . . Polyakov? Really! How wonderful, how miraculous. Oh my." He clapped his hands like a small boy who had received a great treat. "Zoya Polyakov, heavens, yes, this is some news! Brandon, you only told me we had a random Russian girl, not *the* Zoya Polyakov. Indeed, well, this is a moment worthy of true fanfare."

Zoya's eyes grew wide. "I do not know you," she said.

The little man smiled as he waved his finger in the air. "Ah, but I know you, I know everything about you, and about your friend too. What is her name again? Elga. Yes, Elga Sossoka. Of course, who could forget Elga Sossoka? Tell me, where is she these days?"

"I do not know this woman you speak of."

The little man nodded. "Yes, fine, why don't we lie to each other? We can always sort out the truths from the lies back at the lab." He turned to the square-jawed friend. "Well, Brandon, I am afraid this sudden piece of good fortune has altered our plans considerably. Though all to the good, I believe. I am overwhelmed by our luck. Your friend White here is under a kind of spell. You see, she is quite skilled at them—aren't you, Zoya Polyakov?"

The woman said nothing. White looked confused. "No, don't talk about her that way. I won't let you hurt her."

The little man smiled. "Oh you can relax, White, your lady friend here will not die." He drew a small revolver out of the holster beneath his suit jacket. "But of course you will."

Bendix aimed and fired and White's head snapped to the side as he fell. Then, before his body had landed, the shrill sound of a patrolman's whistle sounded and a voice shouted out from the brush, "Police! Ne bougez pus. Lâchez vos armes." The voice was familiar, but before Vidot—who was already bewildered at the great number of people popping up out of the park's shrubbery—could put a face to the voice there was an even greater commotion as a strange and thunderous thumping noise began to fill the air, like rugs being beaten on a balcony, immediately followed by a wild chorus of piercing screeches.

He heard Oliver yell "Run, Will!" and then, despite the policeman's insistence that they stop, all the players in the conflict began fleeing in a variety of directions in what quickly became a blur of frantic action. A woman's voice cried out. More guns were fired. Vidot, craning in vain to see exactly what was happening, could not focus on anything because the skull he was riding on was now tearing through the woods as fast as it possibly could. Navigation was clearly difficult in the dark, and various tree branches came flying in fast at Will's head, almost scraping poor Vidot. Finally Will stopped, ducking behind a thick tree. He crouched down, breathing hard with panic but otherwise perfectly still, not even moving when the shouts and commotion from the now far-away voices began to fade. Vidot instinctively crouched down too, low on Will's skull, as if hiding in his own thick forest.

Nearby, a twig broke in the dark. Sensing what was about to happen, Vidot wanted to cry out a warning, *Don't move, don't say a word.* But he couldn't.

"Oliver?" Will whispered, peering into the dark. "Is that you?"

The small gleam of light, perhaps from a distant streetlamp, caught the edge of the gun as the little man stepped out from the shadows. "No. I'm afraid it is not," he said. "You will stay silent, please. My driver has the car waiting, parked right past the edge of the trees there. See his headlights? Yes, let's go."

Book Four

Really, nobody knows whether the world is realistic or fantastic, that is to say, whether the world is a natural process or whether it is a kind of dream, a dream that we may or may not share with others.

—JORGE LUIS BORGES, *The Paris Review*

I

Maroc had awoken that day feeling desperate. Lying in his bed, he reflected on how he had only meant for this position to be a brief sojourn in his professional life, a mere stepping-stone to a more lucrative appointment. But lately it had appeared as if this post might wind up derailing his career entirely, for beneath his watch the entire district seemed to be breaking apart in uncontrolled insanity—why, only the night before he had received a report of a victim found with his eyes gouged out and his throat ripped open. To make it worse, neighborhood witnesses had reported that the man had been killed by a chicken.

Enough, thought Maroc. He would have to assert himself more forcefully. He could not have episodes like this—along with police officers simply disappearing off the face of the earth—occur without consequences. The criminals must be found and then they must pay or, as his superior, Papon, had told him yesterday in what had been a very short, curt chat, Maroc himself would pay.

But now, only hours later, the wheel of fortune had turned again and Maroc was feeling a sense of radiant confidence and dawning possibility that made him almost ecstatically hopeful that things were changing for the better. After a week in which he sensed the whole world conspiring against him, good news finally began arriving. He learned the first piece of it that morning when, as he came into work, it was reported to him that Bemm and Vidot's police patrol car had been recovered. Better still, the suspected thief was locked up downstairs in his jail. Maroc had immediately grabbed Lecan out of his office and the two headed down to the cells. Ignoring all the hissing and lurid catcalls from the prostitutes, they found the cell with the ancient woman sitting cross-legged on her bunk, chewing on a hunk of dry bread. She did not acknowledge them as they watched her through the bars. None of them said a word, and after a few minutes the two men turned and left her alone again.

Back in Maroc's office they compared notes. "She looks stubborn," said Detective Lecan.

"That's quite a black eye she's got. Wonder who hit her?" said Maroc, sounding uncertain.

"I doubt it was Vidot or Bemm," said Lecan.

"You're right. I don't think an old hag like that could take on two able-bodied police officers. I mean, Vidot was a bit slight, but still."

"Absolutely, she's much too ancient. I can't see her overpowering Vidot. And certainly not Bemm. They were both fit enough to handle an old woman."

"What's her story?" Maroc asked, taking a clementine off his desk and peeling it over the wastebasket.

Lecan looked through the report. "The woman says she first found the car over on rue Dupin. Perhaps she's telling the truth."

Maroc nodded thoughtfully. "Or she's conspiring with Vidot's wife, that's my bet. The widow gets a new lover, the hag gets a new car. Not a bad deal for either."

"If we ever find ourselves in a similar situation, I'll take the car," Lecan joked.

Maroc smiled as he continued: "We should at least grill the old cow, see what she has to say."

"Like I said, she looks stubborn," Lecan said. "I'd let her sit and stew a bit before we try to get anything out of her. Time in the cell will soften her up."

Leaning back in his chair, Lecan read the rest of the file aloud. "She gave her name as Elga Sossoka, though she has no identification. She claims she took the bus in from the country to visit a friend but when she arrived, she says, she found that the friend had moved. Walking back to the bus, she saw the car with the keys hanging out the door. She says her feet were feeling sore and her ankles were swollen, so she took it and drove it around for a few days, trying to track this old friend down. She says she knew it was wrong to take the car, but she's getting older and her mind makes mistakes." Lecan threw the report across the desk. "Ridiculous! Who does that sort of thing? In a police car? Too absurd. I could blow up that story in ten minutes."

"So blow it up," said Maroc.

Lecan picked up the phone and instructed an officer to drive out to the address near Cergy where she claimed she had been living. "See if anyone's there, tell them we have her in our cells. Let them know they might want to send a lawyer, but they shouldn't expect her home anytime soon. Then ask a few questions and see what you can find out about her."

Maroc nodded as Lecan hung up the phone. "You're right, twenty-four hours in a cell should soften her up, then we'll put the screws to her. I bet she's in it with Vidot's wife. I can smell it. Which reminds me"—he picked up a stack of papers and waved them at Lecan—"Pingeot brought these transcripts by yesterday, want to take a look?"

Maroc had placed Madame Vidot and her lover under twenty-four-hour surveillance, tapping their phone lines and watching each of their homes. Though the lovers had not attempted to meet, they spoke often. Which is how, the previous afternoon, Maroc had found himself listening to his very nervous subordinate, the young Christian Pingeot, reading lurid and explicit pornography out loud to him for the better part of an hour. "Then this Alberto fellow says"—the officer had cleared his throat—"ahem, 'I want, um,' ahem, 'I want to thrust my spear deep into you, your' . . . sir, I really cannot."

"Read it to me, officer."

"All right, sir. 'I want to thrust my spear deep into your moist petals'—please, sir."

Maroc had to agree it was pretty bad stuff. But he had made poor Pingeot continue, simply because he enjoyed seeing the officer's discomfort. Now he gleefully handed the transcripts to Lecan.

Lecan read the report with wide eyes. "My, this fellow Alberto is a terrible poet," he said.

"Well, he certainly is Italian," Maroc conceded.

Lecan smiled. "Do the two know we are watching them?"

"Hard to say. But she won't let him come to her flat. And they cannot go to Alberto's, his wife is there. So see what he proposes?" Maroc pointed to a section of the transcript.

Lecan read it and smiled. "Ah-ha, the rascal, he wants her to meet him tonight in the Bois."

Maroc clapped his hands. "Ha ha, such good old-fashioned naughtiness. Makes me feel young again," he laughed. "Well, why not join in the fun, eh? Are you up for a bit of surveillance tonight? Maybe we can catch them with his pants down and her skirt up and then bring them in for some real questioning." He grinned lasciviously.

"Well, between those two and that one in the cage downstairs, we should be able to make some progress," said Lecan.

"I agree, I agree," said Maroc. "It's a very exciting day." And so they made their arrangements.

Later that night, sitting in an unmarked car across the boulevard, they watched as their subject Alberto paced back and forth on a lamp-lit corner of the park. They had followed Alberto from his apartment and now, having waited for almost half an hour, all of them were growing impatient for Madame Vidot's arrival.

Lecan lit a Gauloise.

"You fool," said Maroc. "Put it out; she'll see us if she comes up now."

"She's not coming," said Lecan.

"Impossible," said Maroc. "You read those dirty transcripts, the woman is like a cat in heat."

Lecan looked at his watch. "Maybe her conscience got the better of her. Maybe she feels bad about that nice husband she killed. Who knows? What I do know is we have been here for some time and there's no sign of her. I honestly don't know why he's still waiting. The little slut stood him up."

Maroc stared at the lone silhouette loitering across the street and shook his head in frustration. Where was she? He had felt so tantalizingly close to wrapping up all the strands in one nice, neat package, but now some gnawing sense at the bottom of his stomach was telling him that the simple solutions he wanted were beginning to slip away. "Fine. Let's at least grab him. He must know what she did with Vidot. He must. Even if he's innocent, he'll have a lot to tell us."

Babayaga

"Well," said Lecan, reaching for the door handle, "we'll never know unless we ask."

They got out and crossed the street. Alberto stopped his pacing as they approached; they could tell he recognized them at once. Then, pretending he had not noticed them, he began to nonchalantly walk down the path into the darkness of the park. It was bad enough that his date had not shown up, but a conversation with the police was clearly not the way he wanted to spend the night.

"The bastard's trying to slip away," said Maroc, picking up his pace. He would have run but he hated running, it always made him feel fat, and so by the time they reached the corner, their suspect was gone. "Come, he went that way, we can catch up with him," Maroc said. Lecan followed him into the park.

They walked in silence, listening for footsteps, but the Bois was quiet. They followed the paved walkway until it divided and then, instead of splitting up, they both stayed to the right, going deeper into the park and crossing near the lake. Every so often they would pause and look around, hoping to hear their quarry's footsteps, but as they stood in the silence, it was clear that Alberto had escaped them.

They headed back to the car. Halfway down the walk, Maroc tapped his hand on Lecan's shoulder and pointed into the overgrowth. "Look, is that him?"

"It's hard to tell," said Lecan.

"Who's he with?" Obscured by the brush, they could only dimly make out a group of figures standing in a small clearing about fifty meters away. Maroc and Lecan moved in closer, stepping carefully between the thornbushes and tree branches in an effort not to make any noise. Coming closer, they found a situation of such interest that it made them completely forget their missing suspect.

There were seven people there, all of whom appeared to be frozen as stiff as wax statues. As Maroc and Lecan came to a break in the trees, it became clear why the group of people were immobile, as the majority of them had guns pointed at one another. A small bald man was moving about and talking. Maroc squinted into the darkness, trying to make out what was happening. "What the devil is he—?"

That was when the little man produced a gun and shot one of the men in the head.

Maroc immediately pulled his whistle from his pocket and blew it as loudly as he could, rushing headlong into the middle of the clearing, with Lecan right behind him. "Police! Put down your weapons and stay where you are."

Maroc had, up until this point, served largely in administrative roles, and in his entire professional history he had very little actual experience working in the streets among the citizens of the city's neighborhoods. His long, comfortable career had begun with a desk job in a Paris office; then, during the Vichy years, he'd moved on to more bureaucratic work in Bordeaux, then back to a desk in Paris, where he aided Papon in various departmental roles, and where, over time, he had grown quite comfortable thinking of himself as an important figure of authority and power. Therefore, when he yelled "stay where you are!" he was logically convinced that everyone would do just that. He was, therefore, quite bewildered when his imperious command, combined with his piercingly loud police-whistle blast, had entirely the opposite effect. All the characters in that small clearing, who had, in fact, been standing perfectly still before as they stared down the barrels of one another's guns, all now suddenly flew into a burst of frantic and frenzied motion. Guns were fired, people ran off in all directions, and, to make things worse, the forest itself seemed to spring into life as two broad caped shadows came swooshing down from the trees, blocking his vantage of the fleeing suspects while knocking one of the women to the ground. What the hell was going on? Who were these superheroes swinging out of the sky like some wild characters from the Fantax or Fulguros comics? Then Maroc realized the large swooping creatures were actually owls and the capes he had imagined were their wide wings. Were these the same killer birds that had attacked the man by the Galeries Lafayette? What was this, some mad homicidal falconry? What went on in this damn park? Lecan went dashing off into the forest, pursuing several of the fleeing group, while Maroc chased down one of the men. Grabbing at the man's legs, he forced him to fall forward. The man's gun went off as they hit the ground. When the man started shouting out in English, an infuriated Maroc instinctively punched him hard in the face and knocked him cold. After handcuffing the uncousious man, Maroc stood up, dusted off his coat, and looked around the scene. The birds were gone, frightened by the gun, no doubt. Most of the other people had vanished too. Lecan had not returned. The woman the owls had attacked lay close-by. In her gray suit, she looked ordinary, a secretary perhaps. She was spread out on the ground with her eyes open, staring up at the sky with bloody scratches on her face and a leaking bullet hole in her temple. The dead man, whom the little bald fellow had shot before all the commotion, lay by her side, his legs bent wrong and his arm extended so that the two almost looked as though they were holding hands. Maroc shook his head in dismay. Papon would not like this at all.

Hearing a noise, Maroc looked up to see Lecan coming out of the brush, his hair askew, covered in dirt and leaves. He was pulling another handcuffed man along by his elbow. "I managed to trip him up as he was running by," he said. "He's an American."

"I think this one's American too," said Maroc, pointing at the unconscious figure in the dirt. "You'd better take yours to the car and radio the station for some assistance. Get an ambulance here too. Tell them we have two bodies and two arrests."

Lecan led his prisoner off, leaving Maroc standing in the clearing, looking over the three prone figures. Maroc remembered how when he was little, his overprotective mother would never let him play in the small local park after dusk. "Bad things happen in the dark when God cannot see you," she would say. He wondered what she would think if she could see him standing in this clearing, in the company of two dead bodies and one unconscious prisoner. Yes, Mama, you were right, he thought, very bad things happen in the dark.

II

Elga had the whores all gathered around her in her cell; there were five of them now, three having been brought in during the night. She was regaling them with secrets, tips, and easy tricks, what herbs and teas to drink to avoid diseases, what to scrub yourself with, the subtle ways to spot the crooked policeman who could be bought or seduced, along with simple recipes for lavender perfumes to bring the right kind of customer. She explained the pulls of the night, how understanding the lunar cycles could help them navigate customers' moods (men paid more on the half-moon, fucked longer on the new moon, fell for any flattery on a quarter moon, and could cut you on a full moon). She told them which birds to watch for omens, how to use menstrual blood for curses, and made them laugh and chortle with her stories about the tiny-cocked corporal and the prudish cardinal who shit his bed. She told them about Catherine the Great's sumptuous bedroom and all the proud noblemen the queen had bled dead in return for their affection. She let them know how bergamot oil could clear away pimples, how turnips made skin boils recede, and how to kill boot fungus with long soaks of cider vinegar.

"I'll tell you one important thing," she said. "If you ever marry a man, don't take his name. Tell him you're untraditional, make a scene, have a fight, but"—she shook her finger in their faces—"always keep that one precious thing. Men want to swallow you down, take all of you, even your name, like a big fish gulps down minnows. I tell you, your name is the piece they cannot have. I have been chased by the law and I have been forced into hiding, but I have always used my own name, in every country where I have ever been, even if the police know it, it's no matter. Your name is the only important word there is. If you lose your name, you lose your strength, and here amid the beasts you need all the strength you can get."

She asked which of them wanted a husband. Three of the women, blushing, raised their hands. Elga nodded. "See? That's good," she said, pointing at the giggling ones. "That's the way you get a husband, through laughter and tears, back and forth, all the time, like one of those metronomes sitting on top of a fancy fat parlor piano. Tick tock, tick tock, tears and laughter, play it well and you will confuse and bewilder him and he can be yours. He will try to outthink you, outflank you, calm you down, but you can always dance around him with your weeping and your mirth, ha ha ha, until he is pulled under the same way a great whale drags the massive whalers deep to the bottom of the sea. Of course," she shrugged, "it won't work on the smart ones, but luckily, ha ha ha, the world has no shortage of stupid men."

At this, an awkward silence fell over the group. "What?" asked Elga. "Why so quiet?"

One of the girls spoke up. "But what if I want to be with a man I can love and honor, not a big dumb oaf?"

"Ah, um, I see, so you want a trick for that new kind of love you see all over your matinees and musicals? Boy meets girl and they hold hands, ha, you want that shit?" Elga spat on the floor. "Bah. Those tricks exist, yes. There is a spell for every hunger, every need, mmmn, yes, but, mmn . . ." She shook her head. "Only fools go there." She was quiet for a few moments, stewing in her thoughts. Finally she noticed they were still watching. "Get away, leave me, go!" she shrieked. They huddled off to the far side of the cell while Elga sat on her thin pallet and brooded.

These modern girls were too soft, she thought, even the tough ones wanted to be spoiled and pampered. None of them were warriors. Her mind wandered back to the beginning, when she traveled with the ancient trains of archer and spear. The leader of that first group, Oba, who had allowed Elga into their camp, now showed her the way. The other women welcomed her warily; one, named Temra, loaned her bedding and shared her ration. Another, named Rasha, gave her some torn rags along with a needle to sew her own clothes. They were following a chanyu's army whose name Elga had since forgotten. She did recall how, after many months in the field, this ruler had drunkenly quarreled with Oba over their lot of plunder, and how that night, hours after the victory banquet, Elga was awoken by Rasha and told to quietly gather her things. One by one, the women followed Oba, stepping over the soldiers who lay, unmoving, on the banquet floor. Climbing high up the dry hills above the valley, Elga looked back at the silent camp. "I thank the stars no one awoke to catch us," she said to Rasha.

"Don't thank the stars," Rasha said with a wry smile, "thank poison."

That was when Elga realized how foolish it was to fear an army.

Over the years, they found countless other khans, nizams, rajes, and princes to serve. Each time, victory followed their hire as they traced the armies' paths across the fields, hills, ridges, and steppes, east to west and back again, laying the charms for victory, nursing the wounded, burning the dead, and taking their share of the bounty. The pattern was as constant as the North Star: after every battlefield success, their host's pride would grow and swell until finally the vain and foolish victor wholly believed that it was only his strategic foresight and sharp-eyed skills that had forged all his good fortune. He would grow impatient with the imperious Oba and her crafty tribe, who were, after all, no more than superstitious wenches—skilled with the healing arts, yes, but too ugly to look at. Then requests would be refused and lines would be drawn.

Some died from wild blue lightning fire searing their camps, some found their tents coursing thick with plague rats, some tasted polluted wine; and then there were the fortunate ones whom Oba benevolently indulged, allowing a more glorious end as their heads were sliced off in a clean flash by their enemies' bright, shining steel. But in every case, arrogance and hubris turned once proud armies into simple carrion, lying plenty for a murder of crows, as the women marched on.

With every day, Elga learned more. Her christening bath had been in a pool by the Belaya River. Her dream had been of a snake wrapped around a white marble egg. Oba could not tell her what the egg signified, but the marble meant a long life and the snake, she said, was a very good spirit to have on your side. She taught Elga how to grind up the serpents' sloughed-off skin and inhale it, which brought visions of all varieties: some came as prophecies and predictions; others tore the fabric of reality away, giving her fractured glimpses with meanings far greater than she could comprehend; and others merely widened her perspective and control, letting her chart the paths of her enemies' approach.

She gained other virtues as well, wisdom, strength, and, most important of all, time. The serpents' smoke entwined with the eternity of death, slowing the effect of her years to a mountain's crawl, so that men's sons were born as babes, grew to men, withered ancient, and were buried in the time it took a wrinkle to even hint its presence at the corner of her eye. But age she did, along with all her sisters, centuries slow, but sure, as they passed back and forth between the comforts of the court and rougher life with the army in the field, tending to

Babayaga

the healing tents and bargaining for fates as imperial borders wandered and kingdoms dissolved into dust.

From almost the very first, Temra was her closest friend. Elga had no idea how old she was, only that she had served Oba for eons and could sense from a glance or a footfall the old woman's many moods. Temra cautioned when to stay out of Oba's path and, alternatively, when it was timely to ask for favor. Over the years, she also provided wise guidance on how to master this range of new powers. "You are a different animal now, but you are not evil. Like the serpent who guides you, you can be an ally to many," Temra told her. Elga could not think of any beast allied with the serpent, but she did not contradict her friend. She merely worked her days and lay through the nights as the years fell around them like drops of rain.

Elga stayed with Oba, Temra, and the rest of the tribe for what would have been the span of four lives, studying, listening, watching. To memorize the spells, she mimicked Temra by the firelight and then turned them backward, spinning them into riddle songs that she repeated as she followed the dusty long trains of mules and camels.

Finally, in the end, she was forced to flee, once again alone and frightened. Oba's mind had slowly blackened with a seething paranoia that wrapped around her thoughts like a choking ivy. Obsessive, secretive, and certain that those around her were trying to hurt and betray her, she sulked and brooded and kept to her tent. Then, one by one, the other women of the tribe began taking ill, some mortally stricken with fever, others dying from bloody cramps. Plague pyres burned and suspicions grew. Finally, one night, Oba sent a message for Elga to come to her side. When Elga found her, Oba whispered that she needed help taking the conspirators down, and that the worst of the plotters was Temra. Elga begged to leave, Temra was a sister, friend, and lover to her, but Oba firmly insisted. Elga asked why she could not do it herself, why she needed her help, and that was when she learned her final lesson from Oba.

"I have never told you this but all in our camp, you and me and the rest of the women, our bonds to the darkness give us a stronger hold on life than weakling mortals possess," Oba explained, her fingers working nervously on the edges of her shawl as she chattered on. "A man can stab or choke you to death, but if you are one of us, if you have our blood, your ghost will remain, still capable of a curse and a haunting, still able to track, still able to whisper and curse, until your will is done or the earth finally burns and vanishes. It takes more than one hand to kill a woman of our spirit, you need another with powers to help. Two sisters must act together, one blow for the body, one blow for the soul. So remember, you need a second sister to kill with you or you will never be safe, the witches' spirits will follow you, they will haunt you, and they will kill you." Elga did not like the look in Oba's eye as she said these things.

Before she was allowed to leave, Oba made Elga promise to lure Temra back before the sun rose, but instead, the moment she was out of the tent, Elga ran stumbling, panicked, out through the camp, barely able to breathe, trying to find her friend to give warning. When she got to their pallet, Temra was gone and no one had seen her. Elga wandered the campsite, searching in the dim glow of the vigil fires for her friend. Temra was innocent, she knew that as clearly as she knew where to find her hands. Oba had descended into a madness, time had chewed through the spells and was now tearing apart the old woman's reason the way a swarm of locusts went at fields of summer grain. Perhaps she was talking to Temra at that very moment, convincing her that Elga was the traitor. It might be worse, she realized, thinking it through; perhaps Temra had been the second sister who had helped Oba bring the cramps and the fever to all their fallen sisters. Perhaps Oba was now only covering her tracks. Elga stopped searching for her friend. It was not safe. She grabbed her few belongings and made her way to the edge of the camp, where she hid. Hours later, she took a horse and rode it out bareback, driving hard for four days, up creeks and off trails to confuse any pursuers, until the stallion became delirious and unsteady, almost crushing her as it collapsed from exhaustion. Elga made camp, built a fire, and smoked the horse-meat. She shaved the edges of the ribs against flat rocks until they were sharp as warrior knives and tucked the new weapons into the leather belt of her skirt. Then she continued on through the wilderness, moving steadily north and west, beneath the bleak and pallid skies.

III

"Smoke?" the bald man asked, holding out a silver cigarette case.

"No," Will said tersely.

Smart move, thought Vidot, don't take anything from this man. He reeks of toxins. Of all the hosts he had ridden, Will was the first Vidot felt a certain kinship with, perhaps because he sensed the two of them were equally perplexed by all that was unfolding about them. After so many hours on this scalp, Vidot was beginning to feel like Will's affectionate sidekick, a loyal gundog, or a Sancho Panza to his Don Quixote. He would have enjoyed the camaraderie more if the chiming of his own internal clock had not been growing so increasingly loud. Vidot was feeling painfully certain that every block they drove down was leading him further away from a solution to his metamorphosis. Fleeing the old witch had most probably been an error of judgment, but he had gotten the sense that staying close to Will and Zoya might lead to a possible solution. After all, she seemed to have powers too. But now she was gone and he was in yet another stranger's car speeding across the bumpy streets of the city. He had the feeling that it might be a long time before any potential answers appeared, while at the same time he was fairly certain that he did not have the luxury to wait.

The car slowed and turned into a narrow alley behind what Vidot recognized to be the pharmacy. Once they stopped, Bendix pushed Will out of the car, keeping his gun pressed up into Will's neck as he unlocked the building's door. He gestured for Will to step forward into the darkened room. "Go ahead, I will get the light, it's—" Bendix did not finish the sentence; instead he jumped up and slammed the butt of his gun into the side of Will's skull. Sitting high atop Will's scalp, Vidot was safe from the gun's blow, but not from the aftermath as he found himself reeling down as though he were atop a great falling tree as Will tumbled over, landing hard on his side.

Will lay moaning on the floor while the little man turned on the light, and whistled loudly. There was the noise of rumbling footsteps from above, and Vidot looked up to see two large men descending the stairs. Both were almost grotesquely oversized and muscular, looking like mutant stevedores or errant strongmen from some rustic circus. "Put him in the chair there. Be careful. We'll use him for the next test," said Bendix. They lifted their victim up and dragged him to a wooden chair by the wall, lashing him tightly to it by his arms and legs. Bendix stood to their side, smoking and watching. He seemed to be thinking through his next steps.

"You can leave us alone now, I won't be needing your help," he said, going to fill a tall glass at the water cooler in the corner. The two large men nodded and went upstairs. Looking down at his victim, Bendix took a sip from the glass and then threw the rest of the water into Will's face, thoroughly dousing Vidot. Will woke up with a shock, and the little man smiled a devilish grin. "My apologies, but you must understand, it is important to set the right tone," he said, leaning over his prisoner. "Now, where should we begin? How about we start with you telling me all you know about Mademoiselle Polyakov?"

Will shook his head. "I don't know her."

The little man nodded and took a drag of his cigarette. "Lies never bother me. In my profession, lies are like a wave hello, or a child jumping joyfully to greet his papa as he comes home from work, they are simply another way to begin a happy conversation." He picked up a chair and placed it directly across from Will, sitting so close they were only millimeters apart, though Will was a full head taller. "You know how strange it is?" asked Bendix. "I have spent so much of my lifetime searching for Zoya and Elga, such a very long time, so long that I had even given up. And now, when I am working on a completely different project, I find her, without even looking. It is enough to give me goose bumps, look. See?"

He held out his arm. It was true, Vidot noticed, the man did have goose bumps. Will did not say anything. "I wonder, have you ever asked your friend Zoya her age?" Bendix asked, then smiled. "No, I suppose a true gentleman would never do such a thing. But I can tell you one thing, she is older than she looks. In fact, would you believe me if I told you she is older than me?"

Will stayed silent.

"I see." Bendix got up and went over to the closet. "First you lie and now you don't talk. That is fine. I don't mind. So, how about I tell you all I know about this friend of yours while we get set up here."

From the depths of the closet he rolled out a large, odd-looking device. It was a tall, black, metal tripod composed of a padded arm that rested above a series of rubber hoses that were, in turn, wrapped in a serpentine fashion around a skeleton of steel pipes.

"This was a long time ago," said Bendix, "when I was working as a fresh-faced research assistant in Basel. Now, when I say a long time, it was almost fifty years ago, well before you were born. Like me at the time, my industry was budding young then too, molting free of its cultish alchemical past and burgeoning by leaps and bounds toward a bright and promising future. It was an electric, exciting time of discovery. My colleagues and I sensed opportunity everywhere. Most of my work was laboratory-based; this has always been my natural milieu. But my direct superior at the time, a brilliant man named Claude Huss, believed the next great leap forward could only be made by journeying beyond the antiseptic confines of the lab, out into the field, where we could delve into the myriad mysteries of the organic world. His plan—an ambitious one—was to catalog and distill the world's most ancient remedies." The little man paused to correct himself. "Not distill them literally, of course, but rather to identify, classify, and then methodically strip every remedy down to its most basic chemical components. Then we would rebuild each one scientifically, dispensing with the unnecessary elements and improving upon them wherever possible. As I said, it was an ambitious goal, but what ambition."

Bendix kept talking as he rolled the awkward, rattling contraption over to Will's chair. "You see, Huss was an anthropological pioneer, really, and to him this field of research was of the utmost importance. My job was to accompany him on this safari, uncovering any and every source of ethnobotanical knowledge we could find. Huss and I traveled for well over a decade together, by train across Asia to see the herbal doctors of the Far East and taking passage on the White Star steamer to America to visit the indigenous reservations there. We dove into mescaline rituals, sampled fungal teas, and danced with majestic hallucinogenic lizard kings. Then up the Amazon we went, where we both almost died of malarial fever before drinking deeply of the enlightening ayahuasca. Oh, how we suffered. But it was well worth it for all we were able to sample, collect, and categorize. Wait, one second . . ."

The little man rose and went over to the metal cabinet on the wall. Inside was a stack of white cardboard boxes. Removing one of the boxes, he opened it and carefully emptied the powdered contents onto an aluminum tray. Next he took a tall brown bottle off a shelf and poured its liquid over the powder, mixing it into a paste as he continued his story. "Some secrets took a little prying, but most were quite easily bought—for instance a bone-crowned Polynesian medicine man traded us what amounted to two volumes' worth of jellyfish cures for a single bottle of scotch. Bartering was often simple like that, some took gold, others whiskey. There was, however, a singular group who guarded their herbal remedies so obsessively that, in the end, extracting their coveted secrets became our greatest obsession, especially for poor Huss. It was all the more vexing since this band of ancient women, sometimes called the Babayaga, or sorceresses, or Wicca, or, more commonly, simply witches, were all situated right here in our realm, here in Europe, scattered across the east and the north: primarily in Russia, the Balkans, and Poland. I tell you, these pests were everywhere. Despite centuries of persecution, we knew they were still among us, roaming the land, leaching off our society like parasites, doling out their curses and cures wherever they went. Try as we might, though, we could never make contact with them. We hunted and searched tirelessly. More decades passed, and our new medicines began earning us prodigious profits. Huss's patents alone made him one of the wealthiest men in Zurich, but he never enjoyed his fortune. It bought him a vast mansion, but he stayed buried, locking himself up in its bowels, myopically studying maps, charting their rumored migrations, sending out correspondence to all corners of the continent, obsessed with chasing down their cursed kind. We followed every faint trail, every wisp of scent or clue, putting out ever-increasing offers for rewards, and eventually instructing our budding trade network of small town pharmacists and entrepreneurial suppliers to keep their eyes and ears open for these strange women. It was their shriveling ancient coven versus our prospering new cabal, and I knew we would run them to ground, it was only a matter of time."

Bendix opened a drawer and pulled out two separatory funnels. One he filled with water and attached to a hook and a tube, keeping its valve shut tight. The other he spooned a third full with the wet, gray paste from the tray and then hooked it beneath the water funnel, sealing the higher tube to the lower funnel. "Well, finally we caught one. A telegraph arrived in Bern from a Polish apothecary named Zell informing us that his brother, a local farmer, had trapped a bitch of a thief in his barn. The man was superstitious and, sensing she was trying to slip him a spell, he had gagged and bound her. Huss and I were there in twelve hours, a miracle for travel in those days."

Bendix tightened both of the funnels into place on the contraption. The water began dripping down into the lower funnel, and the paste started dissolving. Opening a metal drawer, the little scientist removed a long hypodermic needle. He fastened it to the tube at the bottom of the device.

At this point, Vidot was growing quite concerned for his host. Will was still groggy and seemed only half unconscious, but his arm was thoroughly lashed to the contraption and the scientist clearly planned to stick that hypodermic needle directly into his vein.

The little man kept talking. "We tortured that Basha for days, a battle of wits and physical endurance I will never forget. She was initially quite recalcitrant, but we conceived of means that, well, I will spare you the details, but eventually we broke the creature, wringing out an immense quantity of valuable information. Huss had been right all along, these creatures knew more than we could have ever guessed, more than we even knew how to put to use. It was staggering, they could actually meld sound to substance, producing remarkable effects. The potential remains limitless. The woman was also extremely well versed in recipes involving skullcap, valerian, Iceland moss, and other lichens. We could only use the smallest bit of what she gave us, so much of it was far beyond our comprehension. But what we did manage to exploit, well, I'd wager you've bought any number of cures for indigestion, headaches, or fever, at least partially composed of ingredients that came from that woman's mind."

He unbuttoned Will's left sleeve and rolled it up.

"We learned about Zoya and Elga from her as well, the only two colleagues that were still alive. Keep in mind, this was forty years ago, in early 1919. Are you beginning to see? Do you understand yet? We sent riders out to trap the two, but of course, they had vanished from their camp by then."

He vigorously massaged Will's forearm until it was pink from his attentions.

"In the end, I burned Basha alive, pouring kerosene on her while she writhed and whimpered. It was the least I could do, the evil creature had managed to hiss out a curse that inspired Huss to stab a fork into his own eye. The man thrust the tines straight into his own brain. Can you imagine that? Well, without him and his leadership, his vision, the entire project lost focus and eventually folded. Finally, I too lost my heart for the hunt, though of course I have always been curious about the fate of those two. Such a long time . . ." Bendix was silent for a moment, concentrating as he adjusted the drip. "I should probably point out, that while the means were certainly extreme, putting Basha down was not pure vengeance. Like any business, we sought to eradicate the competition wherever we found it. It was no different with the others. The Asian herbalists we shot, the peyote shaman we shot, the whiskey we brought the Polynesian was laced with poison, but then we shot him too. He might have had an antidote, after all, and we wanted to leave no loose ends. So I say all this with a very clear conscience."

He tapped the needle's tip and squeezed out a drop. "What we did is no different from what your own Dr. Kellogg has done, taking the peasant's country grain meals and placing it into those cereal boxes that line the bright aisles of your endless supermarket shelves. Remember too, these were not noble victims; each one was truly a pathetic, primordial savage, busily digging through the earth's horrible filth to forage for their unreliable cures. Huss and I, on the other hand, were scientifically accelerating the evolution of mankind. We did the world a favor, honestly, elevating an entire civilization out of the putrid swamps of ignorance. So here we are, yes? Now it is time to find a vein."

Awake enough now to sense the danger, Will tried to struggle, but he was tied down too tightly. "There, there," said Bendix, "I apologize for the needle but so far none of our other delivery systems works quite as well. We have tried blending it with hashish, cutting it with doses of methamphetamine, even baking it with anise into sugary cookies. Every experiment has had its setbacks. Your poor Boris and

Ned, and the others too. All pioneers, all necessary sacrifices. I promise, you will all be remembered as heroes. I am sorry." As the needle broke the skin, the agony of Will's screams sent Vidot's antennae vibrating with such high intensity, he felt engulfed by fire.

IV

Zoya sat in the big Chevrolet beneath the streetlight, shaking from more than the cold. Down on the corner she could see Oliver talking on a public telephone. She felt vulnerable and nervous. A stranger had said her name to her tonight, awakening a fear she had not felt for years. The owls had come to her rescue and then the guns had started firing and she had run, leaping into the thicket and then lying quietly beneath the brush for what seemed like an eternity. Finally, she had worked her way through the thornbushes and crossed over to the far side of the park. She had eventually emerged from the cover of the foliage and, trying to act nonchalant, strode out onto the well-lit boulevard. She saw a solitary man coming toward her and was about to duck back into the park again when he stepped beneath the streetlamp's beam and she recognized him.

"Oh, hullo," Oliver said with a slightly nervous smile.

"Where is Will?"

"I'm afraid I saw that odd little man take him away. I was hidden behind a tree but I saw the whole thing."

"Why didn't you help him?"

"I would have tried but the man had a gun and, well . . ." Oliver held up his empty hands.

Zoya looked around. "And the others?"

"Well, Brandon and the other goon went off with the police in handcuffs. I expect they have some explaining to do. Oh, and Gwen's lying back there in the grass, surrounded by a flock of curious authorities—the phrase 'exquisite corpse' comes to mind."

"Who was the little man—?"

"Let's walk while we talk, shall we?" interrupted Oliver, looking around. She fell in beside him as they began strolling. "We're simply out for our evening constitutional, right?" he said. "I parked the car up the way. So, yes, clearly the whole setup was a bit of a double cross. How Brandon expected to get away with it, I can't imagine. Trying to wrap my mind around the various possibilities. The way I figure it, you were the patsy, Gwen was supposed to serve you up on a silver plate to help get rid of Will and me. An old-fashioned star-crossed love triangle. A desperate gambit that really doesn't make much sense. Poor Gwen, silly girl, I don't know why I took her for an innocent when so precious few are. Obviously, my phone call about the pharmacy triggered all this. But I haven't the foggiest how it all ties together."

"Pharmacy?"

Oliver explained his visit with Will earlier that day. When he was done, Zoya felt as confused as she had felt when Will had first told her about his predicament, only this time she was sober. She did not like the feeling of being outside a mystery, looking in. Usually, she was the riddle that eluded being solved, but now here she was, the one having to be rescued, the one without a clue. There were too many secrets that she was not the author of and did not have any answers for. It made her feel skittish, and now some little man had stepped out of the woods, out of the darkness, out of some past, whom she did not know. But he knew her and that frightened her.

Approaching the corner, they saw a police car coming out of the park. Oliver put his arm around her shoulder. "Don't worry, it's only for show," he said reassuringly as the car passed by.

"We have to find Will."

"Mmmn," said Oliver. "I'm afraid it might be more prudent to—"

"No," she said firmly, surprising herself with the steel of her conviction, "we have to find him, now."

Looking at her, the constant hint of grin he usually wore slipped away. He appeared to be weighing the timbre of her words. "You realize who we're up against, right? I hate to admit it, but these fellows are a weight class or two above me."

"We are going to find Will," she said calmly.

He nodded slowly. "Of course we are, dear." The ember of a smile flickered back. "Never leave a man behind."

After a few minutes of walking, they turned off Avenue Raphael onto Avenue Prudhon, where halfway down the block he led her over to where a parked Chevrolet Bel Air sat between two streetlamps. Oliver opened the door for her, then got in behind the wheel. She could feel the momentum of events pulling her, surging forward out of her control. She did not know why she felt such a strong need to help Will, but the intuition felt overwhelming. In some manner, their lives had become entangled, like accidental knots. She did not know where it was going to end, but she knew that she was willing to fight not to have it end here. It was a strange and unfamiliar feeling, it was debt and obligation, he had saved her, after all, and this was her chance to balance the scales. She had always looked out for herself; men were merely the rungs to be climbed on the ladder of time. She had always taken from them without guilt. But this was of an altogether different nature. Another kind of feeling was lurking in her and she did not want to put a name to it. "Please, we need to go," she said to Oliver.

"I agree," Oliver said, shaking his head as he repeatedly turned the key, "but I'm afraid our car's being a bit stubborn."

"What do you mean?"

"I mean it doesn't work. Could be I left the lights on and drained the battery. Could be the starter. The quality on these Chevys is so damn spotty."

"So what do we do?"

"Well, there's a phone booth right on the corner there. I could call a taxi service, though I'm not sure any cabdriver will be up for helping us rescue Will. They used up all their heroics at the Battle of the Marne. Let me see . . ." He fumbled through a small red notebook he had pulled out of his jacket pocket. "There are a few people I could ring up, though it's hard to figure whom exactly we can trust at this point. For instance, if Gwen were alive she would have been the first one I called. Ha ha. Ah well, we'll simply have to take our chances with whomever answers. Might take a few tries." He dug in his pocket. "Luckily I've got some *jetons* for the phone."

She watched and waited as he went down to the phone booth and started dialing. One call followed another, and with every coin Oliver dropped into that phone, she felt the weight of her conviction to find Will grow. If he were almost any other man she had known in her past, she would have been long gone by now. She knew that she had probably played the situation entirely wrong from the start. She could have stayed with Oliver. He would have been easy to leave when the time came, and leaving was what a majority of her bones was urging her to do right now. But her heart told her to stay.

A hair-trigger instinct to run had always been strong in her: she had charmed her way onto ducal carriages, hidden in the beds of hay wagons and dairy lorries, tucked herself into the claustrophobic baggage holds of freight trains, stolen countless horses, bicycles, and automobiles. She had even once driven a hotwired BMW R75 motorcycle across the Latvian countryside while a bundled and dour Elga rode sullen in her sidecar. Of all her many skills, knowing when to flee was one of Zoya's most pronounced; she would be long gone before the empty vault was discovered, the forged checks reached the bank, or the bloated body washed up on the riverbank. She knew she could slip out of the Chevy now, leave Oliver to his phone calls, and vanish backward into the night, holing up in a nearby hotel or rooming house, sleeping until her strength returned in full. Then, in a few days, she could find her way to some other town, perhaps breaking from her old trail, heading south to Madrid, Milan, or Rome, or maybe finding a berth on a steamer to a distant port, Capetown, Hong Kong, or Buenos Aires. Making the journey alone, with no sister beside her, would be alien and dangerous, though perhaps, like Elga, she could find some poor urchin to train in the arts, beginning the cycle all over again. All she needed to do was pull the shiny door handle right beside her, and then she could go, never stopping, never looking back.

The trouble was, she couldn't. The strange knots binding her to Will kept her rooted in the car seat, waiting impatiently for Oliver to return with whatever scheme he could muster. There was some feeling, some ephemeral spirit working here. She could feel its strange strength clutching at her soul with a grip too strong to resist. It felt like a spell—she knew all the signs of those, but she knew too that this was no bewitching, it was her own choice, born from some kind of affection, which overrode all her old patterns and habits. So instead of bounding off into the briar, she stayed. It was greater than a sense of debt or obligation—Will had shown up in time to save her life, yes, but he had only been her unintentional hero, stumbling in at a lucky moment—the fact was there was more between them, in how their sleeping bodies curled together like a punctuation mark, how his kiss fit against her lips, how their tongues danced along chest and nook and thigh, and how his simple, assured presence calmed her, taking her mind from the constant focus on the hunt, making schemes and stratagems evaporate. It was different than a simple debt. This bond with him made her slightly nauseous, the way all magic did.

Oliver finally came back to the car. "Well, I'm happy to report the cavalry is on its way, though they'll take a bit to get here."

She nodded, saying nothing. Oliver took out a cigarette. "I must say, I find your affections for our friend Will quite touching. I'm not sure there's a soul on earth who would go to such great lengths to rescue me."

She looked up at him. "You have to want to save someone in order to be saved."

"Yes, well, now there's a brain-teaser . . ." Oliver said, pausing mid-sentence as he thought it over. He lit his cigarette and smoked it as they sat silently together. For twenty minutes, nothing happened except for the occasional car passing by.

Finally, a little gray Citroën *deux chevaux* came rattling fast around the corner and pulled to a hard stop in front of them, its beat-up bumper almost kissing the Chevrolet chrome. The doors opened and Zoya watched three large black men draw their sizable bodies out from inside the tiny vehicle's. Moments later, Oliver was making introductions: "Zoya, may I introduce Red, Flats, and Kelly. Gentlemen, this is Zoya."

"*Bonne nuit, mademoiselle*," said the one named Red, tipping his hat. She smiled politely. She had guessed they were American even before they started speaking English. She was not especially skilled with that tongue, but she had known her share of sailors and could follow them well enough. "Okay, Oliver, how about you tell us a bit more about this job?"

"And this had better be good, friend, not some wild fairy-tale goose chase," said Kelly. "We had plans to connect with Basie's crew backstage at the Olympia tonight."

"No, it's no fairy tale," said Oliver, pulling out his wallet and taking all the cash out of it. "First of all, as promised, here's the down payment on the fee. It's all I have on me at the moment, but there's plenty more where that came from. Now, did you bring the jumper cables? I'm going to need them to get this damn Chevy moving."

"Yep, though I'm not sure our little car's gonna be able to get that big ol' Chevy going," said Red.

"Well, let's give it a try. And the shovels?"

"We got 'em," said Red. "We had to, um, borrow them from the building manager."

"Fine, excellent. If all goes to plan you'll be able to return them by morning. Now, let's see, where to next?" Oliver said, taking a folded-up document out of his wallet and laying it out gingerly across the hood of the car.

Kelly looked down over his shoulder. "What you got there, Oliver?"

"Looks like some crazy-assed treasure map," Flats said.

Oliver flashed a grin. "An astute observation, Flats. It actually is a treasure map of sorts. It shows where, back during the war, you see, a man I know hid—"

"—crazy-assed treasure map," said Red.

Kelly shook his head. "And we could be hanging with Basie."

V

The chef looked down at the little girl. Noelle held the egg up. "Fry it on both sides, please, and keep the yolk soft, then place it on a piece of dry white toast."

The chef looked around impatiently. "You should not be here. The house manager will be very upset. And you cannot bring me some random ingredient in off the street and expect me to simply cook it up. If we start here, where will it stop, will you bring in a cow? Will you walk in a pig? If I do this for you, there will soon be a line of people from here to Les Halles asking me to boil their cabbages and bake their bread."

But the little girl did not move, she just kept holding the egg up to his face.

Noelle had found the egg that morning, still warm, and tucked in the yellow folds of her hotel bedcovers. Sitting across the room from her, atop the couch in a pose that was both haughty and aloof, the chicken pretended not to notice that the girl had found it.

The little girl had risen late, feeling rested though slightly nervous that Elga had still not returned. She hoped the old woman turned up soon, before any employees came knocking at the door with questions about the hotel bill. But Noelle did not let herself worry too much, the chicken was there with her, after all, and it had already proved itself very useful in keeping her out of trouble. Noelle picked up the big black phone and called room service, ordering a crème brûlée, some sherbet, a half dozen beignets, and a slice of chocolate cake for breakfast. She ordered a bowl of raw rice for the chicken—that was what Elga had been feeding it and the bird seemed to like it. Then Noelle nestled into the high pillows and studied the egg.

She was still mulling it over as the breakfast cart was rolled in. Sitting on the end of the bed, she carefully tucked the white napkin into her nightgown and gobbled down all the deliciousness, while keeping one eye focused on the egg. She pondered the very real possibility that it was magical and might grant her a series of wishes, like the magnificent genies from the storybooks. She ticked off her possible wishes. First, she thought, she wanted to become the most splendid and celebrated prima ballerina in the world. She imagined a sea of roses falling at her feet as bouquets were tossed up to her on the Opera House stage. Next, she thought, she wished to be a movie star, like her idol Audrey Hepburn, wearing glistening pearls and diamonds that sparkled as the flashbulbs went off, capturing her kissing her tall, handsome husband on the Cannes red carpet. Oh yes, she thought, who will my husband be? Who? Who? With her mouth full of chocolate cake, Noelle was now bouncing on the mattress, tickled by all the possibilities. She quickly ran through her options, deciding she did not want to marry another film star, because they always had to kiss the other pretty actresses in other movies and she did not like to share. She did not want to marry a president or king, they were often overthrown or guillotined; and she did not want to marry a soldier, even a heroic one, because they were always being shot. Businessmen were boring, doctors came home with diseases, and race-car drivers had a tendency to crash and burn. She thought about a young man who worked in her village, helping a local beekeeper. He was a tall, thin boy with curly brown hair whom she knew only from watching him walk through town carrying his smokers and gear, often awkwardly weighed down by his harvested honey. He was shy, and she was shy, but by the time she scraped out the last bit of crème brûlée from the bottom of its ramekin, she had decided on her course of action.

First, however, she had to get the kitchen to prepare this egg for her, which was turning out to be difficult. "Please, sir," Noelle said, "it is only one egg."

The stubborn chef threw up his hands. "I have said no, and little girls need to learn that no means no."

"No only means no until you say yes," she said with a smile.

He returned to the onions he had been mincing.

Noelle thought for a moment, wondering what Elga would do in this situation. "Hmmm, well, I am sorry," she finally said, looking around the kitchen. "The chef at my father's house would cook it for me. You know, his kitchen is a lot like this, only a little bigger." The hotel chef kept chopping at his onions. "He is an old chef, Louis is his name. Sweet Louis," she continued. "I think he has grown half blind and now Papa does not like his food at all, he says his broths are flavorless and watery and his roasts are so dull even salt cannot help them." The chef slowed, listening as Noelle spun her story. "Yes, it won't be long before Louis is gone and Papa needs a new chef. Have you ever been to Monte Carlo?"

The chef put down his knife and came over to the girl. "How do you want your egg?"

"Cooked on both sides, but keep it runny, and then put it on a slice of dry white toast."

He took it from her hands. "You are a silly little girl. I will put it between two pieces of toast, then you can eat it like a sandwich."

"Thank you." She curtsied and the chef shook his head.

A few moments later, she carefully carried the fried-egg sandwich on its white china plate down the long, high-ceilinged hallway back to her suite. There, she hopped into the big, comfortable velvet chair and gave the chicken a conspiratorial wink before opening her mouth wide and taking her first bite.

Within seconds she was lying in convulsions on the floor, kicking her legs spasmodically, flailing her arms, and snapping her neck back and forth. Her eyes had rolled up so that only the whites showed and her veins bulged and pulsed out from her skin as the visions flooded her mind with the force of a storm's foaming waters breaking through an overwhelmed dam.

Over the next two hours, in the muscular thrall of this unrelenting seizure, Noelle saw many things, but she did not see the beekeeping boy.

VI

Will was in Detroit. He wasn't sure how he had gotten there, but it was a sunny day and he was walking down Congress Street toward Woodward Avenue. There was the Guardian Building straight ahead, with the classical Buell Building towering up on his left. He could smell the yeast from the Stroh's brewery and hear the distant clickety-clack of a streetcar traveling down Michigan Avenue. Then Will stopped, puzzled. On the corner where the Ford Building should have been there stood a weathered saltbox farmhouse with white clapboard siding. A little beyond that a Holstein cow grazed on a patch of grass by the intersection with Griswold.

The screen door of the farmhouse slammed opened and Oliver's friend Jake stepped onto the front porch. He had a cup of coffee in one hand and a copy of *Le Figaro* under his arm. He gave Will a friendly smile and waved. Will did not know what to make of this and stood there dumbfounded. He got that he was experiencing some induced form of dreaming (he knew the electric trolleys on Michigan had been out of commission for years now), but it came with a tangible sense of reality that confused him. Jake gestured for Will to come over to the house and then disappeared back inside. Unsure what to expect, Will crossed the street, walked up the flagstone path, climbed the creaky porch steps, and followed Jake into the dark, old home.

Entering the parlor, Will immediately smelled bacon and heard the telltale spitting and sizzling sounds of frying fat coming from a room in the back. Going down the long shotgun hall, he came out into a low-ceilinged kitchen, where Jake had all the gas burners on the cast-iron stove cooking, with scrambled eggs in the wide skillet and tomatoes and thick slabs of bacon on the grill. "I didn't really have time to make anything fancy, the boys only called a few minutes ago to tell me you were coming. But bacon's good, right? That's honestly the only food I miss from the States. America sure knows how to make bacon." He took a plate from the cupboard and, piling the eggs on high and topping it with the mix from the grill, set it on the small table in front of Will. "Eat up. It's hot and delicious."

Will did not know why he felt so comfortable; perhaps it was the odd familiarity of being back in Detroit, or the safe, comforting reassurance of knowing he was in a dream. He sat down and dug in. The food was delicious. He hadn't realized how hungry he was, he could not remember the last meal he'd eaten. "Where are we?"

"Good question," said Jake, pulling up a chair across from him. "Simple answer is that we're in a mix of your mental landscape and mine. Very confusing to move through at first, and tricky to get orientated in, but you get used to it. But basically, like I said, we're wandering around in a blend of my subconscious and yours."

"How's that work?" Will asked, taking another bite.

Jake shrugged. "Beats me. I ain't the pharmacist. As I understand it, the prime ingredient of the drug is extracted from a common root, one plant, and in some way we are both somehow connected back to that single source. I guess this is what lets it blend the different visions of its visitors. Impressive and very deluxe stuff, light years ahead of what the other guys have got. I mean, putting aside how incredible it is that we're commingling our individual and unique hallucinations, there ain't many drugs out there can conjure up a decent breakfast, am I right? That doctor is a genius." He leaned over to the window and pointed past the faded gingham curtains. "Your vision out there. What is it, Chicago?"

"Mmmn, no, iz Detroight," said Will, his mouth full.

"All right, well, see, we're also in my grandparents' house, up in Accord, New York. Upstate. So, this here is a mishmash of pieces of your unconscious world mixed with chunks of mine. Now, I don't know why my mind would conjure up this sad sack memory for me, I've been in plenty nicer places, but I guess it's some sort of symbolic recollection for me. Like I said, it's fascinating. When Bendix described what he was up to, I volunteered right away."

Will mostly wanted more breakfast, but he thought he should ask more questions first. "How do you know Bendix?"

Jake shrugged. "He's been doing various tests with us ever since the war. Initially, he was mixing up Thorazine with variations of crank to try to change a soldier's sense of time, you know, so that things would seem very slow while the GI was actually moving very fast. It had potential, but there were big physical setbacks, massive strokes and coronaries. Then he had an idea for how to interrogate suspects under doses of lysergic acid. That went kinda badly too. Bendix sent over some LSD batches from Bern that were way past the point of potent. Test subjects were flying out of hospital windows to escape the purple dragons and pink elephants. Two strikes were enough, and Washington sent me back here to smoke him. Then he pulled out this ace from up his sleeve, right in the nick of time, too, 'cause his number was up. But he put this on the table and everyone saw the potential right away. This could be huge. If he's got what he says he's got—and it sure the hell looks like he does—then it's going to be the biggest thing since ol' Madame Curie discovered radium. But like I say, I don't know what it is exactly, Bendix is using some mix of ergine, DMT, ibogaine, and other stuff. I don't ask many questions, the guy spooks me, honestly. The lab boys can sort out the details, all I care about is what we can do with it."

"Yes. Very interesting. Really, fascinating," said Will, only half listening while slathering butter on his toast. He felt entirely at ease; it was nice to be back in the States again, even if it was only in a fantasy. He liked Jake too; the man spoke with a down-to-earth straightforward style that reminded him of home. It made sense to Will that Jake came from good upstate country people. He wasn't like the other New Yorkers, with their obtuse, long-winded ways. Will wondered how Oliver and Jake had ever become friends when their personalities were so clearly miles apart.

"It is fascinating," Jake went on. "Think about how a drug like this could affect the entire topography of war. I could be at one latitude, see, and you could be thousands of miles away, but if we're dosed at the same time from the same batch, shazam, we're sharing a single stage together. Like we are now, get it?"

Will nodded, only vaguely understanding.

"What this means," Jake continued, "is that you can fly over one of Ho Chi Minh's camps in the deepest, thickest jungle and dose them by air, like you're irrigating crops. At the same time you carefully dose up your own GI force that's sitting back in, say, West Germany, all gunned up and ready for action. Talk about your goddamn ambush, the Commies will be loony-eyed and drug dreaming, wandering through their ancestral mud-hut homes, when—ka-bam—good ol' Yankee Joe kicks down the bamboo door and scorches a flamethrower in their faces. Then it's like 'Oh, hello' and 'Sayonara, buddy!' all in the same breath."

Will shook his head. "Wow, incredible. I never imagined stuff like this was possible."

Jake smiled. "Right now Bendix is the only one who can do it, no one else is even close. Mark my word, once the kinks are ironed out and the army labs start cooking up their industrial-sized batches, boy howdy, it is going to be a whole new ball game."

"Seems like it works pretty well already. I mean, this bacon tastes really good," Will said, loading up his fork for his last big bite.

Jake nodded. "Yeah, well, the clinical tests are almost done. But like I said, we still have some kinks."

"Like what?"

"Well, finding proper dosage levels and looking at the long-term impacts on the subjects; these drugs can put quite a strain on the system. I'm pretty sure that's what took out Boris, his heart exploded. Then there's the question of how you're affected in the real world when you're hit here. We've got more bodies buried in the basement than we have answers. Also, what if the effect isn't lethal, if it's only a crippling injury, then what? Then we get weird stuff like Ned's muttering coma."

Will stopped scraping his plate and looked up. "Ned? I thought she was working with the Russians."

"Ned was working for Ned; every other loyalty she had died back in Spain when the Fascists shot all her friends. Since then, she's been working with anyone who paid her. She would have betrayed this operation too if she'd had time to figure it out. I'm pretty sure that's why

Bendix gave her a funny dose. His methods are, well, like I said, the guy spooks me, but this is the new frontier, right? There is so much we don't know. We need more experiments, you understand. Sorry."

Wolfing down his food, taking in the surreal atmosphere (out the window a herd of bleating sheared sheep caught his eye meandering up Larned Street), Will had only been half-listening to Jake's story. It was fascinating, but so was so much at the moment, his world had become a grand orchestra of overstimulating sensations, with every sensory section—horns, strings, percussion—all going at full tilt. However, Jake's last point did catch Will's ear, the way a perfectly chimed triangle can cut through a symphony, and at the word "Sorry," he looked up to find Jake aiming a pistol directly at his head.

Without thinking, Will ducked and flipped the table up. Jake fired the gun into the ceiling as he tumbled backward with the remaining eggs, butter, bacon, and scalding coffee spilling, yellow and black, all over him. Jake aimed the gun again as Will dashed out the hallway. A shot hit and splintered the doorframe behind him as he dove out to the porch.

Leaping over the rickety stairs, Will took off down the walkway and ran across the street. Running past a pair of grazing goats, he heard another gunshot as the wig shop window shattered out in front of him. Not waiting for a second shot, he dove in through the revolving doors of the Penobscot Building, scrambled across the lobby with his head low, then ducked into the stairwell by the elevators, slamming the door shut tightly behind him.

Running up the stairs, Will thought through the weirdness and tried to form a plan. He realized that Jake was already an expert in this field, he had probably been hunting in this hallucinogenic terrain for some time. Jake also had a sizable advantage in that he had figured out how to actually get his hands on a weapon, he had a gun, while Will had only his wits, which at the moment were not nearly as focused as they needed to be.

Will reached the third floor and flung open the stairwell door only to find himself facing a rolling green pasture with a picturesque cardinal red barn standing on a knoll off in the distance. There was a creek, and a few yards beyond that a stand of ash trees. With no real notion except an instinct to keep moving, Will ran toward the grove, but the soil was boggy and his shoes quickly got stuck in the mud. Panicked and fumbling, he tried to correct his footing, but he stumbled and fell, slipping sideways on the ground. He started to right himself, but before he could get up, he felt the hard pressure of steel being pressed against his head. Slowly, he sank back down onto his knees.

"Well, pal," smirked Jake, "you can't say we didn't give you a nice last meal."

"Okay. But give me one minute more, just one minute, please." Will shut his eyes and tried to prepare himself for what was coming next. He quickly thought of all the beautiful things he had known in his life: his parents, his mother's two cats sleeping in the sun, Doris Day singing "Shanghai," a glass of whiskey on a winter's night, and the taste of the warm crêpe he had eaten the first day he was in France. Then, finally, Zoya, her eyes, her cheekbones, the nape of her neck, and the way her breasts and bare torso looked as she lay half uncovered on the bed, breathing heavily, exhausted from his kisses.

Will heard the click of the pistol. He opened his eyes and noticed that one of the Paris metro's Art Nouveau entrances had risen out of the meadow. "At least I get to see some of Paris before I go."

"What?"

Will pointed at the metro entrance.

"Oh damn—" Jake started to speak but his words were interrupted by a big, strange crashing and small yelping sound, as if an oak tree had fallen over a dog. Then there was silence. Will stayed on his knees, uncertain of what he should do next. Finally he looked up over his shoulder and found a stranger standing above him, awkwardly wielding a heavy branch in his hands. At the man's feet lay Jake, crumpled up on the wet field, his suit splattered with mud, his skull neatly caved in.

"Is he dead?"

The man nodded, with a shrug.

"Gee, thanks," said Will, slowly picking himself up off the ground. He put out his hand. "My name's Will. Are you French or American? Français ou américain?"

The man shook his hand and seemed about to answer when an enormous blinding white light flashed out and exploded across the landscape, engulfing all their surroundings. The man, the broad field, the distant trees, the whole world, completely vanished. Will tried shutting his eyes to block out the blinding, burning glare, but he had no way to stop the fierce light; his nerves felt scalded and raw as his panicked consciousness was shocked to a bright expansion point from which he was sure he would never return. The only bleak reassurance he had was that he absolutely knew what this was, the moment he had feared for years now, the great A-bomb annihilation. Someone had done it, the button had been pushed, an arrogant prime minister, a prideful president, a crazed stupid admiral or a lethally offended premier, it did not matter, some arrogant son of a bitch had launched the ballistic missiles, from Washington, Moscow, 10 Downing, or out from the bowels of one of the new nuclear submarines, it did not matter; the preemptive solution to every global conflict had landed, and all the wars being waged on the planet, every battle, every argument over justice or injustice, from the greatest of moral struggles to the most petty kitchen debates, conflagrations over the borders of oil nations to ornery grandmothers haggling over the price of thimbles, none of it mattered now, like the sun-scorched scorpions on the shores of some distant Bikini atoll, which had all been irradiated into an iridescent nothingness, it was over. Talk about the meek inheriting the earth, this once proud species, who had risen out of the jungle mud to overcome the mythical dragons of fire, serpent, fang, and talon, who had built spired cities, cleared continents, and were poised to conquer space itself, had been defeated, ultimately, by the fractional split of the tiny atom. All this flashed across Will's tumbling mind as he spun deep into the shrill, screaming abyss. An inexorable vacuum pulled at him, swallowing and sucking him down toward a nodal nothingness. And then it was over.

VII

Witches' Song Nine

Yes, feel this atomic weight bearing down on your dreams,
threatening like some swollen pink organ,

cystic, fevered, prime to burst
whenever a flashbulb pops.
Look how you have forged
your own haunting.

Lyda and I, we had a lover,
the naked professor, who, wrapped up in our blankets,
drew his hieroglyph riddles
across the whitewashed walls
and out onto the broad planked floors,
his nervous enthusiasm cracking his chalk,
and we would stare, wondering,
Where is this going?

Yes, yes, truth is vitality,
knowledge is power,
and we have our own lexicon, seared to mind,
of root and sinew, berry and boil.
Our cause is clear and yet our impact slight,
but you, well, where are you going?

Your scientists dig for answers.
The way pigtails play with matryoshka dolls,
one riddle tucked inside the last,
following it down, winding deeper
into endless, spiraling mysteries
while behind you, the hot winds blow
and the desert sands slip in
under sunny doorsills.

Enough of this, it makes me anxious,
let us instead set our eyes back
to the city of the fool and the crone.
Now there is a pair too, so very like you,
who never doubt their path.

Babayaga

VIII

"Hullo," said Oliver.

Will blinked and looked around. He was back in the pharmacy lab.

Oliver was beaming proud. "Surprised to be here? Well, yes, I always say, never underestimate the possibilities of pure adrenaline," he said, holding up an empty syringe. "Had to dig through the cabinets to find it. I thought it was worth a shot, so to speak. Wonderful stuff. Simply wonderful."

Behind Oliver stood two of the jazzmen, Kelly and Red, wearing their matching blue suits. Both the men were mud-stained and sweaty and both were breathing hard. They each held a smoking Thompson submachine gun pointed down at two giants, who each lay stretched out on the floor, pistols still in their hands and sizable chunks missing from their heads. Blood covered the walls and oozed out from their bodies, pooling across the concrete floor. Flats stood by the closed door, watching out the window with a Johnson rifle in his hands. Bendix himself was nowhere to be seen.

Then Will saw her, she had been standing in the shadows by the staircase, watching the scene shyly with her arms crossed. She stepped forward with a small smile and a look of relief on her face. Moving slowly, depleted of strength, he pushed himself up out of the chair and took her in his arms. He held her for a long time without saying a word.

Twenty minutes later, he watched as the jazzmen stowed the guns and stuffed the shovels into the back of their impossibly small car.

"You have quite a woman there," Red told him, nodding to Zoya, who stayed on Will's arm.

"If you've got any issue coming up with the cash you owe us, I know some Berbers who will take those Thompsons off our hands, along with the rest of the stuff," Flats told Oliver.

Oliver nodded. "No need to bring in the Berbers, Flats, I'm good for the cash. Hold on to the guns till you hear from me."

"Okay, just trying to be accommodating." With that, the jazz boys rumbled off in their car and were gone.

Now Will was riding shotgun with Oliver behind the wheel. Zoya rested in the back. They were driving fast through the night, heading out of town, toward a friend of Zoya's who she said might help them. Oliver filled Will in as they drove: "The whole adventure was torn right from the pages of Poe. Did you ever read "The Cask of Amontillado"? It was like that, only, thankfully, without the fatal immurement. The map turned out to be accurate, you see, the guns were stashed in the sealed-off catacombs over in Montparnasse, right beneath the cemetery. It makes sense, it's close to the station, so I suppose my soldier cached it all away before he caught the westbound train. The catacombs down there are littered with piles upon piles of skeletons."

"I know about the catacombs, Oliver."

"Oh, sorry, of course, I always forget you're not a tourist. In any case, there's a hidden street entrance to the lower levels, and once we got in it was merely a matter of identifying the right crypt. Luckily the map was very good, that fellow must have been well trained by the OSS, because we found the spot in no time. I'll say, though, it was rather amusing watching the jazz boys dig through the ossuary, throwing those ribs, shinbones, and skulls about like mad dogs. At one point I tried doing the 'Alas, poor Yorick' bit but no one was amused."

"Where was she?" Will asked, gesturing toward Zoya, asleep in the backseat of the car.

"At the top of the stairs, keeping watch. We were in and out in half the time I thought it'd take. Then it was simply a matter of dashing back to the pharmacy and coordinating a successful attack."

"How'd you pull it off?"

"Oh, well. I had a rather elaborate charade cooked up involving dressing the boys in overalls and pretending to be EDF electricians, but then Red suggested we simply kick in the front door and start firing. We had them out-armed and we possessed the element of surprise, so his plan made sense. Besides, I don't know where we would have gotten the overalls."

"So, you kicked in the door and started shooting? With me just sitting there?"

"Well, there was a bit of reconnaissance, but I know what you mean. As I said, I would have preferred some intrigue involving handlebar-mustache disguises and whatnot." He smiled. "But it all worked out. The jazz boys are crack shots, you know, they were all front-line infantry during the war. It was a fortuitous team to have on hand for the job. I must say, you are a lucky man."

Will rolled down the window a crack and leaned his head against it. The fresh night air cleared his thoughts a bit, but not enough to make sense of things. He reached his arm over the seat and wrapped his hand around the sleeping Zoya's ankle. That helped.

IX

The guard came for Elga early. She acted as though she were fast asleep when he rousted her, though she was already well prepared. Slowly, she stepped over the sleeping whores and out of the cell, trudging ahead of the officer. She waited as he unlocked the heavily secured doors and took her up the narrow stairs. The main rooms of the station house were mostly empty at that hour; only two officers were in sight, one yawning, one picking at a roll and sipping coffee as he read the morning edition of *La Croix*.

The guard walked her down the hall and around the corner, where they came across three men standing around a desk. Her guard interrupted the conversation.

"I have Elga Sossoka here," the guard said to the man Elga guessed was his superior, a police captain perhaps. "Which room do you want her in?"

"Put her in two," said the captain. Elga noticed that when the guard had said her name, one of the other men in the group, a tall fellow with a bruised cheek who was wearing a rumpled gray suit, reacted almost as if he had been lightly slapped. It was a small and slightly suppressed expression, no one else seemed to notice it. But he eyed her now with a curious interest that Elga did not like. She looked down at her feet and tried to look stupid.

The guard took her arm and they continued down the hall. The exchange had bristled her nerves. She wondered if she was merely being paranoid, but as they came to the door marked "Room 2," she looked over her shoulder and saw that the tall man was ignoring his companions and focusing all his attention on her. She knew this wasn't good; she would have to work fast.

Room 2 was empty except for two chairs and a metal desk. A notebook and a pair of pencils lay on the desk. The guard seated her in the chair by the wall and then departed, locking the door behind him. Sitting alone, she collected her thoughts. She guessed that the man's having noticed her had set off the old impatient celestial clock's ticking, and she knew she would have to act fast to escape the fate it was running toward. She took a deep breath; even pondering the effort ahead wearied her. She had seen too much excitement in the past few days. She remembered back to when she lived by herself in the forest: countless seasons would pass without the need for a major spell; small ones, yes, to lure in squirrels, moles, and tasty field mice, or to catch pheasants and quail, but other than that she had enjoyed the long silence of those years. Of course, that could not have lasted, once the steady industry of man found its fuel and it began burning and digging and wrenching everything in its omnivorous fashion; it was only a matter of time before it burned down her door. Now the world had no silence, it was full of tin radio sounds and fat Victrola tunes and constantly ringing telephones, the voices on the other end of the line always busily killing and clearing for what was to come next. Even the village church bells that once taunted her hourly with their misguided faith were now drowned out by bleating horns and sputtering engines, and she was sure that densely tangled tranquility of forest she had lived in had long ago been cleared for corrugated wheat fields and the hungry harvest threshers that went with them. One had to move fast now to dodge the massive crush of the machinery, the gears gnashing with their atonal screech and grind, as if a thousand grand pianos were constantly falling from the sky and crashing down on the pavement all around her. It was no wonder that she had a hard time concentrating. Alone in the room, she spat on the floor.

A moment later, the door opened and the captain they had met in the hall entered the room with a second officer. She looked at the keys looped on their belts and held herself back from simply grabbing at them. That man back in the hallway had her jumpy, she could feel the clock ticking away, counting down. She always hated that clock. With a condescending tone, the captain explained that they had some questions regarding how she had wound up with Detective Vidot's patrol car. "I already told the other one, why bother me?" she grumbled.

Babayaga

The captain smiled politely. "Your explanation, madame, was slightly less than plausible. But maybe once you've given us more details we will be more ready to believe you. I will leave you here with Officer Aubert so you two can talk."

Elga nodded. She had been through variations of this at many border crossings and city gates and in the camps of captured artillery, and it was always the same mix of formality and stupidity from men who earnestly believed that they were being crafty. Some she confused, while many she killed, and Officer Aubert, who sat down across from her and opened his notebook with a patient smile on his face, would soon belong to the latter category. "Do you mind if I smoke?" he asked.

"Do what you want," she said.

He lit his cigarette without offering her one. She knew this was part of the game: when he had first asked her permission to smoke, he was really saying "We are together," while this subsequent failure of courtesy said "But I am superior." She did not know if this was a trained nuance; she doubted it. All over the world, these interrogators acted out the same rote habits, like woodpeckers working their way down a tall pine thinking they are very clever in their search for bugs. But all the years of dodging questions and dealing with these pesky, prying interlocutors had left her with little patience. Besides, there was that man in the hallway and the clock was running. It was time to play her part. She leaned toward the man. "Now, my friend, do you want me to tell you the real truth about what happened that night? Is that what you're looking for?"

Aubert's eyes lit up. "Why, yes, of course, that is why we're here." He dutifully readied his pencil at the top of the notebook page, prepared to commence.

"Fine, but do not write this down yet. It is important you follow me with your complete attention. You can take notes later, now you should listen and watch," she said, holding her finger up in front of his eyes. "Remember, the path of this story is very critical." She started tracing out a map, an imaginary one that followed the imaginary steps she described from that night. He kept his eye on her finger. He did not know she was tracing out a maze that would enthrall his thoughts. Within two minutes his eyes would dim and he would be utterly spellbound, his mind would be soft, wet, and ready clay. Idiot, I should pity you, she thought, this is too simple. There is no observer looking in from a window, no one is sitting beside you. You are all alone here at this moment that will be your last, your end. The world has utterly abandoned you, leaving you at my mercy, vulnerable to the tricks of an old woman because they think I am so weak, so perfectly harmless. To them I am already dust.

The policeman's eyes grew wide. Elga felt like the mighty spider leaning forward, feeling that tug of the web as the fresh fly arrived.

She knew the path that followed. When the spell caught, Aubert would open the door to the interrogation room and lead her out of the station. If anyone tried to stop them, Aubert would attack them. He would be her blind slave, fighting for her freedom, and once they reached the street he would take his pencil and shove it deep into his own throat. This would start a commotion and amid the confusion she would complete her escape. She looked from his pencil to his neck, eyeing that soft target, thinking of how men walk blindly through their lives, their Adam's apples thrust out before them, unconsciously taunting every weapon. She was only seconds away from escaping this trap.

But then, the door opened and the captain returned, this time with the tall man in the rumpled suit. Aubert snapped to and rubbed himself alert. Elga sat back, dejected. The clock had stopped, the path was blocked. She would have to find another way.

"Excuse me for interrupting," said the captain politely. "I am afraid, madame, that you will have to leave now with this gentleman."

She looked around, trying to act confused. Even Aubert began to protest: "But I was making progress—"

"Ah"—the captain held up his hand, cutting his subordinate off— "these are things we cannot control. Mr. Brandon's superiors believe she is a person of interest, so we must release her." With that, he folded his arms. Elga could sense his frustration with this turn of events.

Ten minutes later she was sitting next to the man called Brandon as they were driven in a black Cadillac across town. He had not yet said a word to her, though hearing him speak at the police station she had gathered he was American. She also could tell that the French captain, a man they called Maroc, had a great distaste for him while at the same time being extremely deferential, even going so far as to give Brandon his handcuffs, which Elga now wore on her wrists. Throughout it all, and even now, she kept her mouth shut. She had learned long ago to be careful around men the police feared.

All in all, though, she did not think much of Brandon. She had always found Americans to be a strange collection, almost as uniquely exotic as the fruits and flora that had come to her from that faraway land. She could remember the day—back how long now?—when a lone passing hunter, trading some venison with her, had told her of the uncharted lands newly found. She recalled chopping the deer meat up and cooking it into a greasy stew, listening as the hunter described this discovery between greedy, wet mouthfuls. She remembered him repeating the words "gold, gold, gold" as she tried to wrap her mind around all the other opportunities this unexplored country might hold, not in metal, but in richer, more powerful treasures. She recalled the end of that visit, watching as the hunter scraped the bowl clean with his thin, stained fingers. "I won't be back," the hunter had said, "I plan to work my way aboard one of those ships to go find my fortune. I am not too old yet for the New World."

"Bah!" Elga had shaken her head. She offered him a cup of mushroom tea before he left. He thanked her again, sipped the tea down quickly and was reaching for his kit sack when the poison hit. It had been an act close to mercy. She had seen the rash on his neck and his brown mottled eyes and, recognizing his illness, knew too that he would not be able to endure the coming pains of the season. So, she pushed this bearer of one New World off into the next. She had emptied his pockets of every kopeck, smoked and packed the deer meat, and left his corpse for the crows.

She was not sure if he'd been babbling fable or fact, but curiosity was enough to pull her out of her woods. Wrapped in the hunter's old coat, she journeyed alone across the countryside, catching rides on serfs' barrel carts and bartering mules until she finally reached the booming port city. As she arrived and her nose sniffed excitedly at the heavily scented harbor air, her heart beat hard, it was nothing like she had ever experienced. Amid the brine, fish, and sewage stench, fresh new fragrances filled her nose, raw and potent aromas she had never encountered before, pungent with possibility. Eyeing the tall-masted carracks parked between their herring buss and dogger sisters—all laden low against the waterline—Elga nodded to herself and set to her business.

Stevedores, merchant runners, shipping clerks, and wharf rats swarmed about the busy docks as the ships' heavy cargoes were unloaded. Shaded in the darkness of their barnacled bows, Elga went to work, bargaining charms to the superstitious in exchange for samples of untested seedpods, wild grains, and dried root, whatever the sailors could bring her, all the while noting other sharp-eyed harridans working their own trades at the edges of the market. She sensed these ladies weren't whoring, peddling, or working the scrimshander trade, these were her own sisters, all answering the same call, sniffing the curious wind back to the source, and it was not long before she fell in with their lot. They each earned their keep by hustling in the taverns, pickpocketing crew, and tricking coins from mates first and second with their lush harlot lures, then regrouping later down the dark dead ends of broken oyster-paved lanes to swap their cribbed kitchen notes and pool their collected bundles of new mystery. Bunches of weeds and clumps of chopped stalks went into their dark variations of stewing slumgullion and red goulash as they rubbed their hands bug-eyed and busy with a simmering excitement. Buckbean, swallowwort, thimbleweed, and sweet gum proved powerful, while hobblebush, coolwort, and black tupelo offered more subtle possibilities. Elga remembered being especially proud of the secrets she coaxed and pried, over weeks, from the sly black persimmon. She stayed there by the sea for more than threescore years, working with her hoyden sisters as they labored over their exotic cargoes like bees in a honey hive: moving from candlelit garret rooms to low-ceilinged brick cellars, slaving over clay ovens, mixing, sizzling, blanching, stirring, reducing, then boiling and basting some more, all the while shouting, whispering, coaxing, chanting, and hissing out roughly hewn phrases and untried incantations, marrying the brews to their tongues, finding the consonants that harmonized and the vowels that stuck wet to the tumescent seeds, stalks, and spoils from the new land.

Finally, Elga left the others and returned to her forest, loading three fresh and healthy mules with the bundles of her hard-wrought bounty. Now that she was done, she gave little more thought to the New World, she had what she needed. Over the years she would hear tales of European exiles fleeing persecution, vanishing beyond the sea's horizon to build their newborn cities of God. Eventually, some returned to the Old World brandishing wordy manifestos proclaiming their right to liberty, along with the finespun white cotton and cane sugar to trade, all handpicked by their land's ebony slaves. To her, this New World seemed like a rough stew of notions that even now, centuries later, seemed unmixed and unblended, too many of the ingredients far too strong in their righteousness and certainty while also much too bitter with contradiction. Elga doubted if she would ever like the taste.

Sitting in the car with the American, she felt it was maybe time for someone to go find another New World, for having built their great cities all the way out to the Pacific, these Americans now seemed to stay busy by constantly running about, bumping into one another like a passel of fattened hogs who had long outgrown their shit-laden sty.

The car pulled up in front of a building that had two men standing out in front. As the car stopped, one of the men knocked on the building's front door and a little bald man with round glasses came out. To Elga, the bald man did not look quite human, he looked more like a white shrewmouse.

As the little man came over to the car, Brandon rolled down the window. "What happened?"

The little man did not answer at first, but looked over at her instead. "Well hello, Elga Sossoka." She stayed silent. He nodded. "It is an honor to finally meet you. You must have great good fortune to have lived for so long and come so far across so many lands. Perhaps we can borrow some of your luck to change our own poor fortunes. That would be a welcome turn of events." Then he returned his attention to Brandon. "You see, we had a serious setback. I'm afraid your friend Jake has died. I don't know precisely how it happened. It was a simple clinical exercise, purely academic. I for one certainly did not foresee any obstacles. This Will fellow did not appear to have that much fight left in him."

"I'm confused. Jake's dead? How?" Brandon asked.

"As I said," the little man replied, his tone a bit impatient now, "I do not know. You see, I was interrupted in my work by a group of enormous Negroes who burst into the laboratory firing tommy guns. Zoya Polyakov was with them. They killed Jarl and Malte and then took this Will away. So, your friend Jake's death is only one part of our problem." He began explaining what had happened, and although Elga tried to keep up, the many details made it difficult to follow. The one word that did catch Elga's ear, sticking like a hungry tick to her ear, was the name "Zoya." The girl had been here, only hours ago. Hearing the name, Elga's blood flared and her brain hummed with violence. She sat forward and tried to listen more carefully. Finally, frustrated with all the words, she interrupted: "You are looking for Zoya?"

The little man stopped talking and turned his gaze to Elga. "Why, yes, we might be, do you happen to know where she is?"

Elga nodded. "Maybe. I don't know. There are a few places to try. I was hunting for her too. We can hunt for her together now."

The little man looked slightly baffled for a moment but then looked at Brandon and smiled. "Yes, Elga, by all means, let us hunt for Zoya together."

X

Witches' Song Ten

Oh I do, I do and I am never done
adoring that which is the automobile.
No, not only one, but all together,
the massive swarm, seething and choking,
teeming and festering, these slithering steel insects,
black, red, and baby blue, swelling veins stiff,
enfolding the globe in their great gray
gaseous cloud of progress's passion.
Mere metal boils bubbling upon the earth's surface,
shuttling and speeding while oh how I adore
being nestled inside, armored against the world,
sinking into the plush ovum of velvet comfort.

Babayaga

Our first rides were with virile old generals
who lured us to seduction, humping us amazed
till their hearts exploded as the tin radio played that fine new jazz.
Yes, yes, this is truly a carriage for creatures such as us.
I know, for you it's your century's most wondrous innovation,
but it is truly no more than the same infernal tale,
man burning for power's gain,
peat and straw, cow pies and corpses,
all manner of forests torn bare,
whole mountains chewed free of their coal,
all this, all that, merely kindling to burn.
Caves and campfires first, then hearths and stoves
sooting your great cities black
before adding a coat of locomotion steam, and now
the inferno trapped, locked in iron, internal combustion,
no different, not a whit,
only wheels on gears on stone on steel,
a new can of burning, always forward motion.
Man inflames everything he finds,
first squatting naked, roasting poached fowl,
then dropping bombs from those droning trumpets buzzing high
as the floating pond geese gaze up in awe
at what is so coming down.

Man was born to char the earth and
when there's no swamp gas, black tar, or proud timber to tap
he sends out his canines hunting rabid far afield.
While, awaiting their return
he solemnly builds the looming tall pyres
that will burn every enemy down.

XI

Vidot regained consciousness as he was hanging out at the end of a
thread of hair, floating in a high wind. He did not know how long he
had been lost in that dream state. In a way, he wished he was back

there now, it had been so reassuring to feel like a whole man again, in his old suit, walking the streets of his neighborhood with two strong legs and a sure and steady gait.

When Vidot had first watched Bendix inject the needle into Will, the flea had nervously wondered what the best course of action might be. After Will's initial ear-shattering scream, his host had collapsed into a deep slumber, only twitching slightly, with no outward signs of pain or discomfort. Vidot had thought it might be fine to simply watch and wait. Bendix was busy cleaning up and putting things away, only returning every few minutes to take notes on Will's condition. As the scientist finished a third observation of his prisoner, one of the gargantuan men came lumbering down the stairs. Bendix pointed at Will. "He's been in the dream state for about ten minutes. I suspect it will only be another five or so before Jake completes his task. Then I'll need you to dispose of the body."

"Where?" asked the giant.

"The basement," said Bendix. "with the others."

This sentence set off all sorts of alarms in Vidot, as he realized the fatal danger Will was in. Immediately, Vidot's professional instincts took over. He was thrilled. As a policeman, he had always waited for this moment, when he would actually protect the innocent from a real looming threat. Policemen generally arrived too late, not because they were lazy or incompetent but because nobody ever called them until the window had already been smashed, the blade had been stabbed, or the head crushed. By the time he and his colleagues arrived, the safe was bare, the blood was cold, and the only thing left for him to do was dry the tears, collect the clues, and help sweep up the shattered glass. This did not bother many of his peers, who were happy enough to simply cash their checks and go home, but Vidot lived perpetually on the balls of his feet, waiting for that desperate moment when his sense of duty and honor would be called into action. He longed to leap in front of a speeding car to save a heedless child or push a bystander out of the path of an oncoming bullet.

What could he do? His options here were even more limited than the dutiful police dogs that offered no more than sniffing, barking, or bites. Still, his sense of urgency was strong. Which is why, though he knew it was an insane and potentially even suicidal act, Vidot the flea did the one thing he could do: he valiantly and forcefully bit into the flesh of Will's skull, sucking up his dangerously drugged blood and plunging himself into the strange and mysterious world below.

Almost immediately, he found himself wandering down through his old neighborhood on rue Mouffetard, which was almost as he recalled it, though now periodically punctuated by curious interruptions: a brook running through an alleyway, an Irish bar with a sign reading "Casey's" standing where the old man Bourdon's barber shop should have been. As Vidot kept walking, the unrecognizable elements of the landscape began to outnumber the familiar ones, the hat shop was now a stand of willows, the watchmaker's now a record store, until, turning a corner by the old library, he came upon the sight of Will kneeling in a muddy field, a man holding a gun against his head. Their backs were both to Vidot as the entrance to Vidot's old metro stop blossomed out of the field in front of them. Distracted by this, the man with the gun did not notice Vidot's approach. Nor did he hear the detective lift the heavy branch from the ground and swing it round his head with all his might.

Moments later, the man with the gun lay at their feet as Will rose and dusted himself off. Vidot felt light-headed with excitement. He was not sure how to explain the situation, there was too much to say, so many odd and unbelievable circumstances had stacked themselves up, one upon the other, but then, at the very moment when he was shaking Will's hand and preparing to start with a simple hello, Will completely vanished, disappearing right before his eyes, leaving the detective alone in a landscape that was now suddenly and completely Paris.

After that, Vidot walked around for what felt like hours, lost in his thoughts amid scenery that was at once surreal and all too familiar. He found himself missing Adèle with his whole heart, completely abandoning the deep hurt of her betrayal. He longed to sit with her again at their little dining room table, where he could relate to her all the colorful details of this incredible adventure. He had just saved a man's life! It was, perhaps, the most richly satisfying act he had ever accomplished, and yet without Adèle there as a part of it, he felt empty and hollow. He realized that for him nothing existed in the world of any importance until he shared it with her. Adèle was his sole audience, his only validation. He had no eyes of his own and he was completely deaf without her. He was nothing, truly, but a vessel that carried his small puzzles and great triumphs home to her. Only after she absorbed them or interpreted them or merely smiled at his detailed and perhaps occasionally tiresome recital of them did the many dimensions of his existence finally bloom within him as well, opening up like rosebuds in water. This was, he realized, a perspective of their relationship he had never appreciated before, because he had never been so very far away from it.

A great wave of exhaustion overwhelmed him and he lay down on a park bench across from a vision of the Place d'Italie. He liked the neighborhood quiet like this, without the cars endlessly running around the city circle. Closing his eyes, he found himself thinking about all those people who were always on the move, continually driving and darting about the city streets and the country roads. Where are they going? What do they need? They wanted bread and cheese and wine, they sought laughter and sex and company, and then they chased the money they needed to start it all over again. It was a mad carousel, rotating faster and faster to an accelerating scream of a calliope song; the music never stopped, never rested, and now he was so very tired.

He did not know how long he slept. He felt the wind blowing softly against his body and heard the distant whinnying of a horse. Coming to, he was alarmed to find that his tiny body was on the verge of slipping off Will's head as the strand of hair he was only tenuously attached to was now waving wildly in the wind out an open car window. Vidot pulled hard and managed to climb up the cord of brown hair back to the safety of the scalp. Gathering himself, he was frustrated by the fact that he was still trapped in the confines of this little flea body, yet his brief sojourn as a human had lifted his hopes considerably, for now he knew that he was still, in his soul and spirit, essentially, a man. The rest was only a trick.

He worked his way up to the peak of Will's brow and took a look around. They were traveling through the night in a Chevy Bel Air, out past the city limits. The passengers were a cast of characters that had by now become all too familiar. Will was in the passenger seat, Zoya lay across the backseat sound asleep, and Oliver was driving, rambling on in his droll, desultory manner. "Impressive, really, I must say. Never had a woman fight like that for me, even when I was truly in love."

"When was that?" Will sleepily asked.

"Oh, some time ago now," said Oliver, "when I was first in Paris. I met her when she was studying at the Sorbonne. You would have adored her, Will. Jacqueline was beautiful, black hair, pale skin, your Zoya reminds me of her a bit. My Jacqueline was more petite, but with the same broad cheekbones and the same perfect nose. I fell hard for her right away. We had mutual friends, all ex-pats, and we would take our wicker baskets filled with fruit, bread, brie, and champagne down and picnic in the Luxembourg, playing boules or badminton and lounging about like creatures off some Bastida canvas. At night we'd sit and play canasta in the Spanish cafés while the Gypsy guitar players strummed. I pursued Jacqueline quite energetically, but she was a wary one. I suppose I had a reputation for being a bit louche, even back then. But eventually my charms did win her over and she started staying at my flat, first a few nights a week, then every night. Things grew fairly domestic. Frankly, until then, I'd always been the sort of boy who races madly about, forever late to the station. But the whole pace of life changed with Jacqueline, seconds seemed to tick slower, and while she stayed busy with her studies, I began writing, real writing, not the trite stuff, but actual earnest stabs at it. I sent packets off to New York and London editors who were honestly encouraging. I have to say, my life was as solid as it's ever been, I was wide-awake in the world. Then, as I grew comfortable, for the first time in my life I was finally able to let my true self emerge."

"That sounds great," said Will.

Oliver gave him a dark grin and his voice dropped a bit. "Yes, it does, doesn't it? Though in this particular case my true self turned out to be a complete ass: sarcastic, remote, and glacially cold. A Jewish psychiatrist later told me it was due to a deep, unformed Oedipal anger, not enough imprinting with Mama, or some such bunk. In any case, it was not the best thing to unleash on this innocent girl. I tell you, I loved Jacqueline as much as I've ever loved anyone, but that doesn't mean I loved her very well. I made her miserable. She began losing weight, dramatically, ten pounds, twenty pounds, as if her entire self was trying to escape from me but only her flesh could get away. Finally, she got so thin doctors got involved. It was heartrending. And then, well, it ended."

This got Will's attention. "She died?"

Oliver looked shocked. "God, no, she shipped off back home, on the Cunard line. Settled into D.C. society and wound up marrying into a family of some prominence. Actually"—Oliver smiled to himself—"I believe her husband Jack's likely to become the next president of the United States." He slowed the small, rattling car and turned it up a bumpy old farm road. "You should probably wake your girl up. I believe this is where she told us to stop."

XII

The priest was awake in his small bed when the car pulled in. He had been lying there, blinking up into the darkness as he did almost every morning. Now somewhere deep into his eighth decade—even he wasn't sure of his age—he savored the beginnings of the day, before early prayer. Most mornings he lay indulgently counting through his deep aches, sorrows, and regrets as the waking thrushes and starlings outside punctuated his silence with their optimistic counterpoint. With arthritic hips sore from his daily bicycle route, the priest had, over time, learned to sleep on his back, a pose that used to bother him, seeming too much like rehearsal for the coffin. His slow respiration mirrored the morning's own breath as the day awoke in soft tones, bird flutters, and tentative stirrings. For some reason, today the world did not hang as heavily on him as it did most mornings, and as he lay there he nursed a fledgling, unsettling feeling that reminded him, eerily, of hope. It was an emotion he had long distrusted. He suspected the cause this time was the night jasmine that bloomed out on his arbor trellis. One of the windowpanes in his bedroom had cracked months before, he wasn't sure how it had happened, and he had planned on replacing it before winter came, but then the arrival of the blossoms had made him delay. Some nights, the gap in the jagged open pane brought in the rain, but more often the pure fragrance came through it, wrapping its essence around his body and filling his lungs as he lay in his bed. He was amazed that it was still blooming so late in the season, and he breathed it in now, deeply inhaling the scent, feeling as if he was wrapped in the romantic arms of its embrace. He had never been with a woman, had actively suppressed that desire for his entire life, but he felt as though some part of the feeling, its profound and reassuring comfort, could be found within the soft aroma of that jasmine. It made the coming day feel ripe with beauty. Who could hunger for any sin, he thought, when so much satisfaction could be found in the wandering fragrance of a simple flower?

He heard the gravel kick as a car turned off the main road and started up the drive; then the engine cut off and a car door slammed. Perhaps it was the police again with more questions, or Elga returning with the girl, or maybe it was a Soviet stranger coming with an ax. (He was always nagged by the slight worry that a stranger from the old land would come after him, not because he was important, but simply because the state was so random in its violence. Even with Stalin dead, the bear still seemed intent on mauling the world.)

The knock came at the door, and he pulled his robe on as he crossed the dark room to answer. He was surprised to see Zoya standing there. She had dark circles under her eyes and gazed at him with a solemn look that was both nervous and penitent. "Come in," he said.

He put the kettle on the stove. She found a chair and sat staring out the kitchen window. It was still mostly dark out.

Andrei tried to open things up with small chatter. "Things have been busy around here. The farmer next door died last month, a flu killed him. One cough and he dropped like a stone. There is trouble with the will so now his sons are fighting over the land, tearing his little empire to pieces."

She was silent. Andrei kept talking. "Yesterday a policeman came out from the city asking about Elga. Have you seen her?" He poured the tea.

"Yes," she said and continued to stare out the window. "I have seen her. Only days ago. Maybe it was yesterday? I can't even remember. So much has happened." She sighed. "I have news to tell you."

Andrei sat down across from her. "What is it you have to tell me, Zoya?"

She looked up. "Max is dead. I am sorry."

Andrei closed his eyes and instinctively prayed for grace.

"There was a fight," she bluntly went on while he kept his eyes shut. "I was attacked by Elga; she was insane and she wanted me to die. She had a girl there with her. They had me trapped in their spells. I needed a distraction to break the girl's concentration. So I killed Max and the girl screamed and I got the time I needed to escape. Again, I am sorry." She stopped talking and he looked at her again, her fingers nervously tapping the handle of her teacup.

For almost sixty years, Andrei had watched his little brown brother scratch and sniff across the continent in a strange otherworldly state. Part of him had been waiting for the spell to end so that they could be reunited, while another part had hoped Max would vanish completely into the ether, taking all this unwanted mystery with him. Andrei had never thought Max would die before he did, he believed his brother was protected, his mortality locked up within the whorls of magic. Hearing the news, Andrei's first thought was not grief but worry that this spell had been sustaining them both, as though participating in the strangeness of Max's adventure had been what kept him going, either magically or because he refused to end his days unsure of how the grim fairy tale ended. How many wars had been waged, how many cities conquered, how many maps redrawn, while his brother was tucked inside wool coat pockets or stashed in steamer trunks or scurrying to and fro across gutters and granaries as the circumstances demanded? Throughout it all Andrei had never lost the connection to his brother. But now it was done. Max was gone. A door unlatched in his heart and Andrei felt something slip out; he wondered if he needed it. Sitting quietly at the table with Zoya, a new emptiness inside him, all Andrei knew was that he was honestly not sad at the loss of Max, he was only aware that his own shadow of time had just grown a full length longer, crossing some unseen line.

He looked up and saw the anxious expression of the woman across from him. She was waiting for his answer. "I must thank you for coming and telling me this yourself. It is surprisingly thoughtful of you. But I guess in a way we were all family. Do not feel bad, though. My brother truly died many years ago, Zoya," he said. "He was drowned in his own black sea even before you met him." Zoya still looked worried, so he told her what she needed to hear, a fact he suspected she knew already. "In his heart, my brother was always a rat." Now she did look relieved. Andrei gave her a half smile and patted her hand, thinking to himself, Well, here we are, a lost witch seeking absolution from a broken priest. These must be modern times.

"Where are you heading to?"

Zoya shook her head. "I don't know. I'm here with some people, we are leaving Paris," she said. "But I'm not sure where we're going."

The priest thought about how many times he had asked that same question and heard some version of that same answer from Zoya. He realized a woman as beautiful and self-possessed as Zoya never needed to know where she was heading, she only needed to know what to do once she got there. "Who are your friends?"

"Two Americans. They're waiting in the car. I told them you could help us. We need to find a place to hide, very serious people are after us."

"You can stay here," said Andrei. "The policeman told me they had Elga in jail for stealing a car. I doubt they will keep her for long, but she won't be here for at least a few days."

Zoya thought this over, then nodded. "We will stay one day, then we will be on our way. We'll take the train."

"Didn't you come in a car?"

"One of the Americans is taking it back. The other is coming with me. You can drive us to the station after we've rested."

Andrei grinned. He knew Zoya was kinder than Elga, but years with the old woman had made her almost as presumptuous and demanding. "I'd be happy to. Perhaps they would like to come in for some tea?"

"They are American, I think they prefer coffee."

"Well, I have tea."

She went to fetch her friends. Andrei rubbed his forehead; he felt guilty for calling his brother a rat. He had only wanted to relieve Zoya's guilt, but he knew it was a truly terrible priest who only says what a confessor wants to hear. Max deserved a better eulogy.

As Andrei put his clothes on he realized it had been three-fourths of a lifetime since he had last laid eyes on his brother's true flesh, but he could still vividly recall Maximilian that last night, his sparkling eyes and devilishly wicked smile bobbing above that sea of unwashed and unruly miners all shouting in a drunken mad din as the roulette wheel rattled round. His brother's expression had been so bright, so flush with joy. Perhaps Max had been lucky after all. If all men could vanish there, thought Andrei, in that moment of pure satisfaction, aglow with good fortune, fiercely confident in their futures, then the benevolence of God's grace would be much easier to acknowledge. Instead, time had rolled on, washing through that barroom door, taking not only his brother away, but all of them, the miners, the gamblers, the witches, and the priest, all torn out into the driving river of war and waste, so many now lying enmeshed in unmarked mass graves or freed to the skies in the steady smoke that wafted through the camps' barbed wire. We assume so much, thought Andrei, and forget how little we are promised.

Zoya came back in the room with two men. Weary-eyed, they looked like a pair of naughty seminary boys, their suits wrinkled, one with a fading bruise on his cheekbone and blood on his arm, the other one mud-stained and tousled. This is what happens, thought Andrei, when you fall in with a girl like Zoya.

As she introduced the two, there was an expression on her face that the priest had not seen for some time. Was that a blush, he wondered. Ah, perhaps she had fallen for one of these two. Zoya had always possessed a persistent romantic streak. Elga complained about it all the time, saying that it made Zoya soft. But Andrei knew otherwise, he had watched her turn too many of her lovers into corpses. She was not soft, but she could be sentimental. Yes, he could see she had something for this one with the bruised cheek. What a miraculous fountain love was, Andrei thought, ever flowing, ever refreshing, with a force too exhausting to even contemplate. He rose and gave them a polite smile. "Welcome," he said in his rough French. "I am making some tea. Would you like some?"

The two both shook their heads. "No thank you," said the taller one, in French but with an accent that sounded somewhere between British and American.

"Fine, then. In that case, you will have to excuse me." Andrei took his old cassock off the wall hook and put it on. "I have a morning service to attend to. You are all welcome to stay, and if you are hungry you'll find dried lentils and some potatoes in the pantry. There's some Cantal cheese in the icebox too, but no bread."

"Thank you, but I think—" the taller one began to say, but the priest was already out the door and did not hear the rest. Climbing onto his bicycle, Andrei started down the gravel road. The sun was not all the way up yet and he was already tired of this day.

XIII

Noelle had the chicken in her lap when Elga finally came back to the suite. The room stank of stale air and ammonia. "Mmmn, mmmn, little girl, what have you been up to?" growled the old woman, who looked beat-up and tired, with her eye now almost swollen shut. She trundled by Noelle on her way to the dresser, patting the girl's head as she passed. "Come now. There's a man out front with a car for us." Noelle did not move.

She had only awoken a few hours earlier, lying on the floor in a pool of her own urine. She had halfheartedly mopped the mess up with bath towels and then left them in a wet pile by the couch. Her stomach felt acidic and hollow. She had climbed into the big yellow chair, determined to wait for Elga. The old woman would come back, she had to. After a little while, the chicken had emerged from behind the couch, approaching her gingerly, with tentative steps. "Don't worry," Noelle had said to the chicken, "I know it's not your fault." She took the chicken in her arms and sat there, curled up around the bird, both of them motionless through the morning. When, finally, the door opened and she saw Elga's stooped silhouette waddle in, a ray of light shot through Noelle's heart, but it was not enough to illuminate the darkness.

Now she sat watching as the old woman dug into the big suitcase, took out the old pistol, and tucked it into her belt. Elga patted the gun and a little smile crossed her lips. Then she emptied all the clothes from the dresser and the armoire into their suitcases.

"So, what?" Elga looked over at her occasionally as she packed. "Your chicken laid an egg?"

The little girl nodded.

"And you ate the egg."

The girl nodded again.

Elga shut the suitcases and buckled them up. "Okay, so now, what, you think the stars are made from the bites of crocodile teeth, the sun is a boiling gob of God's spit, and we are—I don't know—slaves to all the white maggots that are down there writhing in our guts? You think things like that now, yes? The universe is so awful, so black and bad?" She stopped to look at the girl. Amazed, Noelle nodded a final yes. The old woman shrugged. "Ya, well, before you thought ballerina shoes and cream puffs made the world spin round. You are maybe closer to the right answer now. Go backward a bit, find your balance. It takes time." She pulled the suitcases down onto the floor and started hauling them toward the door. "Come on now, I need help."

"I'm not going," said Noelle.

Elga stopped and looked at the girl. Noelle feared that the old woman would get angry, slap her or yank her hair to force her to go, but instead Elga's features softened into an expression that could almost be described as kind, even sympathetic. Leaving the suitcases, the old woman came back and sat on the floor by the chair. She took the little girl's hands in hers.

"Okay, how about I tell you a story? This is a true story, not a fairy-tale fable. Okay?"

"Okay."

"Once upon a time, I had daughters too. I didn't tell you that before, did I?"

Noelle shook her head no.

The old woman moved her lips, as if she were talking, but no sounds came out; she stood there mouthing silently for a few moments until finally her words began. "Well, I had daughters. But I never knew them. They were taken away, it was bloody and simple work, the way a stupid farmer would kill that chicken of yours. My girls were buried in a swamp. When I found out, it made me so angry, angry that I didn't get to hold them, adore and cherish them, they were a part of my heart, torn from my hands, so I was filled with fury that I could not raise these girls and give them all my kindness. You see, I wanted to give them treats, like I give you treats. So what did I do? I bared my teeth and I bit at the world. I bit the guilty, I bit the innocent, I bit the whole ugly world. These things still haunt me. But you know what I think now when I wake up with the nightmares?"

Noelle shook her head.

Elga's voice was heavier now, as if her words might spill into tears. "I think, yes, I was wrong, maybe very bad. Bah, I don't know. An evil was done to me, to my blood, to my soul, and so I hit back, and kicked back, and then I bit back, hard. Maybe too hard. Yes. Maybe. And then I think of how the sky up above us teems with hawks, eagles, and vultures, all with sharp talons, while all around us fierce and quick animals stalk the grasses with their fangs and claws, and then too, below us, the earth, the black soil, squirms with the insects wielding their pincers and bitter venom. All these creatures, all around us, lashing out and biting at the world. We say we are civilized, but most of all, we are dumb animals. We have nice soft pillows and black telephones, and now toothbrushes too, but that does not mean we are not simple, desperate to fuck, to eat, to kill, all the time, never stopping. So don't forget that." She stopped as if she were finished, but then a thought seemed to occur to her. She crossed the room and pulled back the window's thick curtain. "Come, look outside here, I can show you how dumb and simple they are."

Tentatively, the little girl got up and went to Elga's side. The old woman pointed down to the broad Place de la Concorde, which sat right across from the hotel. Automobiles buzzed busily around it. "What do you see down there in that square?"

The little girl squinted; she had been sitting in the dark for such a long time that the brightness hurt her eyes. "Statues?"

"No, no, little one, they are more than statues. That one there, the tall skinny one"—she pointed to the great monument that sat in the middle—"you know what that is?"

"An obelisk?" the girl said, feeling like she was being quizzed by one of the nuns from her old school.

"Bah. Call it what you will, but this is what it is: a great big penis. A big man's giant cock. His fertility. Men have been building these all over the world, everywhere, for as long as they have walked the earth. They are so enamored with themselves, they cannot help it. They put those cocks up everywhere, like little naughty boys shouting, 'Look at my penis! Look at my penis!' And see what they put here all around it outside? See those statues of women encircling that big, massive cock? The men will say they put the women there to symbolize victory or harmony or some such horseshit, but really they put those women around that cock to show how power works. To say men are bigger, to overshadow us." She looked down at the bewildered girl. "That is how it is wherever you go. So, you know what you are going to want, what you are going to need?"

"What?" Noelle asked.

"A way to fight back." She left the window and headed to the door. "And I gave that to you. You have that now; forever you have it. So, okay, let's go."

Noelle knelt and took the bird in her arms, and then she dutifully followed Elga as the old woman dragged their luggage out the door.

As they walked down the hallway, Noelle looked at the prints of landscapes and ancient architectural drawings that lined the walls. These, along with the carpeting and chandeliers, had all appeared wondrous to the simple little girl who had checked in only a few days ago. Now they seemed more complex, and as she followed Elga down the hall her brooding mind dug into these images, chasing new interpretations of the world. Coming into the lobby, with its high ceiling, its decorative nymphs and gilded garlands in the upper molding, its gold-framed mirror, its tall glass doors and long curtains, Noelle thought it was really no different from any cathedral or palace or great museum: they were all splendid exaggerations, a way to fool ourselves into believing that we are greater than the ordinary beasts. All the grand rooms were nothing more than visual tricks, like the rigged and mirrored boxes that stage magicians used, attempts to turn all of these small pale creatures into a gathering of the great and mighty gods they so wished to be.

"Countess? Countess?" A sharp voice interrupted Noelle's thoughts, and she turned to see the hotel manager stepping quickly out from behind the hotel's front desk, wearing a pressed and polite smile. "Countess, excuse me for a moment, pardon me, but are you checking out?"

Without pausing, Elga pointed at the luggage. "I was looking for you," she said. "Take these and come with me." Noelle followed as the old woman led them both out through the revolving doors to where a sedan waited at the curb. Elga walked up to the car and knocked at the window. The window rolled down and a dark-haired man stuck his head out.

"*Que se passe-t-il?*" he asked with a bad American accent.

Elga waved her thumb toward the manager. "We need to pay him."

The American looked at her as if he did not comprehend what she was saying, but she merely stared back at him, clearly happy to wait until she got her way. Finally the man got a checkbook and started to write. Leaning back out, he asked the manager, "How much?"

The manager mentioned the figure and the American shook his head dismissively but then went back to writing. Noelle looked over at the other man, sitting in the passenger seat; he was small and bald and he wore a cream suit and a white panama hat. He did not seem to be paying attention to the curbside exchange. Finally, the American tore the check loose and handed it to the manager.

"Thank you, Countess, we hope to see you again." The manager bowed, stepping back from the car. Elga ignored him and pointed for a hovering bellboy to put the bags in the trunk. Then she climbed into the backseat. Noelle followed.

"So, where to?" said the American.

The old woman did not answer at first, she simply stared straight ahead. Noelle looked up into her eyes and it seemed as though Elga's irises were vibrating ever so slightly. Noelle nudged her gently and the old woman broke out of her silence.

"I have snake dust stored in the priest's barn. It will help us find her,"
Elga said. "His place is not far out of town. I will show you the way."

XIV

Witches' Song Eleven

Oh, right now we're far away from Elga on another ride,
the big engine hums like my busy cyclone mind.
Lyda's growing weary of our ramble,
hoping to remain behind at the farm,
she always had a soft spot
for that dead rat's solemn brother.
But Basha insisted we all stick with this reedy fellow,
pushing us into his cage of a car just as he was pulling out,
leaving his friends behind to their fate, and now
here we go, my one keen eye watching.
The great city's body grows,
we trace its arteries in, watching the beast swell,
its avenued claws grasping the peripheral villages
in a tightening grip,
slowly crushing their hearts dead, feeding its centuries' hunger.
Then its tentacle legs and arms thicken with the long lines
of low stores spanning and radiating out,
busy with entrepreneurial ambition,
followed finally by the porcine, urban bloat,
stuck with spires and antennae;
these guts of the metropolis, ever tumescent,
they glow phosphorescent,
bursting at its buttoned seams as the beast stuffs itself thick daily
with the farmer's fats and grains, and the fishmonger gains
all taken by claw from land and sea,
the iron and stone raped and ripped from distant horizons.
Every day, Paris eats its own nation
as every capital and crown is wont to do.

Babayaga

Every day we call it civilization,
Doll it up it with art and pomp, a trumpet's ta-da.

So this one driving, Oliver,
he's not much of a riddle, is he?
Dancing with shallow musical steps
from one iced oyster tray to the next,
only as constant as a crooning radio signal.
But he makes for a good, soft bullet
as we now aim him true, picking up velocity
as he's shot toward Basha's plotted point.
She is in the front seat and
she thinks I can't see her, but I can,
she is not as invisible as she would like to be.
Her pale silhouette leans over,
whispering what into the driver's ear.
What? I cannot hear her
but he does, doesn't he.
She will keep wrapping him up,
enshrouding him in her ghostly whispers,
until her bidding is done.

XV

High in the barn loft, the afternoon light came through siding cracks in long, diagonal shafts that Zoya thought looked like golden swords leaning at rest. She was curled up naked, her arms wrapped around Will, as they both lay beneath the thick red wool blanket, protected from the autumn chill. She liked the way her naked breasts pressed against his chest, she liked the way her bare hip wrapped around his warm thigh, she liked stroking his leg and feeling its strength. She sniffed at his armpit, he had not bathed for two days and now the rank toxins from all his various adventures filled her nostrils and made her smile. This was literally a part of him, these tiny, stinky tumescent atoms that emanated from his pores and, inhaled and ingested through her sinuses, became a part of her. There was magic in that, a slight and playful communion bonding them together; she sniffed again, deeply this time. She loved how rotten he smelled. Then she fell asleep again.

She awoke to the sound of evening birds, the sun was beginning to fade. She gazed up at the crowded shelves above them, all stuffed with jars and books, sheaves of papers and piles of dried fungus and root. These were all Elga's, though Zoya knew them by heart. For years the old woman had hauled her odd collection around, fashioning potions, cures, and curses as needed, hawking them, for money or for luck whenever they were running short on good fortune. When events were rushed and times uncertain, they traveled light and Elga would hide the lot of it away in dank sewers, attics, damp catacombs, or old root cellars, hexing and stashing them for years, even decades at a stretch, but always finding them again, digging up and hauling away the cache whenever the coast was clear. Zoya felt uneasy lying there now, she could almost sense the old woman's presence and imagined the crone muttering to herself as she searched for ointments, balms, powders, or merely those green tins of crispy grasshoppers she liked to snack on. The priest had said Elga was locked up in a jail back in the city, and while Zoya knew they wouldn't hold her long, she believed they would detain her at least long enough for Zoya and Will to rest some before they ran again.

Looking at Will, she whispered the tiniest of spells and touched his ear to keep him asleep a little longer. They had crawled into bed exhausted soon after Oliver had left that morning. He had departed with a promise to "sort things out proper" with the authorities. "Don't worry, I'll go to the embassy first. I have a bit of pull there." Putting on his hat, he said he would send word when the coast was clear. "Head south," he suggested, "to Antibes. There's a little hotel down there that Scott and Zelda used to stay at. The Hotel Belle Rive. Lovely spot, right by the water's edge. Shut yourselves in your suite, find some dance music on the radio, and order up room service till you hear from me. Shouldn't be long." Then he smiled a perfectly confident smile that reminded her of a lawyer leaving his client at the gallows, promising a pardon that never comes.

She was quite sure she would never see him again, not because he was a bad man, but because men like Oliver, though sincere in their dedications, also suffered from a squirrel's tendency to be distracted by any random acorn that fell on their path. These were the men who committed their betrayals casually and effortlessly, letting people down with little malice and less concern. Promises were simply nice solid-sounding words to them, and so, as Oliver's car drove off, she was relieved to see him go. After all, he had been useful, but he was used up. She did not mean to judge him, she merely observed. But what she saw was what she had seen all too often, a silly, vain creature who had been raised to believe the universe spun around him, when in fact he was the one spinning in the darkness, circling truths he could never hope to perceive.

Besides, she recalled, he was so lazy in bed.

Will stirred in his sleep; she let him rest. When they first climbed up to the loft she had arranged their pallet, laying the priest's spare sheets and blankets over straw and filling buttoned shirts with clean stable rags for makeshift pillows. He sat on a stool, watching her work, telling her of Bendix, the drugs, and the vivid dream he had been chased through. While she was intrigued to hear about the hallucination's landscape and the mystery man who had saved him, she was more interested to hear about this scientist who, she learned, had once hunted her and killed her friend and stolen their secrets. A rage swelled inside her but she bit her tongue: this was not something she could share with Will. "Oliver is right," she said, lying down on the sheets, "we need to go south."

"Where to?"

"Not to Antibes, not to anyplace where anyone knows we could be." She paused to think. "If we cut across the Pyrenees, we could disappear into Spain. Maybe go down near Gibraltar, then we can always cross to Algeria or Morocco if we need to. We should be fine." She gave him a reassuring smile and stretched her body out across their makeshift bed. "I know how to travel." She reached across to her lover. Elga had once told her that no man could run like they could run, pride and weakness always slowed a man down. "We move like the water, they move like fat fish. It looks like it will work, but it doesn't. Their big stupid balls always slow them down." But Zoya was sure

Elga was wrong. Will had tumbled into her life the same way he fell into her arms now, full of vitality and lustful energy. He had no strong ties to any history calling him back and no ambition of where to go. He could be hers, entirely, and she did not plan on letting go. Tightly embracing, they licked, bucked, and bit, rolling over and into each other through the morning until they both lay exhausted again, his chest bellowing hard, her skin chafed raw by his stubble. Soon he had slipped off to sleep. Now, hours later, she ached to wake him again. She wanted the feeling of his hands on her hips and his body hard inside her. She had felt a difference, an awakening, a new kind of appetite, deeper than the simpler one that so often gnawed at her; this was a fresh hunger that she liked, promising a union that filled her heart with warm blood and satisfaction. She wanted more.

Outside, the birds stopped chirping. She noticed the silence immediately. She was feeling cautious, though she knew birds quieted for many reasons. A dog or a fox could be passing nearby, or a hawk could be gliding overhead. Perhaps the priest had returned, though she guessed that he might have come and gone already, returning to his chapel again for his evening service. No, there was no reason to be worried, birds stopped singing for a myriad of reasons. She slipped out from under the blanket and picked up her clothes. Besides, she thought, if a car had pulled into the driveway she would have heard it, unless it was someone who knew how not to be heard. They could have parked up the road and crossed the flat wheat field on foot. She fastened her bra and slipped into her underwear. She looked down at sleeping Will. She had never pulled anyone in so close to the truth before, but then, she had never felt as vulnerable. She buttoned up her blouse. The silence was so complete, even the evening crickets were silent. Still, probably nothing to worry about. She pulled up her skirt and fastened it.

A bird chirped. She exhaled, surprised at how nervous her instinct had been. I am too jumpy, she thought, I must relax. When the bird chirped again she noticed it wasn't the chirp of an evening songbird, a finch or a bunting, it was the cluck of a nearby chicken. Then a thought struck her with the dead weight of certainty, with the sureness of a nail hammered into soft wood: the old priest did not keep chickens, but Elga's little friend did.

Babayaga

She touched Will and he stretched beside her and sat up, rubbing the sleep out of his eyes. "Hi," he said and grinned. She kicked him hard, a sudden blow to the side of the head that knocked him flying, over the edge of the loft and down to the barn floor, safely out of the way, as the door burst open and the guns started firing.

XVI

As he began the benediction, Andrei was relieved to be wrapping up the evening service so efficiently. His two frail parishioners, both well into their nineties, had enormous patience for long ceremonies. The ancient benefactress was blind with glaucoma and wheelchair-bound. Her husband could still walk, but only with the aid of his two silver-handled canes. But they both chanted and sang with full voices, the purity of their lives giving strength to their hymns. The two were always ready to sing.

Andrei was both diligent and modest in his dealings with them. Unlike their maid, who was always leaning in as they sipped their soup to ask what benefice they planned for her in their will, he was respectful. He knew if they both died tomorrow, perhaps perishing hand-in-hand in their sleep, there was a great probability that he would be left poor as a cockroach. He believed this would be fine, a righteous punishment for so devotedly serving a God he did not quite believe in. On the other hand, if they bequeathed him even a small fraction of their wealth, it would only prove to Andrei that if God did exist, he was as indulgent as a drunk uncle at Christmas, throwing out candies and treats to the scattering children, regardless of who was good or bad. Not exactly the spirit you want to build a theology around. But it did not matter, God could do what he wanted to do, the priest would not beg a sou from these two souls who had already piously provided him steady refuge from the world. While they were strict in their rituals and demanding of his time, both of them were kind, and in exchange for a small stipend he delivered a modest service at every sunrise and sunset, along with longer, more elaborate sermons for saint's days and Sunday masses. Clearly these two did not need his spiritual guidance, theirs were spotless souls, and there was scant wisdom he could offer in his homilies that they had not already gleaned from a lifetime's experience. In fact, it was painfully obvious to Andrei that what they enjoyed most about their rituals at this point in their lives was simply how the duties of religious observation filled up their empty days.

At that moment his blessing of their bowed heads was disturbed by loud, concussive thunder booming close-by. It sounded as it was coming from over beyond the east side of their property line.

"Is it a rainstorm?" asked the old woman.

"No," said Andrei, through guesswork measuring the direction and distance of the noises as the thundering continued to boom. "I do not think it is a rainstorm."

"So what is it?" asked the old man, cupping a palm behind his good ear.

Andrei paused, listening to the rumbling as it grew. Rising, falling, shaking, and vibrating in its timbre with occasional loud cracks, it sounded more metallic than thunderous, and more organic than the gears of any farm machinery. Finishing his rough estimation, the priest grimaced, realizing the probable cause. "You will have to excuse me," he said, reaching for his coat. "I believe God is burning down my house."

XVII

Will scrambled to the corner of the barn, bewildered and naked, his ears deafened by the sound of crackling electricity, gunshots, glass shattering, and the screaming of women's voices. Clouds of colored powders—seaweed green, turnip red, and deep orange—ballooned explosively throughout the room, jars smashed onto the floor, hurled down from above, where a ranting Zoya howled out strange phrases in what Will guessed was most probably Russian.

In the fading light, and with all the dust blooming about, he could not make out the attackers. The silhouette of a woman, shouting loudly in a language equally foreign, stood in the doorway as she and the man beside her both fired their guns straight up into the loft. There was a second man standing beside them, seemingly doing nothing but observing. Squinting through the haze, Will could make the first man out as Brandon and was sure the second was little Bendix. He did not recognize the old woman.

Other bullets were firing in from the outside, piercing the walls. The voices seemed to be coming from everywhere. Will desperately looked for a way to help. Another jar exploded, completely obscuring his view of the barn door. He realized they had not noticed, or perhaps could not even see him amid all the clouds of colored dust. He decided to try to sneak out the back and circle around to surprise the attackers from behind; he could possibly tackle one and maybe get a gun. He didn't understand how Zoya was able to survive up in the loft; they kept shooting at her and she kept shouting. He knew he had to act fast.

He grabbed a garden hoe leaning against the wall and ran to the small door at the rear of the barn. Opening it, he found himself standing nose to nose with a little girl holding a chicken. The girl wore a deep scowl and was busy chanting, "Fish coin, fish coin, fish—" Remembering her from Zoya's apartment, Will went into a sudden rage, quickly grabbing the chicken by the neck and hitting the girl over the head hard with it. "Get the fuck out of here!" he shouted at her in English, walloping her again while the chicken wildly squawked. "Get the fuck out!" The girl went shrieking off across the yard, holding her hands to her head as she scurried into the thick woods. Will dropped the chicken, which looked up at him menacingly, aggressively clawing the ground as if readying for a fight. Without a thought, Will kicked the bird, sending it off after the girl, flapping and fluttering its wings.

There was the simultaneous crack of a bullet and a stinging on his ear. "Ow!" He felt the warmth of blood down the side of his neck as he ducked around the corner. Checking, he found it was only a scratch of a wound. Mike Mitchell poked his head around the corner of the barn and took another shot with the pistol. It missed. With a leap, Will lunged back inside the barn and ducked to the side. He didn't think Mitchell was stupid enough to come right in after him, but a second later that is exactly what Mitchell did, stepping cautiously across the threshold and getting clobbered in the face with

Will's hoe. It split Mitchell's nose and sent blood spurting out as he collapsed. Will grabbed Mitchell's gun as he fell and shot Mitchell twice in the head with it. Will had never killed a man before, and it stunned him how quickly Mitchell went from being alive to being dead. He quickly lay down behind Mitchell's prone corpse, using it as a shield as he carefully aimed and fired toward the figures in the doorway.

Under attack, his assailants reacted immediately. Brandon leapt to the side while Will fired two more shots in his general direction. Will then turned in time to see Bendix slip off as well, leaving the woman still chanting while firing her revolver up into the loft. Hearing Zoya's shouting and her footsteps jumping around on the floorboards above him, Will realized she was, against all odds, still alive. He tried to get a sense of where in the cloudy, dusty barn Brandon was, but he couldn't see him. The sound of electricity crackled all around him. He couldn't figure it out. He stood up and aimed the pistol at the old woman, but his chamber clicked empty.

Suddenly another figure slipped up behind her. Will paused. Who is that, he thought, the priest? There was a quick motion and the old woman's arms flew out. Caught mid-shout, she gargled a scream and fell forward into the dirt.

Before he could react, Will suddenly felt a great weight pushing him to the ground, as though a sack of potatoes had landed on him. He collapsed beneath the mass of it. Will rolled to the side, desperate to avoid the next blow, adrenaline coursing through his veins. He was literally naked and defenseless. He suspected that the man who had been standing in the doorway had slipped away and had somehow come up behind him. The bullet would come any second. Again, he thought of Zoya. She was silent now, there were no footsteps in the loft, it was all over. He shut his eyes and winced, ready for the end.

"Hullo, hullo? What have we here?" a voice said.

Will opened his eyes to see Oliver standing over him, pointing past his shoulder. Will turned and saw another man lying in the dust about ten feet away. The man was also naked, his body curled up against the wall, and he was vomiting violently. Will got up and gave the man a closer look. "I think I know him from someplace."

Oliver eyed the two of them. "I certainly hope so."

Will felt bruised, probably from the initial fall. He looked around. There was shattered glass and liquid all over the ground from where a hail of bullets had torn through Elga's collection of concoctions. Brinish and brackish liquids dripped down from the rafters, and the air hung thick with sulfur.

With his remaining strength, Will scrambled up the ladder to the loft. There he found Zoya lying on the floor, unconscious. He put his ear to her lips and listened for a breath while his hand felt around the top of her chest, desperately hunting for a heartbeat. It was there, faint but present. He looked around the loft; bullet holes riddled the ceiling and the back wall, as poxed as the Milky Way, yet she didn't seem to have a scratch. He smiled in grateful wonder.

He found his pants by the pallet's edge and pulled them on. Then he gently lifted Zoya and heaved her over his shoulder. Stepping with care, he cautiously made his way down the ladder to the barn floor. There he laid her down on the straw-strewn ground. Oliver came up to his side. "How badly is she hurt?"

"It's hard to tell," Will said.

"Well, there's no bleeding. Maybe we should just let her rest."

Will looked at Oliver. "What the hell are you doing here, anyway? I thought you went back into the city."

"Oh, I did go back. I got to my flat and picked up the mail, got a coffee and the paper. I was going to relax a bit, you know, before I went over to the embassy. But then I recalled I still had that item I had forgotten to return to you. The thing nagged at me until finally I figured I should just hand-deliver it to you, didn't want you worrying about it while you were gone."

"The knife?"

"Yes, see, I thoughtfully put it over there for you," said Oliver, pointing down at the old woman's body. Glinting brightly in the light of the day, the long handle stuck out of her back. "According to the official report, you'll be somewhat of a hero, as it was your knife that took down the assassin of two U.S. agents, a Russian assassin no less."

"I don't know if anyone is going to believe that," Will said.

"Well, ballistics don't lie," Oliver said. "Just give me a minute to get the right guns into the right dead hands and we should be fine."

Will looked over at Mitchell's body. "You said two people. Where's the other one?"

"Over here," said Oliver, taking Will over to the north side of the barn and pointing down behind a bale of hay. Brandon lay on his back, his eyes looking surprised, the bullet hole in his forehead still leaking a steady wash of blood. "Lucky shot, I'd say."

"Yes," Will agreed, "pretty damn lucky. I thought you meant Bendix."

"No, I was coming up the drive and saw him beating a hasty retreat, running away across the field. It seems that's generally his modus operandi."

They heard footsteps coming down the gravel drive and both turned quickly just as the old priest entered the barn. He ignored them, stopping and kneeling on the rough ground beside the old woman. He crossed himself and said a prayer, then he rose and went across to crouch down next to Zoya. He put his hand to her chest and left it there for a few moments. Only then did he look up at the two men. "She needs help."

"I have a car, we can get her to the local doctor," said Oliver.

"No, no," said the priest. "Do not take her to the doctor, he would have no idea what to do. She needs a very specific cure. Do either of you know where she lives?"

Will was about to reply when a loud, retching sound came out from the barn's darkened corner. The priest squinted into the shadows and then looked quizzically up at Oliver and Will. "Who is that naked man?"

XVIII

Elga looked down at the point of the knife blade sticking out of her chest. She pinched it with her fingers and tried to push it back, but it

seemed she could not apply enough pressure. She tried reaching behind her and pulling it out by the handle, which was sticking out
from her spine at a perfectly perpendicular angle, but the blade was
lodged deeply in an unreachable point between her shoulder blades,
and her short, stiff arms could not extend that far.

"It's stupid to try," came a voice. Elga looked up to find the ghost
of Mazza standing there, a hole of blood still sitting where her left eye
should be. Lyda stood next to her.

"Oh," said Elga.

"Yes," said Mazza, nodding toward the knife. "I could try to pull it
out, but I'm guessing it's in there for good."

The spirit of Lyda opened her mouth and out dropped a smattering of small silver fishes.

"See what I'm up against?" said Mazza. "It's going to be good to
have someone to talk to now. These two are useless."

"Two?" said Elga, itching at her chest.

"Come, you remember Basha?" Mazza gestured toward a spot
where the light seemed a bit crooked.

"Oh, right," Elga said.

"We must go now, there are still some matters to attend to," said
Mazza. "Basha has had us flying around like barn swallows, but now
most of our work is done."

"Work? What work? Killing me? Is that what you stupid bitches
came to do?" Elga said, placing her hand to her chest where the point
of the knife poked out. "Ow."

"Always so easy to offend, Elga." Mazza paused. "But, possibly,
yes. It may have been time for you to go. I do not know. I don't ask
questions and Basha shares so little."

XIX

Vidot sat in the passenger seat of the car, wearing the oversized
clothes he had borrowed from the priest. He had not said a word to
anyone, other than *"Il est très compliqué,"* *"Puis-je voyager avec vous
en ville?"* and *"Merci pour le pantalon."*

Oliver had been pointing a pistol at Vidot when he finally

emerged, naked, from the shadows. Feeling as exposed and vulnerable as he had ever felt, Vidot raised his hands in surrender just as Will stepped forward and told Oliver to put the gun down. "He's okay. I told you, I know him."

"Where in the Lord's name do you know him from?" said Oliver.

"He's a friend," said Will, nodding to Vidot. Then, addressing him: "*Merci.*"

Vidot made a small bow, relieved that Will had remembered him from their mutual hallucination. After a few more awkward moments, the priest had finally gone to get him a set of clothes.

In the car now, he tried to use logic to reassemble the surreal course of events. All he could come up with was that the death of the old woman had broken her spell over him, returning him to his natural state. He wondered if the same thing had happened that day all over Europe. God knows how many others were sprung free. The woman was ancient and had, no doubt, cast countless spiteful spells between Russia and Paris. He imagined legions of bears, squirrels, and tortoises spontaneously becoming men again, awakening naked to their restored form, as bewildered as he was. Driving along in the car now, he scratched his fingers lightly along the top of his hand, pinching himself and pulling at his skin. He rubbed his arm and ran his fingers through his hair. He never imagined the intensity mere existence could cause, but now, as tears ran down his cheeks, he scratched at his testicles and wiggled his ten toes in the old priest's roomy loafers, all while savoring the simple satisfaction of being back in his own skin. He looked over his shoulder at Zoya, lying unconscious with her head in Will's lap. The American was softly stroking her forehead, gazing down at her face with an expression of tender affection that almost made Vidot's heart burst.

Oliver drove fast. As they left the countryside behind, buildings slowly filled in the spaces, crouching together and growing in height, as if they were physically being pulled shoulder to shoulder as they stacked up toward the center of the city, rising taller as they were drawn in by the centripetal excitement of Paris. It was not too late in the evening and the boulevards still bustled with families and young couples out for an after-dinner stroll. Vidot realized his wife, Adèle, was there in the city too, perhaps even now in the arms of her lover. Vidot wanted to run to find her, pull her from her Alberto's arms, box the man's ears and punch him in the nose, and then seize her, kiss her, throttle, embrace, and shake her till she screamed. The impulse was so strong, he had to close his eyes to try to calm himself. Not yet, he thought. I cannot go to her when my heart is so rough. I must wait.

They drove down rue Lafayette and turned up toward Pigalle. "I'll pull up in front of the hotel," said Oliver. "You can help get her upstairs, yes?"

Vidot nodded. He was curious what would happen. They had all listened as the priest, crouching next to Zoya on the barn floor, had explained the necessary steps they would need to take if they hoped to revive her. Will had asked the priest to come with them, but the old man had refused. "You don't need me," he said. "You'll find it by the window."

Oliver stopped in front of the small hotel to let them out. Will lifted Zoya and put her over his shoulder, shaking off any assistance. As they went in, the front desk was empty. Vidot led the way to the stairs, which they climbed quickly. When they reached Zoya's floor, Will pointed down the hall. "It's that one, on the left." Vidot did not bother telling him he knew the way.

The door was unlocked and as they entered neither commented on the state of devastation. Vidot glanced to the corner where the dead rat still lay on the floor with a cleaver stuck in its skull. Flies were buzzing lazily above the bloodstains on the wall and floor.

Will took Zoya over and placed her gently on the bed, while Vidot opened the window. On the sill he found the three owl balls that the priest had told them would be waiting there. Vidot then went to the kitchen and found the matches and pipe. It made him smile, for it was a man's pipe, with a red walnut bowl and a black stem, exactly like the one Vidot's grandfather had used. The old man had never smoked but had always chewed on the end of it to disguise his nervous jaw. What would the old fellow make of this, wondered Vidot, crushing an owl pellet into the bowl of the pipe. He took it over to Will, who was arranging Zoya on the bed.

Will unhesitatingly took the pipe and lit the match.

"Bonne chance, monsieur," said Vidot.

"Thank you," said Will somberly. "We'll need all the luck we can get." He put the pipe to his lips and lit the owl pellet, inhaling deeply. Then, following the priest's instructions, he pressed his mouth against Zoya's. Exhaling forcefully, his breath pushed the smoke down into her lungs. He went back to the pipe three more times before the narcotic took hold and he lost consciousness, collapsing on top of Zoya. Vidot moved Will's body off her and then watched as the pair lay together, jerking gently now and then, the way cats and dogs often do in their sleep.

The priest had said the process could take hours, so Vidot settled in to wait. Hearing a sound at the door, Vidot looked over to see Oliver enter, hat in hand. "Hullo," Oliver said, and then, looking around at the wreckage of the room, "Good grief."

"On sort d'une grosse bagarre," said Vidot.

"Did anyone get hurt?"

"Seulement le rat." Vidot pointed at Max.

"My, that's quite an extermination." Oliver sat down gingerly on the corner of the bed. He pointed at the twitching couple. "Seems to be working."

"Who knows? One must trust the priest, I suppose," said Vidot, now wandering distractedly around the room. Here and there, the inspector picked up small items, hairpins, a pair of dice, two loose buttons, a scrap of blank paper, carefully looking each one over before setting it down again. On the kitchen table he came across a photo. He recognized the face of the man standing next to the girl. Vidot discreetly tucked the photograph into his pocket.

"Listen," said Oliver. "I think I'd better go check in with my friends at the embassy."

"Of course."

Oliver gave him a sideways look. "If you want I can leave you out of the story."

"Yes," said Vidot, "I would be grateful if you could avoid mentioning me."

"How did you wind up out there, anyway?" asked Oliver.

"I was the old woman's prisoner."

"The old woman's . . . ?"

"Yes."

"Ah well, she seemed like a terribly strange creature." Oliver looked at Zoya on the bed. "Have you ever seen the painting by Goya called *Witches' Flight?*"

Vidot shook his head and said "No."

"It's quite marvelous, a circle of witches float in the sky, flying and dancing in their nocturnal Sabbath, while beneath them a poor trapped man cowers, his head hidden beneath a bedsheet, quite desperate not to look up."

Vidot nodded. "He does not want to see the women?"

Oliver considered that thought. "That's right, he does not, and I, for one, don't blame him. Understanding any woman can be difficult, but trying to comprehend a sight like that could drive a man mad. Besides, whom could he tell? Who would believe him?"

Vidot looked at Zoya lying on the bed, her eyes shut, her mouth open in a silent cry, her black hair spilling over the pillow like a dark wild sea. He realized how little he knew, how unimaginably vast the universe was, and how its emptiness was only another word for mystery. "Yes, who would believe him?"

"So, I imagine it might be prudent for us to keep many of these details to ourselves, or else we'll probably both wind up in the booby hatch."

"Yes, I would agree," said Vidot with a slight smile. Only days ago, it would have professionally offended Vidot that someone could seriously suggest withholding elements of an investigation: to him it was the equivalent of stealing pieces away from an unfinished jigsaw puzzle. But now he saw that the questions lying before him led into a sinister labyrinth, a complex and many-storied maze from which there was very possibly no return. That was enough for him. Still, there were duties that needed attending.

Oliver rose from the bed. "Nobody is going to be at the embassy at this hour." He looked at his watch. "I'll have them call someone to come listen to me. I want to be the first one in to give his version."

Vidot nodded. "*Oui, oui.* Go, monsieur. If there's trouble, I can get help."

Oliver put on his hat and gestured to the sleeping couple. "I shouldn't be long. Thanks." With that, he was gone.

Vidot watched him go with some disbelief. Who, he wondered, would ever leave his vulnerable friends in the company of a complete stranger, especially one he had only recently found naked and lying on the floor of a countryside barn? But the recent events had been so disorienting that it was clear no one was thinking straight. Vidot himself felt especially light-headed. He sat on a chair in the corner for a long time, looking across to the bed as the man and the woman lay shaking in their low tremors. Then, Vidot took a deep breath and began looking for a telephone.

XX

Zoya awoke to Will lying only millimeters away, their noses practically touching. His face, angled up to the side, looked smoothly angelic. What a strange dream it had been. His eyelids twitched in sleep, and she smiled groggily as she reached across and gently stroked his cheek. How long had she known this man? A little over a week? Really? The mere sight of his sleeping face made her heart feel as soft as a ripe persimmon.

There was the small cough of someone clearing his throat. She looked up and realized that she was back in her small hotel apartment. At the foot of her bed stood a man wearing baggy, rumpled clothes and a slightly embarrassed expression. Behind him stood a policeman.

"Good morning," said the man in the oversized clothes, putting his hand to his chest, "I hate to disturb you. My name is Charles Vidot, I am a detective with the police here in Paris and I regret to inform you that you are under arrest."

"What?" She sat up in the bed. "I do not understand. There must be some mistake? Why are you arresting me?"

He paused, and it seemed to her as though he were about to break into a smile, but then a shadow seemed to pass across his features and his expression became painfully sad, as if it were on the verge of tears. "Oh, mademoiselle," he said, shaking his head sadly, his voice breaking with emotion, "I am arresting you for the terrible murder of Leon Vallet."

She sat there, staring at him, far too drained and weary for any tricks. She looked down at Will's sleeping body. She knew what this meant. She could not bear to leave him, she felt like a green branch being stripped from its trunk. But what Elga had said so many years ago was true, you can never run far with a man, no matter how strong they are, they only slow you down. She had wanted this though, they could have tried. She could have opened her heart and taught him her secrets. He was not like Leon, he was not like any of the others, she could have spared him. They could have lived on forever. Tears filled Zoya's eyes as she reached to touch Will's face.

"Do not wake him, mademoiselle. Please, let him rest. He has been through so much," said the detective, holding up a piece of paper. "We will leave him a note, yes?"

Book Five

Of course, in present-day France you have to say that everything's fine, that everything's lovely, including death.

—SIMONE DE BEAUVOIR, *The Paris Review*

I

Maroc felt good as he strode down the street toward the office. He had spent the previous night in a room not far from the station with a bouncy, zaftig barmaid, Camille Vermillon. He rarely stayed through to the morning with her but the previous evening had sought her out with the full intention of burying himself deep in the folds of those generous bosoms straight through to the dawn. He had even called his wife before he went to hunt Camille down, telling Madame Maroc that he had important police business that would keep him at the office. Then he went to the bar. Camille was distant and pouty when he showed up, but after he had swatted her ass a few times and pushed her around a bit, she was ready to treat him right. He had needed it. The pressures of the previous weeks had been almost too much to endure. After a long night of great exertion, he had left his Camille a sulking pile of flesh, bruised and sore, smoking a cigarette in her bed and glaring at him as he pulled up his suspenders and left. He knew she would be there for him when he came back, some girls just needed it like that. He was thoroughly happy, reinvigorated, and relaxed, feeling as though he had just spent a week at a Swiss spa.

Approaching the station, he suddenly felt even better. For as he neared the entrance, a familiar figure stepped out from the doorway, causing him to stop dead in his tracks. It was Vidot, right there before him, alive and in the flesh. Maroc was so surprised and relieved, he almost hugged his old antagonist. "Vidot, you silly fool! Where have you been?"

The detective gave him a polite smile. "It is a rather long tale. I will put it all in my report and so I would rather not have to go through it twice. You can read it there later. But you will be pleased to learn that I have made an arrest in the Vallet case; she is resting in a cell downstairs."

"Really? That is wonderful news, and what about Bemm?"

"I currently have some of our people looking into that. But I'm glad I caught up with you, I need your help this morning on another important arrest."

Maroc was even more pleased. "Another one? Is that why you're dressed in uniform?"

Vidot looked down at his clothes. "I needed some clothes, I was in a bit of a predicament. Luckily I had these at the station. Shall we go?"

Maroc shook his head. "I shouldn't. I have work to do, Vidot, get some other officer to help you."

"I'd happily do it on my own if I could, but I believe I will need your authority, for it is a very important arrest. Come, let us go."

Maroc threw out his hands. "Ah, I had forgotten what a frustrating man you can be, Vidot. You reappear out of nowhere, offering no explanation of where you have been or what you have been up to. You have nothing to say regarding the fate of your colleague Bemm. You vanish, lose your partner, and now you're ordering *me* about? Who is in charge here?"

Noticing that officers coming out of the station were staring at the two of them, Maroc grew a little self-conscious. He did not want to make a scene by losing his temper, but Vidot was especially skilled at getting under his skin.

The detective was nonplussed by his superior's outburst. "Of course, sir, you give the orders and I merely carry them out, but when I come across significant crimes being committed in our city that need a timely response, you will forgive me if I expect our leaders to respond forcefully," he said.

Maroc paused, looking Vidot over. The detective's attitude repulsed him. As humble as the detective tried to sound with his "sirs" and his formal manner, there was an insubordinate note of condescension in his tone. The superintendent took a step back and changed the subject. "Have you been home yet?"

Vidot raised one eyebrow. "Why do you ask?"

Maroc smiled mischievously. "I only wondered if perhaps this little adventure of yours might merely be a way of avoiding returning to your apartment. Perhaps this 'mission' you describe is not very so important, perhaps you're only popping up and hauling me off on some merry goose chase so you will not have to explain to your lovely wife why you have been away and out of touch for so long?"

Vidot paused for a moment before he answered. "You are correct about one thing, sir. My wife is a lovely woman." If Vidot's tone had been cool before, it was now arctic. "But I was not aware you had met her."

Hearing the edge in the detective's voice, Maroc decided to leave the subject alone for the time being. He realized it might be a good idea to come along with Vidot on this arrest: Why should the arrogant little officer get all the credit? "Very well," Maroc said, indulgently patting Vidot on the back, "let's look into this lead of yours."

Twenty minutes later they pulled up in front of an ordinary-looking building. Going directly to the front door, Vidot knocked hard. No one answered.

"See if it's open," said Maroc. It was unlocked. "Voilà!" he said with a smile.

Inside the room there was a scientific lab set up along three long aluminum tables. A line of storage cabinets stood behind them. Rubber tubes, glass vials, and various joints, pipes, and screws ran down the length of the tables, past a series of silent Bunsen burners. At the end of the tables sat a pile of loosely arranged thick manila packets. Maroc went over and pulled one open. It was filled with a white powder. "Well, well, what do we have here?" he said, dipping his finger in for a taste.

"I would not do that," said Vidot, grabbing Maroc's hand before it could reach his tongue.

"You want to tell me what's going on here?" asked Maroc.

Suddenly, a loud voice with a broad American accent filled the room. "Well, *bonjour!*" They looked over to the staircase, where a broad-shouldered man in a dark blue suit descended, followed by another man. Maroc suspected the men had been hiding, hoping they would leave. Maroc looked to Vidot, but the detective clearly did not know these men.

The American stepped forward and spoke again, but this time

only in English, which Maroc did not understand. The American took his wallet out of his jacket, pulled out a card, and passed it to Maroc. It read:

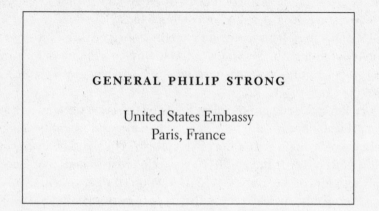

GENERAL PHILIP STRONG

United States Embassy
Paris, France

He said a few more words Maroc could not understand and then he ceased talking and broke into a broad smile.

Maroc looked around a little bewildered until Vidot spoke up: "The gentleman says he is General Philip Strong, and he says he's from the American embassy. He says he is waiting here for his team and he says he would like to know who we are and why we feel we have the right to walk into someone's private property."

"Well, tell him the door was open."

Vidot and the man proceeded to have a conversation in English while Maroc stood there feeling increasingly frustrated. Finally, Vidot turned to him. "He says that he and his team have been working with the United States Department of Defense in conjunction with both NATO and Interpol. He claims he has oversight on a project being run out of this building and says the contents of those envelopes are United States property. He apologizes for his English, but neither he nor his colleague speaks French. And, finally," said Vidot with a be-mused smile, "he is requesting we leave the building now as it is a matter of national security."

This annoyed Maroc even more. "Oh really? Whose national security is he talking about? Ours? Are the Basques somehow involved, the Kabyle, the Pieds-Noirs? I sincerely doubt it. We don't need an American cowboy strolling in to lecture us about his idea of national security. And I would specifically like to know what that substance is in those packets over there, in fact I demand to know—" At that moment, mid-rant, Maroc glanced over at the grinning American and realized there might be some opportunity here that he was missing. "Ahem, yes, let me begin again. Vidot, please tell this gentleman we apologize, but this is a major investigation, and while we respect his credentials, in fact he has no authority here, we are—"

At this, the American cut him off, talking now even more volubly with a great booming voice that echoed through the room. This interruption once again infuriated Maroc, and he started shouting and shaking his finger in the air. "Tell this man to shut up while I am speaking! I am the law here! I want an explanation!" Vidot was attempting to make sense to both sides but neither would be quiet. The American, while still shouting, strode to the middle of the room and slammed his briefcase down on the countertop. Maroc was still yelling, Vidot was trying to translate, but then the American opened up the case and everyone got quiet.

The American peeled two piles of ten-thousand-franc notes off the stack, placed them on the counter, and pushed them toward Maroc. Vidot explained, in a slightly disapproving tone, "He says he would like to pay us, in order to reimburse us both for wasting the Prefecture of Police's time."

Maroc looked at the money, he looked at Vidot, and then he looked at the American. "He is offering this as some sort of a payoff?"

"Yes, that appears to be the case. It is clearly an attempted bribe," said Vidot.

Maroc's face grew red with revulsion and he slammed his hand down hard on the counter. "This is absolutely disgusting, Vidot. Tell him that as an officer of the law I am appalled at his offer. Anyone with even an idiot's sense of justice would see that our time—which he has absolutely wasted—is worth much more than this insulting sum."

Vidot looked at him, stunned.

"Go ahead," said Maroc. "Tell him."

"I will not," said Vidot. "Crimes have been committed in this room, there are bodies buried in the basement, there is a homicidal scientist loose—"

"You tell him what I said, Detective, or I swear I will have you tied up in months of internal investigations for the little holiday you've been off on." Maroc stepped up to Vidot and seethed in his face. "And I promise you it will be a very thorough investigation, an inquest in which even the tiniest stones of your personal life will be turned over, and I am sure you do not want to put your sweet wife through that, do you?"

Vidot's eyes flashed as Maroc let the last words slip out. Maroc felt bad playing so low, it was not his style, but he was not about to let this arrogant detective get between him and the American's money.

Vidot slowly turned and spoke to the American, who without hesitation reached into the case again and unpacked more cash, not stopping until almost fifty percent of the case's contents was stacked high on the counter. The American looked up at Maroc, gesturing with his hands as if to say, "Is this enough?" Maroc smiled and pantomimed that he should put the cash back into the case. The American looked at it, hesitated for a moment, and then refilled the briefcase and handed the whole thing to Maroc.

Moments later, Maroc was walking out with a taciturn Vidot by his side and the case of cash in his hand. The mission was over. He turned to wave farewell to the American and his associate, who both stood in the doorway, watching them go. "What did he say as we were leaving?" he asked Vidot.

"He said he hopes someday he can show us the same hospitality in America that France has showed him here."

"Ha ha, I bet he does." Maroc felt absolutely victorious: like Charles Martel, who had fearlessly fought back the hordes of invading infidels at Tours, he had just taken on the great American army and won.

When he and Vidot got into the car, he did not start the engine right away. They both sat still, facing the small laboratory building. Maroc was waiting for his heart to stop its tremendous and wonderful beating. The case of money sat between them. Finally he looked at Vidot. "You can take your share now."

"Excuse me?"

Maroc patted the case and smiled. "Go ahead, take some." Vidot did not move. Maroc went on: "I was very rude to you in there. I owe you an apology. Besides, I am not as greedy as you think I am. So, go on."

"No," Vidot said, shaking his head, "I cannot take this money."

"Oh, but you can." Maroc turned and faced him while Vidot continued to stare straight ahead. "You can and you should, Detective, for your own protection. You see, if you do not accept my generosity, you will stay absolutely pure, and I do not like pure people. In fact, they make me sick. So, please, Detective, it has been an eventful enough morning, so simply take your share." He pushed the case forward, cracking it open so that the money faced the detective. Slowly and reluctantly Vidot looked down at the cash.

Watching the detective's hand reaching tentatively into the case, Maroc felt calm again. In fact, he felt better than he had all day. Vidot paused. "I do have one request."

"What's that?" asked Maroc.

"Do you think you could drop me off by my tailor?" he asked.

Maroc burst out laughing. There, see, he said to himself, no one is as noble as they seem. In the end, we are all parasites.

He did wind up dropping Vidot off at his tailor's by the Madeleine church and then headed back to work. It was still early in the afternoon, and, after parking the car, Maroc strode in through the station's front doors, feeling as good as he had felt all day and going at full steam. The adrenaline from his little adventure still had his blood coursing and he was thinking up ways to make the most of it. He would only stay in the office a few minutes, he thought, check in with his staff, and then head to the bar again and get his hands on that sweet Camille. Striding down the corridor, Maroc was so distracted thinking about grabbing hold of Camille's perfectly pear-shaped rump that he did not notice the other officers in the station staring as he passed by. He ran through his options with rough logic. He could not realistically spend a whole night again with the barmaid right on the tail of last night, his stupid wife might finally see the light, but the case of money in his hand inspired him to think he could dash out and buy Camille some Ladurée macaroons and maybe some shiny earrings and then get in a quick fuck with her before heading back home to his wife. Of course, though he'd try to buy her off with macaroons too, his wife would also probably be in need of some physical attention; she was always like that after he spent a night away. What was he complaining about? So, there would be a lot of serious fucking ahead? That would not be so bad, he thought with a grin, he only hoped he could get it up for— Maroc's train of thought shuddered to a halt as he came upon the small crowd that was assembled around his office door.

"What is going on, why are you here?" he asked, but the group of policemen standing there did not say a word, merely parted to reveal the shivering, stark-naked man, with a coat wrapped around him, who was sitting alone on the floor in front of Maroc's desk.

"Bemm?" Maroc said, recognizing the officer. "Bemm! What are you doing here?"

"That is what we were wondering," said Officer Pingeot. "The maid says she came in to clean early last night and the office was empty. She locked it up when she left. Then a little while ago, I came to drop off the transcripts from Madame Vidot's phone tapping. You were not here yet, so I got your key from Anna and unlocked the office, and that is when I found him curled up, shivering there, like he is now, only without the coat."

Maroc was bewildered. "How did he get in? Does he have an explanation?"

"He has been unable to speak, he clearly has been through some sort of horrible trauma. We are awaiting the ambulance."

"Well, there must be some explanation!"

The officer gave him a polite smile. "We were hoping you could provide that."

"How would I know? I was not here last night, I was home."

"We called your wife, looking for you, and she said you were not home last night, that you had told her you had to work late, in your office." The last three words came out with a barely restrained emphasis that managed to offend Maroc to his core.

He looked again at the shivering Bemm. This was too impossible and absurd for words. He knew this whole thing was a trap that Vidot had set for him, that was the only explanation that made any sense, and his only thought was to go find the little detective and beat him unconscious. "I am taking personal charge of this investigation, starting immediately!" he announced.

"You were not here"—Pingeot looked slightly nervous as he spoke now—"so I had to call someone . . ."

"So? So?" All the nerves in Maroc's body were now screaming. "What are you saying to me?"

"What I mean to say is, I called the prefect and he is now on his way."

"WHAT DID YOU SAY?" screamed Maroc, shaking violently. "You called Papon's office! He is on his way here? Right this moment? Are you an imbecile? Are you insane?" Enraged, he lunged out furiously for the officer, intending to throttle him. In the process, the case flew out of Maroc's hands. Falling to the floor and bursting open, its contents spilled all over the floor. Maroc was too mad with anger to notice and continued choking Pingeot.

It was at this point in time that the prefect of the Paris police, Maurice Papon, strode around the corner to find his recent appointee, Maroc, standing in the center of a small crowd who were all energetically trying to keep him from strangling some boggle-eyed subordinate. Beneath this eruption of violence, a naked man sat at the foot of Maroc's desk, awash in an enormous pile of loose ten-thousand-franc banknotes. The naked man, seemingly oblivious to the men struggling above him, stared out at the world with a troubled look of awe and confusion. And that was the last day of Superintendent Maroc's once promising career in the Prefecture of Police.

II

Noelle was tired of listening to the old ghosts bicker in the coop. She and her chicken had first found the abandoned, low-roofed building after fleeing from the priest's farm. She had crawled in for shelter and to recover from the shame of the barn fight. She had been hiding too, worried that Elga would find and punish her for running away. She thought about going back home, or even returning to the dreaded asylum, but every avenue seemed to lead to more punishment, so she stayed in the coop. When she grew chilly, she piled a rough bed of dusty old straw over her body and slept. The chicken stayed dutifully by her side, keeping watch.

The first morning she woke, her stomach growled with hunger. Beside her, she found a solitary egg lying on the floor. Her red chicken sat next to it, looking up at her with an expression that held no emotion. She hesitated at first, remembering her sufferings from the last egg, but finally the extreme pangs of hunger outweighed the fears and Noelle snatched it up fast, still warm, cracked it against her knee, and opened it up. She swallowed it in one gulp, catching the yellow yolk and licking up every bit of the clear albumen before any could drip off the shell.

Then she heard voices behind her. Turning around, she saw them standing against the wall. She recognized Elga right away. The old woman had the point of a butcher's knife sticking out through her chest. Much to Noelle's relief, Elga paid no attention to her, focusing instead on the heated discussion she was having with the two other women. One of them, who had a bloodstained hole where one of her eyes used to be, seemed to be baiting Elga with sharp words in a language foreign to Noelle, while the other looked solemnly on, occasionally nodding in agreement with the first. Elga was loudly arguing back, waving her finger in both their faces and then gesturing toward what seemed to be a third person, though no one was there.

That entire first day, none of them spoke to Noelle, though they occasionally gestured in her direction. Tempers flared and at times the coop was thick with the din of their shouting. Occasionally Elga would clomp over to the far corner, where she would sit alone with her back to them, her arms crossed in a pout. The bloody-eyed woman would yell and curse at her and Elga would turn and yell back until finally Elga would come stomping across the coop to shake her finger once more in the other woman's face.

After a full day of this, the sun sank and Noelle lay down again, ignoring the old women and piling up her straw for another night of sleep.

The next morning when she awoke it was so cold she could see her breath. The room was quiet and the women were no longer there. Noelle's throat was parched with thirst, so she crawled out of the coop and into the brush, following her chicken as it wandered through a glade toward the sound of a creek. Once they found it, Noelle leaned over the flowing water and scooped up handfuls to drink. The chicken in turn waded into the shallows and pecked at the creek's surface in a manner that made Noelle giggle.

They walked through the sun-dappled trees up the low slope of the hill, the chicken keeping a few steps ahead of Noelle. Climbing back up into the coop, Noelle lay down on the hay again. She longed for the hotel suite, with its warm bed and chocolate éclairs. The thought rekindled her hunger and she looked at the chicken.

The chicken sensed Noelle's gaze and seemed to grow slightly self-conscious. It got up, shook out its tail, and made its way to the edge of the hay. It walked around in a small circle and then sat down. It remained there, in an almost contemplative manner for a number of minutes, occasionally looking over at Noelle but then looking away again. When it rose, there was an egg.

Noelle slurped it down and within moments the old women were back. They were no longer shouting at one another. Now they were all comforting Elga, who sat on the floor, sobbing into her hands. The one with the bloody eye leaned over and whispered words into Elga's ear as she caressed the old woman's shoulder. After a long time of this, the ghost of Elga finally rose, straightened out her skirt, and, wiping the tears and snot off her face, came over to Noelle.

"Okay, well, it's time to go. You can't stay here," Elga said, clapping her hands.

Noelle felt nervous. She reached over and grabbed the chicken, holding it close to her chest for comfort. "I'm sorry I ran away," she said.

"Ah," Elga snorted, "forget about it. Regretting the past only eats up the future. But now you must go."

"Where?" asked Noelle.

"First, go to the train station and pick a stranger's pocket. Look for someone tall to prey on, their brains and eyes are so far away from their pockets."

"But I don't know how to pick a pocket."

The old woman nodded. "You will. All you have to do is try. You'll be good at it. We'll give you a charm to protect you. Then, take the train to the city. We are going to find you help there."

"But what if I get hungry. How will I get food?"

"Oh, that's easy." Elga snapped out of her gloom and pointed at the bird. "You can always sell the chicken."

Noelle held the bird tight to her chest. "Oh, but I don't want to give up my chicken."

Elga chuckled, her eyes were still glassy and wet from weeping but they sparkled now. "Don't worry, that chicken is smart, it will always find its way back to you."

Noelle looked at the bird. "Really?"

The old woman nodded. "Yes. Believe me, child, you're going to be selling that chicken for a very long time."

III

Slowly coming to, Will reached clumsily across the bed to where she should have been. Finding only the empty pillow, he got up fast, leaping out from the sheets and shouting Zoya's name with an urgency that shocked him. Nobody answered, the room was empty. On the small table he spotted an envelope with his name written on it. Inside, the message was short.

> *Dear friend,*
> *Good day to you! I have asked your friend Zoya Polyakov to*
> *come to the police station on rue St. Denis for some question-*
> *ing. She is technically "under arrest." Please excuse me for not*
> *waking you. There was too much to explain. A desk officer*
> *should be able to help you with any questions once you arrive. I*

may be out of the station on an errand but I hope you will
await my return.
Sincerely,
Detective Charles Vidot

Will was out the door in a shot. Tumbling down the hotel staircase as he buttoned his shirt, he tore through the lobby and out onto the street. There was no taxi in sight so he started running down the sidewalk. Cars flew by and he craned his neck over the automobile hoods, desperate for a cab. Finally he spotted one coming around the corner of rue Blanche. Will dashed across the street and threw himself in front of it, causing a shriek of brakes.

He jumped in and rattled off the address to the driver. Looking at his watch, he saw that it was almost five o'clock. As the driver's radio played a Polish polka, Will tried to piece together what must have happened. He remembered carrying Zoya to the room with the other fellow, the one he had seen in the dream world. Was that man this Vidot? The letter referred to him as a "friend," so presumably they knew one another. And where was Oliver? The taxicab jolted, braked, and barked its horn through the traffic, the Place de l'Opéra was bumper to bumper. Will rubbed his face with both hands in frustration. His memory was cloudy. He remembered smoking the owl pellet as the priest had instructed. Then he must have passed out. He did not remember any dreams or visions, only a deep, soulful rest. He tried to remember what day it was, Friday? Saturday? The traffic on the street was busier than it would have been on a weekend. It must be Friday. At the thought of work, Will shook his head. He had not called in sick, left any sort of message with his assistant, or even checked in. At this rate, his job probably wouldn't be waiting for him.

He leaned toward the driver, *"Je te donnerai cinquante francs de supplémentaire si vous pouvez m'amener au commissariat de police en dix minutes."*

The driver's eyebrows went up and a broad smile broke out on his face. "Okay!" he said in English and they were off. Through a combination of blaring horns, bravado, and inspired sidewalk driving, the cab zoomed, lurched, cut, swerved, and sped down the Boulevard des Capucines, along rue de la Paix, then turned up the Right Bank until it crossed the Pont Notre-Dame and pulled up in front of the police station.

Will threw a fistful of francs at the self-satisfied cabbie and, leaping out, ran up the steps. Inside, he found a desk clerk. Yes, yes, she said, a woman matching that description had been brought in early that morning. The clerk began leafing through the ledger in front of him.

"Well, hello!" said a voice behind him. Will turned and saw the man from the barn, no longer naked or wearing the priest's borrowed clothes but now clothed in what appeared to be a smartly tailored suit. "We never had time for a proper introduction. I am Detective Vidot." He looked down at his clothes. "I am not usually this formal, but I will be reuniting with my wife soon after some time away and I would like to look my best." He offered a tight smile. "I trust you had a good rest."

"Where is Zoya?" Will said.

"Ah," said Vidot, "I have some news there, good news or bad news, I do not know. I had hoped we could keep her longer, but when I returned from the tailor I discovered she had already left."

"She was released?"

Vidot looked uncertain as to how to answer that. "Maybe? Or perhaps she released herself, with some assistance? I am not sure yet."

"You think she escaped?"

Again Vidot paused before answering. "Yes, that is my guess, though it was not entirely unexpected. I was actually on my way to speak with a man who will, I believe, shed a bit of light on what occurred. Perhaps you'd like to join me?"

As Vidot led him down the hall, Will looked around. He had never been in a police station before. The slow clatter of typewriters clicking out reports and the stale cigarette scent mixed with the smell of mimeograph ink permeated all the rooms they passed through. The officers and clerks they passed moved in a slow and steady motion, as if they were assured justice would ultimately prevail, or because they simply did not care. At the end of the corridor they came to a closed office door that Vidot opened without knocking. An older man sitting behind the desk stood up as they entered. He already looked nervous.

"Detective Vidot," the man began, straightening his tie, "it is good to have you back—"

"Lecan, please, be seated," said Vidot curtly, taking a chair across from the man. Then he paused and stared at the older detective. Will remained standing, watching the two and trying to figure out what was going on, until Vidot remembered he was there. "Oh yes, this is my American friend Mr.—I am sorry, Will, I don't know your last name."

"Van Wyck."

"Ah, yes, a Dutch-American? I see. Well, Mr. Van Wyck, this is a colleague of mine, Detective Lecan. Now that we have made our introductions, Lecan, could you please tell us what happened with our prisoner Zoya Polyakov?"

"Who?" Detective Lecan grinned, clearly attempting to look as if he had never heard the name before.

Vidot shook his finger at his colleague in a scolding, almost teasing way. "Now, now, Lecan, do not try to hide it from us, tell us what you did with her. I have found three officers who can testify that she was last seen in your custody, so please provide us with the details of what happened or we will have to go to the authorities."

Will looked confused. "Wait, aren't you the authorities?"

Vidot lifted a pack of cigarettes off Lecan's desk. "Perhaps we are," he said, taking one out, "or perhaps we are simply three men talking about a pretty girl as men so often like to do. So now what do you have to say?"

Lecan looked at him suspiciously. "You are saying this conversation is off the record?"

Vidot smiled and held out his hands. "Of course."

Lecan shifted in his seat, he looked nervous. "No, it's too much. What I have to tell you will sound preposterous. You will think I'm mad. Who knows, I might truly be mad. Maroc's probably right, he says I'm going to kill myself if I keep drinking like a Belgian."

"You will be surprised what my friend and I find preposterous," said Vidot.

"Well . . ." The old detective looked down at his hands as he spoke. "First there is this, I saw her not long ago, I think maybe it was last week. She was walking on the street while I was at Chez Loup. I knew it was her immediately, though it seemed impossible. I had not seen her for years, many years, and yet I swear she had not aged a day. I told Maroc as much and of course he laughed at me."

Lecan shook his head, as if even he didn't believe himself. "Then when I came in to work this morning, I saw her name in the log. I recognized it right away. I'm telling you, my heart almost stopped. I had to go see for myself. Sure enough, there she was, sitting alone in the cell. It was almost as if the angels from above had brought her out from the shadows of the past, to taunt me and show me how old I have become."

"You think too much of yourself," said Vidot.

"Yes, perhaps." Lecan smiled. "Anyway, the officer on duty informed me that you had left instructions that she not be disturbed, but I needed to speak to her. I simply had to. So I pulled rank and had her brought up to one of the interrogation rooms."

Lecan shifted in his chair nervously as he went on. "I came in right away and introduced myself to her. It was only the pair of us, sitting there alone. She was so elegant, so good-looking, she excited me. I started talking at a fast, impulsive rate. She did not remember me at first, but I reminded her of where we had met, way up in Frankfurt so many years ago. I described the nights we had gone out and what she had worn, her feathered cap, her velvet coat, the ermine muff she always carried. Finally she smiled, she remembered, or pretended to. Yes, she agreed, she found it strange that she seemed still so young while I had grown—how did she put it?—'as old as a turtle.' I said the thought had been bothering me as well, for I had been so young then. She said she used a beauty trick that she had learned from an old friend. She asked if I believed in real tricks like that, not merely illusions or sleights of hand. I said I did not know what she meant. She asked if I believed that real magic could be found in magic tricks, and I said, emphatically, no, such things were only found in fables and children's stories. Then she asked if I believed in curses. It was an odd question, but the whole conversation was getting quite hard to follow, she had started with beauty tricks and now she was onto curses. In any case, I answered again, no, curses were the same as magic, it was all silliness. Then she grew quite serious, her eyes grew wide, and I swear a shadow seemed to pass across her face. She said that I would discover I was wrong, because curses do in fact exist.

"Then she said she would prove it to me right there, by placing a curse on me. I asked her not to and she laughed and said I should not be worried, after all, I had said only moments before that I did not even believe in such things. Besides, she said, it was a small and simple curse. She said it went like this: I would gradually disappear, experiencing the absolute gray solitude of death long before I ever expired. First, she said, my wife would stop responding to my voice. Then my children, who are grown but still visit me every Sunday, would stop coming by the house. Colleagues would no longer include me in their confidences. Old friends would forget my name. Letters I wrote would go unanswered, my telephone calls would ring in crowded rooms but no one would pick up. Waiters would ignore my order or always get it wrong. When I went to the cinema, they would refuse to sell me a ticket, not because they were being rude but because they did not see me unless I shouted and waved my hands. In the end, I would wind up destroyed by my own solitude, utterly lost, an empty and invisible shell, abandoned by all those I had ever adored and even the ones I merely passed by on the street, for no one would acknowledge me, I would be a living ghost in their midst.

"I sat there stunned at her explanation, not saying a word. She said, 'Shall we test it? Pick up that telephone and call a person you know, anyone, your wife or a friend, dial them up now and, watch, I guarantee you they will not answer.' I scoffed, because I actually knew my wife was home at that very moment, overseeing our housekeeper's weekly visit—you see, my wife thinks our housekeeper is a thief and she watches her every move like a hawk. So I picked up the receiver and dialed my flat. As I was dialing, Zoya pointed at me and made a few odd whispering noises. I did not pay much attention because now the phone was ringing. It must have rung twenty times but not a soul answered. Zoya was smiling, watching me holding the receiver of that black phone, which suddenly seemed incredibly dense and unimaginably heavy, like a great rock pulling me to the bottom of the sea. I know it sounds irrational, but it felt profound and terrifying. I swear, looking at that ageless creature sitting before me while the phone endlessly rang in my ear chilled me as the threat of death never has. I slowly hung up the receiver and asked her what she wanted. Zoya gave me a small smile and said I should walk her out of the station and take her to the nearest café, there we could say goodbye. So, unbelievably, that is exactly what I did. We got up and I escorted her past the front desk, out the front door, and over to the Café Balzac. I ordered us each a white coffee. I asked her, 'When I walk away from you, please give me your word you'll remove this curse,' and she said she would. And so"—Lecan shrugged—"I left her there."

The men sat there in silence, taking in Detective Lecan's strange tale. Finally Vidot spoke. "And did you call your wife again?"

"Yes, first thing when I returned to my office. She was home, of course. She said she must not have heard the call when I rang earlier. Then she did not understand why I was weeping on the phone." Vidot nodded with solemn understanding. Will looked on in amazement. Lecan sat back, "So, what now, Vidot? Will you turn me in?"

The younger detective shook his head. "No, I do not think that is necessary. You are certainly not to blame. I had suspected Zoya would only stay with us a little while, though I had hoped to speak with her once more before she left. I have many questions. I think your friend Maroc might have been angry with you, but, well, he has his own troubles now. So, I see no reason for you to worry." He rose from his chair. "Thank you for your candor, I sincerely appreciate it. Our business here is done."

With that, he walked out of the office and Will, still stupefied by all he had heard, followed. "I don't get it," he said, trailing behind the detective.

"Nor do I, but there are some answers I do not have time for. We have our lives to live, don't we? And I will not waste any more of your time, sir. It has been a rare treat getting to know you. Now you'll have to excuse me, I have to put a bulletin alert out for your girlfriend."

"An alert? But she—"

"She is a lovely woman, monsieur, but she is very dangerous. Do not worry, I am sure we cannot capture her, she is well rested and extremely capable. But there are, no doubt, other people who are looking for her as we speak, men quite powerful and not particularly well-intentioned. I suspect she is nimble enough to elude them, but still, I believe it would be better for all if she left the city. We do not need a girl like that running loose in our streets. As our poets never tire of reminding us, Paris is already magical enough." He smiled. "Good day, I hope we meet again in more fortunate circumstances."

Vidot walked off, disappearing around a corner of the hall. Will remained standing there, amid the typewriter clatter and cigarette haze of the station's fluorescent bureaucracy, more than a little uncertain of his own direction.

IV

The scientist sat on his metal stool, meticulously attending to the line of test tubes, uncorking their Claisen heads and precisely administering the drops, his careful actions disclosing little of the irritation that was buzzing through his every nerve. He was exhausted and upset, angry with himself for becoming so distracted by the appearance of Elga and Zoya. But who would have ever thought they would turn up again? It was incredible. After how many years? But it was so peripheral, he had allowed these old, vestigial emotions to define his actions when he should have been wholly focused on the business at hand. He felt as though he had sentimentally fallen prey to his old supervisor Huss's obsessions and succumbed to some innate desire for satisfaction. But such justice was never useful, and it was completely unnecessary to the matters at hand. He should have stayed uninvolved, let his colleagues sort it out, for that was their business, not his. Those women were the past, causing predictably what they always caused when you unearthed them: bloodshed, chaos, and tragedy. He was glad to leave that behind, to let them fight among themselves, stirring up their small, provincial evils, they were not his responsibility.

He had made it back to the lab to find the Americans waiting,

General Strong having just paid the French police off with the money that was supposed to be for him. Then there had been all the questioning. Bendix had told Strong only what he thought he needed to know, keeping significant details aside. Strong had guessed there was more to the story and tones had grown heated. At one point, Strong even called Bendix an "evil little Nazi creep" (this accusation came often and always offended Bendix, who was technically Swiss and, though he had advised the Germans during the war, had never technically joined the National Socialist party). In the end, Strong wanted to shut the shop down and take all the packets of formula off with them, but Bendix refused, telling Strong he could have them once he came back with his cash. In exchange, Bendix agreed to cook up this last final batch.

He had hoped to have time for more clinical tests, but there was no time left. Besides, he had run out of test subjects, and without Brandon's assistance he had no idea where to find more. It was fine, though, the important work had been done. There might still be some imperfections, but the army could sort through that on their own. They had plenty of guinea pigs on hand.

He reminded himself of the monumental significance of what he had completed here. What Fermi, Oppenheimer, and Teller had accomplished with the atom, he had done with the mind.

Outside the rear entrance, the two men Strong had placed on duty to watch the building lay writhing and choking on the alley's cold cobblestones, each one purple-faced, each tugging at his throat, desperately wheezing for a last breath.

Along the bench, various tubes of borosilicate bubbled, hissed, and gassed, cloaking Zoya's footsteps. Before Bendix sensed she was there, she had come up behind him and gently touched the potent point in his neck where the occipital and trapezius muscles meet.

He would have reacted, but he could not. He was immobilized.

She stepped in front of him and smiled. "Sorry. You do like to run away and I had to make sure you would stay with me. But don't worry," she said, moving out of his static line of sight, "this will not take long."

Straining every muscle, desperate to see what she was up to, Bendix found he was frozen in place, fastened firmly to the spot, with every muscle he wished to move now absolutely petrified. His eyes darted about with widening terror. He could hear her opening the glass cabinets, removing items and placing them on the metal counter, and then his pupils dilated wide as he heard the familiar clinking of the syringes being removed from their velvet case. "You are fortunate it is me," she said, in a voice that was almost soothing. "If Elga were alive, you would be stone deaf by now, watching while she snacked on your bloody ears. Then she'd stick the tines of a fork through an eyeball and pluck that out too. You'd watch her chew with your good eye for as long as she let you." Zoya returned to his line of sight. "She might even spare your life, so you could suffer in agony. Me, I am not that cruel, I promise I will let you die. But I do think it will hurt." She held up the needle. "After all, your strange equipment is very new to me, so you'll have to be a little patient"—she smiled—"I'm a virgin at this."

It did hurt, and after the first injection, the searing pain was so tremendous he desperately wanted to scream out, but his paralysis prevented even that last great spasm. He knew he only had a little time, perhaps less than a minute, before the drug hit. The shame of his defeat burned at his pride, he wanted some tool, some trick, to smash her, to maul her, to wipe that mocking smile from her lips. Perched on the metal stool before him, she was still talking, calmly, soothingly, looking into his eyes as he endured the piercing agony and strained to break the spell. "Is it not odd to you that our paths would cross? After so many years? Have you given that any thought? I have. Incredible, even for a coincidence. What does your scientific reasoning tell you about this, Doctor? What natural force pulled us together? Was it electricity? Gravity? Was it God?" She shook her head. "No, we have no God, do we? That is a bond we share. But what was it, then? Can you guess?" The room was dimming; he had only seconds left before the nightmares came. He did not want to imagine the visions that were now rising up from his subconscious, racing toward him in a great tumultuous wall like a massive black storm bank descending upon quiet plains. He was intelligent enough to be terrified. He could barely hear Zoya's voice now. "Goodbye," she whispered, reaching out to gently stroke his cheek. It was the last human touch he felt before the darkness of his life exploded.

Over the next twenty minutes, she kept building on the nightmares, methodically filling the syringes and emptying each one into his pale, prone arm. Finally, as he sat there, immobilized with his eyes glaring, lost in the grotesque phantasms of his delirious, macabre mind, she rose and went to the bookshelf. Pulling down the manuals and textbooks one by one, she tore the pages out and covered the floor. Then she held a fistful of paper up to the burner and, after it caught fire, dropped it to the ground. The flames caught fast. As she left, she wondered what the neighbors of the 6th arrondissement would find lurking in their own dreams once the smoke hit.

V

Witches' Song Twelve

One down and done, yes, that hairless goon gone,
real strong venom for that foul cur, making it linger,
making it hurt, his mind dancing mad to cindered ends
his mean mongrel spirit spit out from hell's teeth,
all in fair recompense for all evil done.

So now we elemental sisters exhale,
our most bitter course through,
and now a fair wind will soon take
the dandelion seed dancing
across the blackened, turbulent sea,
on toward shadowed safety,
on toward cherished immortality.

For no one wants to be eternal
and alone.

Babayaga

VI

The priest met the detective at the entrance to the asylum. Vidot was holding a brown grocery bag. "Ah, thank you for coming. And here you are," he said, handing the bag over to Andrei. "I cannot tell you how much I appreciate your generosity."

Looking inside, the priest saw the clothes he had loaned Vidot three days before in the barn, now all neatly folded up. He looked back at the detective. "That looks like a new suit you've got on."

"It is!" grinned the detective. "How perceptive of you. It is much more expensive than I am used to paying, but, well, I must look presentable. I am returning home after all. But come, we are not here to talk of me." He took the priest by the arm and led him into the asylum. "The nurses tell me you assist here occasionally."

The priest nodded, unsure of where this was going. "I do what I can, a weekly mass, last rites as they are needed."

"Yes, yes, that is most kind," Vidot said, a little offhand, clearly distracted by other thoughts. As they approached the two women sitting at the front desk, he presented his identification. "Hello, I am Detective Vidot from Paris, and this is my colleague. I called earlier."

The nurses both looked bright-eyed and willing to help, but it was clear they had no idea what Vidot was referring to. Whomever he had spoken to previously had clearly failed to pass on the message.

"A man was brought here yesterday?" said Vidot, hoping to clarify. "The man they found at the police station?"

At this there was a unison of "Ohhh" and their faces fell into solemn expressions of concern. Vidot gave them a polite nod.

Moments later, the priest found himself looking down at a thin, shivering figure who was balled up and muttering into the corner of his mattress. Kneeling beside the bed, Vidot held the patient's hand. The detective's face held such deep sympathy for the creature lying before them that Andrei had to ask, "Are you related to him?"

Vidot did not take his eyes off the man but nodded. "In a way, yes, he is a brother to me like no other could ever be, in that we have shared a unique and terrrible experience. But he is not a blood relative, no. He was once my colleague. His name is Bemm."

"Bemm. I see. And what happened to Monsieur Bemm?"

"We were on a journey together, he and I. We were heading to the police station where we both work. Then we were attacked and separated. I thought he had died, but he hadn't, he made it there to the station, and waited for me, I suppose, or for some kind of help, slowly going mad in his solitude. That is where they found him, transformed into . . . this." Vidot leaned over and brushed the trembling patient's hair away from his eyes. "He is healthy, physically, his body is fine. But his mind, well, it seems he encountered realities greater than he could bear. Many people need the certainty of solid walls and clear windows, but then they meet mysteries they cannot solve."

The priest knew this all too well. "Yes, there are many."

"And when they envelop and overwhelm you, well, if you are not prepared . . ." He gestured toward Bemm.

The priest looked down at the man. "What can I do for him?"

"Sit with him, talk to him, reassure him," said the detective. "He needs a friend by his side, one who believes in him and, though I do not know you very well, I sense you are one of the few people alive who can help him."

"I can try."

"Good, good. I knew you would. Or at least I hoped so. I will come and visit as often as I can." The detective leaned over and spoke gently to the patient. "Listen to me, Bemm, we are safe now. It is over. You can tell this man, this priest, the truth, he will understand. We are safe now, Bemm." Again, he took the patient's limp hand in his own. "We are safe."

The detective rose and put on his hat. With a warm and grateful smile, he shook hands with Andrei and left the priest alone with Bemm, who had not changed his position or expression and still lay shivering on the cot.

Andrei sat down on the corner of the bed and stared into Bemm's wild eyes. He stroked the man's forehead. He thought about what

Vidot had said about the mysteries. He realized that he himself had stopped trying to comprehend them many years ago, merely attempting instead to stay afloat as the spinning, swirling tempestuous world carried him along through the darkness on its grand elliptical journey.

He had been a victim of strange fortune, but not like this man, and not like his own brother. He imagined he was looking down at Max, who had suffered immeasurable horrors for years as a prisoner in another body, another life. He recalled what he had often imagined he would say to his brother if Max ever returned to him whole again, if they were ever fortunate enough to stand in a room, looking eye-to-eye. He remembered that these imaginary conversations always began the same way, with the same phrase, the words he believed lay at the core of what any human being ever wants to hear from another, what affection is in its primary essence, what the bonds of friendship and family mean above all else. So he placed his hand gently on Bemm's shoulder and, softly, slowly, spoke the phrase, over and over again, as if it were a prayer, "I am so glad you are here."

VII

Will lay in his apartment, listening as the front door creaked open. He was too exhausted to move from his bed. Fine, come in, monster, he thought, whoever you are, spy, soldier, policeman, priest, specter, come on in. He had a fairly good idea who it was.

He had arrived home late after wandering the streets, uncertain where he was supposed to be. He had called Oliver's apartment from a pay phone and when there was no answer searched through the telephone booth's beat-up directory until he found *The Gargoyle Press*'s number. No one picked up there, either. When he finally walked the long distance to his apartment, there was a note in his mailbox from his office asking him to call. It seemed they were worried, or perhaps they merely wanted to go through the final formality of firing him. But he didn't want to call the agency now. He picked up the rest of the mail and newspapers and went inside, where he lit a cigarette, poured himself a whiskey, and collapsed on the couch.

The sun was setting and dusk washed the windowpanes with the pink hues of late autumn. In the last light of the day, he sipped his drink and glanced through the paper. There was no news of any gunfight at any barn. There was nothing that interested him. As the last of the sun slipped away, he kept the lights off and went to lie down. The darkness engulfed the room, drowning him in blackness as a deep sleep overwhelmed him.

He wasn't sure what time it was when he heard the door latch turn, but it clicked his eyes wide open. A floorboard creaked, then stillness. Then he saw her shadowy figure slip into the room. She unzipped her skirt and pulled down her stockings. She crawled under the sheets and he took her warmly in his arms. She smelled like she had been sitting by a campfire.

He didn't ask any questions. He kissed the nape of her neck, he wrapped his arms around her and pulled her close, she shivered and grasped his head in her hands, her actions were fierce and hungry, kissing his neck and cheeks, until finally her lips fell on his lips. They kissed for a long time.

She never spoke. Eventually, they tumbled across the bed until she was lying beneath him. He pulled her close and took her breast in his mouth and she pressed her hips against him, opening her legs. He held her down on the bed and pushed himself inside her. As they moved together, he never stopped looking into her eyes; she tried to avoid his gaze but he held her steady and would not look away. Finally, her eyes spoke to him. Her eyes said, Words are too weak, too small, they are always too small, even the purest and most simple phrases fail. Her eyes said, Look at who you are, you were asleep when I met you, but now you're awake, so stay awake. I did not need you and I did not want you and yet here you are, awake in my body and in my heart. Then her eyes said, This is the last time. Her eyes said, I am leaving you, don't follow me. There is nothing but pain down my path. So kiss me goodbye. Kiss me. Please. Kiss me. And her eyes were crying.

He answered by turning her over so that he lay on top of her, pressing his lips hard on hers and then holding her face tight in his hands. Stay here, he said, without using words, stay with me, he said, pushing himself harder inside of her. Yes, I am awake now, he said. I am awake and I am yours. You have taken me on a journey I can never understand but now you own me, wholly. I was nothing, and now I am a man, and now I am yours.

She said nothing he could comprehend, she clung to his back and increased her passion, scraping him with her sharp nails until the blood seeped out from his flesh. She pulled him tighter still, so that the sweat of their chests smacked. She would not let him go, he would not release her, they thrashed and they thrust and they loudly strained the limits of the bed's strength, until their bodies finally collapsed, intertwined, exhausted, breathing so hard it seemed their hearts might burst. He tried to look and see what her eyes said now, but they were closed.

He fell asleep again, he could not tell if he was dreaming or awake. He thought he heard the echo of women's voices chattering in other rooms, but he could not tell if it was a dream or reality, maybe it was just the cooing of pigeons.

When he awoke, her pillow was empty and the room was dead quiet. He lay there thinking about all he had felt with her, how exposed and vulnerable, yet paradoxically also safe and assured. In the throes of their passion, he felt as though he had pulled back every layer and laid himself open to her, still wordless and yet revealing more than he had ever confessed, even to himself. He knew a threshold had been crossed, and that what he was feeling now was deeper than the various flirtations and romanticism and thoughtless screwing around that had come before. Because now she held some part of him, an indescribable, essential, and secret part, what he was at his best, a knowledge of his true potential, what he was made of, who he could be. He needed to be with her again, perhaps for as long as he remained in Paris, however long that would be, or perhaps for the length of his life, for if she did leave him she would be taking with her that essential part of him, and then he knew he would never feel whole again. The more he lay there thinking about it, the more certain he was. She had become an integral part of him, the person he would not be able to fully live without. He did not know if he lived within her in a similar way, but he suspected he might. It felt too strong not to be mutual. An exchange had occurred, of comfort, of knowledge, of intimacy.

He knew he was not being sentimental, it was more scientific than that, chemical to the point of being elemental, or maybe tribal, he could not say. All he knew was that they were one now. It was as simple as that. You didn't need an advanced degree to figure it out, or a priest to tell you it was so. He rose from the bed and wound the sheet around himself.

Wandering through the dark apartment, he sought a sign of her presence, a note or a clue that she had actually been there and might be coming back. All he found was an irritation from the scratches on his back and the lingering scent of woodsmoke. Other than that, it was as if he had always been alone.

He lit a cigarette and sat on his couch, watching again as the sun came up over Paris. Looking back, he did not recognize the man he had been that morning when he had awoken hungover on the bench beneath the Pont Neuf. Since then, everything about him seemed to have changed. How was it possible for someone to travel such a great distance within himself in such a short period of time?

There was a ringing from the downstairs doorbell and Will rushed for the buzzer. It was her, he knew it, coming back, she could not have left him, it made no sense. He was surprised, moments later, when he opened the door to find Guizot standing there.

"Hello!" The little man burst past him into the apartment. "I went by your office yesterday, they say you are not there, they have no idea where you are. So I called here, I even came by yesterday afternoon. But today, aha, today I got you! I knew if I came early I would catch you, and I did. Where have you been hiding? It does not matter. But, my God, look at you, you look pathetic, we should get some caffeine into you."

He went straight to the kitchen, put the kettle on, and began going through the cupboards, pulling out the coffee, the press pot, and the sugar. All the while he talked. "I met a girl, Will. A lovely girl! I know, I know, you say, 'What of your wife, Guizot? Oh, you adored her so.' Ah, well, my friend, you cannot waste your whole life worrying about one woman. So I am getting a divorce. It is not my style, no, I agree, and it will give my Catholic mother a heart attack—*and* it is going to be expensive—but we only each get one life, right? And this new girl, she is also going to be expensive too, ha ha, I could tell that right away. But worth it! So, I tell you what I am going to do. I am going to make my new girl a new perfume. I've already got a name for it: Eglantine. We are going to sell it by the truckload and make a mint. The best part? My wife's lawyers won't be able to touch the profits, right? Because I made this perfume after she left. My lawyers have it all figured out. Modern romance, Will, it's crazy wonderful, is it not? Wait, what is the matter? You look like I just shot your dog."

"I'm sorry, Guizot. I'm really not up for this right now."

"Of course you are, you are my advertising genius! I need you. I know I fired you, forget it, don't be mad. It's over. We're going to do this together, today, right now."

"I don't think so, Guizot."

"Listen"—the little man shook his finger at Will—"I want to tell you this, whatever shit is going on in your life, it has no place in your work. That is the most important part of any man's life. Work is the only thing that means anything. Ever. Whatever your problem is, you roll up your sleeves, you spit in your hands, you rub them together, and you work. Work can solve the biggest problems in the world. Money issues? Family? Constipation? I tell you, Will, work solves it."

Will shook his head. "It's none of those, Guizot. It's a woman. A woman left me."

For the first time since he entered the apartment, the little man paused. "A woman, eh?"

"Yes," Will said. "A woman."

"So, you like her? You miss her? That's what this is all about?"

"Yes. I gave her my heart and she walked out."

"Oh." Guizot sat down on the kitchen stool and for a moment he was quiet. "What is her name?"

"Zoya."

"Oh, that is a beautiful name." It looked as though tears were welling up in Guizot's eyes. Neither of them spoke; the soft electric buzz of the kitchen clock was the only sound in the room. Then Guizot smiled and snapped his fingers. "Okay, I have a brilliant idea. A spectacular idea. A big, colossal, amazing idea. You know where we can get a band?"

Will sighed. "Yes, I think I know where we can get a band."

Guizot smiled. "Well then, let's go."

Three hours later, Guizot and Will were sitting behind the glass with the engineer at the Studio Pathé-Magellan watching as Kelly, Flats, and Red fleshed out the tune Guizot had written in the cab driving over. The engineer finessed the levels as the little man ran in and out of the booth, barking instructions at the players in between takes. The band took his comments in stride, seeming bemused by Guizot's antics—probably because he was paying them such good money. (When Will had tracked the jazz boys down, the three had been wary of the offer. As Kelly put it, "Singing jingles ain't gonna do much for our sterling reputations." But Guizot had waved enough francs in their faces to convince them, even throwing in a case of perfumed bath soap for Flats to seal the deal.)

As the session slid into the afternoon, Will's faith in their enterprise slowly faded. "This isn't going to work," he said.

"Ah, but of course it is. My guys are back in the warehouse right now scraping the old Parfait d' Amour labels off and sticking on the new Eglantine labels. My trucks will distribute them before dawn all across the city. By the time we get this to the radio station tomorrow, Eglantine will already be on the shelves. I'll have France covered by the end of the week, then Düsseldorf, Hamburg, Milan—boom, boom, boom."

"That's not what I meant," said Will. "The song won't work."

"Ah, of course it will, listen to that background. Nobody will hear it but her. "Zoya, Zoya, Zoya." Ha ha, she's going to love it."

Will leaned back in the studio couch and listened as the little man sang and danced along with the recording, bouncing around like the ball in the sing-along films.

They kept working on the jingle, repeating it take after take; the music was better than a lot of the tunes Guizot had written. Still, Will realized, his funny little client had been right, days before, in his passionate diatribe against his industry. It wasn't only the ads, it was the whole cultural mechanism of manufactured emotion: it had torn down, abused, and then reconstructed the way people lived. Before movie romances, he wondered, how did people kiss? How did they caress before they saw Bogart and Bergman embrace? Before pop songs told them to dance and twist and hold hands, how did they discover their passions, improvising and fumbling and finding their way blindly behind all those closed doors? But now, movies, television shows, radio programs, billboards, and advertisements all swamped, swarmed, and buzzed about them, blinding their eyes and drowning their ears, telling them what to feel and how to act.

The band took a break and came out of the booth. Red lit a cigarette. "Okay now, we can only do this for another hour or so, we've got a gig tonight."

Will nodded.

"How do you fellows like the tune?" Guizot asked, beaming.

Kelly leaned back against the wall. "Well I don't know now. Some music takes you to a nicer place, lifts your spirits up, or maybe only says good luck. Then there's the music that just gets you paid."

Guizot laughed and patted Kelly on the back. "That's good. Now maybe try a little flamenco style?"

The jazz boys went back into the booth and the engineer started rolling the tape. As the rhythm picked back up and Red sang the tune, Guizot became blissfully engrossed in the band's every gesture and beat. Will wasn't listening anymore, he knew none of this mattered now. These canned tricks might work well for Guizot as he flew from one wife to the next, but it wouldn't work on Zoya. She was a woman who knew the weight, measure, and meaning of things. Will could imagine exactly what she would look like when she heard the tune; it would be that same expression she had given him back in the bar when she had asked, "What happens after these victims of yours buy your product and the spell is broken? When they awaken to find their life is as empty and sad as it was before, only now a little poorer too?"

The band was still swinging, and Flats was blowing his horn, as Will quietly rose, put on his coat, picked up his hat, and slipped out of the room without saying goodbye. And that was the last day of Will Van Wyck's once promising career in advertising.

VIII

When Adèle walked into her apartment, she screamed. Vidot sprang up from where he had been sitting on the couch. "Oh no! There is no need to be frightened, my dear. I am not a ghost, I am simply here, I am home."

She looked thin and pale. He knew that no matter what emotions she held for him in her heart, his absence must have been a source of great stress. But though he wanted to, he did not reach out to embrace her. He simply stood smiling at her, a little awkward and formal, feeling stiff in his newly tailored light wool suit. The main room of their apartment felt very small and empty, he had never been more aware that they were the only two living things it contained. Seeming unsure of what to do, she merely stood there too. She straightened her skirt with her hands. "Where have you been? What happened to you?" she asked.

"I honestly do not know where to begin." He shrugged. "I have been working, investigating, solving a crime, tying up loose ends. But I am home now, and I will not be going back in to work for a little while." His smile felt awkward on his face, his stomach churned with worry. "Oh here, look, I brought home a present for you." He pulled a large frame wrapped in butcher paper out from beside the table. He bent over and tore the paper away, trying not to shake from all the emotion he was working to contain. He stepped to the side so she could see the painting.

It was rough and Impressionistic. Done mostly in shades of blue—cornflower, Persian, and cobalt—it showed an older woman with melancholy eyes gazing out a garret window. She looked as if she might be recalling better days, or watching her beloved depart down the avenue. "I introduced a dealer I know to the artist today. He liked the work, picked up a dozen or so of this fellow's pieces. Interesting artist, he mostly does portraits of his wife. He's been painting her for years now," said Vidot. "The dealer, Christof, owed me a favor. He's going to cobble together a show of the work and get them a bit of press as well. I picked this one out to keep, I thought you might like it."

"Oh," Adèle said, studying the painting. "I'm not sure it's very good."

"No?" Vidot came and stood by her side. "Why don't we let it stay a few days and try it out? If we still don't like it, I can return it to Christof." He looked down at her, trying to look calm and serene. "It is good to be home, Adèle."

"I am glad you are home too," she said, looking up at Vidot, her expression unfathomable.

He stood there, trying to guess what she felt. Relief? Guilt? Absolution? The mantel clock's ticking was the only sound in the apartment. Vidot felt torn, his whole soul exhaling with relief at having made it, finally, here to his own apartment. But his heart was twisted and unsure whether, despite both his words and hers, he truly was at a place he could call home.

He reminded himself that he was a Frenchman, he was expected to understand these wanderings of the heart. Perhaps it would be more appropriate to ignore the whole thing and simply find a lover of his own. Perhaps she expected him to, or perhaps she thought he already had. But that had never been his style. He was not moralistic, he was simply a man in love with his wife.

For the past few days he had done all he could to resolve the many complex facets of this case, as well as coming to terms with the parts he would never solve. He had considered paying a visit to her lover, Alberto, repeatedly imagined walking up to him on the street and popping the man in the nose or socking him in the eye, but after he had turned it over in his mind he decided that he did not want or need that kind of justice.

His only desire was to know if this apartment could hold any possibility of being a home for him. If it did, then he could begin again, letting the past grow faint and weak and vanish in that way it naturally does. But this was it, the final riddle of his journey. He did not feel the urge to smile. The emotions he was going through and whatever she might be feeling seemed more unfathomable to him than the secrets of any crime, more mysterious than any mystical spell. Over the past few days he had gone through an incredible, inconceivable metamorphosis and somehow, miraculously, had survived. Along the way he had accomplished amazing feats and overcome grave threats of a scale he could have never imagined, and yet here he was, in the end, standing in a smartly tailored suit, fumbling, awkward, wordless and shy, faced with nothing more than the eyes of the woman he loved. Like an ancient blind weaver who has run out of thread, he felt quite empty-handed.

So, in a gesture that held uncertainty, curiosity, and more than a little fear, he gently reached out to take his wife's small, soft hand into his own. She did not resist, yet her acquiescence did not reassure him. He was uncertain if her heart held any ardor for him or if she was merely giving the appearance of obedience and acceptance. He knew he had the strength to seize, slap, shake, even beat her to wrest a confession, but that was the last thing he wanted. He simply longed for a hint of her small, perfect smile and pined for a sparkling glint of happiness in her eyes. He had come so far to reach this moment, and this was all he wanted, her hand in his, with full trust, steady until the morning. He thought to himself that in these tenuous times, this was perhaps the most he could hope for. He felt the warmth of her skin on his and looked down at both their hands. A riddle's truth lay here, how absolutely large and great one very small thing can be, and how, with sweet, tender vigilance, one can take these small, fleeting moments and build them into something eternal. This is all we are at our best, he thought, tiny instances accumulating up into a greater whole. There is nothing magnificent in this world, he thought, that is not born from an act so slight as to go wholly unnoticed. We must be especially attentive to see them, and to remember to perform them, he thought, yes, that is the crux: we must simply pay attention. He squeezed her hand softly, as if to say, I am here, I am right here for you. Then, with barely a pause, he felt Adèle gently squeeze his hand back. He took this as a good sign.

That night the two of them did not make love, they did not even kiss more than to say good night, but as they lay in bed, their arms draped around one another, their toes tentatively touching, Adèle finally shifted, pulling him close and burying her nose into his nightshirt. Then they both slept, soundly, their breath rising and falling, slipping in and out of unison.

IX

It was late in the afternoon and Oliver had a black eye. He dropped a sugar cube into his coffee and stirred. "Of course I meant to call earlier, but it's been so busy. The embassy had a lot of questions, but it all was manageable, at least for a while. Then French intelligence showed up and insisted on asking their own questions. It became less of a friendly debriefing and more of an interrogation, but I held up well until, out of pride, I suppose, I shared my theory that the French resistance was a bit of a mythical beast. Of course one of my interrogators turned out to be an actual hero of the resistance, and, well . . ." He exhaled his cigarette and sipped his coffee before continuing. "That was only a minor side note, really, the rest of it's all cleared up or shut up by now. I did manage to get my hands on a good amount of cash to pay Red and the rest of the jazz boys, and I'm pleased to say they were happy with that unexpected bonus. They said you got them some money too. Speaking of cash, you ever meet Philip Strong?"

"No," said Will.

"Thought Brandon might have introduced you. Phil's a big honcho, runs the whole theater for the agency, one terrible son of a bitch. Anyway, word is he had to pay an astronomical sum to the Paris police to keep them from poking around Bendix's lab, and then, only hours later, the damn place caught fire and burned to the ground with Bendix trapped inside. Dunno who was behind it, Phil's people or the police or whomever, though it seems rather messy for company work."

Oliver paused for a drag of his smoke. "You know, I almost pity that Bendix, the good doctor had such grandiose plans. Imagine, finding the means to bond the world into one shared consciousness. Incredible stuff, really. If only he had aimed that power in a slightly more peaceful direction, he might have enlightened us all. He could have been a Buddha, but he turned out to be a pest, ha ha. Sounds like something right out of Cole Porter."

He had been rambling on like this ever since he arrived at the station. Earlier, waiting by the small café stand, Will had been unsure if Oliver would even show. When he did arrive, Oliver had seemed listless at first. But then he had settled into his chair, lit his cigarette, and starting talking. Apart from Oliver's rambling monologue, the station was quiet, an off-season calm before the holiday storm, with only a handful of travelers waiting. Porters pulled their carts by, and station agents wandered about, occasionally checking their watches. Will's own train was scheduled to leave on the quarter hour.

"I did want to ask you one question," Will said.

"Really? Okay." Oliver winced, butting out his cigarette. "Though I have to tell you, I am deathly tired of questions."

"I know, but seriously, tell me this, what was the knife for?"

Oliver looked curious. "The knife?"

"Yes, that first night," said Will, "you wanted me to bring the knife to that meeting with Boris and Ned. I figure you couldn't have planned on blackmailing me that early on, you didn't even really know who I was yet."

"Oh, yes. The knife." Oliver nodded. "It sounds silly now but I had planned for us to do a little bonding together, a little ritual with a blood oath, something we boys used to do up at Camp Kinloch when I was young. It was only meant to be a bit of theater to show our commitment to the good fight, a bit of rah-rah."

"What were we fighting for?"

"To remain here in Paris, of course, to stay on the agency dime. It was a time for serious action, Will, they were chopping funding, pulling the plug on us all. Now that de Gaulle's back in, there's no reason for them to stay. The local Communists have been neutered, the Russians are contained, and Germany's quiet, which makes this conflict pretty much over. The big-theater stuff here is done, Washington has no need to keep funding it, which means all of us, the ad men, the journalists, the intellectuals, and even the poets, every single soul of us who's been living on the company's largesse, we're all being cut off."

"Come on, there weren't that many people working for the agency," Will said.

"Oh yes there were. You couldn't throw a copy of *Fodor's* across a Spanish Quarter café without hitting someone on their payroll. In the low season, pretty much every American you saw in this town was a penny ante spook of some sort. I'd rather hoped we could all rally together, all for one, one for all. Ridiculous, obviously, childish stuff, but that was another time, really. A whole other era."

"It was two weeks ago," said Will.

"Was it? Well, it seems like a lifetime, doesn't it?" said Oliver. "Come to think of it, I suppose for Brandon it was."

"So, what about Brandon, what was he was up to?" Will asked.

Oliver raised an eyebrow. "No one at the embassy offered any specifics, but it's not too difficult to deduce. Clearly, his goals for those pharmaceutical experiments were not very different from what I was up to, ginning up the game so that he could stay here, overseeing wave after wave of hallucinogenic assaults against Ho Chi Minh's godless hordes while sitting in the comfort of the Ritz bar. Ordinarily, he would have run that scientist's operation through more proper channels, but doing it the right way would have eaten up too much time and he was desperate. He was going to be shipped out too; he had to rush. I think Brandon only wanted the same thing Ned, Boris, me, even you wanted. We all simply wanted to stay in Paris."

"Looks like you're the only one who's staying."

Oliver shook his head. "Not for long. I'll probably ship home soon. I've got a friend at the *Herald Tribune* who's offered me a spot at the sports desk. It's not ideal. I'll have to find some angle to make it interesting, but I need the job, right now the larder is pretty bare."

"Really? What about your family money?"

Oliver smiled. "Here's a little secret, Will: the money I come from is so old it's dead. The great cod fortunes swam away some time ago. But that doesn't matter, I'm always happy to work, I'll be fine. What I'm curious about is what's next for Paris? Look at this grand station, Will, think of this city, it's been the eye of the hurricane for centuries, a firestorm of ideals, art, and philosophy, a place where fierce arguments became actual revolutions, which then exploded into bloody wars. Think about all that happened here, Pascal, Descartes, Voltaire, Napoléon, the barricades of the commune. This was it, the glistening pearl resting at the center of a grand transcendent battle for mankind's soul. I wanted to be a part of it, to help in some small way to keep it going. But now it's all over, the bullies and the bankers back home need a real war and what we're doing here these days is far too subtle."

"What do you mean, subtle?" Will asked.

Oliver shrugged. "Well, American factories need orders for jeeps and jets, and American politicians need full employment. A cold war doesn't get you that, only a real war will do the trick. After all, every soldier hit with a bullet means another new job listing, and every jeep blown up means another order on the books. So they've got that kind of war now and, well, bully for them. But when we pull out of here, that's it for this place. As funny as it seems, this was the last battle for Paris, the final act, and now, mark my word, this city will be abandoned, not by people but by history. The local intellectuals will go on with their philosophies, and de Gaulle will wrestle with his little Algerian conundrum, but the idea of France as the beating, vibrant heart of the world is over. They will be left with nothing but dull tourists coming over, packed like wet sardines on those new Pan Am and TWA flights, pouring out in record numbers to overwhelm the palaces, plazas, and galleries. They won't have the slightest notion that they're standing where Marat shrieked to the crowds, or where Baudelaire searched for his absinthe, or where a Stravinsky ballet—a *ballet*, mind you—caused a bloody riot. They won't see Degas for the shifty little snob he was, and, my lord, they won't bother reading Proust. For them, all this will be little more than one of those cheap roadside attractions you see up in the Catskills, all will be trivial. The mighty dynamo is dead."

"Okay, well, then," Will said with a grin, "sounds like it's a good time to hit the road." He stood up and looked over toward the waiting train. "They're probably boarding now, Oliver. Thanks for coming, I appreciate it."

"Ah, yes, of course, sorry for going on like that. Ridiculous of me, really," said Oliver, rising to his feet. "But I am glad I could see you off. That's what friends are for, right?"

Will suspected Oliver was only being polite, they weren't true friends. Oliver was too naturally opaque, maintaining a safe distance from the world; and Will was little more than a stray white tennis ball that had rolled onto Oliver's court from some clumsy beginner's match. But there was no one else for Will now in Paris, and so this tall, thin man with the cool smile and his insouciant manner was probably the closest thing to a friend Will had left.

Oliver walked him to the platform. "You really think you can find her?"

"I can try." Will said. "She mentioned Spain, so I thought I'd start looking there."

"You know, Spain isn't particularly small."

Will grinned. "I know that."

"And while your Zoya is an exceptional woman, I have to say—"

"I'm going to find her, Oliver."

"Yes, yes, of course you are." Oliver gave him a bittersweet smile, as if he had done all he could. Will shook his hand and headed down the walkway. Looking back, he saw Oliver still standing at the head of the platform, his hand held up in a halfhearted farewell.

Perched high in the station, a pair of owls sat resting upon the broad steel girders, watching quietly as the traveler made his way down toward the waiting train, his shadow growing long in the low, waning light.

X

It was the last ferry of the night. As the engine started up, its blue-gray diesel smoke blew back across the deck, mixing with white wisps of sea fog. Zoya lay in the lorry's open bed, tucked, unseen, amongst paneling, packing crates, and rolls of insulation. The truck was parked on the deck amid long haulers, buses, and passenger cars. As the ferry eased away from the Copenhagen docks, bouncing softly into the choppy, cold waters of the Oresund Strait, the boat engine's groan matched the ache in her heart.

A narrow crack of the night sky was visible between the bales and tall boxes, and a low orange moon peeked down at her. She tried to distract herself, thinking about a newspaper article she had read a few months before about how the Russians, those old friends from so long ago, had recently sent a rocket up beyond the atmosphere, aimed at the lunar surface. That is so like us, she thought, we are always reaching up, clawing and grabbing, first for the fruits on tree branches and now for the stars. Even the spires of our small town churches and city cathedrals seem to be stretching up, straining to scratch at heaven's peak.

She imagined what the Soviet rocket must have looked like, sailing away from the confines of the earth. The thought reminded her of sieges she had witnessed, long ago, where the long, red streak of cannonballs arced high above the desolate, dusky wreckage of battlefields before falling against the failing buttresses of those great sinking cities.

Ah, you poor stupid moon, she thought, you idiot stone, circling up there, watching over us for so long. You must have thought you were safe from us, eternally remote, discreetly distant. I could have told you it does not matter how far you go or where in the darkness you hide, no place is safe from the fumbling throes of man.

She looked down and stroked Noelle's hair. The sleeping young girl had nestled her head on Zoya's chest, wrapping her arms around her waist. Underdressed for the north, they had been huddling together like this for the last two days to stay warm. Zoya remembered how Elga often used to say a woman's hands had poor circulation because her hot blood was always staying busy in her mind, keeping her out ahead of the brutes.

The russet chicken rested by their side, it seemed to be sleeping too. Zoya had found the girl where the old ghosts said she would be, waiting for her on the outskirts of Paris in a small park near Gagny, but the bird in the girl's arms had been a surprise. Leave it to those women to forget to mention the chicken, Zoya thought. She wondered how she would care for the girl, what tricks she should be taught. The ghosts will help us, she thought, or at least they will do their best to try. She would find the girl a pair of wool mittens in the morning.

Pulling Noelle close, Zoya tried to settle in and rest as the churning ferry boat carried them north. The diesel's thick cloud of exhaust trailed behind the boat, dimming the stars, one by one, as their course bore them deep into the comfort of the coming winter's darkness.

Sleepily, her thoughts drifted back to Will. She had not wanted to leave Paris. She had taken the girl back into the city with her and found them a place to stay. She thought they could be there for a while, perhaps she had hoped to stalk him. Both curious and protective, she wanted to watch her rabbit try to find his way. But instead it was he who had flushed her out, the way the shock of gunfire frightens fowl from the brush.

It was only a few days after she had last seen him, when she and Noelle were holed up in the Bercy Hotel. She went into a baker's shop to pick up a baguette, and there she heard the song. It caught her ear right away, as if it were hunting for her, calling to her. She had glanced around the shop until she found the little transistor radio the baker had perched up in the corner. The song came out of the little speaker, tinny and rough with static:

Zoya, Zoya, Zoya,
the girl with the forever fragrance,
the girl with the magical style,
come back to me,
come back, I need to be near
Eglantine, Eglantine, Eglantine.

It was a jingle for a cheap perfume, but she knew it was really a message for her. He was trying to lure her back. She recalled the way he had described advertising, like a campaign in a war. So he had sent the song out riding the invisible airwaves, raining down all over the city to find her. It was as good a trick as the most skilled witch could concoct. She could sense his desperation: he would use all the weapons he had mastered, everything he could muster. This was merely the first shot from his cannonade.

She went back to the small hotel, got the girl, packed up, and left. She knew there would be no rest for her in Paris. She had to take the girl and go.

Offended and shaken, she knew, too, that Will would never stop trying to find her. Once he had tried and failed with every tool in his arsenal, he would begin to search for her on foot. He would sense that she was gone and then he would go out searching blindly. He would run down endless trails to stone-cold dead ends, he would look for her in empty hotel lobbies and sun-bleached squares, he would wander through twisted warrens of uncountable cities and sleepy port towns, he would stumble across the jagged terrain of a thousand torn horizons. Perhaps the owls would lead him back to her, but probably not. It was for the best if they let him go, for he should never stop, he should always be running the wrong way. Yes, she thought, never slow down, Will, keep searching, fruitlessly, endlessly, let this be your punishment, for my heart burns, like the stinging, raw palm of some lost and drowning sailor when the storm has pulled the last rope from his grasp. Who knows if I will heal or if I will ever be whole. You have softened me, made me vulnerable, creating a weakness here in my heart where I can afford none. You asked a lioness to be a lamb, you asked a crocodile to help you ford the river, you lay with the viper and dared to ask her not to bite, and the sad thing is, I tried, with every fiber, every muscle, I tried, Will. But now, I will live forever and this pain shall never perish, and that is why I curse you. I have made you heroic, and you will stay strong for a long time, broad-chested and sharp-eyed, and my curse will drive you onward, she thought, until, finally, you are broken, like a blind and ruined horse tearing through the briars. Maybe the owls will guide you back to me, maybe not, but I hope with my whole heart they keep you running the wrong way. I hope they make you suffer through it all. It is the oldest and most simple curse on earth, and when properly applied, no cure can be found. Some might call it love.

"Zoya, Zoya, Zoya . . ."

HISTORICAL NOTE

The Central Intelligence Agency's infiltration of various European literary movements centered in Paris has been vigorously documented. The agency's influence on global, especially European, advertising during the same era is more anecdotal, though any serious research would possibly reward the diligent. While popular mythology dates the decline of Detroit as coincident with the '67 Twelfth Street Riot, in fact the "Paris of the Midwest" began losing its sizable population more than a decade earlier (see *Time* magazine's article "Detroit in Decline," published in 1961). As for the immigration of various castes of Russians into Western Europe following the 1917 revolution—including White Russian nobility, Orthodox clergy, and other curious figures—this too has been the subject of both history and speculation.

ACKNOWLEDGMENTS

I would like to acknowledge the coven who coaxed & encouraged, first Liz Boone and my mom & sis and also Stephanie Cabot, Sylvie Rabineau, Jennifer Barth, Carolyn Mugar, Audi Martel, Sophia Rzankowski, Catherine Bull, Kat Hartman, Helen Ectors, Shannon Cobb, Valerie Elbrick, Susanne Hilberry, and the two stars who guide me through the dark, Nora Montana & Carolina Rose.

Much gratitude too to my ever-bemused editor Sean McDonald & the crew at FSG, to Lorin Stein & the gang at *The Paris Review*, and special thanks to Ambassador Hartman for leading me to his tailor.